LET THERE BE LIGHT

ANCIENT ORIGINS BOOK THREE

ROBERT STOREY

In the blackest pits, or emptiest of voids, there is always a guiding light; it's just up to us to find it.

– Robert Storey

FACT:

On the 8th January 2011 an asteroid with the potential to impact Earth in 2040 was discovered by the Mount Lemmon Survey. This near-Earth object was given the designation, 2011 AG5.
A year later, in 2012, the world's international media warned this same asteroid might impact our planet in the year predicted. This warning was subsequently retracted soon after by the same sources, citing a false alarm.
Whether these media channels were privy to the whole truth is open to conjecture, however, true or not, our planet is under constant threat of annihilation and we still have no tried and tested means by which to protect ourselves from this celestial threat.

The governments of the world's most powerful nations have secret contingencies for global disasters. These plans are kept from the public for a reason.

YEAR:

2041 A.D.

PROLOGUE

OUT OF THE earth came the fires of hell, the breath of death licking at the heels of all living creatures. Predator or prey, it mattered not; consumption of flesh and bone was sacrificed to the maw of white hot heat and flame. Rock melted and the air itself burned as the devastation that was the fallout from the arrival of the asteroid, 2011 AG5, streaked out from the impact epicentre faster than a supersonic jet. As predicted, trains of tsunamis sprang into being to arrow into the Indian Ocean, their titanic power obliterating everything and anything in their path.

South Africa, the once proud nation, was no more. Scarred and mortally wounded, the whole southern African continent became shrouded in the blossoming dust cloud that would encompass the whole planet in its choking, suffocating embrace; a cloud that still persisted to that day, a cloud that had brought humanity to its knees and shook the fragility of civilisation to its core.

NASA astronaut, Pilot Commander Tyler Magnusson, stared at the footage on-screen, his thoughts melancholy. While he'd seen these pictures many times before he often found himself watching them again, the force of nature frightening to behold, and yet, equally, mesmeric in its raw power. The potent image of the meteor strike recorded the year before from his own spacecraft, USSS Orbiter One, was a stark reminder of the momentous times he was living through: an epic age of humanity where the culmination of man's endeavour pitted itself against the powers of the solar system and beyond.

It seemed strange to Tyler that only humans bore the full knowledge of what transpired in this era of terrible, apocalyptic transition, bearing witness as the dominant sentient race of the time to the upheaval brought from the stars. The weight of responsibility for the entire planet and every living thing on it was in Homo sapiens' hands. The burden couldn't be greater.

Despite the tumultuous nature of events, as day came after night and dawn reversed dusk, time marched ever onwards, waiting for no one and no thing. The inevitable decay of the world ticked on, animals breathing, breeding, dying; plants growing, multiplying, rotting. It is a curious paradox that all living things must die. What is the point, the purpose, the grand plan of existence? Knowledge gained, darkness fought and light sought, hard-earned wisdom lost to the abyss of death. The fact that we humans appear to be the only creatures on the planet that are fully aware of our own mortality – and not just our own, but that of those we hold dear, too – seems a cruel twist of fate. Or perhaps it is just an evolutionary curse gifted us by our forebears, a trade-off for a so-called superior intellect. Some view this machination of chance, intelligent design or divine provenance as an inevitability that fuels their motivation to live life to the full, fearing little in their quest to savour its sweetest pleasures and fully comprehending their tenuous hold on existence, seeing it as a gift on loan rather than a permanent possession. Others let this burden of knowledge smother and cripple them with dread, stifling their voice and actions beyond comprehension until their days, even their entire lives, are without meaning or direction, except as a dire warning to those who seek to do otherwise. And yet who is to judge what is meaningless and what is not? Everything has purpose, great or small; the sad and perhaps frightening thing is, in some cases, that purpose might not be our own.

Tyler heaved a sigh as the final vision of the great oceans' deep blues, from horizon to curved horizon, succumbed to the veil of black ash and pulverised stone, hiding the blessed planet we all call home from view. Flicking a switch he turned off the display and returned his attention to his surroundings. The United States Space Station, USSS Archimedes, continued to drift through the silent vacuum of space, its orbit uninterrupted by the passage of time and the embattled Earth that continued its own journey through the heavens encased in its thick, undulating cloak of ejected matter from the 2040 meteorite impact.

'Commander?'

Tyler looked to his colleague, Sandy Turner, the spacewalk specialist and station pilot.

'Sir,' she said, 'the final Sabre space-aircraft has arrived from the surface. They're requesting your presence on board the ISS.'

'Are the GMRC's ships still docked?'

Sandy tapped a button to produce a holographic image of the International Space Station, to which the Archimedes was attached. 'They are.'

Tyler's expression grew grim. The GMRC, the Global Meteor Response Council – just the name made him angry. When the first asteroid destined for Earth had been discovered in 2011, misinformation calmed the world's populace about its destructive potential. But when six more asteroids were found to be following in AG5's wake, any one of which had the capability to annihilate the planet's fragile ecosystems, the cover up expanded and it was decided a unified response was needed if humanity was to live on. So, in 2017, instigated by the world's leading nations to combat the unprecedented threat, the Global Meteor Response Council was born, and the GMRC, as it became known, was tasked with the most important of missions: to protect and preserve humanity, civilisation and all life on Earth. And with that remit it had embedded itself into the very governments that had created it. And year on year the GMRC's influence had grown until it answered only to itself, a global organisation of unrivalled power and reach that bent all of the world's nations to its will, regardless of their size or strength.

In 2022, the GMRC cemented its position of authority by advising the United Nations to verify the existence of the first asteroid to the masses, including the full disclosure of how its impact in 2040 would devastate the Earth. This single act allowed the GMRC to operate in public and to unify humanity's purpose, while in secret it plotted to combat the larger threat to come in 2042 and 2045, when the final asteroids would arrive. With the majority of the planet's populace believing only one asteroid was on a collision course with Earth, all but the paranoid could have guessed at the preparations being made behind the GMRC's public façade. Chief amongst the GMRC's plans was the Space Programme and its larger cousin, the Subterranean Programme, the latter of the two acting as a failsafe in the event the former was unable to prevent the predicted impacts.

And since its inception all those years ago, the GMRC was everywhere, sticking its nose in where it didn't belong and interfering with each country's efforts to save the planet like an overbearing parent that refused to take no for an answer. And where that influence was felt the most was amongst the civilian agencies who worked in space, with NASA shouldering the greatest burden of them all.

'Shall I tell them you're on your way?' Sandy said, breaking Tyler's reverie.

He took one last look around to make sure everything was in order. Satisfied, he nodded and left her alone on the control deck as he moved aft towards the umbilical passage that connected Archimedes to the enormous bulk of the International Space Station, which in turn was connected to the slightly smaller Chinese Space Station, Jiùshìzhǔ, and its sibling, the European Space Station, Guardian. In current climes the day for firsts had almost become a regular occurrence, but the fact that the four largest space vehicles in history had moored up to one another like a celestial gathering of metallic angels was indeed a momentous occasion. With their solar panels arching out like feathered wings the *Three Sisters*, as they were called, encircled the parental form of the aging International Space Station. A procession of cutting-edge technology tethered to one another in perpetuity until the powers-that-be deemed it fit for them to go their separate ways once more.

Tyler, with the aid of magnetic boots, strode through the partial gravity generated on Archimedes, the sound of metal ringing on metal echoing at his passing. Reaching the end of a corridor, he switched off his footwear's mechanism and floated up through a hatch to re-emerge on the next level. With a deftness born of a career in space, Tyler pushed against a bulkhead to re-orientate to a new vertical and then re-engaged the mag-boots, which secured him to another walkway.

Spiralling outwards from Archimedes' interior, Tyler found himself moving past the laboratory complex, which had been taken over by the GMRC's nefarious R&D Division at the behest of the United States military and the all powerful GMRC Directorate, the Global Meteor Response Council's controlling division. Unusually no guards were placed at the entrance to the lab modules and Tyler slowed and then stopped. The surrounding corridors, which stretched off in all directions, were eerily empty.

With the oppressive silence setting his senses alight, Tyler felt a compulsion to enter the highly restricted area, the same area which had caused so much trauma to the Archimedes crew ever since the GMRC's R&D Division had brought on board a sinister experiment going by the name of Project Ares. With many of his colleagues still in quarantine on the surface due to exposure to this blackest of scientific projects, Tyler knew the risks involved. Following the recent disclosure by NASA's Mission Command at Houston that many of those under medical supervision had taken a turn for the worse, with two in critical condition, and the sudden death of his captain, Bo Heidfield, who'd all but died in his arms only a handful of weeks before, the stakes were high; but Tyler also knew anything he could learn about Project Ares might aid his comrades, who now fought for their lives on the surface hundreds of miles below.

Steeling himself, he entered an override sequence in the nearby wall console. A six digit number appeared before a small square lit up in neon green to the side of the closed windowless doors. He pressed the button and the obstructions swished open with a gust of air that brought with it a faint whiff of chemicals. Surprised he'd been able to circumvent the security so easily, despite the lack of burly armed GMRC guards, Tyler edged forward, his eyes scouring anything and everything for signs of occupation, information and ... danger.

He wasn't sure what would happen to him if he was caught snooping around; probably a dressing down by his superiors at the GMRC's instigation. Worst case, he'd be reassigned to a desk job back on the surface to await evacuation with his family to the United States Subterranean Base located beneath Colorado and New Mexico, also known as USSB Steadfast. *Although*, he thought, *if the Space Programme played its part they might not need the subterranean bases at all, or at least for a much shorter timeframe than envisaged.* Tyler wondered what life would be like in the underground complex he was to call home, maybe for the rest of his days, before he forced himself to concentrate on the task at hand. Opening another door, the odour of formaldehyde washed over him, stealing his breath away and making his eyes water. Under reflex he gasped for air, setting the back of his throat afire and his head to throbbing. Holding his breath, Tyler moved to another wall console and fired up the extractor fans. The fumes in the room dissipated and his breathing eased.

Remaining alert, he moved forward again and into a room containing an array of windows overlooking a section of the ISS and the Earth beyond.

A strange noise behind made Tyler spin round.

Eyes wide, his attention homed in on a plastic sheet which fluttered in the breeze generated by the fans that continued to whir away in the background. Sighing, he returned his scrutiny to the area before him, an area in which he'd witnessed the curiosity that the GMRC scientists had laboured over day and night. The image of the *object* popped unbidden into his mind's eye and he shuddered in remembrance. The *monstrosity* had captivated both his and his captain's unnerved focus, its plasma field continuously contorting into abstract forms and creating ghost-like faces abhorrent to behold. The thing moved as if alive, almost as if it were aware of those around it who sought its secrets. And it was the audio stream Tyler had accessed to accompany this oddest of visions that had ultimately killed Bo Heidfield, sending his commanding officer into a violent and irreconcilable fit. Medics had rushed to the scene but failed to resuscitate his friend. The GMRC had questioned him to the nth degree about the incident, although for reasons unknown to Tyler they had neglected to initiate any grievance against him for trying to spy on their activities. It had helped that he'd skirted over the fact that he'd actually seen the abomination they harboured in the laboratory complex, only admitting to hearing the sound it had produced. Which was just as well, or else his personal investigation into the matter would have ended before it had even begun.

Grieving for his dead captain, and after rigorous screening and short term quarantine by the GMRC, Tyler had taken some compulsory R&R on the surface under orders from NASA's top brass. Why he'd been unaffected by Ares Tyler didn't know, and neither, it seemed, did anyone else.

The only reason he found himself back at work so soon was the same reason all four of the world's largest space stations were now rafted together, and why his presence had been requested on the ISS. Remembering why he'd been passing by the lab complex in the first place, Tyler prepared to leave, but a mark on the tiled flooring made him pause. Bending down, he ran his fingers over the outline of a five-sided shape that wasn't dirt or any other surface mark, but an outline that had raised the surface of the floor itself. It was almost as if the ceramic composite had melted, or had been drawn upwards somehow.

'Can I help you, Commander?'

Tyler snatched his hand away from its examination and glanced round. A woman dressed in grey GMRC coveralls and matching jacket stood in the doorway. Tyler knew her as one Ms Sylvia Lindegaard, the person responsible for the GMRC's integration on Archimedes, and she looked less than impressed by his being there.

'This area hasn't been properly vetted for NASA personnel,' she said, her expression as severe as her tone. 'How did you get in here?'

Tyler, against his better nature, kept his face neutral. 'As Archimedes' ranking officer I wanted to make sure your scientists hadn't compromised my crew's safety. Considering the number who've already suffered at the hands of your beloved Project Ares I think that was a reasonable motivation to circumvent your security codes, don't you?'

'I'm sorry about the passing of your captain, Commander.'

Tyler could hear the lack of compassion behind the words and the anger he'd been hiding flitted across his face.

'However,' she continued, 'this section of the ship is still off limits for *all* NASA personnel and you'd do well to remember it.'

Tyler let out a snort of contempt. 'Seems to me like the GMRC's clearing out.' He looked around the room, which was void of any equipment, or any other paraphernalia that usually accompanied a scientific research project. 'Let me be the first to say, good riddance.'

The GMRC liaison, who was unusually tall, almost freakishly so, raised an eyebrow in mild surprise. 'Haven't you somewhere to be, Commander?' She moved aside to let him pass.

Tyler stared at her, his hatred undisguised, before he brushed past and on out of the laboratory complex. Muttering to himself and cursing the GMRC, he resumed his journey to the temporary passage that connected Archimedes to the International Space Station. Turning off his mag-boots, he floated through a slowing rotating tunnel with white corrugated walls and moved from partial gravity to the microgravity environment aboard the aging ISS, where he was greeted by a party of two.

'Welcome aboard the ISS, Commander,' said a man, his accent

Russian and smile broad. 'My name's Alexei Denisov and this is Astrid-Hélène Pichon.'

Tyler grunted in response.

'Is there something wrong, sir?' the man's companion said, her Gallic lilt and genuine concern bringing him out of his internal stupor.

'No, I'm fine. My apologies. Bad day.'

The two ISS astronauts exchanged a look, perhaps having heard about the goings-on aboard Archimedes.

'Are you here to take me to the auditorium?' he said, as he shook hands with each in turn.

The French woman, Astrid-Hélène, gave him a sympathetic smile. 'Your comrades are already assembled, as is everyone else. Follow me, Commander.' She turned and floated off down a corridor.

With the Russian following behind, Tyler was led through a maze of interconnecting modules and hatches until they came to the hub of the International Space Station, the central node, commonly known as the *auditorium*. The largest space module ever built, prefabricated on the surface and assembled in space, was a sight to behold. Comprising a flat floor and ceiling, the connecting walls curved outwards, the convex design, if viewed from the outside, appearing like a giant, slightly angular, holeless donut. As Tyler's guide had said, everyone else from all four space stations had already arrived, leaving only skeleton crews behind to manage critical systems.

The babble of noise from the ranks of the planet's finest was an assault on the senses. The quiet calm of life in space and everything that entailed meant gatherings such as this were unheard of. Over a hundred people in one place, in space ... even twenty years ago this would have seemed an impossibility, but with the world's resources channelled into the GMRC's divisions on an unprecedented scale, the Space Programme had benefited like no other – at least, it had initially.

Tyler took his place in a seat built into the wall, loose straps over his shoulders ensuring he didn't float away, and his reception committee, the French woman and Russian, sat down either side of him.

A sweeping window stretched around half the auditorium and Tyler could see the ISS docking ports outside, where two large Sabre transportation crafts had berthed the previous day; emblazoned on their sides was the stark, white lettering of the GMRC's logo:

Astrid, following his gaze, touched his knee and leaned closer to him. 'Don't worry, Commander, I hear the GMRC are leaving us.'

'Some say for good,' Alexei said.

Tyler glanced at the Russian and then turned back to Astrid, whose bright blue eyes twinkled with compassionate intelligence.

'Things will get better now, yes?' She winked and gave his leg a squeeze before removing her hand and returning her attention forward, where a large wallscreen shimmered into life.

Tyler gazed at her for a moment before looking, along with everyone else, at the image now on display. A crystal clear picture of NASA's Control Center, complete with the familiar circular insignia on the wall, filled his vision. Lined up in front of this stood thirty people, wearing a mixture of civilian and military uniforms from various nations, and at their head stood five men. The central figure was NASA's chief administrator, James Davis Jackson, the highest ranking official for the civilian agency. Resplendent in a deep blue flight suit adorned with various emblematic patches, he stepped forwards to survey the astronauts before him as if they were in the same room, not separated by thousands of miles and the vastness of space.

'My friends, thank you for taking the time out of your busy schedules to join together on the eve of what can only be called the most pivotal moment in human history, perhaps even our planet's history. On this most auspicious of days, where our combined efforts to conquer the stars has culminated in the space stations that surround you now, we are one nation, one species, one planet, united in a common goal against a singular threat which jeopardises the existence of everything and everyone we hold dear.

'The six asteroids that, even as I speak, draw inexorably closer to Earth, represent a challenge like no other, a test of our resolve and spirit against which we must – and will – prevail, lest darkness descend and life and light be irrevocably, irreparably extinguished.

'Ever since the year of Our Lord 2011, when the harbinger of our doom, the near-Earth object AG5, was sighted by the Mount Lemon Survey, the Space Programme as we know it today was conceived, an inevitability of union as our great nations came together to form an integrated response in a collaboration of resources and knowledge that may never be matched in this life or the next.

'But, let it be known, the Space Programme's greatest achievement is not the space-craft, computers or specialised equipment we are set to use in defence of Earth, it is the people watching me now, listening to my words – YOU are our greatest advance, our greatest minds, our greatest hope. Without you our technologies would not exist, without you our technologies could not be operated. Without you there is no Space Programme, no hope, no victory.'

The administrator paused for breath and Tyler felt roused by his words. The hairs on the backs of his arms and neck stood up on end as he was reminded of the magnitude of what he, and those around him, were about to undertake. With his usually calm demeanour chastened, a quick glance around showed him that everyone else was similarly entranced, the hush in the room complete. Astrid's eyes glistened with emotion, indicating he wasn't alone in being stirred.

'To paraphrase a famous British politician,' Jackson continued, '*never in the field of human conflict will so much be owed by so many to so few*. When Winston Churchill spoke those iconic words it was to inspire an embattled nation against Hitler's tyranny, but a hundred years on our fight is against a far deadlier foe, force majeure, a superior force, an act of God, the ultimate enemy.

'And yet,' – he looked around at those standing by his side – 'together we stand, shoulder to shoulder with those present and past. Thousands of years of human advance, every step, great or small, by those that have gone before, has led us to where we are now; the creation of the wheel, the internal combustion engine, electricity, the computer, the World Wide Web, every progression a leap forward, propelling our understanding and capabilities to new heights.

'Look around you now—' he continued, his arms held out beseechingly.

Tyler looked to Astrid, then to Alexei, then to those in front.

'—the men and women beside you can help you change the course of history, of our planet's evolution, of every living plant's and animal's evolution; their destiny is in your hands. Yes, we have had setbacks, failures ... some say too many—'

Tyler noticed the defiant tone entering into the administrator's voice, and the fact that the GMRC had not been mentioned once during his speech spoke volumes.

'—and yet we have persevered despite cuts to our funding in favour of other projects. As the final days of reckoning approach, the next few months will prove to be our best window to action our plans to divert the trajectories of two of the four asteroids due to impact Earth in 2042. I understand many of you, especially my countrymen, will disagree with the decision as to why those two asteroids were selected for deflection over the other two; however, the decision has been made and we must abide by the consensus of opinion. What is more important, if our methods are successful, is that we divert the final two much larger asteroids due in 2045.' James Jackson made a gesture with his hand. 'Observe.'

The auditorium darkened and a glowing orb appeared in the centre of the ceiling. The ball of energy expanded as if ignited by some unseen power and flowed outwards, its tendrils of light activating the giant ceiling screen like a cascade of sparkling jewels. The sumptuous 3D image mapped out the solar system in exquisite detail before its focus rotated to the Earth and Moon, with the Sun moving to the far horizon on the opposite side of the room. Traced onto this living display, six red lines depicted the incoming tracks of the rapidly closing asteroids, and projected onto the end of each of those were the forms of irregularly shaped rocks, each with a data tag attached in the form of a graphical box displaying its designation and forecasted impact date. Blossoming into being close to the slowly rotating image of Earth, four lines of silver arced out to meet four of their red counterparts. Where they met, a circular flash of light turned red lines to green which diverted the asteroids past Earth, leaving only two red lines to realise their original destination on the surface of our world.

With the show over, the ceiling display faded and turned back to an opaque white, prompting the NASA administrator to continue speaking. 'You do not need me to tell you that the closer the asteroids are, the greater our chances of success. The first of our manned missions will embark from the ISS in only a few weeks' time, so let me and my colleagues introduce you to the brave men and women who are the tip of the spear.'

The head of the CNSA, the Chinese National Space Administration, who stood next to the NASA administrator, moved to the fore and gave a perfunctory bow. '*Xing hui*,' he said in greeting. 'May I introduce Wang Bo Shi, commander and pilot of mission AG5–B Alpha Intercept and his science officer, Li Yŭ Háng Yuán.'

At the front of the auditorium on the ISS, a man and a woman floated to their feet and turned to give a smile and a wave to Tyler and everyone else in the room. The Chinese CNSA administrator then gave introductions for two more pairs of mission specialists, after which his European counterpart introduced their six representatives, each of whom stood in turn to salute or wave to their fellow astronauts.

After five more teams from the international contingent had been formally named, the NASA administrator took centre stage once more. 'And heading the United States mission AG5–D Omega Intercept, Professor Andrea Brunel and co-pilot Trent Arnold Moss, Junior.'

Tyler recognised the names well; years earlier he'd helped train them both when they'd been fresh-faced to the agency. A sense of pride and joy stole over him at seeing the two of them stand to receive their applause; such a moment would stay with him for the rest of his days. Clapping along with everyone else, his mind began to wander as the remaining U.S. teams were introduced and the address by his superiors, beamed up to them from Houston, wound down. His thoughts returned to the GMRC and to Project Ares.

'—Commander?'

Tyler blinked. 'What? Sorry, I must have zoned out, what did you say?'

'Are you joining us for the reception?' Astrid said, the screen at the front of the auditorium now blank, the speeches and introductions complete.

'Yes, of course. Forgive me.' Tyler glanced out of the window again as one of the GMRC Sabre space-aircraft undocked from the International Space Station. He looked back to Astrid. 'Lead on, Mademoiselle Pichon.'

Astrid smiled and held out a hand to help him out of his seat. With the formalities behind them, everyone in the room made their way to the ISS living quarters where food and alcohol-free drinks awaited. The auditorium darkened and the sounds of laughter and optimism drifted away, the quiet of space reasserting its power as those that sought to save the lives of billions enjoyed some light relief before the hardest and most dangerous of works began in earnest.

♦

Tyler laughed in good humour.

'No, it's true!' an Indian astronaut said to those gathered. 'If you flip the switch back down, everything comes back up and I mean – *everything.*'

'Everything? Surely not ...' Astrid shook her head and chuckled. 'The mess, it would be terrible, no?'

The Indian man grinned. 'Oh, it was, it took us two weeks to get it out of all the equipment. Two weeks!'

Tyler wiped a tear from his eye; the man's tale was unbelievable, but amusing. Who'd have thought someone would design a zero gravity toilet, with a reversible pump?

'So, Commander,' the Indian said, as a few of the onlookers moved away, 'I hear congratulations are in order.'

Tyler gave him a puzzled look.

'You are to be made captain of the Archimedes, are you not? I bet the person you're replacing will be sick to their stomach they've missed out on overseeing the mission of a lifetime.'

Tyler's memories of his captain came flooding back, memories he tried so hard to forget. His face darkened. Draining the rest of his drink he handed the empty container to Astrid who looked at him in dismay.

'I must be getting back,' he said, and without a further word he glided off towards the module's closest hatch.

Alexei, the Russian cosmonaut, looked up from a discussion he was having with two British astronauts. 'You're leaving so soon, Commander?'

Tyler glanced at Alexei as he passed but didn't reply, his sour mood compounded by the joviality surrounding him.

With the sounds of merriment left behind, Tyler slowed and stopped in the auditorium to gaze out into space and the stars that shone bright in the blackness.

Something touched his shoulder, making him jump.

He turned to see Astrid had followed him.

She flashed him a grin, her face apologetic. 'Forgive Sohail, he did not know what he was saying. He always does, how do you say? Put his mouth where his foot is.'

Tyler's lips twitched at her mistake, but the smile faded before it could form.

She put her hand on his shoulder, the touch lingering. 'My quarters are close, stress relief can be good for the soul as well as the body.'

He raised his left hand where a gold wedding ring glittered in the half-light.

Astrid looked upset, but masked it expertly. 'I admire your loyalty. I, too, have a love on the surface, but with times as they are we must take comfort where we can find it.'

Tyler found her attractive, very attractive, but he loved his wife and family and to throw away that trust for lust was, for him, ludicrous. He was about to reply when he saw some movement through the window. Across from his vantage point, a large section of the ISS could be seen, and his eyes were drawn to a long corridor that ran around the edge of the auditorium's outer rim. Eighty feet away, passing through this curved passage and visible through a line of sweeping, nano-fibre windows, a host of GMRC scientists and security personnel manoeuvred two large objects, one of which was a transparent oblong pod used to transport individuals under strict quarantine.

Tyler's expression changed to shock as a jolt of recognition hit him. The procession turned before disappearing around a corner and without a word to Astrid, he thrust himself from the window towards the nearest hatch.

'What's wrong?!' Astrid called out, but Tyler was too intent on chasing the GMRC team to respond; instead, he propelled himself like an arrow through a connecting module.

Flying through three hatches without regard for safety protocols, Tyler activated his mag-boots with reverse polarity to execute a tight ninety degree turn at speed. Bending his knees to absorb the energy of his flight, he flexed his legs to full extension to continue his headlong pursuit. With Astrid left far behind, Tyler passed through the corridor he'd seen from the auditorium moments before. Pushing out with his hands to match the curvature of the module, he braced for impact as the end of the passage came into sight. Unable to slow his momentum, Tyler's shoulder crashed into the closed hatch, the sound echoing in his ears as a grunt of pain escaped his lips. He spun the circular handle round, heaved open the door and went through.

The area was deserted. Looking left and right, he could see no sign of the GMRC contingent. The module in front was also empty, as were those above and below. Unable to hear anything either, the silence total, Tyler moved right to search for signs of his quarry. A dead end led him back to try the left turning, where a locked security door barred his way. Through a small porthole he could see a sign that told him the ISS transport hub lay beyond. This was where the last GMRC Sabre transportation craft was docked. He knew he had to get there, and quickly. Urgency upon him, he tried – and failed – to override the unfamiliar system. He banged the door in frustration.

'Tyler, what's going on? You're scaring me.'

Tyler turned to see Astrid appearing through the aperture behind him. 'I saw—'

'Saw what?' Astrid said, when he failed to continue.

He shook his head and returned to the door to attempt another computer override sequence.

Astrid pulled him back round. 'Tyler, tell me! What did you see?'

'Can you help me get through this door?'

'*Zut alors!*' Pushing him aside, she entered a code. Nothing happened. Trying again with the same result, she looked at him in concerned confusion. 'This code should work.'

'They don't want us seeing what they're up to.'

'Who?'

'The GMRC, who else?'

Letting out a string of curses, Astrid yanked out the computer console to expose its wires and then pulled out a couple and twisted their ends together. Repeating this process twice more, she shoved the panel back in and tapped in a series of numbers. The red light remained, the obstruction unmoved. Letting out a squeak of displeasure, she thumped the screen with the heel of her hand; there was a click and a clunk, and the light switched to green.

Tyler pulled open the door, but Astrid barred his path with her arm. 'What is happening, Tyler?'

With no time to spare, Tyler gently but firmly moved her aside. 'Follow me.'

He pulled himself forwards through another tunnel and Astrid shook her head and moved after him.

It wasn't long before they came to another locked door. This barrier had no window and this time the French astronaut's attempt at an override was fruitless.

Tyler bunched his fists in anger. 'Damn it!'

'I know a way round,' Astrid said, 'but first you must tell me what is happening. This hatch shouldn't be locked, it's a safety hazard.'

Tyler, trapped by circumstance, calmed himself. 'They said he was dead.'

'Who? Your Archimedes captain, Bo Heidfield?'

Tyler nodded. 'He died—' He held out a hand to the floor as if his friend and colleague rested there. 'He died right next to me. I saw him, there was no life. He had no pulse.'

'You tried to bring him back?'

'For a time. Help came, but it was too late. They took his body away soon after.'

'And now you think he still lives?'

'I saw him, I'm sure I did, in a quarantine capsule. I must find out. I must!'

Astrid's expression turned grave. 'Come – this way.'

Floating away, she led them up into another node of the space station. Locating a hexagonal panel on a side wall, she detached it and secured the metal cover to the floor. Now exposed, a narrow tunnel ran off into darkness, pipework and cabling packed in all around. Before entering this tiny entrance, she removed two small breathing masks from a nearby cabinet and handed one to Tyler.

'This will be a tight fit,' – Astrid secured the apparatus to her head and tore off two tags to expose the filters inside – 'but it will bring us out above the decompression chambers and the space station's arrivals module. Try not to knock any levers on your way through, some will trigger a fire breach alarm that will cut off the ventilation system and flood the conduit with halon gas.'

'You don't have fine water mist suppression?' Tyler said.

She shook her head and ducked inside. Tyler removed the tags from his own mask and followed her in. Sliding along, the two made quick progress, the zero gravity environment negating the restrictive effects of the cramped conditions. The mask created a moist pocket of air over Tyler's mouth and nose, and he paused as Astrid halted ahead and then disappeared above. Her hand reappeared a moment later to help him through the hole and he struggled up beside her.

They were now suspended over the entrance to the decompression area of the ship, as Astrid had predicted.

Due to the disorientating nature of space, the area in view seemed to be below them and the people that moved through this adjacent node were unaware of the two astronauts above, looking down at them through a metal grated ceiling.

Astrid put a finger to her mask to indicate they should remain silent. Tyler gave a nod and took in the scene unfolding beneath. A host of scientists in standard GMRC spacesuits congregated at one of the airlocks that led to the large transport space-aircraft still docked to the ISS, the side of the giant vehicle just visible to Tyler through a window off to the right.

As the men and women disappeared into the decompression chamber, he realised they were too late; the pod had already been taken on board. Growing angry, his grip tightened on the grating before him, his knuckles whitening. As he saw the last of the people disappear, he turned to say something to Astrid, whose eyes widened in warning. She shook her head and gestured for him to keep looking. Her vantage point of the corridor was better than his and the reason for her reticence soon became apparent. The tall form of Sylvia Lindegaard, the woman he'd had the misfortune of speaking to in the Archimedes laboratories, floated into view, and beside her was the head of the GMRC's Archimedes security detail.

'Everything is in place?' Lindegaard said to her companion.

'Yes, all the doors have been secured and the charges have been set.'

'The escape pods?'

'Deactivated.'

Above, Tyler swapped a fearful glance with Astrid.

'And the other space stations,' Lindegaard said, 'they won't be able to undock from the ISS?'

'No. We've been very thorough.'

The woman nodded in satisfaction. 'Excellent. As soon as we're clear, give the order for detonation. I'll be in my quarters.'

'Very good, ma'am,' the guard said, as Lindegaard entered the airlock. With one last look around, he followed her inside.

Feeling like he was in some kind of nightmare, Tyler looked at Astrid, who looked terrified. 'We need to move!' he said, through his mask.

The two of them scrambled back into the narrow tunnel and emerged soon after into the corridor.

Tyler tore off his mask. 'Sound a general alert!'

Astrid was already tapping at a computer terminal. 'There's no response, they've corrupted the system. What do we do?!'

'We have to get to Archimedes.'

'What about everyone else?'

'There's no time; this place is a ticking time bomb. Move!'

Hauling themselves through the interconnecting corridors as fast as they could, they reached a six-way junction and headed towards the Archimedes. The rotating umbilical came into view and Tyler glimpsed through a window the GMRC Sabre transport moving away at speed from the ISS. A distant sound came from behind and the flexible connection between Archimedes and the ISS rippled and warped. Through the same window Tyler saw a fireball erupt into space, followed by another and then another. Lights and sirens flashed and a horrific groaning noise emanated down the corridors towards them.

Hauling Astrid past him, Tyler spoke into a com station. 'Sandy, can you hear me?!'

'Sir?' a voice came back through the speaker.

'Fire up the engines and undock from the ISS, NOW!'

'What? Why?!'

'JUST DO IT!!' He pulled his mask back on and turned to Astrid. 'Help me with these clamps.'

Together they pulled back a heavy red handle, followed by a second.

Another, larger explosion lit up the external blackness. Debris flew in all directions and the European Space Station drifted sideways as it twisted and tore itself apart like tinfoil.

'Get into the next module and close the hatch,' he said to Astrid, as he braced himself against the final lever. 'As soon as I pull this handle we'll disconnect from the ISS.'

'You'll be sucked out!'

'I'll be fine, move!'

Astrid moved back and shut the airlock. Tyler heaved with all his might and the final clamp sprang back with a dull clang. A whoosh of atmosphere vented out into space and Tyler sucked in a gulp of air and held on for dear life as the umbilical broke away. The remaining air rushed past and he activated his magnetic boots. With ice forming on his skin and his eyes on fire, he put one foot in front of the other and reached for the button to close the outer doors. But as he did so, time slowed to a crawl. His hand fell short of its target and he sank to his knees. Toppling over, his feet still attached to the floor, his vision grew dim. Tyler's final breath expelled from his lungs and darkness closed in.

In his last moments Tyler heard a voice and felt hands clasp his ice-cold face. Warmth returned and he opened his eyes wide as, with a great gasp of inhalation, his lungs filled with air. A mirrored mask projected a reflection of his face back at him and a white, gloved hand reached up and slipped the visor up to reveal a clear, plastic bubble beneath. Sandy Turner peered at him in concern. 'Tyler, can you hear me?'

He nodded, coughed and then sat up as his pulse rate returned to normal.

'I was doing a routine sweep of the ship's exterior, operating its systems remotely,' Sandy said, as she helped him to his feet. 'You're lucky.'

Astrid reopened the hatch and rushed to his side while Sandy flipped open a computer control panel on the outside of her spacesuit and powered up Archimedes' engines. 'What the hell's going on?' the spacewalk specialist said. 'I saw explosions.'

Tyler got to his feet. 'I'll explain later; you two get to the control deck. We need to shed weight; I'll jettison the science modules.'

Sandy gave a nod and took Astrid with her while Tyler sped through the partial gravity on Archimedes to the now deserted laboratories. Once there he set in motion the separation procedure. Securing an airlock, Tyler pulled down a red lever and a hiss of hydraulics signalled the release of the clamps. Green icons lit up on a nearby screen and a button rose out from the wall. He smacked it with the palm of his hand and watched through the hatch window as the science modules were released into space with a great puff of gas, as jets of air thrust them away from the rest of the station.

Rushing back to join the others, Tyler emerged onto the control deck where Sandy and Astrid stood staring out of the central window in silence at the horrific scene beyond. The ISS, or more precisely what had been the ISS, drifted in pieces, great and small, the heartrending forms of human bodies floating amongst the wreckage. In the distance the similarly eviscerated European station, Guardian, spiralled away into deep space with flashes of electricity sparking in the dark.

Astrid put her hands to her face. '*Mon dieu.*'

'I can't see the Jiùshìzhǔ,' Sandy said.

Tyler scanned the expanse for the Chinese Space Station, but he could see no sign of it. The bottom half of their view was blocked by the ejected science modules, which gradually moved away from the Archimedes. But as the laboratories continued to recede into the distance, a great rent appeared down their centre and the structure exploded into fragments as the stricken form of the Jiùshìzhǔ clove through it at speed, heading straight for them, a host of broken Sabre space-aircrafts drifting end over end along with it.

Tyler's eyes widened and Astrid screamed.

'Go!' Sandy said as Tyler dragged Astrid aft. 'I'll manoeuvre us away from it for as long as I can. Suit up and get out!'

'What about you?!' Tyler said.

Sandy slid her mirrored visor down. 'I'll follow you out, NOW GO!'

Bulkheads and doorways flashed past. Red warning lights sent shadows cavorting through the ship. A door swished open and Tyler and Astrid rushed to the spacesuits and dragged them on. Seconds from destruction, they entered the airlock and switched on their magnetic boots. Tyler hit a button and the air left the chamber. The external doors opened and Tyler led Astrid out into the vacuum of space. They pulled their visors down as the sun rose from behind the Earth, and turned to see the Jiùshìzhǔ's massive form bearing down on the Archimedes.

Sandy Turner emerged from a hatch a hundred feet away and Astrid grasped Tyler's arm and pointed.

'Sandy, move!' Tyler said through his helmet's radio.

She looked round, but it was too late, the out of control Chinese ship ploughed into them. Sandy disappeared in a mass of twisted metal, her scream cut short. Tyler and Astrid staggered back before turning to run along the hull of the fast disappearing ship, while dodging the chunks of space station that rained down around them. Tyler tripped and fell, his visor flipping up. Astrid stopped, ducked a fast moving object and helped him back to his feet.

She lifted her own visor. 'There's nowhere to go!'

Tyler had an idea, but before he could say anything a shadow loomed. On instinct he shoved Astrid in the chest. A look of shock crossed her face as she fell back. A giant solar wing swept past, barely missing her, and smashed Tyler from the Archimedes, carrying him out into the dark void of space.

◆

Astrid watched Tyler's limp form spiral into the black. The Space Programme was destroyed. The hopes of saving Earth's surface and those living on it, lost to sabotage and betrayal. Turning her head inside her helmet, she saw out of the corner of her eye the bulk of the Chinese Space Station rearing up above her. As it came crashing down, her last thoughts were of broken promises and lost love.

CHAPTER ONE

SPIRALLING END over end it skimmed across the heavens, dragged onwards by gravity's hidden all-consuming embrace. On its metallic skin, criss-crossed with pockmarks and deep impact gashes, were the blackened symbol of NASA and a line of scarred lettering that had once formed a word.

Slowing against mounting air resistance, its rotation ending, the remnant of the United States Space Station, Archimedes, burnt up in Earth's atmosphere, its outer edges flaring white hot and folding back on themselves as it fell from the sky – a manmade shooting star. Alongside this forlorn object, spread across hundreds of miles, other sections of trillion dollar spacecraft cut fiery orange swathes through the night skies. Far below on the Earth's surface no one was witness to this metallic meteor shower and the dire prophetic warning of humanity's ruination it represented, the debris from space slicing into and through the all pervasive dust cloud which masked its passage.

Moments later, emerging from the unseen, the brilliant arrows of light plunged into the Pacific Ocean, their intense auroral heat quenched by the cold, dark waters that bubbled and boiled around them. Drifting down, the ruddy glow from the scorched, twisted metal panel grew dim. Spun round in vast currents, the final journey of the devastated orbital vehicle eventually ended as it came to rest in what would be an eternal watery grave set deep on the ocean floor; the sound of its impact a dull thud that resounded against the hard bedrock beneath. Following these shockwaves across hundreds of miles of the planet's surface, descending through layers of sediment laid down eons past, the density of compacted substrate hardened and then vanished. A huge void, located far underground and stretching for miles in all directions, dominated the continental crust under what were the deserts and mountains of present day Mexico.

This far reaching expanse, unlike everything surrounding it, was not born from nature's timeless geological progression; in fact, it was an engineering marvel of ancient origins created long before the earliest of our civilisations, and even before the evolution of modern man. Hewn from the Earth by a means unknown, the builders of this underworld that functioned independently from the surface above were also lost to time's unrelenting and uncompromising embrace. Where for millennia humanity believed itself set apart from the rest of the animal kingdom, sitting atop a pedestal fashioned by its own arrogance, a long extinct species with a similar lineage flourished for a million years, creating a legacy that put paid to our notion of unique superiority. The existence of this race, reclaimed from the past's vice-like grip and from those that sought to keep it forever hidden, had now been allocated its scientific name by the select few learned in its ways, taking its rightful place amongst its closest brethren and slotted into the Hominid evolutionary timeline. What was the name of this creature that so closely resembled our own? Where we are Homo sapiens, they are Homo giganthropsis. And as the name suggests they were a beast whose size surpassed our own and yet they were also one that had become extinct, like all our other closest relatives. Why the demise of our larger cousin came to pass, no one knew, but what was for certain was that their advancement in science far exceeded our own.

Within this decaying goliath of a subterranean world, long silent cities of immense proportions littered pitch-black chambers so vast they had their own climates; and yet amongst these near endless interconnecting cave-like systems, ensconced near its heart, was a smaller, yet no less grand construction. A construction built not by Homo giganthropsis, or the Anakim as they were known, but by Homo sapiens. Home to twenty million souls and built in preparation for the surface apocalypse to come, this United States Subterranean Base, or USSB, was one of forty-five such bases commissioned by the planet's leading nations and located around the world. This base, however, was by the far the largest of these monumental projects, and it was still dwarfed by the abandoned Anakim world that surrounded it, a world from which the USSB took its name and one that would stay in the annals of time as the greatest discovery in human history, the greatest civilisation ever to have graced the planet, a place that knew no equal, a place to those that knew of it called ... Sanctuary.

Inside this underground immensity, under a twenty mile wide dome capable of producing its own sunlight and weather systems, the human city sprawled. The crown jewel in the U.S. Subterranean Programme, USSB Sanctuary consisted of many levels, burrowing down into the chambers built by the Anakim and producing a three dimensional metropolis on a scale unlike anything seen before. At the centre, directly beneath the great dome itself and on the USSB's top level, an ancient tower cut a slender figure through simulated skies. Up and up this Anakim monolith rose, passing through the dome itself and into the dark of the larger chamber of Sanctuary Proper, beyond.

On the outside of this great spire, which had been moulded by the prehistoric vision of Anakim architects, an external lift system, added by human hands, hummed to life as it began its upward journey to the summit. Inside this cylindrical glass elevator stood a single passenger and, as if mirroring the structure he ascended, the man's elegant frame was tall and lean. His self-assured stance, concealed in an upright posture, gave way to a stern, unfathomable expression formed by angular features and flat, cold, gimlet-like eyes that gazed out with a fierce intelligence. Expensive handmade Italian shoes supported his ensemble, their black leather uppers painstakingly stitched together by a master craftsman and setting off a crisp dark grey tailored suit that accentuated his narrow hips and shoulders to form a more masculine appearance. Curiously, despite the current lack of bright light, he wore a pair of sunshades attached to his spectacles which gave him a sinister, yet apt, air of power and influence.

U.S. and GMRC Director of Intelligence Malcolm Joiner surveyed the scene before him, his gloved hands held clasped at the small of his back. He was not a man prone to acknowledging the positives in anything, but even he had to admit the vista spread out below him as he ascended the three mile high edifice was spectacular.

USSB Sanctuary, the subterranean base run by the United States government in conjunction with the Global Meteor Response Council, lay shrouded in darkness. The artificial sunlight from the immense dome had grown dim, simulating night, and in response the underground city, containing over twenty million U.S. citizens, twinkled and shimmered like a star-encrusted galactic blanket. The uppermost section of the monotube rail system wove in and out of the plethora of manmade buildings and towers, which would have appeared majestic had they not been so close to the gigantic monument at the base's heart. At two miles up the great dome glided past and then fell away below, reducing the majestic scene to a crescentic sliver.

Outside the dome the black abyss of the unfathomably large cavern sought to assert its pervasive mass upon the spire which bisected its body like a brightly lit needle. The air in the elevator grew cool, the heat island inside the USSB left behind. Joiner shifted position to ease his back muscles and looked up as a blue glow seeped into the transparent lift he travelled in. The spire's pinnacle approached and his ascent slowed to a stop.

Two doors slid aside with a whisper to reveal a grand high-ceilinged hallway where four armed guards stood to attention on either side of the entrance. Joiner moved forwards and two of the men fell into step behind him in escort, the lustrous purple sheen of their composite armour glittering under the lights installed above.

The corridor, like the building surrounding it, was aesthetically beautiful and unlike anything built by human hands. Curved green crystalline walls, wreathed with intricate engravings, led those that passed through it across an undulating floor that resembled the sweep of rolling hills. The long hallway, echoing to the footsteps of the three people travelling its length, straightened, its features fading to blandness as it continued deep into the Anakim structure until it finally emerged into an enormous multi-sided room where two large red doors glinted and gleamed on the far side.

Cobalt radiance permeated the room's semi-transparent walls from above and Joiner couldn't help but look up again to view a section of the spire from the inside. If he'd been of weaker mind and easily swayed, the sight would have been truly awe-inspiring; instead, the effect made him feel small and insignificant, an experience he didn't care for.

He walked on, noticing out of the corner of his eye that the two men that had accompanied him hung back before retreating into the shadows to return to their previous station. He knew very few people were allowed into this area and fewer still into the room beyond. As he reached the centre, directly beneath the spire, he stopped in the middle of a twenty foot diameter circle that had been sunken into the floor. Beneath his feet, the great seal of Sanctuary, wrought from precious metals, reflected light from its polished surface.

An odd absence of noise made his attention turn to the elaborate metal doors which now swung inwards. A figure passed through the huge gateway and moved to intercept his position.

'Malcolm Joiner,' the woman said in greeting, her voice strong and inflection flat.

Joiner gave a nod of his head in guarded acknowledgment. A waft of incense reached his nostrils as she walked past, her long, flowing dress fluttering behind her like a silken flag. He turned and extended his gait to match her long, measured strides, her height a few inches greater than his own.

'Have you been successful?' she said, her tone aloof and gaze averted as if his mere presence was offensive.

'I will be.'

The woman Joiner knew as Selene Dubois slowed and her head moved a fraction in his direction. '"Will" is not "have".'

'My efforts are ongoing. The task you – the Committee – set is ... complex.'

'Should we be concerned?'

Joiner hesitated before responding, choosing his words with care. 'The war instigated between China and its neighbours has destabilised the Asian block. Their attention is elsewhere, as you desired. GMRC personnel in the region are primed to be influenced or replaced.'

'And the council's Directorate?'

'Since Professor Steiner has been removed, we have three quarters of the GMRC's Directorate subverted to your cause.'

'Your?'

'Our,' Joiner said quickly.

'And yet the Subterranean Programme's Director General still lives.'

'Not for long; the professor's luck has run its course.'

'He has great influence and our actions expose us. One such as him, with the knowledge he holds ...'

'As I said, his time has come. If you are unhappy with my methods perhaps you should find someone else to do your bidding.'

Selene Dubois stopped walking and turned to fix him with an icy stare, her mismatched eyes boring into his. Joiner's own eyes darted from the green iris to the blue one as he inwardly cursed his complacency.

'The power you wield at the GMRC and within the U.S. government has emboldened you, *Intelligence Director*,' she said, emphasising his title. 'You would do well to remember from whence your privileged position originates.'

Joiner didn't respond; he held her gaze until her brow furrowed in warning, then looked away.

She turned her back on him and moved a few steps ahead, the heels of her shoes impacting the polished tiles underfoot, the noise acute in the silence. 'We are aware of your efforts to find out about Project Ares,' she said, after a pause.

Joiner licked his lips as the unfamiliar sensation of fear tore at his mental foundation.

She remained stock still and moved her head a fraction in his direction. 'Did you think we would not find out?'

'It's my job to know all.'

'Except when told otherwise.'

'I didn't realise I had been told.'

'Director,' she said, 'come, let's not play games.'

'How do you expect me to do my job without all the information on which to base my decisions?'

'Project Ares is not pertinent to your goals; take no further steps to finding out its purpose. Is that clear enough for you, or do I need to clarify our position further?'

Joiner knew full well what kind of *clarification* she alluded to. He took a step forward. 'That won't be necessary.'

'Good, it would displease me should our association sour.'

The woman moved off once more in a slow, measured stroll that forced Joiner to follow.

'You know why you were summoned?' she said as he drew alongside.

Joiner remained silent.

A smile twisted her lips as she relished his ignorance. 'There are certain *incidents* that have transpired since your last visit that we need addressed.'

'Richard Goodwin?'

'Steadfast's director, his civilians and Darklight mercenaries will have long since perished in the bowels of Sanctuary Proper.'

'The base's generals failed to locate them?'

'It seems their abilities and resolve are limited.'

'They're resisting the transition of power?'

'It was foreseen,' she said, 'which is why you're here to aid in their motivation.'

'Motivation for what?'

'A recent event within the military's vaults and laboratory complex has come to our attention. An object was stolen that needs recovering.'

'An object?'

'An Anakim artefact.'

Joiner's curiosity rose. 'What is its significance?'

Selene Dubois stopped pacing, once more standing on Sanctuary's impressive seal in the centre of the room. She looked at him, her clasped hands giving away the telltale signs of impatience, *or is it anxiety?* Joiner wondered.

'It holds the key to everything we're working towards,' she said, unable to keep an intensity from her voice.

'It's vital, then?'

She gave a nod. 'The object in question is a five sided metallic pendant that enables its wearer to activate Anakim technology.'

Joiner's eyebrows shot up. 'You're sure of this?'

'The Committee has marked the acquisition of this object as its top priority. No stone can be left unturned in its retrieval.'

'An artefact of such value wasn't protected?'

'We were unaware of its import. Despite this, it was secured in a military vault, but the person who took it was able to breach its security.'

'A professional?'

'It seems not; at least, not a professional thief.'

'How have they not been found?' he said, perplexed. 'The base is finite and everyone's movements are traceable.'

'They're no longer inside the base.'

Joiner's confusion increased. 'The base is in lockdown, how did they make it to the surface?'

'They didn't. As far as we know they are traversing Sanctuary Proper as we speak.'

'Then they're as good as dead.'

Selene paused. 'Not necessarily.'

Joiner couldn't quite believe what he was hearing and it must have shown.

'There are mitigating circumstances which will become apparent,' she told him. 'Needless to say this individual is also of interest to us. A dossier and select video footage awaits in your office. And Director, remember, despite what you see, further enquiries into Project Ares will not be tolerated.'

'What resources do I have at my disposal?' Joiner said.

'Everything. We want this artefact by any means necessary – whatever you need to achieve this goal, it's yours.'

Joiner nodded, the thrill at having such carte blanche tempered by the weight of responsibility he now bore. 'You must know,' he said, 'there's no guarantee, if they're in Sanctuary Proper, of any retrieval.'

The woman gave him an indecipherable look and then walked away to the imposing doors she'd entered by.

Fearing he'd said the wrong thing, Joiner went to say something else, but her voice curtailed his efforts.

'S.I.L.V.E.R. have been recalled from the field. They will arrive within the day.'

'All of them?'

'Yes,' she said, her voice growing fainter as she moved further away. 'They are to lead the operation on the ground, under your direction.'

Passing back through the great archway, she paused and looked back over her shoulder. 'Make sure to use your resources well, Malcolm Joiner,' she said, her voice drifting through the quiet. 'Failure is not an option.'

CHAPTER TWO

THE DOORS CLOSED behind the tall, slender figure of Selene Dubois, leaving Joiner alone, her final words of warning ringing in his ears. Without instigation, the two purple clad soldiers reappeared at the edge of the Anakim antechamber to escort him back to the lift.

On the long descent down the side of the Anakim tower, Joiner contemplated the work he was to carry out on behalf of the Committee. Find and return a precious Anakim artefact, along with the person who'd managed to steal it. No mean feat considering the size of Sanctuary Proper. Even with the help of S.I.L.V.E.R. and with all the manpower within USSB Sanctuary at his disposal, the chances of success were slim; the dangers and difficulties involved when traversing the endless underground chambers, tunnels and cave systems of Sanctuary Proper were legendary. Although, from what the Committee member had indicated, this thief may be more equipped to deal with these obstacles than most.

There must be something she hasn't told me, he reasoned, they wouldn't give me an impossible task to complete – unless, that is, they want me to fail. The idea was a disturbing one.

Avoiding thinking about the implications of such a possibility and eager to find out more about this intriguing turn of events, Joiner strode out of the elevator as its doors opened and made his way towards the shiny black limousine that sat parked a hundred feet away. His entourage of U.S. GMRC intelligence agents, who'd been waiting for his return, fell into step alongside. A door was opened for him and Joiner settled into the electric car's plush interior while his underlings returned to the other SUVs in the five strong motorcade. Sitting in the back of the stretched vehicle as his driver navigated through the light traffic of USSB Sanctuary's New Park district, Joiner's lip curled into a sneer as he recalled his brief exchanges with the woman and the subsequent humiliation he'd been subjected to. A repressed adolescent memory flashed into his mind, elicited by the unwanted emotion. Fury seethed to the surface. *How dare she threaten me. ME!* The knuckles on his leather glove creaked and stretched as he bunched a fist, his eyes burning bright.

He held his clenched hand thus, channelling his anger into it before letting it ebb away. Slowing his breathing, Joiner poured himself a glass of bourbon from a crystal decanter and took a sip, his usual self-control restored. *So the Committee seeks to keep Project Ares to themselves,* he mused. *If they think a simple warning will scare me off, they're mistaken. In fact, it has only fuelled my curiosity further. What aren't they telling me? What are they so keen to hide?* Joiner knew the folly of disobeying direct instructions; however, he'd amassed a lot of power in his time as intelligence director and even more when he'd assumed his position on the pre-eminent GMRC Directorate. He'd also accumulated a lot of allies over the years, willing and otherwise, many of whom were beyond even the Committee's extensive reach. He was no longer the naïve man who'd been coerced into their service all those years ago.

He stared into his glass. His previous efforts at finding out the inner workings of Project Ares had clearly been too overt, and he knew he must cover his tracks better if he was to find out more about this black project that seemed to have more layers than a supersized prizewinning onion. He prided himself on knowing everyone's business – everyone that mattered, that was – and now the Committee had reined him in they would have to be taught that he was not for controlling. He pursed his lips and sighed. That time had not yet arrived, however. He'd worked for far too long to secure their trust; to throw that away was unthinkable. He was so close now; he could taste it. Each step drew him nearer to becoming one of their number and then their deepest secrets would be his. Secrets he wanted ... no – *had* – to know.

When he completed this task the Committee would be forced to accept him into the fold. He'd been promised an opportunity, this must be it. When he secured them this incredible artefact surely they could not refuse him any longer?

Of course, when he entered their ranks they would have to be made aware of just whom they were dealing with. When that day came he would make them feel the fear they'd induced in him tenfold. The thought of bringing them low, of the terror in their faces, brought an inhuman glimmer to his eyes. But as of that moment his and the Committee's goals were still aligned and such fascinations, delightful as they were, needed to be put on hold.

The movement of the limousine ceased, bringing Joiner's attention back to the present. His door opened and a wash of warm air entered the air-conditioned cabin. He exited and made his way into USSB Sanctuary's GMRC Command Complex, where he submitted to the minor irritation of security checks. He then took a super swift vacuum elevator up to his office suite, located on the one-hundred-and-first floor of the functional glass-clad building.

Leaving his minions to their own devices, Joiner entered his office and shut the doors behind him. As if by magic the room's walls, ceiling and floor lit up, their state-of-the-art displays powering to life and producing a seamless three hundred and sixty degree 3D visual marvel. Instead of standing in a mundane office, Joiner was now surrounded by the Brazilian rainforest as it had looked before the dust cloud had stolen away its life-giving sunlight. Vibrant greens of dense foliage filled his vision, from horizon to distant horizon. Above, the azure skies of the Amazon shone like the mythical pellucid seas of Atlantis, picture perfect in their majesty and populated with a rainbow of ornithological plumage.

Joiner closed his eyes and took a deep breath, imagining the sweet scents that would surround him if the image were real. He stood there for some moments, but as hard as he tried no smells could be conjured forth, only the faint aroma of filtered air and the chemicals used to dry-clean his suit registering from reality. Annoyed at buying into the stress management techniques suggested by his overpaid physician, Joiner walked to the screen and tapped it with two fingers. A graphical command grid appeared in front of him. Selecting his network files, a red-flagged, unread digital package stood out from its fellows. Joiner opened it and an array of documents popped up to arrange themselves throughout the grid.

The dossier promised him by Selene, on behalf of the Committee, was detailed and extensive. Moving to his desk, Joiner transferred the information to the wallscreen behind him and settled into his chair to digest the information contained within.

◆

A couple of hours had passed since Joiner had laid eyes on the digital dossier and during that time he'd been joined by one of his top agents. And while their discussions had been grand in scope, talk inevitably returned to a subject that cropped up time and again.

'Project Ares was investigated wholly in-house,' Joiner said. 'No outside agencies were used.'

'You suspect a leak?'

'I don't suspect. I know.'

'You want further enquiries off the books?'

Joiner considered the man before him. Agent Myers, a nondescript fellow of above average height and build, and Joiner's right-hand man, had proved invaluable over the years. A member of the CIA's Special Operations Group with a dual position as a high-ranking GMRC intelligence agent, his skills and professionalism were second to none. Joiner rarely relied on specific people, but Myers was the exception to the rule.

'I'll make it happen,' Agent Myers said, recognising Joiner's silence to be the affirmation he intended.

Joiner went back to perusing the documents provided by the Committee. He frowned. Some of the video files had been extensively censored, minutes of footage disappearing behind a wall of black and white static. Considering the warning he'd been given, he knew the missing segments must conceal vital information about Project Ares. *If I want to reveal what lies beneath*, Joiner thought, *I'll have to ensure anyone working on their decryption is kept in the dark as to their content, especially considering the leak and my tenuous position with the Committee.*

'There's something else,' Myers said.

Joiner looked up, his expression quizzical.

'We've had reports from throughout the GMRC and U.S. military that ...' Myers' voice tailed off.

'That?' Joiner prompted.

'Debris from geosynchronous orbit has been tracked entering the atmosphere.'

'Debris from what?'

'It appears the asteroid intercept missions planned by the GMRC's Space Programme will not be proceeding as envisaged.'

Joiner frowned and sat up straighter. 'Debris from what?' he repeated, concerned.

'The reports indicate that a catastrophic failure in the International Space Station's propulsion system created a chain of events that has induced a series of explosions, destroying the ISS.'

Joiner's eyes widened. 'What?!'

Myers looked grim. 'That's not all; the other three stations attached to it were torn to pieces in the aftermath. The Space Programme is dead.'

Joiner shook his head in shock. Standing up, he paced away from Myers and stared out at the trees without seeing, his mind working furiously to compute the information he'd just received.

With the Space Programme gone, Earth's surface was doomed. All hope of averting the approaching asteroids turned to dust like the veil that still cloaked the planet in its choking embrace. Joiner thought of his collection of houses and apartments, dotted around some of the most affluent neighbourhoods in America. *At least my art collections are safe here*, he thought, knowing his prized possessions had already been relocated to his new home in USSB Sanctuary.

While he had prepared for the worst case scenario, there had always been a part of him that thought the surface could still be saved. Now that chance had disappeared and subterranean life was assured, it was difficult to accept. It was true he cared little for the billions of lives that would be lost, but thinking about the architectural gems that would be ruined by the scorching heat and icy cold of a world without an atmosphere made Joiner feel quite morose.

Agent Myers cleared his throat. 'Two Sabre transportation ships are reported to have left for Earth just prior to the incident.'

Joiner turned around. 'GMRC?'

Myers nodded. 'You suspect foul play?'

Joiner didn't reply, he didn't know what to think, but Myers' assertion might not be wrong.

'Why would anyone want the Space Programme to fail?' Myers said. 'Who could possibly gain from that?'

Joiner wasn't sure, but as the GMRC's Director of Intelligence he knew its infiltration by hidden groups was almost assured, such was the council's scale. Perhaps the question should be who had the resources to pull off such a coup? He could think of a few organisations that could, the Committee being one of them. *Although, surely even they wouldn't devise such a plan, would they?* Feeling disorientated, Joiner sat back down at his desk to collect his thoughts. Myers remained silent as his director digested the news.

'Dig deeper,' Joiner said at last. 'Find out what you can. Run it alongside the Project Ares op. But be careful who you involve. Make sure no one sees the whole picture. Use multiple agencies, civilian and military, but not the GMRC. Make sure any enquiries or data received cannot be traced back to us. Anything you find: my eyes only.'

Myers gave a nod.

Joiner's intercom buzzed to life. 'Sir,' his aide said, his voice sounding fearful. 'Someone is coming in to see you, I tried stopping him, but—'

Both doors to Joiner's office opened wide, the hyper-realistic digital forestscape of Brazil replaced by the silhouette of a man.

'Malcolm Joiner?' the figure said.

'Who wants to know?' Myers said, his hand straying to his sidearm.

The doors closed behind the interloper and the simulated scene of nature resumed. The man, dressed in chrome-like armour edged with gold, held a similarly clad helmet under one arm. At six foot seven and powerfully built, he was a couple of inches taller than Joiner and carried himself with an assured ease. His chiselled features were unnaturally pallid and his long black hair had been pulled back into a neat plait which draped down over one shoulder. Bright eyes and a relaxed expression showed no hint of concern at the threat from Agent Myers; in fact the glimmer of a mocking smile tugged at his lips as he moved his attention from Joiner to the CIA operative.

'My name is Ophion Nexus,' he said, his voice tombstone deep. 'I believe you are expecting my team?' He looked back to Joiner.

'Sir?' Myers said, keeping his eyes on the man before him.

'Leave us, Agent.' Joiner motioned for Ophion to approach.

Myers remained on guard and held the man's gaze as he walked past before taking his leave, a look of uncertainty on his face.

Once the two men were alone, Joiner rose and held out a hand, which Ophion shook. The intelligence director's eyes flicked down to an emblem etched onto the man's chest-plate.

'The Committee has briefed you?' Joiner said.

'They have.'

'I'm to oversee your mission.'

Ophion Nexus shifted his stance. 'That won't be necessary.'

'Your autonomy is legend, but here – now – you will operate solely under my orders. Do we understand each other?'

Ophion's face hardened.

'Well?' Joiner said.

'I'll report back to you, as the Committee requested.'

'And you will action my orders,' Joiner said, 'also as the Committee requests.'

Ophion gave a barely perceptible movement of his head, his reluctance causing Joiner concern. *What has this man been told?* he wondered. Selene, the Committee member, had indicated Joiner would be in charge; S.I.L.V.E.R.'s leader, Ophion, seemed to think otherwise. *Is he just unused to taking orders or has the Committee undermined my position?* Either way it didn't fill Joiner with confidence; if his success rested on another's actions, someone over whom he had no control, his destiny, and perhaps his very life, was out of his hands. It was a status quo he could not allow to stand. Measures would have to be taken – fast.

'The thief and her two companions have a week's head start,' Ophion said in his rumbling baritone. 'The repairs need finalising; each hour, each minute, reduces our chance of success.'

Joiner sat back down in his chair. 'I'm well aware of the state of play. Matters are in hand.'

'If they were in hand there would not be a problem. If I was in command there would not be a problem.'

Joiner gritted his teeth. 'Is that so?'

Ophion held his gaze. 'It is.'

The two men remained thus for some moments in an unspoken battle of wills before Ophion relented under Joiner's determination to continue the frosty silence ad infinitum. *I can't afford to cede the upper hand,* he thought, *not now; my position of power is already tenuous.*

Ophion turned to leave.

'Wait!' Joiner said, his voice ringing with authority.

S.I.L.V.E.R.'s leader stopped and looked back, his expression dark.

'I haven't given you your orders ...'

Ophion was obliged to wait as Joiner paused. He wanted the man's full attention to ram home his position of power. 'Once I've spoken to the facilitators of this fiasco,' Joiner continued, 'you can liaise with them to form the search teams. When you're out in the field, messengers and tethered relays will be utilised to coordinate under my direction.'

Ophion didn't respond, his hooded eyes bleak.

'Are we clear,' Joiner said, 'or do I need to draw you a diagram?'

The muscles around Ophion's hawklike eyes tightened. In the blink of an eye and a blur of motion, a narrow blade slammed into the desk, mere fractions of an inch from Joiner's hand, making him jerk back in alarm.

'You forget to whom you speak, Intelligence Director,' Ophion said, his tone ice cool. 'You'd do well not to do so again.'

Before Joiner could respond, S.I.L.V.E.R.'s leader, Ophion Nexus, stalked from the room, his dagger left behind, embedded in Joiner's desk like some kind of medieval proclamation, its message clear – a message of warning.

CHAPTER THREE

MALCOLM JOINER, one of the most powerful men on the planet, eyed the weapon sticking out of his desk; a weapon that had been close to severing the fingers on his right hand. He leant forward and grasped the blade's grip and – with some difficulty – wrenched it loose, the wooden surface groaning in release. Holding the dense metal object before him, he angled it back and forth, allowing the surrounding light to glint along its razor sharp edge.

He considered his dilemma. In any other circumstances he would have such a physical threat nullified, but S.I.L.V.E.R.'s leader was in the pay of the Committee and was therefore their agent and representative, as much as Joiner himself. To attempt to have Ophion put down would likely lead to his own demise – S.I.L.V.E.R.'s reputation for retribution in the event something happened to one of their own was well known to those that knew of their existence – but if he let it stand he would appear weak, an affectation the Committee saw fit to excise from their ranks with ruthless efficiency.

Feeling trapped, Joiner recalled Myers to his office.

'Sir, may I ask who that was?' Myers said, after he'd returned.

Joiner placed the blade down to one side. 'He's a S.I.L.V.E.R. operative.'

'S.I.L.V.E.R.?'

'It's an acronym; Stealth, Infiltration, Liquidation, Verification, Extraction and Reconnaissance.'

Myers' expression turned to one of distaste. 'A hired kill squad?'

'If you like,' Joiner said. 'Some call them assassins, mercenaries or hunters, although I think of them more as a multidisciplinary elite taskforce available to the highest bidder.'

'Which is who?'

'They're here on my orders to ensure a successful outcome to our problem,' Joiner said, sidestepping the question.

'The missing artefact. I thought it was a retrieval mission?'

'It is, but S.I.L.V.E.R. are the best at what they do, the best at everything, in fact. They're recruited without deference to national borders, race, colour or creed. They're selected solely on ability and paid handsomely for their work. Only the very best, the most skilled, are considered for their ranks, which always number twenty-two.'

'So few?'

'Leaders all and highly motivated, they are the perfect choice to ensure any mission's success.'

Myers looked unconvinced and – unbeknownst to him – his cause for concern was not without foundation, considering Joiner's recent run-in with Ophion Nexus. The image of the chrome-clad assassin returned to the forefront of Joiner's mind as he racked his brains for solutions to the threat to his leadership and the retrieval of the stolen Anakim artefact. An idea popped into his head, an extreme idea, but one that might just work in his favour. *If I can pull it off*, he thought. He'd need to yank quite a few strings and put the backs up of some powerful people, but then many of those would soon be dead anyway, when the next wave of asteroids hit in 2042.

'I need you to go back to the surface,' Joiner said.

Myers looked dubious. 'Should we keep breaching Sanctuary's lockdown protocols so freely? The military have been vociferous in their opposition to it.'

'To hell with the military, they'll do as they're told. Lockdown can always be circumvented for small parties. Besides, considering

General Ellwood's monumental fuck up last year they're in no position to judge.'

'What is it you want me to do?'

'I need you to acquire something for me.' Joiner flipped up a display tablet from his desk and tapped away at its keyboard to bring up the relevant information for his plan. Once he had what he wanted he angled it towards the CIA operative.

Myers' eyes grew round and he looked back at Joiner. 'You can't be serious?'

'Deadly. This is what I want. Can you make it happen if I get you the necessary clearance?'

Myers puffed out his cheeks. 'It's an ask. Perhaps you should get one of those S.I.L.V.E.R. mercs on it if they're as good you say.'

'They're not an option in this instance.'

Myers frowned as he thought about the ramifications of such a task.

'Well?' Joiner said, as Myers continued to deliberate.

'If you can get me the relevant clearance, which will be a feat in itself, then, yes, I can make it happen. I take it you have a good reason for such a move, as it won't go unnoticed?'

'I have two very good reasons, each worth the risk in isolation.'

Myers nodded and then raised an eyebrow when Joiner remained looking at him over the tops of his glasses. 'You want me to go now?'

'This is top priority. By the time you get to your destination I'll make sure you'll have everything you need to get it done.'

'Okay,' Myers said, his expression still dubious, 'I'm on it.' Without another word he departed, leaving his director alone with his thoughts.

Picking up his portable computer for a secure connection, Joiner dialled the first number on a list of many and switched the video feed to his wallscreen.

The image of a woman in a suit appeared. 'Attorney General's office, how may I direct your call?'

'This is GMRC Director of Intelligence Joiner, put me through to your boss.'

The woman's eyes widened as she realized who she was speaking to. 'Certainly, sir, I'll ... patch you through ... immediately.'

Joiner waited until another feed replaced the first. A man finished speaking to a legal aide, who left the room, then looked up at the camera.

Joiner stood up. 'I need a favour.'

The AG's relaxed demeanour turned guarded. 'Do I have a choice?'

A cruel, self-satisfied smile broke Joiner's deadpan expression. 'No,' he said. 'Now, this is what you're going to do—'

CHAPTER FOUR

DRESDEN LOCKE, commanding officer of the secretive Sanctuary Exploration Division, the SED, shifted in his seat as he waited to be seen by a high ranking GMRC official. Across from him sat one General Stevens, a U.S. Army officer who oversaw the SED's operations out in the dangerous environment of Sanctuary Proper, beyond the safety of the USSB. Stevens, a larger than life individual with an extensive gut stretching his officer's uniform to bursting, sucked on a similarly fat cigar, the end glowing orange as the packed leaves crackled and popped as they ignited under combustion. Between the two men, a pall of smoke hung in the room's reception area and General Stevens' eyes had closed in apparent relaxation.

Locke, on the other hand, was far from at ease. As a civilian he rarely mixed with the upper hierarchy, be they U.S. government, GMRC or dual role chameleons who held positions within both power structures; however, he'd received a video call earlier that evening requesting his attendance at Sanctuary's giant GMRC Command Complex and ever since he'd been on edge. Getting impatient, he stood up and walked to the window to look out at the dark landscape of the Dome level's New Park district. Simulated night reigned and his reflection stared back at him in mute contemplation.

In his fifties, Locke had short silver-grey hair framing an uncompromising expression. A strong jaw, broad shoulders and narrow waist indicated he worked out, while his white and red SED uniform hugged his athletic figure in a complimentary fashion.

The GMRC dignitary's personal aide, who'd introduced himself as Grant Debden and sat at a curved reception desk, cleared his throat. 'The director will see you now.'

Locke gave a nod and nudged the foot of the general, who'd failed to stir from his slumber.

'What?' he said, sitting up in his seat, a lump of ash from the end of his cigar drifting to the floor.

'Time to face the music,' Locke said.

Stevens grunted and stood up, his paunch bulging out like some vast, personal airbag, fit to burst. The general held out a hand for him to lead the way.

Opening one of the large double doors, Locke's expression changed from guarded apprehension to surprise. The room inside glowed with the warmth of a summer's eve at dusk, the beautiful rays of a setting sun sinking down in multicoloured skies to caress the verdant foliage of a lush, tropical forest beneath. Walking inside it seemed as if he'd been transported to another world, a world where the high altitude dust cloud did not exist – a world at peace in tranquil splendour. The experience felt real, immersive and more than a little uplifting.

The tall, slender figure of a man rose from behind a desk that blended into the background. 'Take a seat, gentlemen,' he said, his voice cutting, the tone verging on nasal.

Locke and Stevens did as instructed and the general leaned forward to offer his hand in greeting, but the moment turned awkward when the gesture failed to be reciprocated.

The man eyed each of them without saying a word, the discomfort of the situation palpable against the background of the forest sounds that surrounded them.

'You know why you are both here?' the man said, still standing.

Locke glanced at General Stevens who looked less than impressed by how things were proceeding.

'It would help if we knew who you were,' Locke said, feeling the need to say something – anything to get some meaningful dialogue moving.

'The general knows who I am, don't you, General?'

Stevens took a drag on his cigar but failed to respond, his eyes narrowing.

'My name,' he said, looking to Locke, 'is Malcolm Joiner and I'm the U.S. and GMRC Director of Intelligence.' He turned away from them. 'I also have a seat on the GMRC Directorate.'

Locke tensed at the word *Directorate*, knowing full well the power wielded by those on the Global Meteor Response Council's controlling assembly.

'It has come to my attention,' the director continued, 'that the two of you have a lot to answer for with regard to recent events within Sanctuary's Exploration Division.'

The general ran the back of his hand across his mouth. 'I wasn't the one who hired her.'

Joiner turned back round, a sneer distorting his face. 'Excellent tactics, General. Lay the blame for your own ineptitude at the door of another. I'd expect nothing less from an incompetent such as yourself.'

General Stevens didn't respond, but his blotchy face had turned a brighter shade of red, his jowls taut with anger.

'It's true I hired the woman,' Locke said, feeling he might as well lay it out as it was, 'but the military gave me the green light, they vetted her. This is a U.S. military base, is it not?'

'Ah, touché, Mr. Locke,' Joiner said, his voice dripping with venom, 'touché. Perhaps I should record this meeting as a lesson in how to pass the buck.' The GMRC director looked from Locke to Stevens and back to Locke again. 'Nothing else to say?'

Locke remained silent and Stevens followed suit. Both could see where this conversation was going and it wasn't going to be pretty.

Joiner switched his attention to the screen on his desk. 'Let's start at the beginning, shall we?' he said, glancing up at them. 'How did this interloper enter Sanctuary in the first place?'

'She told us they entered by a series of tunnels,' Locke said.

Joiner sat down in his chair. 'Only these mystery tunnels were never found, were they not?'

Locke shook his head in affirmation.

'So,' Joiner continued, eyeing the general, 'when these three civilians turned up miles underground in the most secure facility on the planet, instead of keeping them locked up indefinitely until we found the gaping hole in our security grid, you decided to let them walk free around the base as permanent citizens?'

'Do you know how big this installation is?' Stevens said. 'Twenty million souls live and work down here; you think I'm the only staffer in charge? I had nothing to do with their release, or with the interrogations. Ask one of my colleagues the whys and wherefores and then you'll get your answers.'

Joiner looked back to his screen. 'It seems we already have and said colleagues have been reassigned to surface duties. If you continue to renege on your responsibilities you'll soon be joining them. And believe me when I say, General, the surface will soon be a place you most certainly won't want to be.'

General Stevens turned a whiter shade of pale, clearly aware of the implications inherent in the director's words. Locke frowned; he knew the surface was bad, what with the dust cloud and civil unrest, but judging by Joiner's threat and Stevens' reaction it seemed like there was something else to fear. What that could be he could only guess, but whatever it was, it didn't sound good.

'Now,' Joiner said, moving his attention back to Locke, 'this woman, free to wander as she pleased, then managed to break into Sanctuary's restricted Exploration Division, the illustrious SED; but rather than have her thrown into prison for the rest of her days you conspired to have her released from military custody for a second time and ...' Joiner paused and shook his head and gave a snort of derision, his expression incredulous. 'Forgive me, I find this hard to believe ... and then you gave her a job *in* the SED. If I were a crass man, Commander Locke, I'd probably say something like: are you *fucking* kidding me?' At these words Joiner's false mirth fell from his face, which had turned white with anger.

Pinned down by the director's fury, Locke's words caught in his throat. What could he say? The man had a point. While Locke hadn't come up with the idea, he had sanctioned it and seen the sense in the woman's induction into his operation. She was perfectly suited to becoming a part of SED operations, having both the qualifications and potential to go all the way to the top. That was until she'd thrown the opportunity back in his face, bringing down with it the mother of all shitstorms.

Locke dropped his gaze and Joiner's lip curled with contempt before he continued his summation. 'With her training in the art of traversing Sanctuary Proper complete, her skills at evasion increased, this woman, who was no doubt marvelling at the ineptitude of the halfwits in charge, then took it upon herself to break into the Smithsonian's secure vaults and from there into the military's vault array. There, she helped herself to various priceless Anakim artefacts and proceeded to disable the security grid within a square mile radius. She then waltzed into the level ten restricted access area of the U.S. military laboratory complex housed beneath and stole an object of supreme scientific interest.' Joiner paused for breath and then stood up and paced away to gaze out at the majesty of the surrounding flora and fauna as darkness fell.

'After completing her heist,' he said, resuming the monologue, 'said individual assaulted a Smithsonian worker and then murdered an SED employee before fleeing the base in a stolen air-shuttle with her two co-conspirators. In the process she detonated a device which obliterated the shuttle track and accompanying launch mechanism, rendering the possibility of any pursuit nonexistent. Have I missed anything out?'

Locke and Stevens avoided Joiner's gaze.

The intelligence director shook his head. 'You couldn't make this mess up.' Walking back to his desk, he removed his glasses and began cleaning the lenses with a soft cloth. 'So, gentlemen,' he said, continuing the task of polishing, 'what do you propose we do to rectify this issue?'

'Repairs on the shuttle track are already underway;' Locke told him. 'They'll be finished within two weeks.'

'I've briefed a Special Forces squad from the Subterranean Detachment on a seek and capture mission,' General Stevens said. 'They'll be ready to go as soon as the track is operational.'

Joiner replaced his spectacles and leant forward, his eyes afire with fettered wrath. 'The track will be finished within three days; I guarantee it, and General, a squad – really? Let me tell you how it's going to be. I want teams out searching Sanctuary Proper for how this person infiltrated this base. I want units on the surface scouring the land for entrances. I want every Special Forces regiment and all SED personnel ready for deployment by air-shuttle at a moment's notice. I—'

'You can want all you like,' Stevens said, looking belligerent, 'I don't have the manpower.'

The blood drained from Joiner's face. 'You will have, General, because when you leave this office you'll give the order to mobilize this entire base.'

General Stevens choked on his cigar smoke. 'The entire base? You're out of your mind. I won't back that!'

The director snatched something up and slammed it down.

Stevens cried out in pain and Locke jumped up from his seat in shock. The handle of a knife stuck out from the back of the general's hand, pinning him to the desk. Stevens groaned as he attempted to remove the blade, but the pain was too great as blood pooled between his fingers.

Joiner grasped the general's other hand, preventing him from making further attempts to free himself, as Locke looked on in horror.

'I'm going to flood Sanctuary Proper with every man, woman and child if that's what it takes to bring this woman in, do you hear me, General?' Joiner said, through clenched teeth.

The general, captivated by the intelligence director's intensity, continued to squirm in pain.

'I – you – we all won't rest until this woman, this English archaeologist, this thief is found, do you hear me?!' Joiner released his hold and raised his manic gaze to Locke. 'I'll have this person, alive or dead, whatever it takes, JUST BRING ME SARAH MORGAN!'

TERMINOLOGY / MAP

USSB – United States Subterranean Base
GMRC – Global Meteor Response Council
Darklight – World's largest private security contractor
SFSD – Special Forces Subterranean Detachment (*Terra Force*)
SED – Sanctuary Exploration Division
Deep Reach – Special survey team working within the SED
S.I.L.V.E.R. – An elite military unit available to the highest bidder
Sanctuary Proper – Ancient underground structure built by an extinct species of Hominid, Homo giganthropsis (the Anakim)

USSB
STEADFAST
NEVADA
UTAH
COLORADO
CALIFORNIA
Las Vegas
USA
Los Angeles
ARIZONA
NEW
MEXICO
TEXAS
MEXICO
USSB
SANCTUARY

CHAPTER FIVE

Crumbling buildings of Anakim origin rose out of the gloom like phantoms in the night, their arcane forms striking alien visions to those that passed them by. Huge abandoned highways and tiny narrow paths wound their way through the enormity of Sanctuary Proper, that stretched out eternal. Untrodden for untold millennia, the three dimensional nature of the subterranean relic induced a kind of sensory overload to any person travelling within its boundless realm; the darkness, all-consuming, all-encompassing, accentuated the eerie silence that permeated the very air, the very fabric of its nature. The endless procession of tunnels, caves, crevasses and cliffs ate into the psyche as the choice of direction for the unwary wayfarer spun off every which way; an array of options each with a fatal potential leading to ends suitable for the dead. A loss of concentration or misplaced step, a sudden turn or ill-timed leap, a disaster waiting to happen, a disaster as unforgiving as the rocky foundations above and beneath, behind and before.

Echoing footsteps and depressive thoughts, beckoned forth by solitude and suffocating stale air, brought to the fore hallucinatory dreams and maddening lucidity. To the minority, who knew of its existence, the way was known to be fraught with danger. To the few who dared traverse its forbidden halls, its mountainous hollow shell, the passage could never be surpassed in scope or threat.

At the summit of a monumental climb – that started a kilometre down in the deep – a hand appeared over a sharp ridge. Feeling about for purchase, fingers dug into thin, dusty soil loaded with gravel. With a final exertion from weary limbs, the explorer heaved herself up, the scrape of clothing and rattle of climbing gear loud to the ear. Rolling onto her back she lay there, chest rising and falling, sweat dripping and heart pumping. All she could hear was the thump thump thump of blood pumping through her veins.

Her breathing eased and she sat up to see a hand extended towards her. She grasped it and accepted the force that pulled her to her feet. 'Where is she?'

He pointed. 'Up there.'

She sighed and focused on the area he'd indicated. High above a small figure traversed a precarious ledge, her long blonde hair peeking out beneath her high-tech helmet, its inbuilt torches lighting her way. 'I think she's losing the plot, this is a dead end.'

'She didn't seem to think so.'

'*She's* taking too many risks.'

The man shrugged. 'It's what she does.'

'I don't like it. I don't like any of this.'

'She's got us this far.'

'Which is where?'

'That's what she's trying to find out.'

She frowned. 'She's not wearing her safety harness again.'

'She said she needed to move quickly. Our water is running low, or hadn't you noticed?'

'It's all I ever think about.'

His shoulders dropped. 'Losing the aerial drone didn't help.'

'That ceiling could have collapsed at any time. It wasn't your fault.'

He gave a derisive snort. 'Our luck sucks.'

'Maybe. It depends which way you look at it.' She looked back up and winced as her blonde friend leapt across a sheer drop, sending loose sediment cascading down the side of the rock face.

Adjusting her helmet visor, she brightened the image of the pitch-black cave, grateful for the technology that enabled its wearer to see in the dark – without them they'd be blind and in even deeper trouble than they already were. 'I'm getting a really bad feeling about this,' she said, 'we're past the point of no return.'

'Give her a chance, she'll come good.'

'She better or we'll die down here.'

'When has she let us down before?'

She looked at him and considered the question. 'There was that time in Pakistan, and then on Easter Island when she—'

'Recently,' he said.

'Oi, you two!' A voice echoed in their helmets, making them look back towards the person they'd been discussing.

'Stop your yakking and give me a hand.'

'Keep your hair on!' Jason said, through his headset's microphone.

'What do you want us to do?' Trish asked, also using her inbuilt communication system.

'Grab this rope and pull, but make sure you're out of the way.' She threw a rope down to them, its coils unfurling on the long descent.

'Are you sure this is going to work?' Jason said, walking forward to collect the line.

'I hope so,' her voice crackled over the radio, 'or we're going to have to find another way through.'

'This doesn't look very safe,' Trish said to Jason. 'You're sure she knows what she's doing?'

'Of course I know what I'm doing,' the voice said through her helmet's earpiece. 'I've had Deep Reach training, haven't I?'

'We're not in the SED now, though, are we?' Trish said.

Her friend failed to comment; instead she finished tying her end of the rope around a boulder and moved back the way she'd come, once more jumping over the knee trembling drop. She gave them a thumbs up signal. 'Good to go!'

Jason and Trish grasped the rope with their climbing gloves and took the strain.

Jason looked back at her. 'You ready?'

Trish grimaced. 'I suppose.'

'On three. One – two – three!'

Trish leant back and pulled as hard as she could. The rope creaked under tension while the dirt underfoot formed tiny mounds as their climbing boots dug into it. With her lungs fit to burst, Trish let go. 'There's no way we're budging that.'

'Hang on,' Jason said, and moved off.

A moment later light blazed forth as he returned with the Centipede, their multi-wheeled, remote controlled, all-terrain supply vehicle. Manoeuvring the fifteen foot long, yellow-clad, insect-like machine into position, Jason proceeded to attach the rope to one end.

He gave Trish a grin. 'No point breaking our backs when Bob can do it for us.'

Trish shook her head. 'If you had to give it a name couldn't you have chosen something better than Bob?'

He waved her out of the way. 'What's wrong with Bob?'

'What's right with it?'

'You've got no imagination.'

'Says the man who came up with Bob.'

Jason peered at a button on the supply vehicle's control console that read: *auxiliary engine*. He glanced up. 'Shall I use the—'

'No.' His friend's voice echoed in his ear. 'Do not use the power boost, if the rope snapped it'd be out of control. How many more times?'

'Spoilsport. Okay,' – he pulled back on the joystick – 'let's see what he's got.'

The Centipede, aka Bob, gained speed before jolting to a halt as the rope snapped tight. Wheels spinning, dirt flying, the low slung vehicle weaved from side to side as it sought purchase.

Trish waved to Jason as the vehicle's motor whined and its wheels slipped and spun. 'It's not working!'

Jason ceased its movement.

'Try pulling at the same time,' their friend's voice said, via their helmets.

'Try pulling at the same time,' Jason said in mimicry. 'It'd help if she came down and helped.'

'I heard that,' came the reply.

Trish chuckled and grabbed hold of the rope, with Jason just in front of her.

Locking the Centipede's joystick into position, the sound of the machine's propulsion filled the air once more and Bob, Trish and Jason heaved back on the rope in unison.

'Keep going!' came the command over their com system. 'It's moving!'

Jason grunted in exertion and Trish felt her grip failing before the rope went slack. She fell to the ground and Jason landed on top of her, knocking her helmet into the dirt with a clonk and sending her visor image to a momentary fuzz of pixels.

A scream of warning caused the two of them to scramble back to their feet. Behind, Bob careered off into the immense blackness of Sanctuary Proper, straight towards a yawning crevasse. Jason made a dive for the control device and knocked the joystick back to neutral. The Centipede slid to a stop inches from the edge.

Jason looked at Trish. 'Jesus,' he said in shock, 'that was close.'

She nodded and heaved a sigh of relief.

'Good work,' said their friend's voice. 'I think I can see a way through now.'

'Is it safe?' Trish looked back up to see the tail end of a pair of legs disappear inside the entrance they'd just created. Before she could voice her concern at the obvious lack of caution, a deep rumbling shook the earth beneath their feet and great cracks zigzagged out from the hole.

The shaking continued and the sweeping cliff face crumbled. Huge swathes of rock toppled free and the shape of a woman moving at high speed, burst back into view to leap out into midair, a hundred feet up, limbs flailing. A scream rang out over the thunderous noise of the landslide and Trish watched in horror as her friend fell to certain death, before the rope they'd been pulling twanged tight, shooting up between them and dragging a beleaguered Bob back the way he'd come.

The woman, holding on for dear life, slid down the arc of rope at speed, chased by a mass of falling debris. The giant cavern gave a final groan before the whole side came crashing down. The deafening noise engulfed them and a wall of dust swallowed the fleeing climber in its heaving midst.

The ground lurched and Trish and Jason staggered backwards towards the yawning abyss behind. Teetering on the brink, Trish grabbed Jason's arm as death approached. A whoosh of air swept over them and a cloud of debris filled their vision. Trish shut her eyes and braced for impact. The rumbling grew louder still and then faded away. She cracked open an eye as the sound of small stones and pebbles trickling down signalled an end to the calamity. The dust cleared and, feet from the wall of collapsed rock, where Trish and Jason were huddled, their friend stood in stupendous victory, a victory of survival and indefensible fortune.

◆

Sarah Morgan threw aside the frayed end of the rope that had, without doubt, just saved her life. Sending a silent prayer of thanks to the gods of chance and fate, she removed her helmet and shook out her long blonde locks under the floodlit glare of the Centipede's headlights.

She approached her two friends, her dazzling blue eyes bright with life. 'You two okay?' she said, her East London accent resonating with concerned confidence.

Trish removed her own headgear. 'Are you out of your damn mind?!'

Sarah frowned. 'What're you talking about?'

'You may not give a shit if you live or die, but when you risk your life, you risk ours; without you we're as good as dead. What were you thinking, going in there without checking its stability?'

'Of course I care if I live or die!' Sarah looked to Jason for support. 'I'm doing everything I can to get us to the surface, or hadn't you noticed?'

'I noticed you didn't answer my question,' Trish said.

Sarah huffed and walked away to check the Centipede for damage. 'Of course I checked for stability. The visor highlights areas of structural weaknesses automatically.'

'Does it?' Trish asked Jason.

'Don't ask me.'

'Even if it did,' Trish said, 'you couldn't have checked it properly,' – she waved an arm indicating the huge landslip behind her – 'or it'd have picked up that.'

Sarah swung round, her expression fierce. 'Will you stop lecturing me! I'm doing all I can, but we've lost half our water supply and we're too far from the shuttle station to return!'

Livid, Trish strode forward. 'Lecturing you? Lecturing you?!'

Jason stepped between the two women and raised his hands. 'Ladies, come on, this isn't helping anyone.'

'Shut up, Jason!' they said in unison, their eyes locked.

He bowed his head and stepped back again.

'You're losing it,' Trish said, her gaze unwavering. 'You could have just killed us all and for what? There's no way through, we'll have to retrace our steps anyway.'

'If there's no way through, then what's that?' Sarah pointed up to the newly created mound of rock.

Trish turned. Before her, near where the cave wall had once stood, the final particles of pulverized stone had settled to reveal a new tunnel system beyond.

Trish faced her friend again. 'Just because it paid off this time doesn't mean jack, we're still screwed.'

Sarah couldn't take much more of this. 'Perhaps if you weren't whining all the time, distracting everyone, we wouldn't be.'

'What!' Trish lunged for her, but Jason intervened to hold her back as she tried to get at the object of her fury.

'Calm down!' he said, struggling to restrain her as Sarah primed for a fight.

'Calm down? Did you hear what she said?! She nearly killed us, AND BLAMED ME!!'

Continuing to vent her anger, near hysterical, arms flailing, she caught Jason in the mouth, drawing blood, and he slapped her round the face.

Trish stopped as shock registered. Tears welled and she turned and clambered away over the fallen debris, holding her cheek.

Jason followed. 'Trish, wait! I'm sorry!'

'Let her go,' Sarah said and returned to her inspection of their lifeline, the battle worn yellow supply vehicle. Crouching down, she ran a critical eye over it. It seemed to have avoided the rock fall unharmed, its intricate internal and external mechanisms showing no signs of damage. Their remaining water canisters, secured to one of its cargo plates, had also made it through unscathed.

Sarah glanced up to see Jason conversing with Trish some way away, arms gesticulating and voices raised. It wasn't long, however, before tensions calmed and the two shared a reconciling embrace.

Jason turned to pick his way back across the rock strewn landscape and Sarah looked back down to continue her inspection.

'You need to make up with her,' Jason said, coming to stand by her side.

'She needed to let off some steam. It'll do her good.' Sarah stood up, her long legs straightening. At nearly six foot she could look Jason squarely in the eye.

'None of this is helping.' He looked worried and glanced over at Trish, who remained where she was, sixty yards away with her back to them. 'You need to make this right.'

'I'll speak to her,' Sarah said, not feeling like speaking to Trish at all, but knowing it was what he wanted to hear.

Jason, reassured by her words, carried on yabbering, his Welsh trill musical to the ear, but something that Sarah zoned out as she double-checked the rest of their equipment was secure on the snake-like machine.

It had been over a week since they'd fled the U.S. Army enclave known as USSB Sanctuary. Deep underground, the massive subterranean city had been a revelation when they'd initially stumbled upon it the previous year; however, success had been marred by capture as they'd been thrown in a military prison quicker than they could blink. Many weeks passed and interrogations were endured before they'd been released and, through a series of miraculous breaks, Sarah had found herself working at the SED, Sanctuary's amazing Exploration Division.

The job had suited Sarah down to the ground and she'd revelled in the opportunity to explore outside the base and far into Sanctuary Proper as a member of an elite Deep Reach team, the pinnacle of SED operations for any ambitious archaeologist such as herself. She'd excelled at the work and lapped up the incredible scientific and archaeological discoveries she'd been privileged to witness. At the time it had seemed like everything in her life had led her towards those moments, an experience carved out by destiny and one unlike any other – an experience that she'd cherish until the end of her days.

The SED, of course, had been fantastic, as had the glory of the United States Subterranean Base itself, and the Anakim treasures contained within and without, but there had been something else that Sarah had found deep down in the Earth's crust, and that thing was love, or at least the blossoming beginnings of it. The man in question, Riley Orton, her Deep Reach SED team leader, had grown close to her during her stay and one thing had inevitably led to another. Responsible for her induction into the SED and for the intensive training regime that enabled her to pass the tests to qualify for Deep Reach duties, Riley had proven to be an amusing and uplifting companion in a foreign world; a world that she had, at first, striven with every fibre to escape from.

Sarah, wary of trusting her own judgement when it came to men, her track record poor, had deliberated long and hard about leaving behind the man she'd grown to care for. But leave him behind she had; her quest to expose the existence of the Anakim and their creation, Sanctuary itself, had proved too great a pull. It was her life's ambition to prove Homo gigantis – or Homo giganthropsis as they were also known – existed, and one that she could not put aside for anyone or anything.

The wrench of separation had been great and she still felt the loss like a knife in her heart, despite what she'd found out afterwards. However, there had been another motivating factor to her leaving the base and setting off for the surface. The death of her mother years before had left a blight on her life, a blight that she couldn't shake. The shadow of her parent's demise followed her wherever she went, an apparition at the edge of vision that refused to leave her be. Her life had now taken on dual purpose; expose the Anakim to the world and bring her mother's murderers to justice.

Combined with the fact that to stay in the U.S. Subterranean Base Sarah would have had to relinquish the notion of ever returning to the surface, she had decided to leave a dream job and the potential of a lifelong partner for ambition, freedom and justice; powerful ideals individually, but undeniable in union.

For years Sarah had believed the fire that had stolen her mother's life to be an accident, but events the year before in 2040 had transformed her perception from that of a horrific tragedy into one of deception and murder. The Anakim maps Sarah had unearthed and then stored in her mother's house for safekeeping had been an act of targeted destruction by agents of the Catholic Church – or at least, that's what she'd thought until she'd found one of the very same maps on display in Sanctuary's secret vaults.

The sad fact was the whole operation, the USSB, the SED, Deep Reach and Riley himself, had turned out to be a lie. They weren't the champions of archaeology and humanity as they proclaimed, but the users of it, abusing their roles for the good of the military and personal gain with no thought for the significance of history and everything that entailed. They even stooped to murdering the innocent to acquire the artefacts they desired.

When Sarah had voiced such reasoning to Trish and Jason, her friends had been quick to voice their opinions.

'How do you know they were responsible for stealing your maps?' Trish had said. 'They could have bought them from the Vatican's agents, or somewhere else.'

'And even if they did,' Jason added, 'you can't blame Riley, he's just some poor sap taking orders like everyone else.'

'Jas is right,' Trish had said, 'and I don't think Riley was a manipulator, either, he's not that type.'

Sarah didn't care for such thoughts; they made too much sense and fed her anger. She also refused to believe no one could have known where or how those Anakim parchments had been acquired. And that made those complicit in their retrieval and use as much to blame for her mother's death as those who had set the fire, and as much to blame as Sarah herself for hiding such precious artefacts in her mother's home in the first place. Not a day went by when she didn't curse her selfish stupidity for chasing a dream that had ultimately resulted in her worst nightmare. Except now that her mum was gone, that dream was the only thing she had left, that and the resulting quest for justice born from the ashes of her own guilt for her leading role in the whole sordid tale. The taste of it physically manifested like a pus-riddled boil on her tongue. Sometimes she even retched when the thoughts came, such was the intensity of the emotions involved. When she found herself in such a moment, her mood turned foul and a vicious side reared its ugly head, a side of her that she disliked, but one she seemed unable to control. It didn't help, though, when Trish and Jason tried to console her or alter her perspective on matters. In fact it was like a red rag to a bull and down in the depths of the Earth where tensions were already fraught, relations tended to sour, as she'd just witnessed.

While Sarah dwelt on such things a memory of Riley's smile sprang to mind, catching her unawares. Angry at the reminder of his betrayal she willed the image into oblivion, but if anything the thought grew stronger. Handsome features, the touch of his embrace and a familiar sense of safety filled her soul. Shutting her eyes, she grasped the pendants that hung round her neck, wishing the heartache away.

'You okay, Saz?' Jason said.

Sarah looked up and shook her head. 'I'm fine.'

Bemused by her conflicting signals, Jason scratched his head. 'You gonna speak to her then?'

'Who?'

'Err, Trish?'

'Yeah – yes – I'll do it now.' Sarah rose, put her helmet back on and made her way over the boulder strewn landscape to her friend. The grey silhouette produced by Sarah's Deep Reach helmet visor highlighted Trish's frizzy afro, a gift from her mother's side of the family. Slightly shorter than Sarah, and a fellow Londoner, Trish had also chosen a career in archaeology, which was how the two had met. Sarah could still remember their first encounter like it was yesterday.

Sarah had been late – no surprise there – for her very first university seminar and had rushed headlong into the lecture hall. Unfortunately for her, she'd misjudged the top step and had fallen, head over heels, down thirty more, ending up in a heap at the bottom in front of the whole class. Sporadic tittering had added to Sarah's physical pain, which had consumed her whole body. It was at that point a face had appeared above her. Sharp features framing kind eyes, Trish's expression had been one of deep concern. Helping her to her feet with the assistance of the lecturer, Trish had taken a bruised Sarah to the university nurse, where she was prescribed painkillers and plenty of rest. Without hesitation, Trish decided to skip her classes for the rest of the day to take care of her and they'd been firm friends ever since.

Back in the present, inside a cold, dark cave, miles beneath the mountains of Mexico, the sound of Sarah's approach made Trish glance back. Slipping her own headwear back on, she turned round.

'We still friends?' Sarah said.

Trish wiped away traces of tears from her face and shrugged. 'Does it matter? You'll do what you want anyway. You always do.'

'I only do what I think is right. It worked, didn't it?'

Trish seemed like she was about to say something, but instead she moved past Sarah without another word, the tension between them unresolved. Sarah knew she'd come round eventually, and she also knew she'd done the right thing. The clock was ticking and they had to find the Anakim temple so they could use its transportation device to get back to the surface, assuming that's where it transported them to, anyway. Thinking about the things that could go wrong with their plan, which were still many, Sarah told herself to get a grip. *I can't afford to lose focus. Not now. There's too much riding on this.* Everything was on the line – not just their lives, but justice for her mother, justice for history and justice for the people. Her expression became determined, her purpose resuming its crystal clarity. Find the temple, get to the surface. Get to the surface, change the world.

Sarah switched on her helmet's twin torches and pressed a button located near her temple to open the coms channel to her friends. 'Time to move,' she said, and gestured towards the route ahead.

Behind, the lights from the Centipede traced her shadow on the rocks as Trish and Jason followed her into another long dark tunnel, the bonds of friendship tested, the route ahead uncertain. Putting one foot in front of the other, tired muscles aching and her climbing boots biting into loose deposit, Sarah resumed her journey into the bowels of the Earth, the call of the surface an all-consuming vision.

CHAPTER SIX

SHADOWS DANCED ACROSS ROUGH, cracked stone walls, the sheen of a mysterious substrate on the cave roof reflecting the Centipede's main beams like thousands of tiny diamonds. The three companions moved through Sanctuary Proper, their footfalls echoing loud as the way ahead narrowed.

Sarah called a halt to proceedings, the time for rest a necessity. 'Grab some sleep,' she said, 'I'll wake you in a few hours for some food and water and then we'll get moving again.'

Too tired to respond, Jason slumped to the floor with a great sigh. No sooner had he slipped off his helmet than he'd fallen asleep, his breathing slowing to a shallow rhythmic rise and fall. Trish, quick to follow his lead, lay down close by, her eyes also drifting closed. Sarah powered down the supply vehicle, selected a place to rest and switched off her helmet visor. The ice blue display gave a bleep before fading to transparency and the blackness of the subterranean catacomb closed in around her. Blinded by dark she sat down against the curve of a curious Anakim structure that emerged from the ground. The finger of rock could not be a natural formation and neither, for that matter, could the cave system itself, unless Sarah was missing something. The ancient builders of Sanctuary, nearly a million years before, had somehow mastered the moulding of the Earth's crust into formations that looked to be of a geological composition, a synthetic construct simulating natural progression. It was a feat of engineering that she continued to marvel at and one she didn't care to dwell on as sleep eluded her. Despite tired eyes, Sarah felt wired, an anxious mind inside a weary shell of flesh and bone.

Feeling she needed to do something in order to promote mental apathy, she reached down inside a pocket on her red and blue Deep Reach uniform and withdrew an object wrapped within a piece of thick, white cloth. The rough fabric appeared grey under the dim light of the Centipede's low level night light to which her dilated pupils had now grown accustomed. Placing it on the ground, she peeled aside the material to reveal the contents within. An orb-like artefact lay before her. Each of its twelve metal sides, made up of yellow and green flecked surfaces, was in the shape of a pentagon, a form that seemed to be of great significance to the race of giants – our long extinct cousins, Homo gigantis – that had forged it. The orb was no normal Anakim object, however, as its recent history suggested it was as far from normal as normal could be. When Sarah had first laid eyes upon it, it rested amongst nine of its fellows in a restricted chamber within USSB Sanctuary's super-secure U.S. military laboratory complex. At the time Sarah had been on a return journey from reclaiming other ancient artefacts that had been confiscated from her upon entry into the subterranean base. In an attempt at avoiding being discovered, she'd stumbled across a treasure trove of Anakim technology undergoing complex scientific study. Unwilling to pass by such an opportunity, she'd decided to steal one of the orbs, which weighed as much as a lump of solid lead. It was a weight she'd considered bestowing on their mechanical supply vehicle many times in the last week, but the artefact was one she'd vowed to keep close, such was its significance in proving the existence of the Anakim and Sanctuary itself.

She couldn't afford to lose it, this strange and otherworldly orb, although Trish and Jason had both voiced their unease at her having it with them at all. The reason for their continued concern was perhaps understandable. Sarah could still remember the agonising sensations that had rendered her unconscious when she'd held the orb against the skin of her palm for more than a few seconds. But that was nothing to how it had reacted to another's touch, a woman who'd been trying to prevent Sarah from fleeing the base with her prizes. Her name had been Cora, a member of Sarah's Deep Reach team Alpha Six, and when she'd held the orb it had sent her into a seizure that ended in a broken spine and death. That the woman was – *had* – been ten steps beyond the wrong side of crazy and had been trying to kill Sarah prior to this was beside the point, the object had shown what it was capable of and that was all her friends needed to know. Sarah on the other hand felt differently, this small, yet dense object had saved her life and she felt a strange kind of empathy with it.

She reached out to brush her fingertips against its side, caressing it like a lover, tender and light. She noted its rough corrugated surface, which turned smooth when activated. Activated to do what she knew not, only that to be holding it when it did come to life was not a wise move in anyone's book; anyone that didn't want to chance dying, that was.

With her memories lingering on that time, she remembered the silver script that had once adorned the orb, script that had transferred to the skin on her hands prior to the darkness taking her. In the present, she looked at her palms before rubbing them together with the faint hope of bringing the vanished lettering back to the surface. Like anyone would in her position, she hoped the transposition of the Anakim symbols to her body didn't represent a threat to her well-being. So far she'd felt no ill effects from the process, but it did leave a niggling doubt in the periphery of her mind. *What has this thing done to me? Is it permanent? Could it render me unconscious at a later date?*

Dispelling such thoughts with a shake of her head, Sarah yawned and felt the chain that hung around her neck move; reaching inside her coveralls she pulled it out. Two disc-like, pentagonal pendants dangled before her, both cast from a smooth, silver-grey metal. The smaller of the two was plain, with a small circle set into the centre on one side. This she had found a few years before; however, the second pendant was her prize possession and it was also what was going to get them back to the surface, or so she hoped. With intricate symbols embossed onto it, the larger pendant measured two and a half inches in diameter and, like its sibling, had a hoop at one end. Unlike the other it had a small clip at the bottom, covering a cylindrical hole which contained a tightly furled Anakim parchment – a kind of digital paper – something that Sarah had returned to its original home after she'd retrieved it from the U.S. Army's military vaults, just prior to their escape from the base.

Sarah felt the temptation to use the pendant to power up another, smaller, parchment, one of many secured in her Deep Reach jacket. She knew, though, that doing so on her own would mean the device would use up her energy reserves as the pendant was in actuality not a power source at all, but rather a conduit to power Anakim technology using the wearer's own bioelectricity. Of course this meant that the device was limited by its owner's physical capacity, which by definition was finite. It also meant that some Anakim technology could not be powered by humans, or at least not a single human anyway, unless they weighed north of four hundred and fifty pounds.

To activate an ancient device the pendant needed to be touching a person's skin, and then usually a hand, finger or bare foot would be placed on a circular indent of a size the Anakim had deemed appropriate for the object in question. With Homo gigantis weighing in at least three times that of an average human, their power reserves and thus potential were much greater; however, if the pendant's operator had contact with other people, skin on skin – a hand on a bare arm, for instance – then the capacity of the power source increased. This allowed Anakim devices to be activated with less drain on the pendant's host, or alternatively it enabled smaller operators to manage larger devices.

Sarah gave a wry smile in the dark, never believing she'd be thinking such thoughts. Even in her wildest dreams she couldn't have imagined what they'd discovered. She would have been happy with part of a skeleton, a single parchment or artefact. To have been witness to the wonders of Sanctuary blew her mind. If it hadn't been for the extreme dangers that went with that knowledge, she would've had to pinch herself to see if she was dreaming.

One thing was for certain though, without the pendant Sarah could never have activated the transportation device that had sent her, Trish and Jason down into the depths of the Earth. It was, without doubt, unique. She still wondered why the smaller pendant didn't work in a similar fashion. Jason had suggested it was broken, or just a fashion item, symbolic in nature, perhaps to be used as part of a ritual or ceremony. Whatever the reason, it had become obsolete in terms of comparative usefulness. It was still an Anakim artefact, though, and thus an object to be cherished.

With a last look, she tucked the pendants away, their hidden forms resting back against the skin of her chest. Patting them three times in OCD-like reassurance, Sarah then gave the orb one last stroke before returning it to her coveralls. Settling down, the sound of Jason's snoring a monotonous choral backdrop, Sarah drifted into slumber.

◆

A spark of light tempted her forward, coaxing her into its warm, protective grasp. It commanded and Sarah obeyed. With a touch of her hand the heat increased. *Why do you fear me?* A voice echoed in her mind. *Am I not what you desire?* A dagger of pain sliced into her head and Sarah screamed. Recognition bloomed and she ran, desperate for escape. Through a tunnel and down she fell. No bottom, no up. Her mind spun and her terror rose. Fleeing into delirium, she fought for release. Darkness compressed her, pulling her back, back from the light, back from freedom. Held by hands unseen, Sarah struggled. Her skin tore, blood trickled and bones broke. She couldn't escape. The heat grew stronger and the spark of fire enveloped her mind. Choking black smoke gushed into her nose and throat, filling her lungs, the taste of ash and death burning her tongue. Her mother's scream echoed her own as the house collapsed in an inferno. Hair afire, skin melting and peeling back, Sarah watched her mother burn. Sobbing in torment she screamed again, the torture of her soul complete.

Sarah jerked awake, the remnants of her pitiful squeals of fear echoing in her ears. Drenched in sweat, eyes darting every which way, she breathed deep, the intensity of the dream causing her lucid mind to mirror the horror of the fallacy it had created. And yet the false imagery was based on the reality of her life and a vivid reminder of her underlying guilt.

She swore and wiped the salty perspiration from her face. A noise in the distance made her swing round. Jason remained where he was, but Trish was nowhere to be seen. Getting to her feet and slipping on her Deep Reach helmet, she powered up her visor. The OLED display sent a glow of light across her face as the spectral enhanced image turned an endless subterranean night to a clear scene of detailed grey.

Sarah knew the folly of going anywhere in a dangerous environment alone and without another's knowledge, and so she bent down and shook Jason awake.

Uttering a grunt of protest he rolled over, his state of sleep reasserted.

Another noise made Sarah pause. Ears straining and with anxiety still fresh from her recurring nightmare, she stood stock still, waiting, listening.

Nothing could be heard.

'Jason, wake up!' Sarah dug her boot into his ribs.

'What?' He opened his bleary eyes.

'Trish has gone. Get up, we need to find her.'

'Gone?' He sat up and switched on his own helmet. 'Gone where?'

'I don't know.' She walked away and turned on the Centipede, its motor whirring into life. Turning back round she let out a yelp. Trish stood a few feet away, looking at her.

'Fuck! Where have you been?'

Trish frowned. 'I heard a noise and went to take a look.'

'How many times have I told you not to go anywhere alone?'

'That's rich coming from you, a person who dives into danger quicker than you can say dead.'

'I've had extensive training, Deep Reach, SED training, you haven't.'

'Well, I'm back and I'm safe, no training necessary.' Trish walked past her and opened an enclosure on the supply vehicle. Removing a flask, she took a swig of water while at the same time avoiding Sarah's glare.

'Look, can we just stop?' Sarah said.

'Stop what?'

'This.'

Trish made a face of indifference.

'This place screws with your mind,' Sarah said, 'it's tearing us apart. You've been caving before; you know what its like.'

'It was a grade two, for one day, so no, I don't know what it's like.'

'Dehydration, paranoia, disorientation,' Sarah said. 'If it wasn't for these helmets and the Centipede—'

'Bob,' Jason mumbled.

'—we'd be hallucinating, sleeping for twelve hours straight and God knows what else.' Sarah looked to Jason, who'd also decided to take on some water.

'She's right,' he said, 'these places can really mess you up. It's the lack of light and fresh air. The constant silence, too. We've been down here over a week. Even I'm feeling it.'

Trish humphed and Sarah took that to be a sign of weakening resolve. 'Truce?' She held out a hand.

Trish hesitated and then accepted the offering.

Sarah searched her friend's face for the hint of a smile, for anything that signalled a warming of relations, but nothing was forthcoming. It was a start, though.

Jason handed a small energy bar to Trish. 'So, what noise?'

'Eh?'

'You said you heard a noise,' he said. 'What noise?'

Trish gestured ahead. 'I'm not sure, something. Sounded weird, like—'

'Like what?'

'I'm not sure.'

Sarah refrained from commenting in order to preserve the new found peace. 'Whatever it was we need to get moving again. According to my helmet we've stayed for too long, we were asleep for six hours.'

Jason swore and Trish looked shocked. 'Are you sure? I set my alarm.'

Sarah nodded. 'Me, too. I must have just switched it off and gone back to sleep. I'll turn up the loudness; we can't afford to lose more hours like that again.'

'So, which way now?' Jason asked her.

'There's only one way; forward. We don't have the supplies to get back to the shuttle station and even if we did—'

'When they found us they'd lock us all up and throw away the key,' Trish said, finishing her sentence.

Jason collected the Centipede's control unit and slipped on the strap. 'How far to the next waypoint beacon?'

Sarah removed an energy gel from her backpack, swallowed it down and then consulted the map on her visor. A detailed schematic of the route to the Anakim temple appeared, along with information on the various hazards between them and it. 'About three quarters of a mile,' she said.

Jason's expression brightened. 'Nice.'

'Straight down.'

His smile faded.

'Welcome to Sanctuary,' Trish said.

Sarah, buoyed by her partial reconciliation with Trish, slapped him on the shoulder. 'Come on, doofus, the sooner we start the sooner we'll finish.'

'Doofus?' he said, peeved.

Trish snorted. 'Sounds about right to me.'

Sarah walked away with a small smile on her face while her eyes scanned the path ahead with care. Trish followed and, bringing up the rear, came Jason; the all-terrain vehicle, aka Bob, trundling along by his side.

◆

A noise echoed down the cave from behind and Jason slowed the Centipede to a halt. Looking back, he searched the pitch-black by filtering through the different visual spectrums provided by his visor's operating system. He zoomed in on an area in the distance. Nothing stirred. *Get a grip, Jas*, he told himself, *you'll be seeing little green men next*. With a shake of the head he switched Bob back into forward motion with a flick of the joystick and followed his friends into the never-ending darkness of Sanctuary.

CHAPTER SEVEN

SARAH PEERED down the enormous rent in the Earth's crust. She knew the bottom lurked far below but from her vantage point, even when using her visor's magnification, a visual confirmation of its existence proved elusive. Hanging a hundred feet down from the lip of the small plateau above, Sarah held onto the rock wall as Trish and Jason edged down alongside her, their ropes dangling onto a ledge located a further fifty feet down. To her right, the black and yellow form of the Centipede hung suspended by its winch cable, which had been anchored into the rock face using its custom built automated deploy and retrieval system. Sarah had hoped to have left the Centipede behind at this point in their journey, but since the large aerial drone had met an early end, they'd have to make do with scaling future obstacles as best they could.

Negotiating Sanctuary's crumbling landscape proved difficult enough, but with the bulky all terrain vehicle along for the ride it slowed their progress to a crawl. With supplies running low, Sarah knew they had to pick up the pace. The time for caution had passed. If they didn't get to the five transportation devices in the Anakim temple in the next seven days, they might never reach them.

The fact that the devices represented their only chance of getting back to the surface wasn't lost on Sarah. Nor was the fact that none of the five might lead to where they wanted to go. There was a chance they might not even work at all. But, when they'd devised this plan back in the safety of the USSB, it had seemed more than feasible; they had after all encountered such adversity before and if they ever wanted to see the surface again this had been their only option. Now that reality had sunk in, doubts had grown with each passing day. *Have I made the right decision? Have I led my friends to an early grave? Why did I ever think this could work?* Whenever these thoughts emerged, Sarah suppressed them. She knew she could do this. She had to do this. *Trish and Jason wouldn't have agreed had they not thought it viable. Would they?* She knew she could be quite persuasive when she wanted to be. *Have I deceived them, have I deceived myself?*

NO! came the angry response. This is the only way, the way to freedom, the surface, justice for my mother and exposure of the Anakim and Sanctuary. There is no other option, it was this or nothing. It was all in; the gamble had been made. Now all I have to do is make sure the dice land in our favour.

Adjusting her harness, mental preoccupation resolved, Sarah continued her descent, the soft clinking of her assorted climbing gear echoed by that coming from her two friends nearby. Reaching the ledge, she disconnected herself and turned her attention to the Centipede. Using its control console, she manoeuvred it onto the same rocky outcrop before Trish and Jason landed alongside moments after.

'You two okay?'

Jason puffed out his cheeks and nodded.

'I'm not sure I can keep this up,' Trish said, rubbing a shoulder.

'Here.' Jason turned her round and began massaging her.

'Ow, not so hard.'

'If it doesn't hurt, it doesn't work.'

'Who told you that, the Spanish inquisition?' She let out a grunt of pain and Jason smirked as he moved to knead her back.

Sarah retrieved the Centipede's anchor with the touch of a button, the wire rope going slack as the mechanism at its end detached from above. A high-pitched whine indicated the winch span round at speed, the cable retracting faster than gravity's invisible pull. Repositioning the spider-like device, Sarah initiated its insertion into the rock. A whir of servos forced a spike deep into the substrate while smaller versions repeated the process on either side. Happy, she reversed the Centipede over the lip, each set of its small wheels leaving behind terra firma for another mid-air ballet. With the next leg of the descent underway, the three friends followed their supply vehicle over the edge, abseiling down over the craggy drop.

Five more times they had to redeploy in this fashion and their supply of abseil anchors had shrunk to half. Sarah had taken to climbing down in order to retrieve her friend's cams and self-piling bolts for re-use. More time they could ill afford wasted.

On the final section, everyone was halfway down when a horrendous noise shook the ground.

'Earthquake!' Jason shouted.

Trish screamed and Sarah clung on for dear life as the cliff face shifted.

Rocks rained down upon them, bouncing from helmets and bodies alike. Looking up, Sarah saw a large boulder heading straight for her. She swung to one side. Pain tore through her as it clipped her shoulder. Letting out a shout she fell ten feet before her safety line jerked her to a stop. Spinning in circles, she heard Jason shout, but she only had eyes for the wall which appeared, reappeared, disappeared, reappeared – BANG! A fist-sized stone bounced from her helmet as the deafening shaking continued. Her rotation slowed and she made a grab for the wall. Slipping a hand inside a deep crack, she pulled herself back in just as another massive boulder whooshed past behind. Pulling herself flat against the relative safety of a tiny overhang, Sarah saw Jason had also managed to secure himself. Trish, however, swung out in dangerous arcs while behind her, appearing out of the gloom, the Centipede tore through the air towards her.

Sarah's eyes widened. 'WATCH OUT!'

Trish turned.

Too late! The supply vehicle swatted her into the rock wall like a rag doll. Knocked out, or worse, Trish rotated, limp, while the Centipede careered into the cliff, the force of its momentum broken by its canisters, which exploded with precious water.

After what seemed an eternity the tremors subsided and Sarah was able to reach Trish's lifeless form.

'Is she hurt?' Jason said, his voice desperate.

Sarah felt for a pulse and her friend's eyes opened at the touch.

Sarah let out a grateful gasp. 'You okay?'

'I think so,' she said, her voice shaky.

Awash with relief, Sarah helped Trish down to the floor of the crevasse.

Sarah looked at her friend in concern. 'Are you sure you're okay?'

Trish gave a small smile and nodded, but before Sarah could say or do anything else, Jason was there and hugging Trish to him.

As her two companions embraced, Sarah regretted the missed opportunity to repair the frayed bonds of her friendship with Trish. And then she remembered the Centipede that still swung from its tether above. She lowered it to the ground and inspected the damage.

'What's the story?' Jason said, coming up behind.

Sarah shook her head and stepped aside. 'The story is, we're in big trouble.'

CHAPTER EIGHT

BEFORE THEM THE two water canisters that had saved the Centipede from becoming a lump of scrap metal stood torn and empty, the remnants of their life saving liquid barely enough for one drink.

Trish looked in despair at Sarah. 'What do we do now?'

Sarah raised her visor and rubbed a palm against one eye, searching for inspiration.

'We'll have to go back,' Trish said.

Jason gave a near hysterical laugh. 'We can't go back, remember, only forward.'

Trish frowned. 'How long can we go on without water?'

'We've already been on rations.' Jason wetted his parched lips. 'No more than three days, max. With this kind of exertion, probably less.'

'How far to the temple?'

'At the rate we've been going? Seven days, who knows?'

'Then we're screwed.'

'Pretty much.'

Trish and Jason's voices, getting increasingly fraught, faded into the background as Sarah walked away to think. Pressing a button on her helmet and sending her visor back down, she controlled the screen with her eyes, selecting the Deep Reach map to the Anakim temple. Searching along the length of the route, interspersed by waypoint beacons, she expanded a section that doubled back on itself. Selecting another option, she brought up other pre-mapped sections.

Due to the remoteness of their location, no other area nearby had been explored by the SED; however, after the Deep Reach team had discovered the temple they'd decided not to retrace their steps. Instead they took a different path which created a giant, circuitous loop on the map. The point of intersection had long since passed, Sarah deciding at the time that the shortest way to the temple was the same path taken by the SED explorers on their way out from the shuttle station. Now, though, this alternate plotline grabbed her interest.

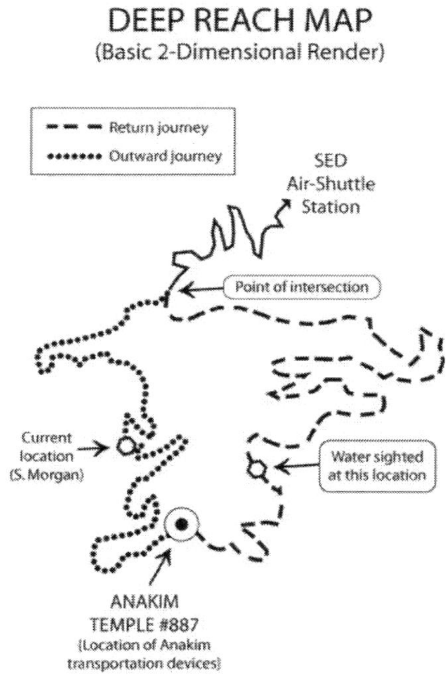

DEEP REACH MAP

(Basic 2-Dimensional Render)

Return journey
Outward journey
SED Air-Shuttle Station
Point of intersection
Current location (S. Morgan)
Water sighted at this location
ANAKIM TEMPLE #887 (Location of Anakim transportation devices)

Its nearest point was a few '*Sanctuary*' miles away, but crucially one symbol indicated water had been found there. Drilling down into the data revealed water had been reported to seep from the rocks. *Perhaps enough to refill a repaired tank*, she reasoned, *or part of one if they were lucky*. There was just one problem.

'That's great!' Trish said when Sarah told them, but her elation faltered when Sarah's expression failed to mirror her own. 'Isn't it?'

'The area between us and it is uncharted. Well, almost uncharted.'

Jason frowned. 'Almost?'

'It looks like the team who was down here before us did a preliminary recce with aerial drones. They seemed to think, according to the report, that there might be a way through, but—'

'But what?'

'But it was deemed too dangerous.'

Trish sighed. 'Why was that?'

'Unstable, potentially impassable obstacles and dangerous temperature spikes.'

'Temperature spikes – caused by what?'

'They don't say what they were caused by, only that some of them reached over a hundred degrees.'

'That's not so bad,' Trish said.

'Centigrade.'

'Ah.'

'It's either that or make for the temple and end up dying of dehydration before we get there.'

Jason looked more than a little anxious, as did Trish. 'Not much of a choice,' he said.

'Can you repair those tanks?' Sarah asked him.

He glanced over at the Centipede. 'One of them I can, using the material from the other one and the right welding torch.'

'There's a repair kit in the rear compartment, you should find everything you need inside.'

Jason gave a nod and moved away to start the task. Meanwhile

Sarah and Trish went through their supply inventory and made sure the Centipede wasn't damaged beyond the obvious.

An hour later they set out once more, but this time into the mystery of the greater unknown.

◆

Four hours of gruelling hiking, climbing and abseiling followed before the three battered and bruised explorers, or Sancturians as they'd become during their stay back in the USSB, found their path blocked by an impassable void. Even with their visors, nothing could be seen beyond where the ground ended in a sheer drop; nothing, that was, except for the remains of a narrow bridge jutting out of the rock a hundred feet down, leading to nowhere. The top of the crumbling structure stood broken, with large swathes of the walkway gone and only the supporting lattice framework left beneath.

A laser rangefinder device aimed down the escarpment's vertical face produced a grim picture. The reading on its small screen read:

10.267 Kilometres

It seemed their luck had finally run out. For all intents and purposes, considering their dwindling supplies, the drop was bottomless. Pointing the laser ahead and above resulted in similarly distant numbers of just over one kilometre, and two kilometres, respectively. The chamber was enormous. When angling the laser out diagonally, there was some good news – there was a floor, after all – but it was little consolation as it was too far away to be accessible.

'End of the road,' Jason said.

Trish leaned over to look down. 'What about the bridge?'

Jason adjusted a setting on his helmet visor. 'Not a chance, there's no way across and even if there was it's too damaged. I wouldn't send my worst enemy out on that thing, it's a death trap. We'll have to find another way round.'

Sarah had other ideas. 'Okay, let's set up camp and grab a few hours rest.'

'Shouldn't we keep moving, try searching for another route?' Trish said, sounding weary.

Sarah shook her head. 'There was a fork in a tunnel an hour back which had potential. I'll check the maps, but we need to recoup first, you especially, you may have a concussion.'

A look of concern flashed across Jason's face and Sarah felt a pang of guilt for manipulating them. *It's for their own good*, she told herself, *they'll thank me when they've had time to think about it.*

While Jason bustled about tending to Trish's needs, Sarah manoeuvred the Centipede to a position of her liking. She then started a small fire to keep them warm, suppressing the memory of her infernal nightmares as she did so, before suggesting they get some sleep. With Trish and Jason in agreement, she settled down with them in an attempt at heeding her own advice.

It wasn't long before Trish let sleep take her; however, despite Sarah pretending to drift off herself, her deception failed to induce Jason into a similar slumber. She cracked open an eye to see he remained wide awake, much to her annoyance. She needed another tactic.

Sitting up, she yawned. 'Can't sleep?'

Jason shook his head. 'Do you think that other tunnel will work out?'

'Pretty sure,' Sarah said, trying to keep his hopes up despite her own fears and the knowledge that there was no other tunnel. 'We just took a wrong turn, is all.'

His expression brightened and her guilt deepened. She hated lying to him, so she changed the subject.

'You care for her a great deal don't you?' She made a move with her hand toward Trish.

'That obvious, huh?'

'A little.'

'I don't think she feels the same way.'

'What makes you say that?'

'Stuff.'

'You made a pass at her and she blew you off?'

'How did you know?'

Sarah shrugged. 'I know Trish. She doesn't let many people in.'

'I think she likes me, though.'

'I think you're right.'

'So what's her problem?'

'Time and place.'

Jason made an odd face. 'What's that, then?'

'If she was up on the surface living her life and without all this crap going on then you'd still find it difficult to land her.'

'And down here, I've got no chance.'

''Fraid so.'

'What if I'm patient?'

Sarah thought about it and gave a downturn of her mouth. 'Maybe.'

'That's not very helpful.'

'Lay the foundations. If she's worth waiting for, which she is – you'd be lucky to have her – then that's all you can do.'

Jason looked into the fire and juggled something from hand to hand in silent contemplation.

'You found any more of those?' She gestured to his hands.

He opened a fist to reveal some blue stones that glowed in the half-light, stones he'd collected on their journey through Sanctuary Proper. He shook his head.

Sarah groaned inwardly, she could tell Jason wasn't about to shut his eyes in a hurry. 'Let's have a look, then.' She held out a hand.

Jason tossed one to her. She caught the small object and

inspected it. Shielded from the light of the fire it shone even brighter, its iridescent blues shimmering as if alive.

'It looks more like crystal than stone,' she said, holding it up to the light of the fire, 'but it doesn't look natural.' She flipped it over in her hand. 'They're not radioactive like Trish said, as our visors would have flagged it up. They could still be dangerous, though, so I wouldn't touch them too much.'

'They can't be any more dangerous than that orb of yours.'

Sarah grunted.

Jason sat up straighter. 'Let's see it, then.'

'Trish wouldn't like us messing about with it. Whenever I take it out she gives me one of her looks.'

'You do seem a bit obsessed with it,' he glanced over at Trish, 'but, what she doesn't know won't hurt her.'

'I hope that philosophy doesn't apply to your love life or you're on the road to nowhere with sleeping beauty there.'

Jason looked anxious. 'Eh? No – hey, stop playing with me, get it out.'

A small smile crossed her face. 'Why so interested?'

'What, you afraid I'm going to steal it? Is it that *precious* to you?' He made an odd noise with his throat, like he had whooping cough.

Sarah chuckled. 'You watch *way* too many films.'

'Says she who knew what I meant. And anyway, I always preferred the books. So come on, let the dog see the rabbit.' He raised a suggestive eyebrow.

Sarah laughed. Whatever the situation Jason could always lighten her day, even when they faced the worst of situations as they did now. It was one of the reasons she loved him as a dear friend and was probably one of the main reasons why Trish reciprocated his feelings towards her, at least in part. Reaching inside her coverall pocket, she withdrew the orb and its cloth cover and laid it on the ground between them.

Jason leant forward and liberated the Anakim artefact from its protective sheath of white material. Sparkling with a metallic sheen, it looked a little like a spherical Fabergé egg, although with less of the ornate and more of the art deco about it. That it seemed unfinished, its surface rough and corrugated, gave it a sinister air, but that might have been because Sarah knew what it was capable of: rendering a person comatose, or worse, dead.

Jason touched it with the tip of a finger and then moved his hand back as if he'd gotten a shock.

'Scaredy-cat.'

He grinned.

Sarah couldn't help but touch it too, her fingers compelled to caress its surface. The pentagonal side she'd made contact with turned smooth and then lit up with a white light before sinking down to slide aside, revealing a dark, hollow interior.

Jason looked as shocked as she must have done. 'How did you do that?' he said, mouth agape.

Transfixed at this unexpected turn of events, Sarah shook her head. 'I don't know. My pendant didn't heat up either.'

'Touch it again,' he said.

Reluctant, Sarah reached out a hand. Cupping the orb's side, she held her hand there, perhaps longer than advisable. The orb grew warm and, one by one, each of the remaining observable sides lit up in turn. She snatched her hand away, not daring to incite whatever danger might lurk within. Nothing else happened for a moment before the side that had disappeared returned and the orb's light faded until the same yellow and green flecked surface could be seen once more.

She tried to recreate the effect, but it appeared reluctant to repeat the process. And not wanting to anger it, she decided it best to leave it be.

'I wonder what it does,' Jason said, after watching for some moments to see if it did anything else.

'Hmm.' Sarah had no idea. How could one hope to know the mind of the person who'd created it, perhaps hundreds of thousands of years in the distant past?

They sat in silence for a time before Sarah felt the pendant grow hot against her skin. She pulled out her neck chain to find the pentagonal artefact shone with a strange hue.

'I thought you said it didn't heat up?' Jason said, as the artefact faded and became cold, much like the orb.

'It didn't, at least not at first.'

'Has it ever done that before?' he said, intrigued. 'Get warm *after* you activated something I mean.'

'Never.' She turned the pendant over to see a new symbol had appeared in its centre. 'Its surface has changed,' she said, amazed.

He held out a hand and she showed it to him.

'It doesn't look like much,' he said, disappointed, 'just a bunch of lines. What do you think it means?'

She shrugged her shoulders and gazed at the alteration for a while before she realised she still held one of his luminous stones, with a flick of her thumb she launched it over to him.

Jason placed the cerulean gem-like stone back into his collection. 'How did that entrance to the cave system get blocked?' he said, changing topics.

Sarah looked up at him. 'What do you mean?'

'Well, we were following the same route as the Deep Reach team that found the temple we need to get to, right?'

Sarah nodded.

'So,' he continued, 'they must have passed the same way as us. I don't see any way that boulder could have got lodged in that hole by itself, can you?'

Sarah thought about the question and realised the same thing had occurred to her at the time, but worrying about the mission had overridden her focus on it, until now. 'Perhaps the Deep Reach team blocked it for a purpose?'

'There is that possibility,' he said. 'If that's the case, they went to a lot of effort to stop anyone getting in again. Or out.'

Sarah gave him a look of consternation. 'Out?'

'Didn't that professor guy – what was he called?'

'Steiner,' Sarah said.

'Yeah, didn't he say in that induction video, ninety-eight per cent of Sanctuary is still uncharted?'

'Yeah, so?'

'Then surely that means this place could still be occupied somewhere.'

Sarah laughed, but her smile ceased when she realised he was being serious. 'What, you think the Anakim are still alive? They've been extinct for millennia. The fossils indicate nothing else.'

It was Jason's turn to mutter an interjection.

'I'm sorry, Jas, Homo gigantis is history, the same as Homo floresiensis, Homo neanderthalensis et al. There's nothing else down here but us and a lot of ancient relics.'

'I suppose.' He gave a yawn and lay down on the ground.

Finally, Sarah thought, her hopes rising, *he's getting tired.* She pocketed the orb and then lay down herself, although her desire was not to seek out sleep, but to wait.

CHAPTER NINE

A FEW MINUTES later Jason's muffled snores confirmed to Sarah she was good to go. Careful not to make a sound, she got to her feet and switched on her visor. The display lit up, the ice blue dials and controls populating the tinted exterior, while the centre produced the selected enhanced visual spectrum of the user's current terrain. Taking a look around, she saw the entrance to the tunnel system that had brought them to their current location was stark and empty. Sarah wished Jason hadn't reminded her of the blocked passageway; it made Sanctuary feel more menacing – and her, tiny and vulnerable. She shuddered.

Making her way to the Centipede, which sat dormant close by, she opened a compartment and removed a med kit. Opening it, she found what she was after, a small cardboard box that read:

Ammonia Inhalant Ampoules

More commonly known as smelling salts. Opening the box, she

extracted an ampoule and stuffed the rest into her jacket's top pocket. The weight of the orb against her leg reminded her of its latest party trick, making her wonder about its function. *Not now, Sarah*, she berated herself, *you have work to do. The time for thinking has passed.*

Moving round to the supply vehicle's winch, which she'd strategically placed facing the cliff edge when they'd arrived, Sarah pulled a lever and flicked a switch so it would spin free when pulled out slow, but would lock up when she activated a verbal command through her helmet. She then disconnected the anchor mechanism and secured it to the back of her climbing harness. Next, she clipped the eyelet at the winch cable's end to her belt. She then ensured the Centipede's wheel brakes were on.

It took some time to carry out her preparations as she had to make sure her climbing gear remained as silent as possible. She couldn't afford to wake them now.

After adding a couple more pieces of equipment to her utility belt, Sarah felt ready and approached the edge of the precipice. In front, above and below was the dark void, a subterranean chamber of immense proportions and intense, unforgiving isolation. Switching through a variety of spectral visor combinations, Sarah returned to the original, which best highlighted the ancient ruins of the Anakim bridge. Reaching up a hand, she depressed a button on the side of her helmet. Tiny circles popped up on the central screen, automatically attaching to the terrain's most prominent features. When she moved her head these visual reference points switched to wherever she looked, increasing or decreasing in number as necessary. When she moved her eyes to look at one of these circles a data box appeared, each remaining visible until she decided otherwise. The data available was as follows; distance from origin – that being Sarah herself – angle from origin, stability factors, warning messages, and a variety of other critical, yet concise information, displayed in semi-transparency so as not to impede her vision.

Staring out at the task ahead, she fought down the rising fear that tried to swamp her tired mind. Going on the analysis from her visor, the remnants of the Anakim bridge below – certain sections of it, anyway – wouldn't be able to withstand her weight for long; she would need to move quickly. It meant securing the winch cable to these areas was also out, but with a limited number of climbing cams available, this was a moot issue anyway.

Even with the Centipede's ton of weight acting as a brake, any fall would likely end with her crashing into the cliff face at a rate of knots. She grimaced; *at least the ground won't be a problem – at first anyway.* The further she went, the greater the risk, as the longer the length of cable behind her, the bigger the pendulum swing would be. If she was lucky, she might get away with breaking half the bones in her body – if she was lucky.

I have no choice, she told her rebelling mind. I got them into this mess; I need to get them out of it. We need water. Water will give us time – options.

The situation was out of control and her friends needed her to deliver.

Everything had come down to this.

It was now or never.

Lifting the smelling salts, she crushed the ampoule and lifted it to her nose. POW! Eyes wide and senses shocked, Sarah's head jerked back as clarity chased away the fog of sleep deprivation and fatigue. She inhaled again and winced. Throwing the ampoule aside, she grasped her pendants and sent out a prayer. *I know I don't deserve this, Mum, considering ... well, you know why, but I'm asking, so if you can help me up there, now would be the time.*

Sarah took a deep breath and then stepped off the ledge.

CHAPTER TEN

SARAH MORGAN WALKED down the shadowy face of the vertical wall of rock, the winch cable maintaining its tension as it aided her perpendicular descent. The ruins of the Anakim bridge loomed before her and she stepped onto its ancient surface. Various hazard symbols appeared as her eyes scanned the way forward, while warning messages scrolled down the side of her visor. The road ahead was a myriad of obstacles fit for the suicidal.

To her left, the bridge ended abruptly where it had once continued parallel to the cliff face – destination unknown. She wondered who the last person to tread upon its surface had been, in a time when mammoths and humanity's ancestors had battled for survival on the surface. *Who fucking cares,* screamed her rational mind, *get on with it!*

Unable to put it off any longer Sarah trod with extreme care out into the black, every step inching her away from the wall and safety.

♦

A persistent click click click stirred Jason from his dreams. Eyes flickering open, he focused on the strange noise. *What is that?* The clicking grew louder and then stopped, before starting again slower than before, but continuing until suddenly increasing in intensity. Heart racing, Jason reached a slow hand up to his helmet to turn on his visor. A scraping sound close by made him scramble to his feet. Scared, he saw Trish standing a few feet away.

'What's that noise?' she said, sounding sleep addled.

The clicking continued and Jason realised it emanated from the Centipede's direction. He traced the source of the sound to the remote vehicle's winch, where the cable fed out along the ground. Following it, he saw it disappear out over the cliff edge.

Trish looked around. 'Where's Sarah?'

Jason frowned as he traced the metal line through his visor, zooming in along its length until he found the answer to her question. Half a mile out onto the Anakim bridge, Sarah climbed across the crumbling latticework that had once supported a walkway above. How she'd made it so far without falling, God only knew; one thing was for sure, though, she couldn't go much further without making that fatal error. Ahead of her the bridge ended, a huge swathe of its centre span missing, before continuing again on into the distance. Jason knew she'd have to attempt a return and that she'd risked her life for nothing.

Trish came to stand next to him. 'Oh, my God, what's she doing?! Is she insane?'

Jason shook his head. 'I'm beginning to wonder.'

◆

Sarah eyed the break in the bridge ahead; she couldn't believe she'd made it so far without a mistake, although there'd been a few close calls when she'd thought she was a goner.

Sweat from her exertion soaked her Deep Reach coveralls and her palms also glistened with perspiration, although she realised this secretion may well have been fear-induced. She wiped her face and then cracked open another ampoule of ammonia and breathed deeply.

Coughing, her waning clarity forced sharp, she sought purchase as she aimed to return to a section of walkway that still survived above. As she hauled herself up a chunk of stone broke free, sending her falling. Spread-eagling herself, she slammed into a crossbeam. Her helmet bounced from the surface and pain exploded in her body. Terrified, she scrabbled to hold on as momentum carried her towards oblivion.

Sliding to a halt, dust and debris drifted in the air around her and she looked down to see her legs dangling over nothing, only the tumbling piece of architecture growing smaller and smaller as it fell.

Feeling sick and hurting all over, she dragged herself back to relative safety.

'Fucking hell, Sarah,' Jason's voice crackled in her ear, 'are you out of your mind?!'

Sarah turned her head towards the cliff and her visor zoomed in on the distant figures of her friends. Too shaken up to speak, she looked back up at the bridge she had to conquer. It seemed more impossible than ever.

'Are you okay?' Trish's voice said.

Sarah adjusted her position. 'I'm fine.'

'Sarah,' Jason said, 'there's no way across the gap, you have to turn back.'

Sarah gave a shake of her head. 'There's no way I'll make it back. Some sections collapsed behind me, the supports are hanging by a thread, this whole structure could go at any moment. I have to go on.'

'Just jump,' Trish said. 'Jason reckons the winch could pull in half the length of cable by the time you reach the rock wall; if we could reverse it back, too, you might—'

'That's a last resort.' Sarah got to her feet and resumed her climb. 'Just be ready if I fall. Now stay quiet, I need to concentrate.'

A few minutes later and somehow she'd made it up to the top of the bridge. Navigating the final section, she looked out across the expanse blocking her way. The hundred and fifty foot gap seemed far bigger up close. A warning icon appeared on her visor.

CAUTION!
Noxious Atmosphere Detected

A distant rumble like thunder broke the silence and Sarah peered over the end of the bridge to see a ruddy orange glow blossom into being. Growing in brightness, a rush of air swept past, followed by a wave of heat. Alarms sounded in her ears and her helmet's breathing mask automatically deployed to seal her face inside. The temperature dial on her visor shot up to sixty degrees centigrade. More warning icons appeared as the temperature continued to rise. At seventy degrees, her skin felt like it was on fire. Stumbling back from the edge, her breath came in ragged gasps as the heat penetrated her helmet's breathing apparatus.

'Sarah, what's happening?' Trish's said.

Hot air filled her lungs. 'Can't – breathe.' Sarah clawed at her throat.

The rumbling ceased and moments later the heat receded.

Jason came on the com. 'Sarah, it's a heat plume. There must be some kind of outlet for a magma chamber down there. If you're going to do something, you need to do it now. The next one might be hotter and last longer.'

Sarah deactivated the mask and sucked in cool air, relishing the sensation as it soothed her throat. Disorientated, but with no time to spare, she detached a small cylindrical canister from her belt and unscrewed the lid. A tripod popped out from the bottom and the aperture at the other end revealed a shiny, metal spike. Reaching to her backpack, she unhooked a dense coil of nano-cord. Securing one end of the super-strong line to her harness, she attached the other to the mechanism on the device, which she placed on the ground. A green light appeared on its side. Her helmet synced with it and a message appeared:

Propellant Primed

Crosshairs displayed on her visor. Aiming it with her eyes, she locked it onto her target and pressed a button on the side of her helmet. With a whoosh and a burst of flame, the projectile sailed into the air, the fine cord on her belt feeding out behind it like a party streamer. Moments later the bolt punched into the bridge on the opposite side.

Pulling the cord tight, Sarah took a breath and jumped.

◆

Jason watched his friend drop from the edge, her blonde hair streaming out from beneath her helmet as she cut an arc between the two sections of Anakim bridge. The Centipede's winch reel span faster, letting out more and more cable. Trish grasped his arm and turned away, unable to look, while Jason's heart was in his mouth.

Sarah flew past the base of the opposite structure, her momentum carrying her upwards before she let go in mid-flight to latch onto an outcrop of stone. A few feet from where she landed, a large swathe of the bridge crumbled away into the abyss.

Jason's finger strayed over the Centipede's winch control, his thoughts full of fear. *She's not going to make it.*

◆

Sarah, heart pumping, blood rushing, grasped a balustrade with two hands and heaved herself onto the top of the bridge. She'd made it! Hazard symbols popped up all over her visor before a single flashing message appeared:

WARNING!!
UNSTABLE STRUCTURE
Collapse Probability: 95%
Alternate Route Advised

Sarah glanced back. *There is no alternate route!* A deep rumble from the depths made her look down. An embryonic larval glow broke the darkness. Black eddies swirled in its midst and a rush of air swept past. She activated her breathing mask before heat engulfed her. Unable to do anything else, she ran.

◆

Trish, sensing Jason's increased tension, turned back to see Sarah leaping and dodging around obstacles as she ran flat out across the bridge. Behind her the structure shuddered and with a tremendous groan, its end collapsed and the rest followed in a domino effect, the falling walkway hunting Sarah down like a giant monster.

♦

Breathing hard, Sarah leapt over a gaping hole and crashed to the ground before rolling back to her feet, her momentum unbroken. A roar of noise set the ground vibrating.

WARNING WARNING WARNING

A tiny window appeared on-visor showing the scene behind. Her eyes widened as the bridge disappeared from view. Adrenaline rocketed and her speed increased. Jumping, running, dodging, the ground lurched. Heat consumed. Lungs burned. Gasping, crying, gripped by terror, the collapse was at her feet and time slowed. Death had arrived. *Why do you fear me?* The voice of nightmares echoed in her ears. *Am I not what you desire?*

♦

Trish made a grab for the Centipede's control unit. 'Press the button!'

'No, she can make it!' Jason saw Sarah leap and he held his breath before the bridge vanished in a cloud of dust.

Trish screamed and he pressed the button.

'Why didn't you press it?' A sob escaped Trish's lips.

In shock, and still pressing the button over and over, Jason looked at the device, confused. 'I did.'

CHAPTER ELEVEN

PELICAN BAY, California, USA

The heavy, reinforced door slid closed with a resounding boom. A buzzer sounded and a green light switched to red.

'Cellblock A1 locked and secure.'

'Cameras and failsafes?'

'The grid's operating at full capacity. All security measures are in the green.'

'What's the old one up to?'

The prison guard, Jayden Connor, known to his friends as Jay, brought up a picture of a cell on the wallscreen. 'Taking a nap by the looks of it.'

'And the son of Satan?'

Jay switched to another image. A powerfully built man, stripped to the waist and wearing prison issue orange trousers, hung from one of the horizontal bars that supported the transparent walls of his high-tech cell. 'He's just about to start.'

'How many do you think he'll manage today?'

The inmate pulled himself up with his arms and extended his

effort until his waist met his hands and his arms locked out. He then lowered himself back down again with effortless ease before repeating the process over.

Jay glanced at his colleague. 'Four fifty.'

'What? He did six hundred two weeks back.'

'Yeah, but he's been out of it since then. Enough drugs to kill a rhino.'

'With good reason; he bit Wilson's fingers off.'

'And he got a good beating for it, that's why four fifty.'

'They're lucky they didn't kill him.'

Jay gave a grunt. 'He deserved it, everything that's happened he's deserved.'

'I don't know,' – the other guard shifted in his seat in discomfort – 'some of the stuff they've done ...'

'What, you don't feel sorry for him, do you?'

'Not sorry, exactly.'

'Then what?'

'It just doesn't sit right. I know what he did was all sorts of wrong, but torturing the guy won't bring back the people he killed.'

Jay shrugged. 'If the cops had their way he'd be dead already and the FBI couldn't have made it any more obvious they'd turn a blind eye to their treatment.'

'I think Wilson got his comeuppance.'

'How'd ya figure?'

'He was tormenting him. And it was his idea to take away his meds.'

'Yeah,' Jay said, 'not the best move. Who knew, though? We have no files on them. We don't even know their names. If Wilson had known what would happen if he stopped his pills he'd never have done it.'

The other guard looked back at the prisoner in question. Muscles rippled and sweat ran over his bruised skin while military tattoos on his arms stretched in time to his exertion. 'He's obviously insane. I don't know how he's not in a mental facility. And they employed him in the army, how crazy is that?'

'Pretty damn crazy.'

'I'm surprised his defence team didn't try for the diminished thing.'

'Diminished responsibility?' Jay said. 'No way. He knew exactly what he was doing; he's as sane as you or I when he's got those little red poppers of his.'

His colleague gave him a dubious look, a *speak for yourself* kind of look.

'Well, maybe not,' Jay conceded. 'But over a hundred people dead, most of them federal agents and police officers. There was no way in hell they were gonna give in to a plea bargain. Some were calling for the chair. If anyone deserves to fry, it's him.'

'I doubt they'll reinstate it for one person.'

Jay sat back in his chair. 'Shame.'

The door to the security office opened; the warden entered and both men rose from their seats.

'Gentlemen,' the warden said, 'we have a contingent of VIPs coming to speak to the prisoner.'

'Which one, sir?' Jay said.

The warden pointed to the screen and the exercising man they'd just been discussing. 'As before, they'll need complete control of all security and that includes all recording equipment.'

Apprehensive, Jay looked to his superior. 'I take it this lot know who they're dealing with? It took us hours to clean up the mess last time.'

The warden wandered over to the console to gaze at the prisoner. 'They're U.S. Army officers accompanied by a couple of GMRC officials.'

'Shall we subdue and sedate beforehand?'

'No. They said they'll handle it. Just run them through our protocols and then leave them to it. We'll make sure the outer corridors are sealed off in case there's any trouble. They seem capable, though, ex marines by the look of it, so they should be able to handle him.'

'That's what they said last time,' Jay said.

The warden made a face. 'As they say, that's their problem. We just do as we're told. I'll just be glad when these two aren't here anymore.'

'Any more problems with the press, sir?' Jay's colleague said.

The warden glanced at the prison guard. 'Yes. We had to arrest two more reporters this morning. Cheeky bastards were trying to come in disguised as a cleaning crew. I don't know if you saw, but the number of news vans outside has increased. The closer we come to the sentencing, the more intense this circus becomes.'

'Yeah,' Jay said, 'I saw them on the way in. They're going nuts. I almost ran one down when they tried to stop me for questions, damn fool jumped right out in front of me.'

The warden looked grim. 'It would help if the authorities, the GMRC, the FBI, whoever, revealed who these men were. The longer they try and keep it under wraps, the greater the furore.'

A knock on the door made everyone turn. The security chief ducked his head inside. 'They're here.'

The warden nodded. 'Right, let's get this show on the road.'

CHAPTER TWELVE

Professor Steiner lay on the bottom bunk, his head resting back on a pillow and his vision engulfed by the bland underside of the mattress above. After twenty years of leading the world's response to the meteor threat as a member of the GMRC Directorate, he often wondered how his life had come to this, locked up in a supermax prison for the crimes of another. Granted, he'd helped Colonel Samson during his insane rampage through Los Angeles, but his part had been enforced by his need to save the lives of hundreds of thousands of people still trapped underground in USSB Steadfast, put there by the unfathomable actions of Malcolm Joiner, the GMRC's duplicitous intelligence director. Furthermore, he'd never intended for *anyone* to get hurt, but Samson had instigated a plan of his own making, a plan that saw him risk everything to secure the safety of his daughter, an FBI agent who loathed her father as much, if not more, than Steiner himself. Steiner had tried his best to prevent more deaths by guiding Samson to safety so that he might help in the liberation of Steadfast's entombed GMRC residents. Of course, none of this had any bearing to those that had imprisoned him, the FBI and civilian judiciary. They were out for his blood, no more aware of his contributions to the future welfare of the human race than the majority of the populace, the billions who remained blissfully unaware of the meteors that closed in on their position with every passing second. Only the dust cloud that had resulted from the impact of the first meteorite the year before ensured mass panic hadn't already destroyed the tenuous illusion that was human civilisation.

A small sound, a steady tap tap tap, squirmed its way into Steiner's awareness. Moving his head to the side, he looked up at the skylight on the cell's high ceiling. On the glass pane, a bird pecked at the window. After it stopped its attention seeking noise, it returned to the task of preening its feathers. Steiner continued to watch the animal, lost in its simplicity, until a cell door slammed, causing the bird to take flight into the freedom of the skies. Steiner wished he could join it. He shifted on the mattress and winced at the pain that racked his body every time he moved. The guards that *looked after* him had ensured his stay had been as uncomfortable as possible. However, his luck had improved a little in the last few days. Instead of daily rounds of verbal abuse followed by the occasional brutal beating, he'd been left pretty much alone. The reason for his reprieve was the same individual who'd been complicit in his current incarceration. Colonel Samson had proved as indomitable in prison as he had without and it had been his actions that had ensured Steiner was merely a forgotten appetiser to the main course. From the screams Steiner had heard emanating from Samson's cell, the colonel had been subjected to horrific practises of torture. These sickening sounds had repulsed him so much on one occasion he'd shed a tear for the monster who'd taken the lives of so many. He could have warned them the colonel was one man they didn't want to antagonise, but he'd decided they could have the joy of finding that out for themselves, such were the pleasures afforded him, such had become the bitterness in the broken shell of his mind he called home. And it wasn't long before Samson had duly delivered, dishing out some of his own medicine despite the efforts of the guards to keep their distance. Samson was nothing if not resourceful. Steiner remembered the small smile that had crept onto his face when the tables had been turned.

He frowned. That those times had given him enjoyment had disturbed him more than anything else. It felt like he was in a continuous fight against the oppression of darkness. Time and again his calm was broken by an array of frightening thoughts, thoughts so bestial he didn't recognise them as his own. He could not let himself be corrupted before ... before what he knew was an inevitability – life imprisonment, which on the surface meant he'd be dead, if not within the year, then within four when the final asteroids made landfall. He intended to go out of life with his head held high and his dignity intact. He would not give Malcolm Joiner the pleasure of his destruction. As far as he was concerned he was still Director General of the GMRC's Subterranean Division and he was damned if he was going to let his last breath be one of torment. He would embrace death as he had life, with courage, optimism and a measured resolution.

His greatest fear was that if he allowed himself to be consumed by hate and despair, Amelia wouldn't recognise him when they met beyond the veil. As he was wont to do, his thoughts turned to his wife, taken from him thirty years ago, stolen by fate's cold, chaotic hand. His fingertips strayed to the gold wedding band that still adorned his ring finger. Touching it conjured up Amelia's beautiful smile. Her features had grown indistinct over the years, despite the photos of her he'd kept in his wallet, offices and home, his memory couldn't secure the outlines he could have once drawn with his eyes closed. But then Amelia had never been the body she'd inhabited, not to him; her soul was what he loved and, as everyone knew, the eyes were the window through which to view the spirit within. The body was a vessel, a biological construct for the mind. Steiner, with an IQ through the roof and enlightenment beyond most, turned his focus to the questions that he often posed himself. These had initially been ones of escape and retribution, but as time progressed such futility had fallen by the wayside. He'd decided that his days should be spent on something constructive rather than the impossible, so he'd resolved to address the fundamentals of the human consciousness and the riddle of the power of man. Why was it some people were capable of such great advances in science and knowledge while others weren't? There were a few central principles he knew to be true—

The familiar wail of a siren halted his deliberations. Steiner rolled over to see a group of men entering the segregated compound that housed Samson's cell and his own. Four of the group were military – ranking officers by the looks of their uniforms – and the other two men, dressed in the garb of GMRC officials, wheeled along a substantial square container. Curious, Steiner got to his feet and moved across his cell to watch these visitors pass by, his hands pressed against the clear walls of his prison.

One of the GMRC men glanced in his direction before disappearing from view around a corner and the opaque barrier that separated Steiner's cell from Samson's. Steiner sat back down on his bunk. He was sure he recognised the man, but he couldn't place him. With a shake of the head, he lay back down to resume his ponderings of reality and the power of the mind to control it.

Half an hour passed before the sound of voices brought Steiner back to his surroundings. The group of men that had entered now departed. Once more the sensation of familiarity sparked in his mind; the GMRC official definitely rang a bell in his head, but Steiner had never been the best with names and faces and he'd seen so many GMRC officials ... he could know him from anywhere.

The smell of something burning made him sniff to confirm its presence. He looked round and then up to see a waft of smoke drifting across the top of the enclosure's transparent walls and the bars that supported them.

'Hey!' He waved his arms at the people leaving.

None turned, even though Steiner banged on the walls and shouted at the top of his voice. The smoke above continued billowing through. Coughing, he covered his mouth with a forearm before tearing a piece of cloth from his thin bed sheets to wrap round his face. Dark, acrid clouds flooded in through the ceiling to roll down into Steiner's cell in waves. Orange light flickered on the far walls and a sudden barrage of shouting and banging emanated from Samson's cell. Steiner waved at the cameras he knew watched his every move, trying to get the attention of the guards. The fire burned brighter and flames licked at the ceiling. Steiner could feel the heat now and he backed away to the far wall.

A scream of agony pierced the air. Again and again Samson's terror-stricken, horrific shrieks fell on deaf ears. No sprinkler system kicked into action and no help came rushing to the prisoners' aid. The fire continued unabated and Steiner was forced to the floor in search of clean air. A final strangled screech ended in silence as Samson succumbed to the inferno that sought to smother Steiner with its black fumes. Seconds passed like minutes and minutes passed like hours as Steiner clung to life.

Finally a siren sounded, lights flashed and water cascaded down. The sprinklers doused the flames and giant fans whirred into life to extract the cloying smoke. Guards stormed into the compound and Steiner felt consciousness slipping as his eyelids slid closed.

◆

'What do you mean, the system didn't work?'

'It was disabled; whoever set the fire wanted it to burn. In fact the fans had been activated in reverse to ensure the fire had enough oxygen. They also used some kind of accelerant. The flames were far hotter than a normal fire, hence the condition of the body.'

The warden peered down at the blackened carcass. The man's ridged limbs had contorted into a fearful posture, his teeth bared in an animalistic grin of death. 'Have the people responsible been found?'

The chief of security wagged his head. 'They took a helicopter out, same way they came in. We've reported the incident and the FBI are en route. They're not happy, questions will be asked.'

The warden cursed and rubbed his eyes. *As if I didn't have enough paperwork already*. He gave a sigh. 'How's the other one doing?'

'He's still in the hospital wing, smoke inhalation. They say he'll recover. The FBI said they want to speak to him as soon as they arrive.'

'What about the military?'

'The U.S. Army rep said they sent no officers to this location. We're still getting the run-around from the GMRC, although the police were quick to distance themselves from the incident, perhaps too quick.'

'I don't think they'd pull a stunt like this, no matter how many of their number were murdered by Mr. Crispy here.'

'Maybe,' – the chief scratched his head – 'I don't know what to think, to be honest. This whole thing's been a mess from start to finish.'

The warden swore. 'And we're the ones who're gonna get it in the neck.'

'There is an upside, sir.'

The warden looked at him, wondering if he'd lost his mind. 'And what's that?'

'At least we won't have to look after this fucker anymore.'

The warden looked down at the grim spectacle and realised he was right. A broad smile spread across his face. 'And who said there were no silver linings?'

CHAPTER THIRTEEN

USSB Sanctuary, Mexico

GMRC Intelligence Director Malcolm Joiner sat in his office. In his hand he held the remote control for the three hundred and sixty degree immersive screen that covered every surface of his office walls, ceiling and floor. He'd been pleased when it was installed; it gave him a sense of control over his surroundings. At the flick of a finger he could be anywhere on the planet. He pressed a button and the wastelands of the Sahara filled his vision, its arid beauty seeming real enough to touch. He selected another view. The vastness of space resolved into being, the essence of the farthest galaxies giving him a yearning for the solitude such heavenly bodies enjoyed on an eternal basis. Beneath his feet the joys of the Milky Way rotated like a giant Catherine wheel, the celestial dance a visible reminder of how tiny the solar system and everything on Earth really was. Joiner frowned and switched to another image. Blossoming trees of a temperate forest swayed in the breeze. The crests of mountains stood tall on the horizon and low lying clouds nestled at their feet, while the setting sun sent rays of light dappling nearby meadows and streams. He stood up and walked around the room, savouring the simulated grass at his feet. The upgrades he'd added to the virtual system had been worth the money; Richard Goodwin's screen, which he'd acquisitioned from USSB Steadfast, had been good, but Joiner felt it lacked in certain places. *A bit like the man himself*, Joiner thought, thinking about Steadfast's deposed base director. He wondered where Goodwin and his Darklight and civilian entourage had ended up within Sanctuary Proper. Crushed beneath a mass of rock, perhaps, or dead at the bottom of a ravine, or just holed up in a cave, withered and dead from starvation or dehydration. Any which way, it was a relief to know that particular problem had resolved itself; having Goodwin and his merry men running around in Sanctuary could have proved quite detrimental to his work, and more specifically the Committee's. The transition of power was at a critical point and any outside influence could put back their carefully laid plans by decades.

Thinking about the people who sought to control him, Joiner's thoughts returned to the main focus of his desire. *What do they want to hide from me so badly? What is Project Ares really about?* He would have to remain patient until he found answers. Myers would no doubt turn up something, but for now he would have to make do with what he had. Joiner tapped at the keyboard on his desk. The dossier on Sarah Morgan popped up on a section of the wallscreen. He pressed a button on his intercom.

'Sir,' said the voice of his primary aide, Grant Debden.

'I want a secure connection to the decryption department.'

'Yes, sir.'

Joiner waited before another voice spoke.

'Decryption, secure line delta, eight five two zero confirm.'

Joiner checked the spooling code on his screen. 'Eight five two zero, delta confirmed.'

'Very good, sir, how may I be of help?'

'I sent down some files two days ago.'

The man on the other end of the line paused. 'Sir, I've just checked our logs and we don't seem to have them.

Joiner grew concerned. 'Check again.'

A longer moment of silence ensued before the man spoke again. 'My apologies, Director. The files had been sectioned into a digital vault as requested and weren't showing up on the main system.'

'And?'

'We've been successful in removing the redacted sections, although due to the sensitivity of their nature we are relying on A.I. to inform us of the successful recovery of data. If you want human confirmation we can—'

'That won't be necessary.' Joiner twizzled a pen with his fingers. 'This artificial intelligence ... is it also aware of the security protocols involved?'

'It is, sir, yes.'

'And as soon as the data is transferred from your system—'

'They'll be irretrievable. The only copies will exist on your personal system.'

'Excellent. Transmit the files to my location.'

'Very good, sir. They'll be with you shortly.'

Joiner hung up and waited for the delivery of the digital packet.

Joiner's intercom buzzed. 'Director, there's a woman from the central bank asking to see you, a Ms. Selene Dubois.'

Joiner froze. Selene, here? A Committee member gracing me with their presence outside of normal channels? It's unprecedented.

'Sir?' his aide's voice said.

Joiner shut down all his data windows and sat up straighter in his seat. 'Send her in.'

Moments later the internal mirage of a setting sun broke in two as the doors to his office opened to reveal the woman he'd seen in the Anakim tower on his arrival at Sanctuary. By her side was the dread form of S.I.L.V.E.R.'s leader, Ophion Nexus, still encased in his chrome armour like a medieval knight lost in time. Behind him were two of his team, similarly garbed in gleaming metallic panels with their weapons attached to back-plates visible above their shoulders. Unlike Ophion, who held his distinctive helmet in the crook of his arm, these individuals wore sculpted headgear which was much like that of the Terra Force commandos, only these were sleeker and, if anything, even more formidable than their U.S. Army counterparts.

Joiner rose and moved round the table, and felt the disturbing and unfamiliar sensation of being amongst people taller than him. 'Ms. Dubois, this is unexpected.'

'Is it?' She walked past him to observe the scenery on display.

Ophion held Joiner's gaze before the intelligence director returned his attention to the Committee member, who continued to gaze out into the 3D imagery.

'You'd like a progress update?' Joiner's tone was uncertain.

Selene remained with her back to him. 'You thought I wouldn't?'

'Of course, but—'

'I made you well aware of the importance of this task and you have proven as ineffective as those you replaced. What do you propose I should do to solve this indifference? Ophion, perhaps you have some ideas.'

'I have one,' Nexus said, in his deep rumbling voice.

Joiner approached Selene. 'My preparations are nearly complete, as Ophion well knows.' He flashed S.I.L.V.E.R.'s leader a look of fury. 'The personnel have been assembled, along with all the equipment needed to ensure the fastest route through Sanctuary Proper. No expense has been spared. The track is nearing completion as we speak and the first shuttles will be out within the next twenty-four hours. I was going to provide you with an update as soon as we'd launched. If you'd have waited another day then this inconvenience would not have been necessary.'

'Inconvenience.' Selene turned to face him. 'You think I've been inconvenienced?'

Joiner didn't know what to say. He glanced at Ophion, whose enigmatic expression showed no hint of humour, though Joiner could tell the assassin was enjoying his discomfort.

'This is beyond inconvenience,' Selene said. 'That you think otherwise compounds the issue. It was decided for you to take the lead on this most important of acquisitions. It seems our trust was misplaced, once again.'

Joiner cleared his throat. 'If you—'

'Enough!'

Joiner clenched his jaw, cowed by the anger in her eyes.

'You have one day, Malcolm Joiner, one day to rectify your mistakes. Make another and it will be your last as a functioning member of the GMRC Directorate. Do I make myself clear?'

Joiner felt his blood boil, his top lip curling into one of displeasure. It was all he could do to contain an outburst, his nails biting into the palms of hands, the pain serving to quell the rising tide of anger as red rage distorted his vision.

The Committee member and her armed retinue swept from the room, the doors closing behind them. Joiner snatched up a glass and hurled it at a wall. The crystal shattered in an explosion of glittering shards, leaving behind a fractured crater on the high-tech screen.

CHAPTER FOURTEEN

JOINER GLOWERED at the doors through which his tormentors had departed, his sense of self threatened beyond toleration. The infuriating and excruciating irony was that Joiner had compromised his own position by delivering to the Committee a means by which to destroy him. Now they had subverted the majority of the Response Council's Directorate, he could be voted off like any other. *I should have seen this coming. How did I not see it?*

'Because you're a wretched fool,' he said aloud.

He'd been manipulated, pressurised and bombarded with work, he could see it now, a choreographed assault designed to swamp him, ensuring he was too busy to realise what transpired under his very nose. The manufacturer of his own vulnerability. If he'd played such a hand himself he'd have seen it as a defining conquest, a sculptured attack of subtle yet simple beauty. That he had been the recipient of it, a victim – he shuddered at the thought – only served to fuel a desire for vengeance so powerful he felt it in his bones. All his years of graft, long hours and sacrifices had led him to this point. *And I'm damned if I'm going to let it slide now.*

Returning to his desk, he reached out to his keyboard. His hand trembled from the surge of adrenaline caused by the confrontation.

He shut his eyes and breathed deep, in and out, deep slow breaths like his physician had taught him.

Moments later he opened his eyes; the shaking had ceased and he resumed his task. A few key strokes locked his office doors and brought up the secure transfer server. Having completed a host of security measures, Joiner saw the requested files lay waiting for him as the decryption analyst had promised. Switching the folder to his wallscreen, he stood and extracted the contents. Three video files appeared, files he'd acquired from the Committee, files that were incomplete. Now he'd see what they'd been hiding from him. He made a gesture with his hand and flicked the playback window onto a new section of the wall.

A video stream appeared, filmed by an array of cameras inside the military vaults located beneath USSB Sanctuary's museum complex.

The woman at the centre of Joiner's woes, Sarah Morgan, descended from the upper level of the large circular vault. He'd already witnessed what had happened before; she'd collected her confiscated artefacts, including the precious pendant that meant so much to all concerned. The scene continued to unfold and Joiner knew the process of redaction reversal had been a success, as previously unseen footage carried on without pause or break.

The lithe form of the English archaeologist went from room to room, deactivating the opacity walls to transparency until she decided to enter a room full of ancient parchments. Stealing a few of these precious documents, she then stopped in front of a display cabinet. The image automatically spun round to capture the thief's progress. Letting out a scream of frustration, Morgan heaved over the stand, creating a domino effect which trashed the whole room. Not stopping there and incandescent with rage, she then stormed into an adjoining room and grasped a massive Anakim shield suffused with jewels. No sooner had she grasped the object by its handle, than a faint ripple shimmered across its face. Unable to move the seven foot tall artefact, the woman made to rest the shield down, but before she could do so a wave of purple energy erupted from its surface, blinding the cameras with a flash of light so powerful it rendered the screen blank. Joiner assumed whatever had transpired had disabled the cameras in the vicinity as that was the end of the video. He rewound it and watched it back. *Why was she so upset at seeing the Anakim parchment on display?* He zoomed in on her face at the time of the event to see an expression of recognition. She'd seen this parchment before.

Joiner searched through her dossier and found an intelligence profile that revealed Sarah Morgan was said to have claimed to have found similar maps some time back. Information gleaned from friends and colleagues by GMRC agents had revealed they'd been lost in a fire which had also claimed her mother's life. Joiner began to understand his quarry's motives. He turned to another document. From what he'd read before, this woman's lifelong mission was to find evidence of a lost race of Hominid, Homo gigantis. Now that she had such evidence she would be attempting to reach the surface and release her discoveries to the world. He shook his head at her folly. The stupid girl was fleeing to her death, escaping from a facility that would protect her from the next wave of asteroids. Sometimes, it seemed, restricting the truth could prove detrimental to the bigger picture.

Joiner moved on to the section where the shield had activated, slowed it down and rewound it before viewing it again. He ran the footage through a spectral enhancer. At the time of the shield's activation he could clearly see the pendant concealed beneath the woman's clothing grow hot in response, the outline of the pentagonal disc revealed under operation.

He spooled up the next film, where the woman entered the military's highly restricted laboratory complex.

His eyes grew wide and he stopped the stream and enlarged the image. He'd seen a small amount of this file but, like the other two, all three had revealed very little of note with regard to Project Ares, despite Selene indicating otherwise when she'd warned him off the subject. Had she been unaware that Joiner would be receiving a limited view of what had transpired? *If she had,* Joiner thought with satisfaction, *her warning backfired as it only served to tell me the files contained useful information about the project.* A mistake he hoped she might live to regret.

On-screen he could see a cluster of logos and signs on a transparent door. Two of the signs read:

U.S.S.B. SANCTUARY
in partnership with
GMRC R&D DIVISION and
The National Aeronautics and Space Administration (NASA)

WARNING!
RESTRICTED AREA
Level 10 Alpha
Special Access Personnel Only

And beneath these, sandwiched inside the glass itself, were the emblems and logos of the respective partners, one of which consumed Joiner's attention like no other, the symbol he'd been chasing ever since he'd seen its name:

He took an involuntary step closer to the screen and resumed the footage, his eyes transfixed on every detail.

The thief continued into a large chamber, her Deep Reach helmet deploying its breathing mask as she passed through a set of decontamination jets. Inside, she ran from an area which held a number of self-contained laboratories and into an adjoining chamber. The angle switched to a new set of cameras, following her progress. She approached a fifty foot high monolith, the only object on show. Surrounded by a pool of light and a host of monitoring equipment, the ancient piece of architecture had the form of a giant pentagonal prism. At its heart, a large, transparent rectangle had been built into the artefact and Joiner realised it was the front panel of a three dimensional container which housed some kind of fluid. Sarah Morgan placed her hand on one of three circular indents located on the front of this curiosity. The liquid inside darkened and a glow bloomed at its core, intensifying into a dazzling star of light.

Like Morgan before him, Joiner hadn't noticed a scientist who approached her from behind; disturbing her from the wonder Joiner now shared. The light died and Sarah Morgan proceeded to interact with the man, before distracting him with a computer readout and then knocking him out with a well-executed bash to the head with a heavy piece of equipment. Joiner rewound the footage and completed another spectral scan, identifying the glow from the pendant as again it activated on cue. He switched his attention to the massive Anakim relic. Heat signatures failed to reveal anything interesting, the viscous fluid contained inside the structure appearing as uniform as it did from the outside.

He knew further analysis could be undertaken, but he didn't have the software or inclination to tackle such a time-consuming process himself. There was also another problem; he didn't want anyone else to be privy to his actions, especially not the Committee. This meant he would need to requisition an artificial intelligence console for his personal use. It was the only way he could ensure full concealment. But such units were expensive and few in number, and results were by no means guaranteed. Plus, acquiring one might raise suspicions – although, upon deliberation, he decided that was a risk he had to take.

Moving on, the next section of video showed Sarah Morgan stealing yet another artefact, a small orb-like object which induced some kind of fit, sending her collapsing unconscious to the floor.

Joiner fast-forwarded the stream, finding nothing further of note, just the woman recovering to flee from the restricted complex.

The final file revealed little new material, apart from a similar incident to one he'd just seen. This time another woman, an SED employee, had attempted to stop Morgan from fleeing the base. After catching the orb that had been thrown as a last resort, this new character had been sent into a violent seizure, ending in death. It seemed the murder was anything but, more a case of self defence leading to a fortuitous result, at least for the thief.

Joiner returned to his desk to ponder over what he'd seen. He brought up the footage again, this time on his workstation. He paused the stream at the point where Morgan activated the shield. He then introduced the next file alongside at the instant where the giant prism had glowed from within. He leant forward, running each one side by side in slow motion, stopping them time and again to rewind and replay. Slower and slower he ran them until they crept along, a frame at a time. Joiner's vision narrowed into tunnel-like intensity, fixating on the power that flowed from the devices. His pupils dilated, he could feel, smell, sense, the infusion of power on display. A power such as that could make a powerful man almost invulnerable. He licked at his dry lips, his desire to wield the device, this pendant, all-consuming.

CHAPTER FIFTEEN

So, Joiner thought, Project Ares is intrinsically linked to Anakim technology. This is what the Committee sought, personal power, not a watered down version wielded through administration, media and money. Project Ares is the power of the Anakim, the power of the Gods.

A spark of motivation ignited in his mind, a glimpse of what could be, a sensation of truth extracted from the ether.

'I have to have that pendant,' he whispered to himself. With it he could turn the tables on the Committee, run his own programme off the books, a personal black project. He'd operated such things before, normally coined 'a civil servant's wet dream' by the parliamentarians that strove to cull the excessive spending of taxpayers' money. Of course, Joiner knew, like most of the establishment, this was the greatest illusion of them all. Money could be created when needed; it was then down to the redistribution of debt to those beneath to ensure the system remained functioning. The process wasn't perfect, but then neither was humanity, so the world continued to spin and the people continued to work – without it only chaos and war would rule, as without control, those that needed power, lusted after power, needed to maintain power, would do anything they could to secure it, regardless of the consequences to the masses. It had been theorised that in the future artificial intelligence might be able to produce a system that would negate the destructive impulses of man, but until that time, Joiner knew the current system would continue uninterrupted, at least as long as money persisted, which was where Professor Steiner had been so dangerous. *A world without money.* He shuddered at the thought.

The intercom buzzed and Joiner's face twitched in anger at the interruption. 'What is it?'

'Director, Agent Myers requests an audience.'

'Then send him in!'

'I would sir, but it appears your doors are locked.'

Joiner let out a curse and deactivated the mechanism.

Seconds later Agent Myers entered, his eyes straying to the smashed glass and damaged screen.

'Report,' Joiner said.

'I'm no further ahead on the leak, but I've put in place a number of misdirections, so anyone looking to capitalise on them will inadvertently implicate themselves.'

'The task, what about the task?'

'Completed, plus I've sent out feelers regarding Project Ares and the space station incident. So far I've been able to acquire snippets of information, but I'm hoping to get a bigger picture as time passes. Covering our tracks from our own people has proven more difficult than I'd envisaged, the GMRC is a formidable machine.'

'Good.' Joiner's expression relaxed. 'Very good.'

'When did you want to set things in motion?'

'Give me fifteen minutes.'

Myers' manner became concerned. 'I'm not sure that's possible. It's a matter of security.'

'It's not a request.'

Myers gave a chastened nod and waited for further orders.

Joiner banged the table. 'Get on with it, then!'

Agent Myers scuttled from the room and Joiner glared at his retreating back before re-securing the doors and resuming the footage on-screen. His eyes narrowed as the woman made the

Anakim shield glow with power. 'I know who you are, thief,' he murmured. 'I know what motivates you; I know where you're going.' Joiner paused the image and touched where the pendant rested at the base of her neck. 'You have what I want, Sarah Morgan, and there's nowhere on this planet I can't find you.'

CHAPTER SIXTEEN

A PILLAR OF ROCK, weathered by time, emerged from the gloom as dust from the collapsed Anakim bridge settled around it. Clinging to this stony column, covered in pulverised masonry, was a small figure.

The heat plume receded and Sarah Morgan deactivated her Deep Reach helmet's breathing apparatus and brushed the debris from her visor.

Jason's voice crackled over the com system. 'Sarah, thank God. I tried to activate the winch but it didn't work.'

'The signal must have been blocked by the heat and dust,' she said, gazing out to where her friends stood on the distant bluff.

'We thought we'd lost you.'

'I thought I'd lost me.'

'Are you okay? Can you see a way down?'

Sarah checked her vital signs on the visor. 'I feel okay.' She looked down at herself to make sure all limbs were present and accounted for. Her heart raced when she couldn't see her left leg, but before she could accept the bad news she realised it was just bent back, wedged in a cleft and disguised by the remains of the bridge. *Idiot*, she thought with a wry shake of the head.

Peering around at her surroundings, she saw the ground at the base of the tower was only a couple of hundred feet down, well within climbing distance.

Getting to work and feeling more alive than ever, Sarah deployed the winch anchor into the rock face and attached the cable to it.

Meanwhile, Jason attached a zip wire handle to his end of the cable. He then helped Trish mount it from beneath and with a fearful screech and a flailing of legs, she flew across the great void to a waiting Sarah. Jason then went about setting up the Centipede's winch mechanism – under Sarah's instruction – before receiving the handle back from Trish, sent via its pulley wheel and tiny inbuilt motor.

With Jason joining them, Sarah consulted Bob's manual on her visor and entered a sequence of commands. The Centipede crept forward off the ledge and crawled along the winch line much like its namesake.

After the crossing was complete, and having avoided any further heat funnels, the reunited company climbed and abseiled down to the chamber floor below.

Despite her near death experience, Sarah's plan had worked as she'd hoped. The path ahead was still uncertain, but the obstacle encountered by the Deep Reach team preceding them had been conquered. The method of her choosing, however, had not gone down well with her pals.

'Do anything like that again,' Trish said, furious, 'and we're no longer friends, do you hear me?'

Jason just glared at her, his expression as powerful as any words.

Undaunted, Sarah felt no remorse; she'd done it for them, after all. She turned her attention to the Centipede, which she lowered down from its position above. 'I knew you wouldn't let me go,' she said, knowing to reveal her true feelings would only incite them further.

'With good reason,' Jason said. 'There could have been another way round.'

'Not in the time we have to reach that water, there wasn't.'

Sadly for Sarah, the arguments continued at varying intensities as they journeyed onwards, Trish and Jason unwilling to let her recklessness – as they saw it – go unpunished.

An hour later, with relations frosty, they entered an adjoining chamber, as immense in scale as the first. This one, though, contained a system of intact bridges and walkways that led them a mile down. The architecture glistened under the grey imagery of their visors, mirroring the ceiling high above. Sleek in style, these Anakim marvels cut simple patterns in the air around them, interconnecting with plazas of varying shapes and sizes.

On reaching the far side of this cavernous space their passage was halted by an imposing wall inside an arch that made the Arc de Triomphe look like a postage stamp. Sarah craned her head back to take in the arch's majesty. Beautifully constructed, the cracked surfaces seemed to glow against the dull shades around it. Unable to contain her curiosity, Sarah, deactivated her visor, which slid up into her helmet. She felt compelled to view the scene with her own eyes.

Under the Centipede's lights the material shone translucent, the rays refracting into a myriad of colours that sparkled deep into the structure.

Trish and Jason also raised their visors.

'How do we get past that?' Jason gestured to the rear of the arch which remained shrouded in darkness a hundred feet away.

Sarah had no idea. Striding forward to investigate, her form cast giant shadows on the barrier to their progress. Like the arch itself, the wall before them gleamed with an ethereal depth, the pool of light from the Centipede's lights tiny in comparison to its immensity. She removed a glove and ran a hand over the surface, which felt rough to the touch.

'Did either of you see that?' Trish said from behind.

Sarah turned, the tone of her friend's voice indicating tensions between them may have thawed. 'See what?'

'I'm not sure, like a ripple?'

'Moving across the wall?' Jason said.

Trish nodded. 'You saw it too?'

'I'm not sure what I saw.'

'It happened when you touched it, Sarah. Try again.'

Sarah removed her other glove and placed both palms against the ancient surface. Up close her view was limited. She glanced back. 'Anything?'

Trish pointed. 'There!'

'I see it!' Jason said, excited.

Sarah leant back to see if she could glimpse the phenomenon.

A distant noise made her snatch her hands away.

'Why did you do that?' Trish said, annoyed.

Sarah stood motionless, ears pricked. 'What the hell was that?'

'What was what?'

'That noise, didn't you hear it?'

'I heard something,' Jason said.

Trish looked at him. 'What are you two talking about?'

Sarah moved away from the wall and lowered her visor. She scanned the way behind them. 'It sounded like a scream.'

Jason came to stand by her side, also looking out into the darkness before switching to his visor.

A black shape blocked Sarah's view and she stepped back in alarm.

Trish stood before her, hands on hips. 'Can you both stop? You're freaking me out.'

Sarah saw the fear on her friend's face.

'It's probably just the air from that heat plume,' Sarah said to Jason. She waited a moment longer, listening, but no further sound came. 'We're tired and dehydrated; we can't afford to get paranoid as well. It's time for our water ration anyway. Let's take a short break.'

While Trish and Jason stayed by the Centipede, Sarah approached the wall again and brushed her fingertips over the Anakim substrate. She paused and then pressed her hands onto it.

'It's doing it again,' Trish called to her.

'Stay there longer,' Jason said.

Sarah held the position and Trish and Jason told her the ripple effect kept repeating itself, without change, every ten seconds. After a couple of minutes passed, and just as she was about to pull away, a prickling sensation ran down her arms and a strange smell, like damp earth and dead flowers, washed over her. The pendant against her skin grew warm and the wall under her hands shifted and turned liquid. Falling forwards, her arms sank into cold distortion. She let out a screech. Unable to stop her advance, she drew in a breath of air and shut her eyes as her face entered the surface. The sound of raised voices sounded far away as the liquid crept over her head. Hands grabbed her, pulling her back. The pendant turned hot, and with a whoosh of air, Sarah found herself standing next to her friends, dry and unharmed. Before them a tunnel had formed, its interior like a funnel of moving water.

'Are you alright?' Jason said.

Sarah gave him a nod in reassurance, before turning her attention back to the wall. Together, the three friends stared in stunned silence at the revolving whirlpool before them. Sarah lowered her visor and zoomed in to the end of the tunnel. 'I can see another chamber on the far side.'

Trish touched the interior, her hand disappearing into the fluid. She withdrew it again, unharmed. 'You think we should go through?'

'I'm not going through that,' Jason said, incredulous, 'it could go anywhere. Haven't you heard of parallel dimensions?'

Trish laughed. 'Don't be a moron. This isn't one of your films. Besides,' she pointed inside the swirling wall, 'you can see the arch inside, look.'

Trish was right; Sarah could see the structure around them through the inside of the wall, continuing unbroken to the other side.

Jason didn't look convinced. 'It could be an illusion or a trick for you all you know.'

'Sorry, Jas,' Sarah said, her face set, 'there's no time for ifs and buts, this takes us in the direction we want to go. We have to take it before it closes again.'

'But what if it stops working while we're inside? We'd be sealed in solid crystal.'

Sarah knew he was right, but she also knew they weren't in a position to look a gift horse in the mouth. 'Without water we're as good as dead anyway, we have no choice.'

Sarah collected the Centipede and drove it into the tunnel, small rivers of translucent wall lapping at its wheels. Hesitant but determined, Sarah followed it inside, the tunnel expanding to her height as she moved. Trish came after, letting out the occasional yelp when the liquid rose too high over her ankles. After what felt like an eternity, but was in actuality only around twenty seconds, Sarah reached the other side and turned round to see Jason had remained where he was.

◆

Jason watched Trish and Sarah exit the other end of the tubular torrent of water. Not normally averse to danger, he eyed the spinning vision with trepidation. When he mentioned the possibility of the tunnel transporting them to another world, he'd been covering for a dread of something far more primal. As a child he'd enjoyed swimming in the cold waters of his native Wales, specifically those found at the Brecon Beacons National Park; a magnet for those seeking some of the most idyllic locations within the British Isles. One summer day, much like any other, he and a friend decided to ignore the warning signs surrounding one of the reservoirs. Swimming and cavorting, the two boys had been caught unawares by a strong underwater current. Dragged out into deep water, Jason had seen his friend disappear beneath the surface, swallowed by the swirling arms of a whirlpool. Although he had made it safely back to shore sometime later, exhausted and in shock, the vision of that day had haunted him ever since. His friend's body had never been found and as he looked into the tunnel now, his childhood trauma made real, he found himself frozen by fear.

'Jason, stop arsing about!' Sarah waved at him to follow.

Something made him turn to face the way they'd come. A breeze blew past him, bringing with it a distant noise. His eyes narrowed. Walking away from the tunnel and ignoring the angry words from Trish and Sarah that came through his helmet, he searched the far reaches of the chamber and its many bridges and walkways.

He saw something move in the distance, but his helmet's technology was unable to resolve it.

Raising his visor, he could just make out a shimmering light travelling across a bridge, from right to left. The light slowed to a stop at an intersection as if aware it was being watched. After a moment it blinked out.

Jason stood there, his eyes straining to see whatever had disappeared.

A shout from Trish, calling him back, echoed out into the silence. The light returned and surged forward, its course heading straight for him. Faster and faster it came and Jason took a step backwards, and then another, before running headlong back to the Anakim arch.

CHAPTER SEVENTEEN

'PISS OFF, Jason; you're just trying to scare me.'

'Think what you like, that's what I saw.'

'I thought you heard it?'

'I heard something.'

'Bollocks.' Trish looked at Sarah. 'Are you buying this crap?'

Sarah didn't know what to think. Jason had shot out of the passage like a scalded cat, ranting about some kind of light. Before they could go and investigate the newly created tunnel shrank to nothing, leaving behind a solid wall.

'I saw what I saw,' Jason said, 'and I heard what I heard. I'm not seeing things. I'm not hearing things. And don't blame it on my over-active imagination because of the films I watch, either.'

'Who said I was going to blame it on that?' Trish sounded angry. 'If I was going to blame it on anything, it'd be your stupidity or lack of sleep.'

Sarah zoned out as Trish and Jason argued. According to the Deep Reach map the water they were after couldn't be too much further, although because this part of Sanctuary had never been mapped, it was hard to tell. Distances in Sanctuary were more than confusing, half a mile could mean a time-eating climb or descent, or quite easily turn into a marathon diversion if the way was blocked.

Feeling weary, Sarah decided they all needed another rest. Forty-five minutes sleep would do everyone some good and might calm growing tensions.

So, at her suggestion, the three friends lay down on the hard surface beneath the arch, the dark of the new chamber seeming as bleak as that of the old. While Sarah felt uneasy about Jason's sighting, of – whatever it was – she was too tired to dwell on it. No light lurked on this side of the structure and that was good enough for her. As her mother had always told her, '*there's no point worrying about something you can do nothing about.*' When Sarah had asked what if she could do something about it, her mother had smiled and said, '*then there's even less reason to worry.*' On that happy thought, Sarah drifted into sleep.

◆

Trish groaned and stirred awake.

Where am I? she thought and then remembered. She sighed before a tickle of hot air brushed her cheek. Her eyes flickered open to the pitch-black of Sanctuary. The foul breeze came again and a growl made her scrabble for her helmet's torch. The light blinked on and big, round, bloodshot eyes stared back at her, inches from her face.

She screamed.

◆

Sarah jumped to her feet, Trish's terrified screeches sending her heart thumping. A light moved in the darkness.

'What's going on!?' Jason's voice came out of the void.

Sarah switched on her visor to see Trish standing ten feet away, leaning on her knees and gasping for air. Nothing else could be seen apart from the Centipede, and Jason, who crouched on the ground, looking frightened.

Sarah approached Trish and put a hand on her shoulder, making her start. 'It's me, what's wrong?'

Trish shook her head and switched on her own visor. 'Jesus Christ, Jason!'

'What? What did I do?'

'You know fucking well what you did! Scared the living shit out of me!'

'Eh?'

Trish looked to Sarah. 'I opened my eyes and there's this hideous creature lying right next to me, right in my face, staring eyes and filthy breath.'

Sarah put two and two together. 'Jason's face made you scream?'

Trish nodded.

Jason stood up. 'Sometimes I sleep with my eyes open. I don't do it on purpose.'

'I always thought you were a freak,' Trish said, 'but now I know you are.'

'Hey! And what's with the hideous creature?' Jason's expression was one of confused outrage.

Sarah couldn't help but chuckle.

Jason's scowl morphed into a smile as he saw the funny side. 'Your face,' he pointed at Trish, 'you almost wet yourself.'

'Did not.'

He grinned. 'Yeah, yah did.'

Sarah's own smile faded as the reality of their situation returned. She looked at the time. 'Come on you two, we've had enough rest, we need to kick on.'

The momentary jubilation passed and the companions moved out into the darkness once more, Sarah, as ever, leading the way.

CHAPTER EIGHTEEN

A SMALL BEACON pulsed white in the darkness, its glow revealing the cave walls around it every five seconds like a strobe with a run-down battery. Sarah bent down to inspect the waypoint marker, which consisted of a metal rod with a light on top. The device drilled itself into the rock when deployed and once secured in place it acted as a permanent reference point for those that followed in the tracks of the Deep Reach survey team that had laid it.

Sarah, Trish and Jason had been travelling for some time, but they'd made good headway after the pendant had helped activate the strange tunnel beneath the Anakim arch. The terrain had been on a level, and only a few short climbs had been needed to bypass some deep cracks and vertical shafts.

Jason approached with the Centipede at his side. 'So, where now?'

More than pleased they'd been able to intersect the return route plotted by the Deep Reach team that had discovered the temple, Sarah consulted her map.

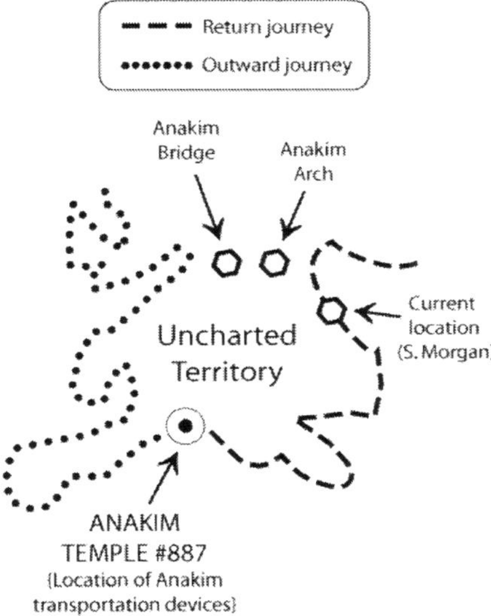

Zooming in on her visor, she analysed the terrain ahead and the location of the water they desperately needed. She turned on the spot, viewing the multitude of tunnels that led away from them. She pointed with an arm. 'That way, about five hundred yards.'

They set off again with renewed vigour and it wasn't long before trickles of water seeped from the rock walls of the cave system they traversed. Soon, the flow of crystal clear liquid could be heard, and then seen, running through small channels cut out of the rock floor. The smell of damp stone made their mouths salivate and Sarah decided the time to stop was now. The repaired canister on the Centipede, all but exhausted, remained forgotten as the three friends got down on their hands and knees to scoop fresh water into parched mouths.

'Oh my God,' Trish said, as she'd drank her fill. 'This is the best water I've ever tasted.'

Sarah had to agree, although its warmth surprised her. Far from cold, the liquid was mineral rich and left a metallic aftertaste on the tongue. Splashing some over her face, she then took some time to replenish the Centipede's reservoir.

'Does that look like steam to you?' Trish pointed down the tunnel.

Sarah squinted in the direction. 'I think so. And according to the Deep Reach team that were here before, it's also the way to the temple.'

Jason hesitated. 'I think I can see light down there.'

Sarah heard the anxiety in his voice. 'Jas, there's nothing down here. Whatever you saw must have been a reflection. We'd just activated the Anakim wall, a technology beyond our understanding.'

'It wasn't a trick of the light, trust me.'

Trish moved off down the tunnel, thirst quenched and spirits lifted. 'It was probably just the Centipede's main-beams reflected by the surface of the arch, or you were hallucinating. You both said these underground places mess with your mind.'

Sarah nodded. 'She's right. Come on, we may have water but we still need to find the temple, light or no.'

'The sooner we get to the surface, the better,' he said, giving in to their reasoning.

They moved forward, and a few minutes later turned a corner.

Sarah switched off her visor. The chamber they'd entered glowed a deep orange, the light flickering over the crumbling ruins that adorned its surround. In the centre a grand piazza led off into the distance, lined either side with rivers of boiling water that shone bright. Peering into one of these steaming basins, Sarah saw the glow emanated from underneath the water itself.

'It looks like there's larva underneath the river,' Trish said. 'Isn't the temple with the transportation devices supposed to be in a hotter part of Sanctuary?'

Sarah nodded. 'We must be getting close.'

Jason joined them. 'There must be a barrier beneath the water stopping the lava evaporating.'

Sarah didn't care, despite its beauty, the heat was intense and she could already feel the damp of sweat on her skin. They needed to move lest they burn off the precious resource they'd just consumed. Carrying on, they passed into a strange dome-like building with curved triangular points sprouting from the roof like a lopsided stegosaurus. The air cooled and they found themselves once more in the dark. Visors back on, they worked their way forward, following the directions on Sarah's map.

They passed the dusty tombs of giants, long dead, their feet leaving trails in the sediment of eons. Huge stone walls and pillars towered above them in the dark, the features covered in fabulous abstract carvings. One particular image caught Sarah's eye, an Anakim priestess spearing a fearsome beast, while another stalked her from behind.

Jason, perhaps still unnerved by whatever it was he thought he'd seen, walked on by, oblivious. Sarah checked her visor. A weak signal from the next waypoint beacon guided them left, out of the building and down yet another cave system, its entrance half-shrouded by a partial collapse.

A few hours later the route had turned into a veritable labyrinth that seemed to go on forever. Sarah stopped. Ahead, half a dozen passages led down into more of the same.

Jason halted the Centipede by her side. 'Something wrong?'

'I don't know. This doesn't seem right.' She brought up an image of the route they'd just taken. The screen on her visor flickered. She banged the side of her helmet and the image resumed, uninterrupted. Running her eyes back over the map, she tried to retrace their steps in her mind.

Moments came and went and Trish moved closer. 'Sarah?'

'Perhaps we took a wrong turn,' Jason said. 'There was a section half an hour back where we could have gone either way.'

Sarah shook her head. 'I don't understand, the map says the next waypoint beacon should be right here.'

'Perhaps its light's broken.' Jason walked around the perimeter, searching, and Trish followed his lead.

After they'd each inspected the surrounding passages in all directions, multiple times, Sarah removed her helmet and ran a hand through her hair. 'This doesn't make sense, it should be here.'

Crouched on her haunches nearby, Trish looked up at her. 'Well, it's not. We've looked everywhere.'

'We'll have to go back and try again,' Jason said.

And that's exactly what they did; however, it soon became apparent finding the way back was a lot harder than they'd envisaged.

'What the fuck is going on!' Sarah stamped a foot in frustration at another dead end.

'We're lost,' Jason said. 'That's what's going on.'

Sarah breathed deep and tried to regain her calm. 'You both looked at the map, too; it's not just me, is it?'

Trish sat down on the Centipede. 'The map's wrong. We've all seen it.'

'It can't be wrong.'

'Well, it is.'

'What I want to know is,' Jason said, 'how is it we can't retrace our steps?'

Trish and Sarah looked at him.

'Regardless of where the beacon is, we should be able to find our way back. Why can't we?'

Trish sighed. 'Because we took a wrong turn.'

Jason shook his head. 'That shouldn't make any difference. We've been working our way through Sanctuary from day one and I've lost count of the number of times we've had to double back. Why can't we do that now?'

'You're saying what we already know,' Trish said, 'there's a problem with the map.'

'No, I don't think that's it. I think there's something wrong with the helmet itself.' He looked at Sarah. 'Didn't you say Riley or someone told you Sanctuary messes with our technology?'

Sarah nodded. 'It's something to do with the material the Anakim used to stop the Earth's mantle from frying everyone inside.'

'So, we're down deep, aren't we? Not just deep, super deep. We've been heading down almost the whole time for days.'

'What's your point?'

'My point is, before we entered this maze, what did we see?'

'Water.'

'Boiling water,' Trish said.

Jason pointed to her. 'Exactly, and what was underneath that?'

'Lava!' Sarah finally saw what he was getting at. 'You think the lower we go, the more interference there is?'

'Sort of. It makes sense, doesn't it? The hotter it gets, the greater the walls of Sanctuary have to work to keep it at bay.'

'And whatever was separating the lava from the water must have been working *really* hard.'

He nodded, his expression grim.

'But none of this helps us,' Trish said, sounding angry, 'does it?'

Sarah didn't agree. 'Well, we know what the problem is, that's something. Now all we have to do is find our way out and try again.'

Trish hopped up from her seat on the Centipede. 'Then let's stop yakking and get started. I'm beginning to really loathe this place.'

With no arguments from Sarah or Jason, the three friends set off once more, turning back the way they'd come, determined to find their way out.

Behind them, unseen around a corner, a single metal pole lay wedged behind a rock, crumpled and bent; on its top was a small transparent shell where a light had once pulsed forth. The missing Deep Reach waypoint beacon remained unfound, but as those that had sought it returned from whence they came, a shimmering blue-green light emerged from the dark to illuminate the area. And moments later, a strange clicking noise began.

CHAPTER NINETEEN

'SERIOUSLY, we're totally lost and you think now's the time to take rock samples?'

'We're better off than we were before. At least we have plenty of water now. Time's on our side again.'

Depressed, Trish gave Sarah *that* look, while Jason, ankle deep in cold water, struggled to pull out his prize.

It had been two days since they'd entered the system of endless tunnels and they were still no closer to finding their way out than when they'd started. They had, however, found a spring of water, an oasis in the middle of their open and ever-changing prison.

With a grunt of exertion, Jason fell back onto dry land with a large chunk of rock clasped in his hands. Setting it down on the ground, he withdrew a knife and whittled away the soft outer layers.

Piece by piece, Jason revealed the interior until he levered out a large chunk and a blue glow washed over his hands.

Trish leaned in for a look. 'Wow, that's huge.'

'That's what all the girls say.' He glanced at Sarah and winked.

Trish tutted, but remained gazing at the luminescing object as keenly as Sarah herself.

Jason continued his work, revealing more of the treasure within. 'I think there's a whole seam of this stuff running through the rock.'

Trish gave a snort and moved away. 'Why do you want it, anyway? You've got those stones.'

'Yeah, most of them went funny. And this,' he waggled the rock in the air, 'is way better. Look at the size of it!'

Sarah cocked her head to one side. 'Went funny?'

Jason put down his tool and dug into his coveralls. 'Yeah.' He chucked some stones at her. 'Look; they went all normal.'

Sarah caught a couple and saw he was right. The stones he'd had before were now ordinary, no glow, just a dull, dirty grey mixed with black. Turning them over in her hand, she returned to thinking about their predicament. How could they find the temple if they couldn't get out of this never-ending rabbit warren? They might have struck it lucky with water, but they were all suffering from hunger pains as their food supply ran low. She tossed a pebble into the water and watched the ripples expand out towards the small shoreline.

Jason stood up. 'There, check it out; sweet, eh?'

Sarah looked at the glowing perfection he held aloft in a gloved hand. The rectangular brick of crystal pulsed a deep, ocean blue with veins of lighter and darker shades criss-crossing its surface.

A shriek of noise echoed down the tunnels, filling the air.

'What the fuck was that?!' Trish stepped back towards Jason, who'd gone stock still.

Sarah, heart beating loud, stood up, listening, ears pricked.

Silence reigned as they all stood immobile.

The noise came again, sending goosebumps prickling along her arms.

Trish looked at Sarah, eyes wild. 'Tell me that's the wind.'

'That's no wind.' Sarah lowered her visor, and looked down to see her climbing axe already grasped beneath white knuckles.

Jason stowed his glowing brick and pulled Trish away from the direction the noise come from. 'I think we should go.'

Sarah spun up the Centipede's motor, its main beams blinking forth as she manoeuvred it to a tunnel entrance.

Another terrifying screech echoed down to them, louder than before.

'Go!' Sarah said, and she followed Jason and Trish as they ran before her, the Centipede speeding along at her side.

A T-junction appeared.

Trish hesitated. 'Which way?!'

Jason dragged her left.

The noise came again, sounding even closer.

They picked up the pace, running full pelt down tunnel after cave after tunnel. Entrances flashed past. The Centipede careered into a stalagmite, demolishing it. Sarah slowed to regain control, and glanced back to see nothing pursued them – if there ever had been. Trish and Jason cut down another fork in the passage and disappeared round a bend.

'Guys, slow down!' Sarah rushed to catch up.

Flying round a corner, she nearly knocked them from a ledge as she skidded the Centipede to a sideways stop at their feet.

Jason moved aside and pointed. 'End of the line.'

Sarah saw a black expanse before them, her visor showing it as a canvas of grey. She peered over the edge and then looked back with anxious eyes.

Trish, one step ahead, aimed the rangefinder at the ground below. 'Half a kilometre.'

Sarah looked at them. 'We're running blind; we have no idea where we're going. The further we go, the more likely we'll never find our way back.'

Another bloodcurdling shriek sent them scurrying. With abseil and Centipede anchors deployed in a flash, they dropped from the ledge. Sarah, more experienced, sped downwards, almost in freefall. Looking down, her visor relayed the distance to the ground enabling her to slow for a cushioned landing. Switching focus to the Centipede, she was joined soon after by Jason and then Trish.

'What the—' Jason looked up in fear.

Sarah followed his gaze. Above a shimmering light had appeared, fluctuating on the ledge before blinking out.

'What is it?' Trish sounded terrified.

'It's that damn light,' he said. 'I told you!'

Sarah faced them. 'Whatever it is, its chasing us, let's move!'

Not needing to be told twice they set off again at a maintained run. Angling left, they passed beneath an Anakim gateway and out onto a massive stairway which led to a central road hundreds of feet across that cut straight as a die for as far as the visor could see. Not stopping, they pounded down the stairs with the Centipede's wheels bobbling down beside them ten to the dozen, the sound of its rubber tyres reverberating like tiny drums. In full flight, they each kept glancing behind to see if the mysterious light followed, but as time passed and the frightening phenomenon failed to materialise, complacency and exhaustion crept in and they slowed to a jog and then a walk. Sarah remembered her visor's mirror function and switched it on, the tiny camera concealed at the helmet's rear saving them from a crick in the neck.

Ahead of them, the mighty thoroughfare they now traversed sparkled like jewels in the night, the expanse lit with a steady glow of bioluminescence that twinkled like millions of tiny stars. Either side towers reached up into the subterranean sky, interspersed with monumental statues in varying states of decay.

Moving ever forward, they tried to put distance between themselves and the thing they'd encountered – Jason's dreaded light – and they soon found themselves passing through the glowing fields they'd seen from afar. Crushed underfoot, the tiny plants released tiny spores that hung in the air around them. The smell reminded Sarah of crushed willow blossom in the autumn fall.

Movement in her visor's mirror caught her eye. She spun round. Back at the top of the steps a light hovered, shimmering blue-green like a swarm of fireflies in the night. Trish and Jason backed away as the light flickered and vanished, before it reappeared, travelling at speed down the stairs, heading straight towards them.

Trish screamed and ran, with Sarah and Jason hot on her heels.

Already tired, they soon slowed again, Trish being the first to fall behind. Sarah ran back to drag her friend onwards and Jason returned to help.

Half a mile away and closing fast, the light bore down on them.

Trish stumbled on, before stopping again, gasping. 'It's no good, I can't run anymore.'

Sarah had an idea. Bringing the Centipede back, she unclipped two large containers and heaved them to the ground. 'Get on!'

Trish stared at her.

'Hurry!'

Trish hopped onto the Centipede's back and Sarah whacked it back into gear. The machine shot forward with Trish clinging to it while Sarah and Jason ran alongside.

Trish looked back. 'It's gaining!'

Sarah increased the Centipede's speed and her own, while Jason laboured on.

Sarah pointed to the Centipede. 'Get on!'

He shook his head. 'What about you?!'

'I'm fine, get on!'

An ear shattering noise like dying thunder propelled Jason into action.

He jumped on board. 'Fucking hell, Sarah, it's almost on us!'

Sarah looked in her visor mirror to see the light looming large.

Swerving right, she reached for the water canister's retainers. Jason saw what she was doing and leaned back to help. One clamp popped up and then the other. They hit a bump and the Centipede left the ground, throwing the black container into the air. The machine landed back down and Sarah jumped.

Held on by Jason's outstretched hand, she turned to see the canister explode in a shower of water as the light tore through it. Sarah stared at the shimmering form as it leapt towards her; death descended and she slammed her hand down. A red button depressed and fire shot from the Centipede's exhaust. Its auxiliary engine ignited in a flash and a roar and the light landed on empty ground.

The speedometer on Sarah's helmet shot up to fifty, and then sixty miles an hour. The Centipede flew across the landscape, its wheels juddering over the terrain and jarring its passengers to pieces while the power bar on its console shrank as it thrust them onwards. Behind, the light increased its speed to match their own and Sarah's eyes widened in horror before it dropped back. And then, moments later, she saw it stop and its light blink out.

Knowing they were far from safe, they carried on, the Centipede transporting them through the grand thoroughfare of Sanctuary Proper and leaving a trail of glowing pollen drifting in their wake. Further back, the thing that pursued them lurked, its presence revealed, but its unfathomable desires unsated. It seemed Jason had been right, they weren't alone after all.

CHAPTER TWENTY

THE CENTIPEDE's auxiliary fuel supply petered out and the engine roar dropped to a whimper. The electric powertrain kicked back in and Sarah slowed their travel in order to preserve the diminished battery life. After a while they got off to walk, each lost in their own thoughts after fleeing the mysterious light that had pursued them.

Trish was the first to break the silence. 'How far have we come?'

Sarah consulted her visor. 'Nearly ten miles.'

'This must be some type of main highway.' Jason looked around at the vast, sunken avenue that had been carved out between the ancient Anakim buildings, shrouded in gloom on either side. 'We're lucky; if that thing had cornered us in the caves we'd be dead.'

Trish looked scared. 'You really think it would've killed us?'

'I don't think it was chasing us for a kiss.'

Trish glared at him. 'It could have just been trying to scare us off. Perhaps we wandered into its territory or something.'

'Whatever – *it* – is,' Jason said. 'What do you think, Saz? Any ideas?'

Sarah pondered the question. *What could it be?* There were a myriad of answers, but none seemed particularly plausible. Although considering what they'd just witnessed and where they were, Sanctuary itself, then perhaps anything was possible.

When Sarah failed to respond, Trish spoke up. 'Perhaps it's some creature that the Anakim found when they built this place.'

Jason shook his head. 'Unlikely. I've heard of creatures in the deep ocean being able to biofluoresce, but nothing on land; at least, nothing that size.'

'We didn't actually *see* anything, though, did we?'

'Your point being?'

'What if it was an illusion, created by the Anakim to frighten away unwanted visitors?'

'Illusions don't obliterate water canisters,' Sarah said. 'Whatever it is, it's after us. We escaped it once, we got lucky. If it comes again—'

'We're screwed,' Jason said, taking his cue to glance behind, as they each did in fearful regularity.

Trish then asked the question they'd all been avoiding. 'How are we going to get to the temple now? If we can't go back because of that thing, and we don't know where we are, we're already screwed, or am I missing something?'

Jason grimaced, his expression downcast.

'I'll think of something,' Sarah said. *I have to,* she thought, *otherwise we're as good as dead.* She looked at her two friends, who searched her face for reassurance, making her feel even more wretched than she already did. *Why had they put such faith in my plan? Because I deliver*, she told herself. *Because I make things happen. I will get us out of this mess. I've done it before. I'll do it again.* The strength of her own internal voice shored up her flagging resolve and sent her mind into overdrive to seek a solution to their plight.

If the only way to get to the surface was by using an Anakim transportation device, then they'd either need to find one somewhere else or find the temple. They were the only choices, save that or somehow get back to the USSB, where, despite the lifelong incarceration they'd be subjected to, at least they'd still be alive. She swirled around the options in her mind, savouring the pros and cons of each one like a fine wine.

Thinking about it in detail, there was no real finesse to the choices at all. Finding another transportation device, while feasible, was akin to chucking a dart into a dartboard with your eyes closed and hoping you'd hit the bullseye. Returning to the USSB meant returning to the route on the Deep Reach map, which meant locating the waypoint beacons they'd need to get to the temple. Therefore, by simple deduction, that option automatically rendered itself secondary to actually finding the temple itself. That meant only one thing – they'd have to go back, which also meant dealing with the light. But how do you overcome something that you know nothing about? That was the question. If they knew what its motivations were, or even had some basic knowledge on its behaviour, then it'd be a start. The only thing they knew about it was that it didn't like their company and would chase them down whenever it sensed their presence. At least that seemed the most likely assumption.

A spark of an idea grew in her mind. A dangerous idea, but then what other choice was there? *None*. She'd think on it further, refine it, and then put it to the vote. Although regardless of their decision, it was the only way, like it or not this is what had to happen if they were to ever see the surface again, if they were to stay alive longer than a few days. The time had come to make a stand and roll the dice. She just prayed they were loaded in their favour.

CHAPTER TWENTY-ONE

USSB SANCTUARY

'Where is he?'

The soldier gestured with the tip of his rifle. 'Through there.'

Malcolm Joiner stalked across the metal floor, his footfalls echoing in the confined quarters of the army barracks. He opened a door and stepped through.

Agent Myers and ten other U.S. GMRC intelligence agents turned as he entered. At the far side of the room a number of Special Forces Subterranean Detachment commandos stood in relaxed disinterest, rifles in hand.

'Let's get it over with, then,' Joiner said.

Myers gave his men some last words before moving to Joiner's side. 'Sir, are you sure you're comfortable with this? I can't guarantee your safety. If I had more time—'

Joiner gave him a withering look. 'I arranged this; you don't think I know the risks? Besides,' – he waved a hand at all the armed men on show – 'we have our finest at our disposal.'

'It only takes a second.'

'If I didn't take risks I wouldn't be where I am today.'

'I still don't like it.'

Joiner's jaw tightened. 'Noted.'

Myers nodded. He'd voiced his concerns and his director knew the stakes; what more could he do? He waved at two of his men, who in response disappeared into a hallway, followed by six SFSD 'Terra Force' commandos.

Seconds passed before a host of shouting echoed back through to Joiner.

Myers glanced in his direction, a look of concern on his face. 'It's not too late for a more secure environment. We could postpone until—'

Joiner shook his head. 'I haven't got time for secure. It needs to be now.'

Myers sighed and waved two more agents forward. They ran in to assist their colleagues.

More shouting followed before a gunshot startled everyone, the thunderous noise setting ears to ringing.

Myers swore. He raised his arm and wagged a finger at the remaining commandos. Their leader acknowledged the gesture and moved his men through into the hall. More commotion ensued before a cluster of men emerged, struggling against a writhing shape in their midst.

A fearsome bellow and a guttural growl made Joiner take a backward step.

The group approached and he held his ground as around them the remaining intelligence agents aimed their guns, ready to shoot and subdue if required.

A marine staggered back with blood gushing from his nose.

'For fuck's sake.' Myers snatched a rifle from a nearby agent, reversed it and waded into the melee. With a swift jab, followed by another, the commotion ceased and the men stood back in a circle to gaze at the source of the disturbance.

Joiner pushed his way forward. He looked down and turned to Myers. 'What is that? *That* is not what I asked for.'

'It's what you wanted.'

'No, it is not. I wanted motivation. I wanted determination. I wanted results. This ... this *thing*, is not fit for purpose.'

'With some time—'

'I don't have time!' Joiner said, furious.

Myers was lost for words, unused to seeing his director so agitated.

Joiner hung his head, his plan for control slipping from his grasp. He'd thought his idea would work, but from what he'd just seen he should have concentrated his efforts elsewhere.

Myers came to stand by his side, the noise in the room subdued. 'Sir, we can find another way. Perhaps I can be of use? Or we could reach out to another service; there are plenty of alternatives, surely? This was always a gamble—'

Joiner put up a hand to silence him. He needed to think and his brow furrowed in concentration. 'I wanted this,' he said, coming to a swift conclusion. 'This was the best option, the only option.' He made a decision. 'Have you got it?'

Myers looked shocked. 'After what you've just seen, I don't think—'

Joiner gave him a look that could melt iron.

Myers stopped talking and waved an agent to him. The man presented him with a small grey case. Myers opened it, removed the single needle inside and attached its shiny length to a glass cylinder containing a green liquid. He then held it up for Joiner to see.

A marine gave a shout of warning and a shadow rose behind them. Weapons were raised and fingers moved to triggers.

'Stick that thing in me,' a gravel-laden voice said, 'and it'll be the last thing you do.'

Joiner and Myers turned. Before them, surrounded by a ring of guns pointing at his chest, battered and bruised, cut and bleeding, was the dishevelled figure of the man Joiner wanted to lead the search for Sarah Morgan. The man who could bring him what he craved.

Joiner's expression changed, a glimmer of hope bringing with it a smirk of pleasure. 'Ah, so there is someone in there after all.'

Colonel Samson took a step forward, burning madness in his eyes. 'I'm still here,' – he coughed up some blood and spat it on the floor – 'but I'll make you wish I wasn't.'

CHAPTER TWENTY-TWO

'Hold him!'

Samson surged forward, knocking aside two marines before four more grappled him to the floor. Snarling like a rabid beast, he twisted, and a scream rang out as he bit into a man's shoulder.

Joiner moved back as they fought to subdue the tortured beast he'd gone to so much trouble to acquire.

'I said hold him!' Myers moved in close, needle at the ready.

A huge marine grasped Samson round the neck, while many others pinned him to the floor. Samson's insane eyes rolled like a maddened animal, teeth bared, skin red, tendons and veins fit to burst.

Myers bent down to rest the needle on Samson's neck and he struggled again. Myers cursed. 'Tighter!'

The marine's biceps bunched and shook with tension. The skin on Samson's face turned purple and Myers stuck the needle in his neck, pressed down the plunger and extracted it in a heartbeat. Samson gave a final twitch before going limp, a trickle of froth seeping from his mouth.

Joiner relaxed.

'He should be out for ten minutes.' Myers gave his Director a look of reproach. 'It would have been a lot easier to do this before he came out of sedation.'

'I needed to see if he could listen to reason.'

'Could he ever?'

Joiner removed his glasses. 'The man's been taken to the brink; we need to bring him back if he's to be of use. I have to admit, though, I didn't expect him to be that far gone.'

Myers nodded. 'The surface is starting to buckle, civilisation is breaking down. The people may not realise it, but base desires and behaviour are asserting their grip. The FBI turned a blind eye and the police encouraged the guards to inflict as much pain and suffering as they wanted.'

'And Steiner?'

'Some of the same, but nowhere near the extent that Samson received.'

'That's not what I meant. Did he survive the fire?'

'Our priority was Samson, you made that clear.'

'So he lives?'

'He does.'

Joiner gave a nod, his emotions mixed. He disliked the professor and would see him dead, but even he had limits. The treatment Samson must have received he wouldn't have inflicted on a dog – on a dead dog. He knew he enjoyed the suffering of others, sometimes at a whim, and sometimes under torture, but he'd worked with Steiner for many years in the early days of the council and he felt an unusual sense of sympathy for him. *Perhaps that's because I may find myself in the same position*, he thought. The Committee seemed to have him in their sights for whatever reason. However, now they'd shown their hand he could prepare his defence.

'Shall we secure him before he wakes?' Myers said.

Joiner gave him a look. 'Considering what we just witnessed, what do you think?'

'I'll see to it.'

Time passed and Joiner found himself sitting on a stool, waiting for Samson to reawaken. He looked at Myers. 'How long now?'

'Eighteen minutes.'

'I thought you said he'd be out for ten.'

'I may have given him too much,' Myers said.

'Will it affect his ability to function?'

'It shouldn't, it'll just extend the effects.'

'Good. And his mind will be clear and focused?'

Myers gestured at Samson who'd been strapped upright to a vertical slab. 'We're about to find out.'

◆

Samson opened his eyes to see two men looking at him. Both he recognised. He frowned as he tried to recall their names.

'Do you know who we are?' the older man said, his face gaunt and sharp, his voice grating.

Samson shook his head, trying to dispel a buzzing sensation that cloistered his senses like a lucid dream. A flash of light flared before his eyes and a spark of remembrance ignited his brain. His eyes narrowed. 'Malcolm Joiner ... what did you do to me?'

Joiner smiled. 'A little medication is all.'

'We need you to be all you can be,' Myers said.

Samson switched his attention to the CIA operative. 'You injected me.' He struggled against his restraints. 'Release these straps and I'll show you what I can be.'

'That's good,' Joiner said, 'very good. We want the beast harnessed, not dead.'

'I'll give you the fucking beast.' Samson bunched his arms and the straps creaked and stretched.

Joiner looked at Myers in alarm.

Samson ceased his efforts and laughed, exhausted.

A flicker of annoyance crossed Joiner's face.

'What, no longer enjoying yourself, *Intelligence Director*?' Samson stared at his captor, his smile gone. 'So,' – he looked at Myers and then back to Joiner again – 'what do you two fucks want with me?'

Joiner folded his arms. 'You're here to retrieve something.'

'What?'

Joiner gestured at Myers, who unfurled a tablet screen and held it up for Samson to see.

Samson looked at the picture of a slim blonde. 'Pretty. Who is she?'

'Someone I want.'

'Say I give a damn.'

'Then I'd tell you she is in possession of an ancient artefact, an object many people – many *important* people – want returned.'

Samson couldn't believe what he was hearing. 'So, let me get this straight. You broke me out of a supermax prison to help you find some trinket found in a ditch?' He shook his head. 'You expect me to believe that?'

Joiner grew angry. 'I don't *care* what you believe. Only that you do as I say.'

'What I don't understand is why a suit like you wants some relic. What is it, the cup of life, the spear of destiny, the fucking Dead Sea scrolls?'

'It's an Anakim pendant of significant scientific value.'

'A what pendant?'

Joiner considered Samson for a moment. 'The Anakim are an extinct human ancestor, who once populated the Earth. It turns out we weren't the first ape to turn creative.' Joiner got up and looked to Myers. 'Fill him in while I take a break.'

Joiner walked from the room and Samson turned his attention back to the CIA operative, his expression quizzical.

◆

The annoyance that was Malcolm Joiner returned to the room sometime later after Samson, resigned to being bored to tears, had listened as Myers brought him up to speed on the fantasy that was Sanctuary Proper and the Anakim themselves. The truth, which he still doubted to a certain extent, was hard to accept. *Although why would they make up something so fanciful? There's no purpose to it.* Unless they'd pumped him so full of drugs he was experiencing a full blown hallucination. In some ways that would have seemed the more likely, had the video footage of this decaying subterranean world not been so detailed and extensive.

'So,' Joiner said, reclaiming his seat, 'can we proceed?'

Myers nodded.

'Excellent. Right, Colonel, now you're one of us, so to speak, let's get down to business. I want this pendant and you're going to go out into Sanctuary and find it for me. You'll lead the search, commanding all SFSD and U.S. military assets, along with SED and mercenary support.'

'Why me?'

'Because you can provide the motivation I desire.'

Samson chuckled.

'Something amusing, Colonel?'

'You might say that.'

'Do you care to enlighten us?'

'Well, seeing as I couldn't give a rat's ass what you want or where you want it – and I'm damn sure I'm not going to do it – the fact that you think I can motivate others is pretty fucking amusing, yeah.'

Joiner sat back in smug satisfaction. 'That's where you're wrong, Colonel. You see, you will help and you will do so as if the mission were your own.'

'Is that so? I no longer care what happens to me – send me back to prison, kill me; in fact I welcome it over this bullshit, at least I won't die of boredom.'

Joiner adjusted his spectacles. 'I am aware that death has little meaning to you, your actions in Los Angeles made that abundantly clear. Although according to our findings, we are the intelligence service after all, it seems we're aware of some details that have eluded the FBI and LAPD.'

'And what's that?'

'That the FBI agent you abducted, and who ended up as your captor, is in fact your flesh and bone, a daughter, correct?'

◆

Joiner watched Samson with interest as the man struggled with the information he'd just received.

The colonel's blazing eyes held Joiner's as if he could burn him into ashes with a stare. A roar of fury erupted from his lips and he thrashed violent, the vertical slab holding him swaying in response.

Joiner stepped back as Myers moved in with a tranquiliser gun. With a hiss of gas the sedative entered Samson's arm, leaving a circle of red on his skin. Seconds later his motion calmed.

Joiner looked at Myers. 'I need a moment alone with the Colonel.'

Myers shook his head. 'Sir, I—'

'That's an order, Agent.'

Myers held his ground, before conceding defeat under his director's unwavering gaze. After he'd left the room Joiner turned his attention back to his prisoner, who watched him like a shark eyed its next meal.

'Colonel, this was not my idea. In fact, I advised the Committee against such action. They insisted, however; after seeing your show in LA, they wanted to utilise your talents. They instructed me they would kill your daughter if you didn't comply with their wishes. All they want is the woman, preferably alive, but most of all they want the pendant. Bring them the pendant and they guarantee your daughter won't be harmed.'

A drip of drool fell from the corner of Samson's mouth. 'Who is the Committee?' he said, his words slow.

'They are the power behind everything, the new ruling order. The global elite, half hide in plain sight and the other in the population's blind spot. They control the media, education, the financial system ... everything is geared to their future success, everything.'

'I know—'

'You know?'

'—about the asteroids.'

Joiner was surprised, but it put Samson's past actions into perspective. 'Steiner told you?'

Samson nodded. 'I gave him no choice. I want ... I want my daughter here, safe haven in Sanctuary.'

Joiner gave a bob of his head. 'A fair request – done.'

'One ... condition.'

'Name it.'

'Who is to carry out the order for—'

'Who is tasked to kill your daughter?' Joiner could have crowed, but he remained aloof and full of gravitas. 'Have you heard of S.I.L.V.E.R., Colonel?'

He nodded.

'Their leader has been given the task; he seems to revel in such work.'

Samson, his fervour fighting off the effects of the drug, strained forward. 'Tell me.'

'His name is Ophion Nexus.'

CHAPTER TWENTY-THREE

'COLONEL,' Joiner said, 'you will be working alongside this man, along with his team. The best course of action will be for you to find this woman and return the pendant to this base. Harming Ophion will be counterproductive to your cause.'

'What about after I have the woman?'

'That's for you to decide.'

Samson, returning to clarity, gave a grim smile. 'Says the snake of snakes.'

'Why would I lie? I sent Myers away so I could tell you the truth about the Committee. If I was behind this I'd hardly let you go – like I'm about to – arm you to the teeth, put an army behind you, and then offer up one of our best operatives. It would make no sense. I'm your best chance to keep your daughter alive, save from yourself. I'm not the enemy, despite what you may think of me.'

Samson's mouth twisted into a leer. 'We shall see.'

'We shall.' Joiner called Myers back in.

The CIA operative came to stand by Joiner's side.

Joiner waved a hand. 'Remove the colonel's restraints.'

Myers looked dubious.

'Now,' Joiner said.

Myers eyed Samson who glared back at him. 'At least let me sedate him again.'

Joiner sighed. 'Very well.'

Myers produced the same dispenser and sent another shot into Samson's arm.

When the colonel's head dropped, Myers called six of his agents into the room, ensuring they had weapons drawn and Samson in their sights. With a final glance at his boss, he unclipped the straps and released the chains binding Samson's limbs.

Samson's hand snaked out to grab a shocked Myers round the throat before dragging him into his vice-like grip.

The CIA agents advanced as one, shouting at Samson to release their leader while Joiner lurched to his feet. 'Let him go, Colonel, don't forget your daughter!'

'Inject me again,' Samson said, his lips pressed against Myers' ear, 'and I'll rip you a new mouth.' He thrust the agent away from him, making him stumble. In his hand he held Myers' sidearm.

Samson turned on Joiner and moved forward with menace. 'Seems like you need a stronger sedative, Director.'

Myers seized a weapon from an agent and aimed it at Samson's head. Joiner held up a hand to halt him.

'If my daughter dies, Joiner, you die.'

'Her life is in your hands, Colonel, not mine.'

Samson held his ground before glancing at the array of guns pointed in his direction.

Hesitating a moment longer, Samson relented and held out the gun, grip first, which Myers snatched back from him.

Joiner moved closer to the irate SFSD commander. 'Colonel, you will have every resource from this base available to you, resources that make USSB Steadfast look like a thrift shop. Whatever you want, it's yours. Manpower, weapons, anything. Find this woman and retrieve the pendant, that's all you need to focus on, that's all any of us needs to focus on.' Joiner produced a small container from a pocket and held it out for Samson to take.

'We went to a lot of trouble to bring you here,' Joiner said, 'don't let that effort go to waste.' He gestured to the open door where a Terra Force commando waited. 'Your men are ready, we debrief in eight hours, you ship out in twelve.'

Samson accepted the offering and flipped open the pouch. He looked at Joiner in suspicion before extracting a small red pill, which he placed in his mouth. Then, without a backward glance, he stalked away.

◆

Joiner watched the bulky form of Samson disappear into a corridor. 'What happens when the medication wears off, will he revert to the same state?'

Myers shrugged. 'Your guess is as good as mine. The lab techs said it would normalise extreme psychosis and trauma, I didn't ask what would happen afterwards.'

Joiner collected his overcoat and pulled on his soft leather gloves. 'He won't get a chance to turn; he won't leave Sanctuary Proper alive. I've taken measures. He knows too much.'

'About what?'

'Everything,' Joiner said. 'He knows too much about everything.'

CHAPTER TWENTY-FOUR

Civilian traffic in USSB Sanctuary's New Park district parted like the red sea as the flashing lights of military police vehicles bore down on them from behind. Above, unmanned aerial drones aided their progress, ensuring pedestrians were diverted and traffic signals turned to green. Escorted in the centre of this twenty strong, fast moving motorcade was a cluster of five sinister SUVs, grills snarling like fierce demons and blacked out windows hiding the occupants within. In the back of the longest of these aggressive vehicles sat GMRC Intelligence Director Malcolm Joiner, who gazed out at the simulated dusk produced by the enormous dome that encased the U.S. subterranean base's top level.

More road signs flashed by and the scenery altered. Soldiers lifted barriers on a blockade and the cars bumped over a lip in the road before hurtling into a low-lit tunnel, its six lanes empty in both directions. Still in formation, the high speed vehicular caravan stormed on, the roar of hybrid engines reverberating through the large downward spiralling road.

Moments later they emerged into a bright chamber, once full of civilian residencies but now turned into a massive staging area for U.S. Army personnel. Drones hovered, floodlights shone, trucks manoeuvred and troops assembled. Joiner had shaken the nest and the termites had swarmed.

Powering on, the military led procession slipped into single file, the lead truck whooping its siren in warning. More barriers raised and they thundered into a narrow tunnel without slowing, a whoosh of sound accompanying each vehicle as it flew by. Down and down they drove through this dark passage before light dazzled again. A glimpse of another chamber either side, full of activity, disappeared in a flash as another black hole consumed them.

A minute later their progress slowed, the darkness replaced by a slow creep of fluorescence. The lead vehicles peeled away into service roads while the SUVs swept into a massive, well-lit atrium. Reaching journey's end, they glided to a stop and formed up in a line on a circular driveway in front of a futuristic building full of glass walls, shiny steel and many floors.

Malcolm Joiner's door opened and he stepped from his limousine. He looked at the expansive main entrance to the building and the large sign that hung above it:

Joiner walked forward with his agents by his side. Inside, the building heaved with military and SED personnel rushing about their business in preparation for the mission to come.

Two men waited for Joiner by the main doors. One he knew as

Dresden Locke, the SED's grey-haired civilian commander. The other was a taller, younger man Joiner recognised from Sarah Morgan's dossier of crimes. He frowned.

'Director,' Locke said as he approached.

Joiner removed the sunshades from his spectacles. 'Is everything ready?'

'It is. Everyone is assembled as requested apart from the S.I.L.V.E.R. contingent, who are still en route.'

'Of course,' Joiner said, while wishing Ophion a long and tortuous death. His eyes flicked over to the other SED man, then back to Locke. He gestured Myers forward. 'Agent, arrest this civilian.'

The man stepped back in shock while Locke moved to block Myers' path. 'Director, what are you doing?!'

'This man,' Joiner jabbed a finger at his target, 'is the reason we're all here, the reason for this damn mess.'

'Riley is no more to blame than I am,' Locke said. 'It was the military who sanctioned Sarah Morgan's employment at the SED, it was the military who let her out of custody and the military who failed to track her movements. If you want to arrest someone, arrest General Stevens.'

Joiner put a hand on Myers arm, stopping his advance. 'You seem to forget, Commander Locke, your Riley Orton here admitted to showing Ms. Morgan around the vaults, which enabled her to carry out her infringements. His carnal relations with her also exposed SED, GMRC and U.S. security, leading to the theft of his multi-function card, the death of a colleague and the destruction of a shuttle track. This man is a liability, an accomplice, and the fact he remains on your staff continues the culture of denial and general incompetence that has resulted in this storm of shit you see around you now. If that isn't reason enough I don't know what is.'

Locke held his ground. 'Riley is a top asset, Director; if you want this woman found he's your best option.'

'Is he, indeed? Is he not also the progeny of General Ellwood?' He looked at Riley. 'It seems defective decision-making runs in your family.'

Riley didn't know what to say, but Locke continued in his defence. 'He knows her better than anyone here. He helped train her. He knows how she thinks. He's also one of our best Deep Reach team leaders, who will be critical in leading the military into Sanctuary. The more SED personnel you have, the more military personnel we keep alive. But if you want to damage your chances of success by all means arrest him.' He stood aside.

◆

Riley Orton tensed, waiting for the GMRC Director of Intelligence to respond to Locke's justification. The agent identified as Myers stood waiting for orders, handcuffs at the ready.

The director stared at Riley with dispassionate eyes. The Deep Reach team leader shifted in discomfort as the silence continued and he glanced at Locke, who remained resolute.

'Very well,' the director said. 'But both of your tenures will be under review within the month, which will be dependent on the success of this mission. Fail, and your chances of continuing your work will be nil. Succeed, and things are more likely to go in your favour.'

Riley breathed a sigh of relief and he could tell Locke felt the same way. With the moment having passed, the director moved on into the SED with his agents in tow.

Locke looked at Riley. 'Remember what I told you, this man answers to no one. Be careful what you say and how you say it and we all might get out of this in one piece.'

Riley nodded and heard Locke mumble, '*literally*' as they followed the agents inside before leading them up a set of escalators and on into the building's main complex.

◆

Little time passed before Riley found himself standing in the Exploration Division's central command suite. The room housed a thirty foot wide circular desk, its surface acting as a digital screen and holographic projector.

Around him, grim-faced men and a number of women waited for the meeting to begin, dim lighting casting deep shadows across their faces. Locke stood to Riley's right, speaking in low tones to General Stevens, who was on his other side. The general held his customary Cuban cigar and the smoke wafted around him like a personal cloak. His usual demeanour of assured arrogance seemed muted, his brash manner quelled, perhaps by the presence of the high ranking individual from the GMRC's all powerful Directorate, the director who'd just threatened to have Riley arrested. Stevens shot the tall, reptilian intelligence director the occasional nervous look while fiddling with a thick bandage that covered the palm of one hand.

A few of Riley's SED colleagues conversed with one another in a huddle off to his left, most of them team leaders for the Deep Reach survey teams who would lead the chase for Sarah out in Sanctuary Proper. The thought of the woman he'd come to care for during their time together sent a host of emotions swirling round his head. In the few months he'd known her she'd evolved from a colleague to a friend to a lover. Now he didn't know what she was, apart from being wanted by seemingly everyone in a position of power. He knew one thing, he still cared for her, but her inexplicable actions had thrown him into a spin and into a world he didn't know. Everything had changed and he had no idea how to regain control.

Riley turned his attention back to the room, forcing such feelings down lest his distraction become obvious. Across from him various armoured Special Forces Subterranean Detachment commandos, the fearsome SFSD, or Terra Force as they were known, stood in patient silence, the stripes on their armour indicating various ranks from captain through to colonel. Riley recognised most of them, used to, as he was, working alongside them out in the field. And then there were the GMRC agents, many of them garbed in tactical gear, apart from a couple, including Agent Myers, who stood next to his boss like the right hand of God.

The twin doors to the office swished open and everyone turned as three people entered.

The chrome armour of the newcomers glinted under the room's diffused lighting and at their head strode a giant of a man. Built like an ox and with eagle-like eyes, he exuded strength and power, his long black hair tied back into a tight plait that draped down over one shoulder. The faces of his two companions remained concealed behind fierce helmets that matched their metallic suits; both, however, were female, the obvious curves in their armour leaving much to the imagination.

The GMRC director moved to the fore, giving the three late shows no hint of welcome, and switched on the desk screen, its light bathing those around it in campfire-like illumination. The room went quiet and he waited until he had everyone's full attention.

'For those of you who don't already know, my name is Malcolm Joiner. I'm the U.S. and GMRC Intelligence Director, a member of the GMRC Directorate and, for anyone who falls short of my expectations, your worst nightmare.' The director let that information sink in, his eyes raking the room before he continued. 'You all know why we're gathered here.'

Agent Myers pressed a couple of buttons and sent duplicated images of Sarah cascading round the table so each person had an image of her to view. In the centre, video footage played in various overlapping graphical windows. Footage as Sarah trained with Riley in the SED, as she ran through the corridors to the Smithsonian's vaults, as she fled the base under a hail of gunfire. Riley dragged his gaze away.

'We are here to find this woman,' Malcolm Joiner said, 'one Sarah Morgan. We are also here to ensure this facility's integrity is maintained, along with the integrity of the entire GMRC subterranean programme, and to return priceless objects of scientific importance back into the hands of the U.S. government, which we all serve.

'As everyone in this room should already be aware, we have brought in the services of an outside organisation to assist us in this task.' The director indicated the three chrome-clad warriors. 'S.I.L.V.E.R. will lead SED and SFSD personnel in the field, making decisions as they see fit to ensure mission success. However,' he continued, 'since original instructions were disseminated a new power structure has been arranged, whereby this mission and everyone in it will answer to my newly designated field commander, an SFSD colonel flown in from USSB Steadfast—'

'That is not acceptable,' said a deep voice.

The intelligence director turned his head towards S.I.L.V.E.R.'s leader. 'I'm sorry, what did you say?'

'Those are unacceptable terms. We were promised full command, no less.'

'I promised you no such thing.'

The chrome-clad man hesitated and looked around at those present. 'Others did.'

The intelligence director removed his spectacles. 'And what *others* are these? I see no one here that outranks me. In fact, the only people I answer to are the GMRC Directorate and the President of the United States, in that order. If you have orders from them I'm unaware of, then please, produce them now so we can move on.'

S.I.L.V.E.R.'s leader took a step towards Joiner. 'This is not a wise decision; you'd do well to reconsider.'

'And you'd do well to do as you're fucking told,' another voice said.

'Ah, excellent.' The director extended an arm towards the Special Forces officers, who moved aside to reveal an armoured figure lurking in the shadows. 'This is the man in question. Ophion Nexus, meet Colonel Samson. Colonel, Ophion.'

The Special Forces colonel marched forward; he was shorter than S.I.L.V.E.R.'s leader, but stockier. His grizzled features, stubble and battle worn armour the complete opposite of the immaculate appearance of S.I.L.V.E.R.'s leader, who had been revealed as Ophion Nexus.

Riley wondered where a man with such an exotic name hailed from. He could have cut the tension with a knife. He glanced at Locke, who along with General Stevens looked on in bleak fascination. The U.S. Army colonel stopped inches from Ophion, his manner aggressive, his eyes manic – feral, even.

Ophion Nexus considered the man who'd superseded his command, his expression cool. He turned back to Malcolm Joiner. Behind him, his two S.I.L.V.E.R. colleagues had moved closer, perhaps sensing the danger Riley could see written all over this Colonel Samson's face. If ever there was a man not to turn your back on, it was him.

'If you want this mission to succeed,' Ophion said to Joiner, 'if you want this woman found, then I'm your best chance of success.'

'I think you'll find Colonel Samson more than motivated. You are, after all, aware of what happens if he fails.'

A look of confusion flickered across Ophion's face.

The colonel's expression darkened and he made to grasp Ophion's arm.

The S.I.L.V.E.R. commander reacted with lightning reflexes, spinning round to clamp his hand onto Samson's wrist, halting him mid-reach. The colonel bunched his fingers into a fist and forced Ophion's arm down before the S.I.L.V.E.R. assassin resisted. Locked in a battle of strength, their arms shook under tension.

One of Ophion's lieutenants stepped forward, a hand straying to a wicked looking knife on her utility belt.

Samson saw the movement and his top lip curled back in contempt. 'I hear you enjoy hunting women, Nexus. You'd better relax your guard or I'll take your friend's knife and cut you in half.'

A dangerous glint entered Ophion's eyes before he realised where he was. He looked around the room and released his hold. 'You'd be wise not to touch me again, Colonel, or you'll have no hand with which to do the cutting.'

Ophion moved away while Colonel Samson continued to glare at him with undisguised hatred, the ferocity of his manner undiminished.

'Excellent,' Malcolm Joiner said, resuming his address to the room as if the confrontation had never happened. 'And now the issue of command has been cleared up, let's move on.'

◆

With the colonel and Ophion separated, the room relaxed and Riley listened as the intelligence director outlined their strategies and how they would utilise special equipment and vehicles to negate the effects of the slow and tortuous route through Sanctuary Proper to the Anakim temple, where it was thought Sarah was headed. It seemed no expense had been spared in the gadgetry on offer, equipment the SED had been after for years had suddenly appeared out of nowhere at the click of Malcolm Joiner's well-connected fingers. Why such efforts couldn't have been made before to aid in Sanctuary's exploration, Riley didn't know. *Perhaps those in power thought they had enough Anakim treasures to be getting on with*, he thought. A fair assumption, considering the amount of archaeological finds that crammed the Smithsonian and military vaults.

'So,' Joiner said, 'as you can see the time it would have taken to reach the temple has been significantly shortened. The original Deep Reach map before you,' – he indicated the depiction of the route which hovered in their air in the form of a hologram – 'has been replaced by a more direct path. Terrain that would have proven impassable has been made possible by the new equipment available. Make good use of it and your progress will be swift.'

'But more dangerous,' Locke said, interrupting. 'And the supplies and equipment you're using are stockpiles earmarked for future exploration; you'll put back the study of Sanctuary by decades, all wasted on this one route.'

Unfazed, Joiner gazed at the SED facility commander. 'There's always a trade off, and the one you mention is of no consequence.'

Locke shook his head. 'You do realise, the number of people you're sending out there has never been attempted before. The risks are immense. As I have said before, surely a smaller team would be more effective, a—'

Joiner waved away the suggestion. 'No, we need to trace their steps. While some teams will take the new route, others will continue by the original path to ensure nothing is left to chance. They'll move fast and with precision. A communication network will also be set up, utilising shielded cable, enabling Colonel Samson to keep a rein on the search and its progress and to adapt as necessary. Regular reports will also be relayed back to SED command, where I'll oversee the whole operation.

Joiner looked around at those present. 'SED Deep Reach survey teams will take the lead, accompanied by a S.I.L.V.E.R. operative and SFSD units. I've been informed, Mr. Orton,' – Joiner pointed at Riley – 'is best qualified to pre-empt Ms. Morgan's actions, and so he will accompany Colonel Samson, Ophion Nexus and Commander Locke in the lead expedition.'

'What?!' Locke looked at Joiner as if he was mad. 'I'm the commander of this facility, I need to be here, controlling operations.'

'Come, come, Commander. We all know this facility can operate without you and I'm perfectly capable of filling your shoes. Your experience in Sanctuary Proper is second to none. No one has racked up more field time. Who better to ensure mission success than you?'

Stunned, Locke didn't reply.

'And besides,' Joiner said, 'it'll give you the opportunity to remedy your mistakes, which contributed to this whole sorry mess.'

Locke opened his mouth and then shut it again. Riley had never seen his superior spoken to like that, and it was disturbing not to see him retaliate. Something had spooked him regarding this Malcolm Joiner, something that told him this was a man to be feared. Riley looked around the room and saw Colonel Samson looking at him. Riley held his gaze before looking away, only to glance back a few seconds later to see the man still gazed at him. Riley felt a ripple of unease and turned his attention elsewhere. This whole mission was giving him a bad feeling.

◆

The mission debrief continued to whisk along, with orders given and questions asked, before Riley saw one of his SED colleagues raise a hand.

The intelligence director pointed at her. 'Yes?'

The woman said something Riley couldn't quite hear.

'Speak up!' Agent Myers said.

'Why is she heading to this temple?'

The director frowned. 'What?'

'Why is Sarah Morgan heading to the temple? Someone said before they only had enough supplies for a one-way trip, so why the temple? If they only had limited supplies, why go in the first place? It's suicide.'

The director seemed flummoxed by the question, which was strange as it was a perfectly reasonable one. Riley wondered why he hadn't thought of it himself, or why no one had mentioned it before.

'There are a number of reasons why,' the director said. 'First, they could have misread the map or chosen the wrong shuttle track. Second, they may be heading to the place where they entered Sanctuary. We discovered a search protocol conducted by Ms. Morgan on a computer database within the SED. As far as we can tell the temple is their target, although any number of routes off the pre-plotted course could be relevant, hence we're covering every eventuality.'

The woman nodded, satisfied, although Riley didn't feel it added up. Sarah wasn't stupid, far from it. She had one of the sharpest minds he knew and an uncanny intuition when it came to exploration. He hadn't realised at the time, but her Deep Reach tests had been off the chart in some areas, the fact only coming to light in a delayed report submitted to Riley's desk after Sarah had fled the base. A breakdown of her results had been interesting reading, although some warnings on her psychological state were raised, including depression, hypomania, and perhaps more worryingly, risk-taking. But then, in their profession everyone needed that edge. Heck, when he'd done the tests his results hadn't been perfect, either.

Malcolm Joiner continued: 'As you know, the target has in her possession certain Anakim artefacts which are as much a priority as Sarah Morgan herself.' He displayed the items on the holo-projector.

Riley looked at the floating, semi-transparent objects before him, which included a weird orb-like artefact, two pendants, a number of parchments and a Mayan tablet.

The director reduced the images back onto the desk's surface screen. 'Be aware, the orb in Ms. Morgan's possession might be dangerous to the touch. You've been warned. You will find more details on the size and form of these items, along with other information pertinent to the mission, in a digital package sent to your personal server accounts. It will be available to download to your helmet visors prior to launch. Study these well when you can, your lives may depend on it.'

Malcolm Joiner powered down the screen and looked around the room. 'Any questions?'

No one answered.

The director nodded. 'Good. Facility Commander Locke and Colonel Samson will address your teams prior to mission start. You all have your orders, and every resource of this base to draw upon. Make it happen!'

CHAPTER TWENTY-FIVE

DEEP REACH TEAM leader Riley Orton and Dresden Locke left the command suite behind and walked down a familiar corridor to the SED facility commander's personal office. Once inside, Locke slammed the door shut, moved to his desk and leaned onto it with his head hanging down.

Riley felt like he should say something, but he was lost for words.

Locke straightened up, his face livid. 'Jesus H. Christ! That man, that fucking man!'

'He gave you no warning he wanted you out for the search?'

Locke moved to his locker, where he yanked out an old set of SED coveralls, the logos and emblems fifteen years out of date. 'Do you know how long it is since I wore this?'

'Ten years?'

'Try eighteen. What is that man thinking?! I'm the facility commander. He thinks he can just swan in here and assume control of the biggest operation the SED has ever seen, while he puts me out in the field.'

'He must have his reasons.'

Locke gave him a furious look. 'He's a fucking idiot, a lunatic with a God complex. Do you know how many people he's sending out into Sanctuary?'

Riley had a good idea, but kept quiet.

'Over ten thousand – ten goddamn thousand! The most we've ever had out there is nine hundred and that was spread over multiple sites.' Locke removed a dusty box from the back of the locker. 'Mark my words, people are going to die out there, a lot of people.' He shook his head and muttered, 'Ten goddamn thousand.'

Removing the cardboard lid, he pulled out his well-worn dark red Deep Reach helmet. His call sign, 'Torch', had been emblazoned on the front above the visor, and his first initial and surname detailed on the right hand side in block lettering: 'D. Locke'. On the opposite side was a holographic image of an archer with a bow, the notched arrow drawn back and its head alight with flame.

'That's a mark eight, isn't it?' Riley indicated the helmet. 'Will it be up to the job?'

'It'll have to be, there's no time to get a new one fitted. I'll need a new battery pack, though.'

Riley nodded. 'I'll get you one.' He moved to the door, paused and then turned back. 'Sir, you don't believe Sarah murdered Cora, do you?'

Locke held his gaze and then shook his head. 'No. The girl was a loose cannon, but no murderer.' The SED commander slid the outdated helmet onto his head and moved to a full-length mirror to assess his appearance. 'I've been around enough soldiers to know a killer when I see one ... as should you.'

'So how did she die? There's something they're not telling us.'

Locke gave a snort. 'There's a lot they're not telling us.'

'And where is Sarah going? The temple, it makes no sense. If she wanted to get to the surface, surely they'd try and work their way up, not down? There's no way she would have taken the wrong shuttle, or chosen the wrong route, either.'

'As I said, there's a lot they're not telling us, and we never did find that tunnel of hers.'

Riley made a face. 'She swore blind that's how they found their way into Sanctuary.'

'And you believed her?'

'You didn't?'

'Maybe, but there was always something off about that girl. I'm sorry, Riley, I know you were fond of her, but that's the way of it. How well did you really know her? How well do we really know anyone?'

Riley didn't think there was anything off with Sarah at all, she was just a lost soul in need of rescuing and, until recently, he'd been hoping he'd be the one to do the saving.

'One thing's for sure,' Locke said, 'we'll have to watch our backs out there as the military sure as hell ain't gonna watch them for us.'

'What do you make of Colonel Samson?'

'Compared to who? Nexus? I get the feeling we're out of the frying pan and into the fire.'

Riley couldn't have agreed more. The intensity in the colonel's eyes – it was hard to pin down, unnatural, feverish, disturbing, to name a few.

Locke tapped his Deep Reach headwear. 'Battery?'

Riley gave a nod and left to source the item. Walking back the way he'd come, he saw the intelligence director's lap dog, Agent Myers, leaving the command suite. Riley slowed to a stop beside the glass wall, the high-tech panel opaque, the door just ahead – ajar.

He could hear voices within and edged closer.

'You saw what I'm dealing with?' Malcolm Joiner said, the rasp of the intelligence director's voice unmistakable.

'I saw,' Colonel Samson's gruff voice replied.

'Can you work with him?'

'Yes.'

'You know what you have to do?'

'I do.'

'Push them hard, push them fast. Leave behind any who falter. No compromises. Locke and his SED teams will try to slow you down; they'll also try and protect their precious Sanctuary. Ignore them.

Tear Sanctuary apart if you have to – whatever it takes, whatever the cost, that pendant must be retrieved.'

'The woman?'

'Secondary,' Joiner said. 'Alive is better, dead will do.'

'The other two?'

'Of no consequence. If you fail, Colonel, don't bother coming back.'

'If I fail, I'll be the only one coming back.'

'Is that a threat?'

Heavy footfalls approached and Riley scurried back to hide behind a pillar.

The armoured form of Colonel Samson appeared in the doorway and he stopped to look back into the room. 'No,' he said, 'it's a promise.'

CHAPTER TWENTY-SIX

COLONEL SAMSON DISAPPEARED down the corridor and Riley stayed where he was until the tall figure of the GMRC Intelligence Director emerged, moments later. Malcolm Joiner paused and Riley ducked his head back, holding his breath, until he heard footfalls fading away in the opposite direction. Relinquishing his hiding place, Riley stood in the middle of the corridor, the words he'd just been privy to ringing in his mind. *Alive is better, dead will do.* Thinking of Sarah imprisoned was one thing; he'd almost resigned himself to the fact, although, he secretly hoped she'd escape and make it to wherever she was heading. *But dead?* The thought made him nauseous. With a sense of dread he continued on his way, the feeling clinging to him like the cloying hands of disease.

♦

Sanctuary's Exploration Division heaved with personnel and the circular command centre at its heart hummed with activity. Holographic computer screens and mapping systems glowed bright, while huge sweeping wallscreens displayed a mind-boggling array of data.

Two large areas stood on either side of this building within a building; one was a large staging area and the other the shuttle bay itself, which all teams would pass through on their journey into Sanctuary Proper.

Since the debriefing, final preparations had been made and Riley stood on a platform in the command centre, next to the staging area where a few thousand people had congregated, the babble of voices a collective wave of noise. Outside the SED's main complex, in the massive atrium which enclosed it, large screens had been erected for the thousands more Special Forces commandos who were also primed for deployment.

Riley gazed out at the men and women ready for departure. Many were SED employees. Every Deep Reach survey team had been prepped and primed in readiness for the off, their high-tech helmets in hand and specialised climbing harnesses strapped on. Interspersed amongst these teams were the formidable forms of the SFSD, Terra Force, their armour, helmets and weaponry an imposing sight for those that witnessed it.

At the front and off to one side, the small number of S.I.L.V.E.R. operatives stood resplendent in their armour plate chrome cladding, their glittering panels a stark contrast to the dull greys, greens and browns of the commandos close by. Unlike their U.S. Army counterparts, Ophion's mercenaries held a wide variety of weapons, including wicked curved swords sunken into moulded back-plates; strange rifles, each customised to the owner's preference; and clusters of strange-looking gadgetry attached to various parts of the body. Riley's fear for Sarah's life, already high, climbed higher with each passing minute. This wasn't a simple seek and capture as they'd been led to believe, it was a full-scale military led assault, its target: a single, unarmed woman in the company of her two friends in the vast darkness beyond.

Locke joined him on the raised dais. 'Nearly show time.'

Riley glanced up to see Malcolm Joiner looking out of the control centre's uppermost window, his posture imperious, his dark glasses covering his all-seeing deadpan eyes. Either side of him agents of the GMRC stood at his beck and call, ready to action anything he commanded. Also nearby was General Stevens, looking anything but at ease, his trademark cigar absent.

'So,' Locke said, 'you say they're only after the pendant?'

Riley looked at his superior. 'That's what he said.'

'Whatever it is or does, it must be important to go to all this trouble over.'

'Does?'

'It must be Anakim tech of some sort,' Locke said, 'that's the only thing that could create this kind of response. Even if Morgan compromised the existence of the Subterranean Programme, the fallout could easily be contained on the surface; easier than this, anyway.'

'All the shuttles are ready,' a voice said.

They looked round as a large bearded man climbed up beside them, his barrel chest and massive arms filling his oversize Deep Reach uniform. Following Cora's death the huge, bald-headed Jefferson Church had been promoted to deputy team leader of Deep Reach survey team Alpha Six; Riley's team. The lead archaeologist and skilled climber was a comforting sight at even the most tense of times.

'Have you seen Colonel Samson?' Locke said.

Jefferson shook his head. 'I hear they call him the Reaper. I tell you what; I wouldn't want someone like that after me. Not many men scare me, but there's something wrong about that guy, something in the eyes.'

Riley revised his previous thought on his friend; he wasn't a comfort at all.

Jefferson handed Locke a microphone and the speaker system in the chamber buzzed to life.

Locke passed his helmet to Riley and stepped to the fore. 'Quieten down!' he said. 'QUIET!'

A flurry of whispers dropped to silence.

The explorers and troops inside, and surrounding, the SED

building waited for him to begin. The SED commander paced to his right and looked down at the floor before facing front. 'Fellow Sancturians,' he said, 'many of you will have heard these words before, but I'll say them again to those amongst the Special Forces who've never ventured beyond the base's walls. All of you will have been briefed on this mission and its importance. We have been told speed is of the essence, but in our fair Sanctuary, speed can get you dead, speed *will* get you dead. To all the U.S. servicemen listening to me now, trust in those that lead you, trust in the SED and the Deep Reach teams to keep you on the safest paths, the surest routes. Keep to the path and you will return, stray from that path and you may pay for it with your life. Sanctuary is one of the most dangerous places on the planet. A wrong step or misplaced jump and you could be on a one-way trip to the centre of the Earth, thirty miles down to hell.

'Normally our expeditions focus on unearthing Anakim sites and analysing ancient burial grounds, which exposes us to all manner of toxins and potential biohazards. Some may think that because this is a seek and capture, those dangers don't apply. Those people are wrong. Dig around at your peril; if it looks dangerous, it probably is. Make sure all visor gauges and detectors are checked regularly. Seismometers and structural stability maps should be consulted at all times. Take heed of hazard symbols and warning messages. Sanctuary's composition limits long range transmissions, so stay in radio contact with your team-mates. If you find yourself in trouble, call for help; egos will get you dead, and get you dead quick.

'Due to the nature of this trip, emergency response teams will be unavailable. However, due to the number of personnel in the field, help will never be far away. Some of you will have noticed my unusual attire,' he looked down at his SED field uniform, 'and that's because I'll be out there keeping an eye on you all—'

A murmur of surprise rippled through the Deep Reach teams.

'—so rest assured I will do everything in my power to keep you all safe.' Locke looked at his watch. 'We are a go for deployment; each team will be called to the shuttle bay via a visor message. Godspeed and good luck!'

◆

In a ready room reserved for officers, Colonel Samson listened to the SED leader's speech while attaching his armour a piece at a time to his newly acquired exoskeleton. Completing the task, Samson secured weapons and equipment, before striding out through the command centre and onto the stage with his helmet in one hand. Locke passed him the microphone, which he lifted to his mouth.

'Ten-hut!' An officer shouted and every soldier snapped to attention.

Samson paused, looking out at the people waiting to hear his words. 'My name is Colonel Samson. Most of you won't know me. Those of you that do may wish you didn't. I suffer no fools. I demand obedience and I take no prisoners. Cross me and you'll wish you hadn't.' Samson pointed to Locke. 'This man says speed will get you dead. I say the fear of death makes you alive.'

He gestured to someone in the control centre and a cluster of lasers produced a holographic scene on the stage. Sarah Morgan appeared, acting out a fight with another SED employee, the deceased Cora Islanovich. The image switched to Cora's dead body, arched and broken, eyes staring and mouth agape in agonised terror.

Samson approached the image of the corpse. 'Our target is a woman, a murderer, a thief and a foreigner,' – the image changed to footage of Sarah with her two friends – 'who has compromised the security of this United States Subterranean Base. Commander Locke is not leading this mission, I am, and what I say goes. These fugitives have a ten day head start. I'm gonna push you hard, then I'm gonna squeeze you till your eyes burst and your veins bleed.' He walked through the hologram. 'I say we hunt down these terrorists and bring them to justice, American justice!'

Samson bared his teeth and held his helmet in the air. 'No depth too difficult, no height too great!'

The thousands of Terra Force soldiers raised their helmets and guns as one and roared, 'NO DEPTH TOO DIFFICULT, NO HEIGHT TOO GREAT!'

'Honour and country!' Samson shouted

'OOYAH!' came the response, the Terra Force battle cry reverberating through the SED and beyond.

Samson pulled on his helmet and pressed a button to send its visor and mask snapping into place. A green glow emanated from the eye-like sculpturing and an army of green eyes blinked into existence in response. The scent had been laid. Weapons were locked and loaded. The hunt was on.

CHAPTER TWENTY-SEVEN

Sirens wailed and lights flashed. Inch by inch, foot by foot, the metal shuttle bay floor retracted, its dense star-shaped points disappearing into the concrete surround to reveal a gaping oval shaft beneath. Two hundred feet across and cutting down into the Earth's crust, this entrance to the underworld descended into darkness.

A loud boom announced the end of the process and the first air-shuttles crept into position. Riley sat at the rear of the lead vehicle, while up front the bulky form of Colonel Samson was flanked by his fellow officers. Riley's helmet clicked back onto his headrest and his Deep Reach helmet visor lowered into place, its plethora of ice-blue dials and gauges populating the interior with a healthy glow.

'T minus fifteen seconds to launch,' SED Command informed them through their helmets.

The air-shuttle twisted on its track and Riley's view spun one hundred and eighty degrees upside down. Suspended above the sheer drop, Riley sagged against his restraints, pulled down by gravity's invisible embrace. Below, the huge hole disappeared into nothing.

SED Command spoke again. 'T minus six seconds—'

'Here we come, Sarah,' Riley murmured, 'ready or not.'

'—three, two, one – launch.'

The clamps released, rockets fired, and they flew down into the pit, their passage a streak of fire in the black. Destination: Sanctuary Proper.

CHAPTER TWENTY-EIGHT

'IF YOU THINK I'm going back there, you're crazier than I thought.'

'Who's going to lure it in?'

'Me.'

'And you think you can outrun it? It can reach sixty miles an hour; it'd be on you in a second.'

'As long as we find the right area it'll work, trust me.'

Trish stood up. 'I'm sorry, Sarah, this seems too much like ...'

'Like what?'

'A one-way ticket,' Jason said.

'If that's how it turns out, so be it; at least you two will have a fighting chance.'

'What?!' Trish's expression grew fierce. 'What kind of plan is that?!'

'Do either of you have a better one?'

Trish and Jason swapped looks.

'I didn't think so. It's either this or slow starvation. The choice is yours.'

Jason paled. 'There must be another way.'

'There's none. This is the only way.'

'Then I should be the one to lure it in. You're our navigator and Trish is too slow. I'll do it.'

'NO!' Trish whacked him.

'Shhh!' Sarah said. 'It could still be following us for all we know.'

Anxious, Trish looked behind, but when the phantom light failed to appear, her mood switched back to anger and she jabbed a finger at Sarah. 'This is bullshit and you know it.' She turned on Jason. 'How can you go along with this? It's madness!'

Jason put his hands on her shoulders. 'Look, I don't like it. God, I really don't like it, but what other choice do we have?'

Trish shrugged him off and Sarah decided to defuse the situation by moving away to look back the way they'd come. As she searched the flat landscape she could hear them conversing in angry tones and her thoughts strayed to her idea. She knew her plan would work. Lure the light to them, which would open up the path behind, allowing them to head back the way they'd come. Then they could – hopefully – find their way to the temple and the Anakim transportation device. Of course that would mean someone attracting the light in the first place and keeping it occupied long enough to secure the other two safe passage. It then came down to luck whether the third person, Sarah herself, could make it back to rejoin her friends in one piece.

A mild breeze ruffled her hair while she scanned the terrain with her visor to see if the shimmering light lurked in the shadows or amongst the fields of glowing flora. She switched to another visual spectrum and repeated the process, and then she tried another spectrum, and then another after that.

Minutes had passed before Trish and Jason returned.

'We've come up with another idea,' Trish said, looking determined and more than a little exultant.

Sarah frowned and glanced at Jason, who looked at her expectantly.

'Don't you want to hear it?' Trish said.

Sarah shook her head. 'I don't know what you think you've come up with, but it's not going to work.'

Trish's face darkened. 'You haven't bloody heard it yet.' She looked at Jason. 'I told you she wouldn't listen.'

'Just tell her.'

Trish made a noise of annoyance before turning her attention back to Sarah. 'Do you remember when we left South Africa, before the asteroid hit?'

Memories of an aeroplane journey came to Sarah's mind and along with it the sense of relief and jubilation she'd felt in those heady days of success; Anakim treasures located and unearthed in a daring raid under the threat of annihilation from the skies above. How could she forget? Little did she know at the time such joy could lead to where they were now, lost in the dark pit of despair.

She nodded.

Trish glanced at Jason again; he encouraged her with a gesture. She looked back to Sarah and continued, 'Do you remember what we saw that day on one of the parchments?'

'A map of Honduras.'

'Before that.'

Sarah thought back. 'The Earth, that city – a massive, beautiful city, full of spires.'

'Yes, but before that, too.'

Sarah couldn't remember seeing anything else. So much had gone on in such a short space of time, the whole episode had turned into a blur. Mix that with recent events and her mind was a blank. 'I don't know, just tell me.'

'A schematic, don't you remember? A kind of blueprint. We didn't know what it meant at the time, but I think I do now.'

Sarah looked into the distance for any signs of the light. 'What does it mean, then?' she said, tight-lipped, her patience wearing thin.

'The schematic, we've seen it somewhere else. It came to me just now. Maybe not exactly the same, but the same outline. That Professor Steiner showed it to us in his induction video. It's Sanctuary. The schematic is Sanctuary!'

'She's right,' Jason said, unable to contain himself any longer, 'it's Sanctuary, I'm sure of it, too!'

Sarah didn't remember the image in the detail Trish and Jason seemed to, but their hearts were in the right place, along with their conviction; both of these things, however, failed to help their situation. 'So, say it's Sanctuary, as you say. We couldn't power that part of the map for long between all three of us, what makes you think it'll be any different now?'

'We had another idea,' Trish said. 'Well, this is more Jason's than mine—'

Jason flashed her a smile and took over. 'You said the interference to human technology, our technology, might be greater down in Sanctuary the deeper we go. What if, now we're *in* Sanctuary, the opposite were true for Anakim technology?'

'Your pendant has more power,' Trish said. 'Don't you think it weird how we opened up that tunnel through the arch so easily? That must have taken massive power, but we did it without even feeling the after-effects. None of us felt exhausted afterwards and our energy reserves were already depleted.'

Such reasoning hadn't occurred to Sarah. Probably because I'm tired, she presumed, before instantly regretting the thought. Have I become so arrogant to think I'm always right, always one step ahead?

Sarah contemplated her friends. 'Okay, even if that's true and we could see the map of Sanctuary, we know how big this place is. How can we hope to find where we are? We'd still be looking for a needle in a haystack.

Jason looked around them. 'You sure about that?'

Sarah followed his gaze, the Anakim highway, if that's what it was, was indeed immense. It had to go on for at least thirty miles, possibly more. Something that large and straight, regardless of what level it was on, had to be easier to locate than virtually any other place they'd been – in theory, anyway.

Sarah had to admit, their assumptions had merit, but there was only one way to test them. She dug into her pocket and withdrew the collection of Anakim parchments she'd stolen from the military vault. Amongst them was the parchment in question, the one that they'd originally recovered from the red Anakim canister near Johannesburg and the Cradle of Humanity.

Sarah rolled up her sleeves and placed her thumb on the small circle found at the top of the paper-like material. She looked at her friends who put their hands onto her bare arms to boost the bioelectrical power for channelling through the pendant. As soon as they did so an image of the Earth appeared on the page. The giant sphere of green and blue slowly rotated, the clarity of detail and colour stunning.

'It worked!' Trish said, excited.

Manipulating the image using the familiar control symbols down one side, Sarah zoomed in using her free hand. Once she had the virtual Earth where she wanted it – positioned over central Mexico – she zoomed in again, further and further until the ground filled the screen before fading from view.

Jason shifted his grip on her arm. 'I hope this works.'

A strange set of symbols emerged before the schematic Jason and Trish had reminded her about materialised.

'There,' Trish leaned in, 'that's it, that's Sanctuary; tell me I'm wrong.'

Sarah may have wanted to, but Trish was right, the shape of the structure displayed on the ancient digitised parchment was reminiscent of that shown to them on their first day of freedom in the USSB.

She zoomed in on the image and once again she couldn't help but be amazed at the intricacies on display; the detail was astounding.

A whisper of noise on a breeze made all three of them look up in alarm.

'I've just had another thought,' Trish said, looking worried, 'what if the Anakim technology is what attracts the light?'

Jason swore and Sarah almost lost her grip on the parchment.

'You two keep an eye out,' Sarah said, 'I'll search.' She hunted through the image, looking for signs of the massive Anakim structure that surrounded them.

A few minutes later her quest continued and Jason glanced down. 'Any luck?'

Sarah shook her head. 'No, you try.' She passed the parchment over and the image disappeared before returning when everyone had readjusted position and Sarah had given Jason her pendant.

More time passed and Sarah could have sworn she'd heard another noise in the distance, possibly the same noise they'd learnt to fear.

Jason looked up. 'I have it!'

Trish and Sarah peered at the image.

'Are you sure?' Trish said, sounding sceptical.

'There.' He traced a straight line on the parchment with a finger, before rotating it further and expanding the view.

'Zoom in further,' Sarah said.

He did so and the resemblance to their surroundings became clear, even down to the stairs they'd descended after their abseil.

'Fantastic!' Trish kissed Jason on the cheek.

But Sarah saw a flaw in the plan. 'How do we find a transportation device?'

'They must have put them at locations where a lot of people congregate,' Trish said, 'like the temple. Large places or areas like the one when we entered Sanctuary, that large circular cavern. You can't tell me there won't be some around here. Also, they should show up on the map when we do find one, like the canisters and that square platform at the Ruins of Copán, remember?'

Sarah felt they were clutching at straws again and her doubt must have shown.

'I'd rather hunt around on this map looking for transportation devices and water than go up against that bloody light. Wouldn't you?' Trish looked at Jason, who nodded.

Sarah stayed silent, thinking.

'Well?' Trish said.

'Okay, we'll do it, but now we're without water again that should be our first priority.'

Trish and Jason's expressions were of sheer relief that they'd averted Sarah's plan. Sarah on the other hand felt disappointed. She still believed her option was the better of the two, but now her friends had an alternative in their minds there'd be no counselling them. And yet another thought worried her more. *I'd wanted to face the light, head on, to face my fear rather than flee from it. Is that so wrong*, she wondered, *or is it the danger I seek?* Flashes of her recurring nightmare came to mind and she felt the days of sleep deprivation and lack of food press down upon her like an anvil. Leadership, and the burden that came with it, had drained her, body and soul, and yet they were still far from safety, the job only half done. If only they could catch a break. Since they'd left the base, virtually the entire journey to the Anakim temple had been one crisis after another, progress followed by calamity, followed by disaster. It almost seemed like Sanctuary itself was conspiring against them, lusting to hold on to those that dared traverse its dark domain.

Now a decision had been made, Sarah was compelled to make it work despite any misgivings she had about it. With the three of them still working as one to channel the power of their bodies through the pendant, they spent some time searching the parchment schematic for signs of water. However, such a hope was soon dashed when it became clear such resources weren't displayed on the map, at least none that they were able to find. They then switched their attention to looking for the temple, their original destination, reasoning there might be another way to reach it. An alternative route also meant they could avoid any confrontation with the light. Unfortunately that failed to work too, due in no small part to the three dimensional complexity of the map, but also because, on further inspection, many features shown didn't correspond to present day Sanctuary. Undeterred, Trish and Jason insisted there was still enough correct detail to be of use, and it was with this persistence that their searching finally bore fruit.

'What's that?!' Trish stabbed a finger at the parchment.

'Careful,' – Jason gave her a stern look – 'we can't afford to damage it.'

Sarah leaned closer. 'It looks like another temple.'

'And what does that look like to you?' Trish said, indicating a specific area.

Sarah squinted. 'Zoom in further.'

Jason made the image larger.

'It could be a transport device,' she said, 'or it could be something completely different.'

Trish gave Jason's shoulder a congratulatory squeeze. 'We won't know till we take a look.'

'What's that around it?' Sarah gestured for Jason to alter the perspective.

'It looks like it's on a hill,' he said.

Trish eyed the image, her expression full of concentration. 'Looks more like a mountain than a hill.'

'Who cares,' Sarah said, 'let's just find it.'

Working out its location in respect to their own, they set off again, desperation strong but optimism renewed. Sarah just hoped it didn't turn out to be another nail in a coffin of their own making.

◆

A few hours later and Jason fired up the map again to see how close they were to the new temple.

'It should be through there.' He pointed over to the right at a group of crumbling ruins surrounding a spire that must have been over a mile high, its point a distant shape through their visors.

The map disappeared and Jason let out a squawk of protest. Trish had turned away to look back the way they'd come.

Sarah moved to her side. 'What is it?'

'I'm sure I just saw movement.'

'The light?'

'I don't know.'

Jason joined them. 'Where?'

Trish indicated an area on the far side of the highway, a mile behind them.

Sarah searched the terrain with her eyes and scanned across before stopping and returning to a section she'd just passed. Her eyes narrowed. A curious fluctuation in the air hovered in the shadow of a fallen statue. 'Don't make any sudden moves,' she said, 'but I think I see it.'

'What?!' Trish sounded terrified.

'I think it's stalking us. You two start moving to the temple.'

Trish hesitated. 'I'm not letting you be bait.'

'Don't worry, I'll be right behind you, let's just not give away that we know it's there.'

Jason took charge of the Centipede and with Trish at his side, made his way under a shattered archway. Sarah pretended to look in the opposite direction to where the light hunkered, while on her visor she watched its position in the mirror. Giving Trish and Jason time to get well into the complex, Sarah followed at a slow walk. Reaching some steps, she almost tripped as her attention remained focused on the light with increasing intensity, the image seeming to fill her whole mind.

At the arch she paused, waiting to see if it moved.

It didn't.

Reluctant to relinquish her advantage, she activated her helmet communicator with a touch of a button. 'How far are you inside?'

A crackle of noise buzzed over the speakers and then Trish said, 'About a kilometre, where are you?'

'I'm still outside.'

'What, why?!'

'I don't want to let it out of my sight. We know where it is, that's an advantage.'

'Not for you, it's not,' Jason said, 'get in here!'

Sarah failed to say anything and Trish spoke again. 'Sarah, you have to come now. The way ahead splits, you won't be able to find us.'

Sarah swore, took one last look at the hidden light and ducked into darkness.

CHAPTER TWENTY-NINE

WITH ONE EYE on her visor's mirror window, Sarah Morgan ran through the remains of the ancient Anakim building, curious carvings and frightening statues jumping out of the dark as she passed. Ahead, the lights of the Centipede traced the silhouettes of Trish and Jason as they waited for her in the pitch-black. Rejoining her friends moments later, she took charge of the supply vehicle and they ran as one, trying to put distance between themselves and the thing that pursued them: the ethereal shimmering light.

A pile of rubble blocked their path. Panicked, Sarah scrambled over the obstacle, slip sliding down the other side while trying to keep the Centipede moving forward. Trish and Jason soon joined her and they sped into another hallway. Huge, twisted tree roots narrowed their path and shattered masonry hung down from above, forcing Sarah through a myriad of twists and turns. She guided the Centipede before her, following the elusive forms of her friends, their faint shapes appearing and disappearing like mist demons in the fog.

Emerging into another open area, the small fellowship regrouped, each casting fearful eyes back the way they'd come.

'Where now?' Trish said.

Sarah pointed up. 'Your mountain.'

Jason and Trish looked in the direction she indicated. Dominating the view, the grey shades of their visors depicted the single spire they'd seen from the Anakim highway. A slender tower at its peak, the base of the structure bulged out in a spectacular web of supports like the legs of a giant insect, each strand swirling upwards to merge into the single body above. This great, monolithic temple had been built atop a rocky mound wider than a city block which was in turn encircled by a massive, moat-like chasm. But as they drew nearer it soon became apparent that the surrounding obstacle couldn't have been further removed from said medieval defence. Wider than a football pitch was long, the barrier that prevented them from waltzing up to their intended destination fell away into the depths.

Completing over half a circuit of the fissure revealed it left the temple in perfect isolation, cutting off any access to it and creating a mountain where ninety per cent of its mass stood sunken into the Earth's crust. Far below, the familiar orange glow of lava flowed in steady spirals along a meandering river.

Despite this massive obstacle to their progress, there was some good news; the fearsome light had yet to reappear.

Jason approached the edge. 'There's no way across.'

'What about that?' Sarah gestured ahead at a structure that had been built inside the crevasse.

Moving closer, they came to an ornate gateway leading to nowhere, except a one-way trip down to the lava, thousands of feet below.

'What is that?' Trish peered out. 'An aqueduct?'

Sarah nodded. 'I think so.'

The crumbling structure sat slap bang in the middle of the expanse that prevented access to the temple beyond.

'I can see bridges down there,' Jason leaned out further, holding onto a granite pedestal. 'I think some are aqueducts, too, one still has water flowing across it!'

'There are tunnel entrances over there,' – Trish pointed behind them – 'they probably lead down to the bridges and then go up inside to the temple.'

Sarah didn't fancy going into more tunnels, especially if the light returned and decided to follow them inside, but something else had grabbed her attention. 'I think there's an Anakim device on the aqueduct.' Sarah zoomed in her visor. At least it looked like it could be part of one, the strange shine of the ceramic-like substance seemed indicative of at least some of the ancient builders' technology.

'You're right,' Jason said, 'but it's a bit closer than you think.'

Sarah followed his gaze down to her feet. The glint of ceramic sparkled from beneath a covering of loose sediment. She scraped her foot across the surface to reveal it further. Dropping to her knees, she swept it clear with her hands. Standing, she looked at a circle indented into a pale flecked surface about a metre square.

Sarah removed her climbing boots and socks, but before she could step onto the circle Trish grabbed her arm. 'Wait! We can't just keep activating this stuff; we don't know what it does.'

'And the light,' Jason said, 'it might attract it.'

'And you'd both prefer to go through more tunnels, unable to see round the next corner, with nowhere to run?' Sarah, fed up with their caution, stepped onto the circle.

Nothing happened.

She rolled up her sleeves and looked at Trish and then Jason. 'I need your help.'

Trish snorted. 'You're unbelievable.'

Jason wilted under Sarah's gaze and grasped her arm. Her pendant warmed against her chest and a tingling sensation spiralled up her legs. A flash of light from the aqueduct transformed into a seething mass of red electricity that flowed out towards them, crackling bolts of blue lightning flashing to Sarah's platform like a Tesla coil.

Trish backed away and Jason swore as the wave of deafening energy closed in. Sarah flinched before the electricity flickered over the ceramic platform and tendrils of tiny lightning licked at her feet. Light flared and died and the noise subsided. Glimmering in the dark was a pathway to the gods; a bridge of blue light spanning the gap to the aqueduct.

Dumbstruck, Jason's hand slid from Sarah's arm.

Sarah raised her visor and gazed out at the incredible vision. She held out her hand and Jason, reading her mind, passed her the cable from the Centipede's winch. Attaching it to her harness and steeling herself, Sarah stepped out onto the Anakim creation. Beneath her bare soles the pulsating energy rippled and crackled and pinpricks of discomfort like pins and needles attacked her skin. Each step brought with it a swell of electricity, the tiny branches clinging to her feet as she moved.

A distant screech stopped her dead.

'The light!' Trish said. 'He told you!'

Sarah rushed back to her friends. Detaching herself, she clipped Trish onto the cable and pushed her forward. 'Go!'

Trish resisted. 'What are you doing? There's no way from the aqueduct to the temple!'

'Yes there is, now go!' With a shove, Sarah thrust her out onto the bridge.

Sarah snatched a rope from her back and secured Jason to the Centipede and sent him after Trish.

Another roar echoed into the chamber, sending fear coursing through her limbs.

Trish had made it across, but Jason was only halfway over. A movement caught her eye. A shimmering glow of blue-green moved towards her at speed. With no time left, she drove the Centipede onto the bridge and no sooner had it touched the surface than steam rose from its tyres. The rubber melted, leaving black trails that smoked until vaporised. Running on its rims, the remote vehicle ploughed onwards chasing Jason onto the safety of the aqueduct ahead. Trish screamed a warning and Sarah felt a guttural growl reverberate through her chest. Stranded in the centre of the bridge without any harness, Sarah glimpsed the stomach churning drop below as she turned to face the thing that dogged their steps.

A shimmering form hovered just above the ceramic platform that had activated the walkway, the air around it distorting and contorting, preventing the eye from resolving what lay beneath. Sarah found herself backing away and she stopped her retreat.

'What are you doing?!' Jason shouted. 'RUN!'

Sarah held her ground. Perhaps this thing was like a wild animal, unable to resist fleeing prey. If she turned tail she could be dead in an instant. She also felt some strange compulsion to look it in the eye, or at least where its eyes should have been. She took a step forward. A sick thrill of horror at her own insanity resonated into a voice within her mind, a voice that sounded like her own. *Am I not what you desire?* it whispered, the silver tongue laced with an insidious hunger, *why do you fear me?*

Sarah thought she heard her friends shouting to her, but she only had ears for the crackling electricity beneath her feet, her eyes drawn to the beguiling light.

The spectre glided forward, its indistinct outline inching onto the throbbing bridge of energy. Light flared and an ungodly screech shook Sarah from abstraction. Blinding blue pulses enveloped the entity. Its light flared red and Sarah glimpsed a writhing form within. Terror struck, she turned tail and ran. The bridge flickered in failure. A blast of air threw her forward and she leapt toward Jason's outstretched hand and grasped it as the support vanished from under her.

Heaved to safe harbour, Sarah turned to see the chasm resumed, the bridge gone and the light nowhere to be seen. Breathing hard, she dropped to a crouch, sweat beading on her brow.

Jason put a hand on her shoulder. 'Fucking hell, Sarah, what were you thinking?'

Sarah looked up at him and shook her head, she wasn't sure she'd been thinking at all.

'I can't see it anywhere.' Trish stared out into the black.

Sarah rose and scanned the area.

Nothing could be seen.

'Perhaps it's dead,' Jason said.

Sarah hoped that was the case, but right now they had to reach the temple. With the possibility of an Anakim transportation device so close to hand, the fresh air of the surface beckoned like the promise of Elysian Fields.

Still spooked by the confrontation, Sarah assessed their surroundings. The temple mount was a hundred feet away with only the yawning crevasse between them and it. They were closer than they were before, but not close enough.

She focused on the aqueduct, which had once cut a semi-circular path out over the abyss from the mountain where it originated. Most of the structure had collapsed eons past, leaving just the tip of its arch held aloft by immense curved supports that disappeared down into the darkness below. And it was on this lone section of the aqueduct on which they now stood, stranded in no man's land.

The shattered ends of the broken structure terminated at the cliff face opposite, its water-bearing channels long since blocked with the debris of fallen rock.

Jason peered over the edge. 'That looks a long way down.'

'Too far,' Sarah said. 'We lost most of our climbing gear when the light chased us on the highway.'

Trish joined them. 'And you didn't think of that before we crossed over?'

'Of course I thought of it.'

'But you said there was a way across!'

'And there is.' Sarah pointed at a single, stone pillar that stood between their current location and the mountain's edge. Like the supports that held up their section of the aqueduct, the pillar – a remnant of the same structure – curved up from the rock wall a few hundred feet below. That it still remained standing was a miracle in itself, although its gravity defying design intimated some hidden Anakim wizardry was at work within its otherwise mundane exterior.

Trish stared at her. 'You're kidding, right?'

'What's wrong? We can launch the Centipede's anchor onto it, climb across the cable and then rope over to the cliff.'

Trish raised her eyebrows in a show of disbelief, but rather than comment further, she returned to investigate the other end of the ceramic Anakim device that Sarah had just activated.

'There's no circle,' Sarah said. 'I already checked. We can't go back, we have to go forward.'

Trish ignored her and continued shifting aside chunks of stone in the hope of uncovering a way to power the energy bridge from that side.

Jason remained looking at the single support column Sarah had proposed as their route across. 'It does look unstable, Saz. My visor is throwing up all kinds of hazard symbols.'

'I know, mine is, too, but it'll hold. When I crossed the bridge that collapsed it had way more warnings than that and I still made it.'

She could see Jason remained sceptical and with good reason, the pillar looked far from secure; cracks littered its façade and two significant undercuts bit deep into its core. But as she saw it, they had little choice.

Rolling the Centipede into place, its bare rims slipping on the uneven ground, Sarah hopped across the central channel where water had once flowed and synchronised her visor to the winch mechanism. She aimed the targeting graphic at her intended target and pressed a button on the Centipede's console. A blast of compressed air sent the anchor soaring out over the gap, its mechanical maw arcing down to latch onto the pillar's top.

With the winch cable taut, Sarah attached herself to it with a carabiner clip and cord.

Trish, resigned to Sarah's plan, came to stand by Jason's side to watch.

'As soon as I'm over to the temple,' Sarah said, 'follow me, but one at a time; that rock won't take two people's weight.'

'It might not take one person's,' Trish muttered.

Sarah, intent on the job in hand, mounted the cable, balancing on top of it while holding onto Jason's shoulder.

'Wouldn't it be easier to climb underneath it?' he said, concerned.

'The faster I go across, the less time the pillar's under load.' She gave her safety cord a final tug to ensure it was secure. 'Don't worry, the SED had special machines to help train my balance.' She extended her arms to either side and then walked out into mid-air. Wobbling a little, she gained speed to smooth out her deviation from vertical and reached the pillar without falling. She crouched down and sank a bolt loop into the stone and secured a rope to it before attaching a grappling hook to the other end. Sarah looked over at the far side and then swung the rope round and round, faster and faster, before launching it out. The metal claws clanked down and Sarah pulled it towards her, but the points failed to bite and she had to repeat the process twice more before she found a solid lock. She gave it a few yanks to ensure it would hold and then transferred her safety cord from the winch cable to the rope.

Ready for the final crossing, Sarah climbed down the side of the column, sending loose sediment sifting down into the chasm below. She reached out and pulled herself onto the rope, and a flurry of small stones fell clattering into the depths. Praying the pillar would hold, she hung upside down on the rope and wrapped her legs around it before pulling herself along bit by bit, hand over hand, inch by death-defying inch. After heavy exertion, she reached the far side and clambered onto the solid base of the temple mount, the building's spire soaring into the heavens behind her. She waved over to Trish and Jason, who seemed to be arguing about who was to go next.

'Trish wants me to go first,' Jason said, his voice coming through her helmet's speakers. 'She wants to see how I do it.'

Sarah gave them the thumbs up; her nerves getting the better of her as he latched onto the winch cable. Unlike Sarah, Jason wisely chose to hang underneath the cable, like she had on the rope, and all went well until he neared the pillar.

A warning flashed up on Sarah's visor. 'Jason, stop!'

He ceased his motion, while beneath dust and debris fell from one of the undercuts, further eating away at the column's stability. The degeneration dribbled to nothing and Sarah got back on the com. 'Keep going, but go slower, try to keep your body as steady as possible, no side to side motion.'

A grunt of affirmation was his reply and he moved forward again, inching across so slowly it felt to Sarah like someone was pulling her teeth out a with a pair of pliers a nanometre at a time ... without anaesthetic.

When he finally reached his target without further incident, he kept his movements slow and with care hitched himself onto the rope and begun the whole process over.

After what seemed like an eternity, Sarah helped Jason up beside her.

'Trish, it's your turn.' Sarah waved her over. 'Just take it nice and slow and you'll be fine.'

'Hook your legs together like I did,' Jason said, 'and keep your elbows in, it makes it easier to stop the sideways motion.'

Trish didn't reply, she was too in the zone and full of nervous energy. Fiddling around and triple-checking she was attached, Trish edged out, moving even more slowly than Jason had.

Another warning message appeared on Sarah's visor and Jason saw it too. He covered his helmet mic so Trish couldn't hear. 'That column's ready to go.'

'You need to speed up now,' Sarah said to Trish, trying to keep her voice calm.

'You said to go slow,' Trish said, 'make your mind up.'

She moved forward a little quicker and more warnings appeared on Sarah's visor. 'You need to go faster, sweetheart.'

'I'm going as fast as I can,' Trish said. 'Is something wrong?'

Sarah could hear the anxiety in her voice.

More rock tumbled from the overhang and the column rocked sideways. Trish screamed as the winch cable sent her swaying.

'Stop moving!' Jason shouted.

Trish did as she was bid and the pillar steadied.

Sarah palms were slick with sweat. 'Very slowly now, Trish, very slowly, move forward.'

Trish pulled herself along again and once more rock fell and the cable swayed. Trish froze in place, mere feet from the unstable column.

Seconds passed and Trish began again, stopping each time the stone pillar moved, until finally she reached the top of the precarious finger of rock.

'Switch over the safety cord,' Sarah said, 'quickly!'

Trish's hands shook as she fought to unlatch herself. Managing it on the fourth attempt, she snapped the clip onto the rope.

A mass of hazard symbols appeared on Sarah's visor and the column lurched sideways. A shriek echoed into the chamber as Trish clung on for dear life. The overhang disintegrated and the column sank a metre before toppling toward the cliff.

'Trish!'

Behind, the Centipede jerked forward and smashed into the aqueduct channel as the cable bit into stone. Held aloft by the winch and sheered in two, the column teetered on its own foundation while Trish dangled from the rope, which was still held fast by the anchor bolt.

Jason grabbed Sarah. 'DO SOMETHING!'

A screech of metal on stone drew all eyes to the Centipede as it crept onto the lip, sparks flying from its wheels as it was dragged forward.

The column let out a groan and shattered.

Clinging onto the rope, Trish flew through the air and slammed into the cliff face, the top of the column beneath exploding into pieces as it thundered home a millisecond after. The rest of the structure smashed into the remnants of the aqueduct that entered the temple's mount and a gush of lava spewed forth, dousing the rock close to where Trish hung, fifty feet beneath Sarah and Jason. Out of the gloom the Centipede spiralled end over end through the air, its lights appearing and disappearing until it hit the wall a hundred feet down. Its main beams flickered out and its crumpled carcass broke into pieces as it disappeared into the depths, clattering downwards towards the river of lava at its nadir.

CHAPTER THIRTY

HEAT FLOODED up the rock face in waves as the lava continued to pour from the side of the mountain on which the Anakim temple towered. The aqueduct had turned out to be a lavaduct and even now it threatened those who fought for life beside its coronal glare.

Sarah and Jason heaved on the rope, sinews standing out in agonised exertion.

A weep of fear escaped Jason's lips as he gritted his teeth and Sarah felt her grip failing as the weight below dragged them back to the edge.

She let go. 'It's no good, it's too heavy!'

Jason continued pulling, his eyes full of feverish tears.

'Jason, stop!' Sarah grasped his lacerated hands as blood seeped through his gloves.

'NO! I can do it!'

'You can't. There's half a ton of rock on the end of the rope. I need to go down and cut it off.'

Before he could argue, Sarah attached the rope to her harness and dropped over the side.

Trish clung to the cliff face below, her head averted from the fiery heat of the lava coating the nearby rock.

The lower Sarah climbed, the hotter it got. She tried communicating with Trish via her Deep Reach helmet, but it must have been damaged in the fall as she failed to respond.

Waves of heat consumed her and Sarah deployed her breathing mask to try and filter out the hot gas that wilted hair and singed lungs.

Moments later, now just above her friend, Sarah reopened her mask and called out. 'Trish, are you okay?! You need to climb!'

Trish didn't respond.

Sarah dropped lower and brushed the top of her friend's dented helmet with a foot.

Trish looked up, her eyes wild with fear. 'My arm's broken!'

Sarah leaned to one side. A bone jutted from Trish's limb.

She inched closer. 'It's fine. You need to cut the rope below you so we can pull you up.'

'If I cut the rope I'll fall!'

Realisation dawned. Sarah craned her neck. Beneath Trish hung the remains of the top of the column, still attached to the bolt anchor and rope. Trish stood on the stone; the very thing that had prevented them from pulling her up also served to keep her alive. What was more, if the rope was cut Trish's safety line would just slide off, and with just one working arm there was nowhere else to go but down.

A chunk of earth bounced from Sarah's helmet and she looked up. The lava was forcing out more rock, the flow expanding, creeping ever nearer. The heat increased. Burning fire splashed from nearby rocks and a drop of molten liquid landed on Trish's leg, searing through cloth and flesh. Trish screamed.

Out of time, Sarah tied herself off and held out her arm. 'Grab my hand!'

Trish shook her head.

More debris fell around them and the lava crept closer. 'TAKE IT!'

The temperature soared and Trish reached out to grasp Sarah's wrist. More flaming droplets showered around them, half a dozen hitting Trish.

Terror flared in Trish's eyes. 'I don't want to die!'

Sarah gritted her teeth as she braced herself. 'I won't let you, trust me!'

With her free hand, Sarah withdrew a knife and cut the rope beneath her. The rock anchor fell and Trish's dead weight dragged Sarah down against her harness. She dropped the knife and grabbed onto Trish with both hands.

Fire took hold of Trish's jacket, smoke billowed up and flames licked at the hair beneath her helmet.

Sarah grimaced and clawed a few fingers inside her friend's collar. 'Jason, pull! FUCKING PULL!!'

They inched up, but Sarah knew they were too heavy for him. The sight of sizzling, burning nightmares immersed her vision and fire crept up her arms.

Trish's eyes locked to hers, terror turning to pity. 'Let me go!'

Sarah shook her head. 'NO!'

Shimmering flames reflected in the tears of their eyes. Trish released her grip and she slid half a foot. 'Look after Jason.'

Pain seared Sarah's mind, but she held on.

Trish prised loose one of her hands and Sarah clung onto her cuff.

Grip failing, Sarah stared into her friend's eyes and shook her head. 'No!'

'Love you,' Trish said, and fell.

CHAPTER THIRTY-ONE

California, USA

'And it's true, never has the United States of America seen the like, and it may not do so again for a thousand years. The rules have changed, perhaps forever. Democracy has returned to our great nation from the halls of despair and corrupted dysfunction. Out of the ashes we have risen like the phoenix to show the world the way, the way to emancipation from tyranny, a true liberation from elitist rule and the repugnant, manipulative machine that is corporate capitalism. Freedom from the hidden new world order masking themselves behind the biggest evil of them all.' The speaker cupped a hand to his ear. 'Who is that evil?'

The people roared the name.

'What? I can't hear you?!'

'GMRC! GMRC!!'

'Long has the Global Meteor Response Council ruled our nation through the back door. The GMRC, this tyrannical beast, this goliath of dread and suppressor of hope, has forced upon us draconian sanctions and protocols agreed over twenty years ago by corporately elected politicians now retired or dead, leaving us behind to pay for their misdeeds. Sanctions that control our fundamental resources. Resources that are our God-given right as American citizens!' The man clenched his fist and slammed it down on the lectern. 'I'm not talking about the filth of money, but the precious necessities of water, food, shelter and electricity. While ordinary citizens, like you, like us, suffer at the hands of these unelected GMRC officials who bask in comfort and plenty, people die in the streets, in their homes, on their knees, put there by the GMRC Directorate and the mighty divisions of power they wield.

'But change is coming, the people have voted! The old system of bought presidencies by corporate donors has crashed and burned.'

The speaker raised his fist in the air and cheers rang out. 'Where there was oppression, I will deliver freedom. Where there was deceit, I will deliver truth! And where there was corruption, I will deliver JUSTICE!'

The crowds in the stadium roared approval, flags waved and the chanting began once more. 'John Henry! John Henry!! JOHN HENRY!!'

The image and noise of the celebrations receded and in a separate window on the screen a newsreader addressed his viewers. 'And there you have it, folks, not once since George Washington gave his farewell address in 1796 has this nation boasted a president outside of the two-party system. It was during his speech almost two hundred and fifty years ago that The Father of His Country warned against the dangers of a political system based on such limited choice. But now, in the year of Our Lord 2041, the American people have handed the presidency to our Commander-in-Chief in waiting, president-elect John Harrison Henry. A rank outsider only two years ago, he has been propelled to power on a wave of discontent. No one knows what the political fallout will be from this former democrat turned rebel, but there is little doubt the ramifications will be resounding throughout Capitol Hill for years, perhaps decades to come.'

FBI Special Agent Brett Taylor switched off the wallscreen. She'd seen and heard enough. Of course, the news was sensational. The next president of the United States would be an independent candidate, the first since Washington himself. Perhaps the most amazing thing was how he'd gained power in the first place. Crowdfunding had long been an institution where individuals, businesses and even countries could call upon anyone, anywhere, to donate money to their cause, be that for profit or otherwise. To use such a scheme to fund a presidential campaign had been tried before, but never on the scale that John Henry had been able to foster. When transparency was complete and donation amounts limited in order to preserve the candidate's impartiality, it seemed the general public's finances, be they American or otherwise, far outweighed that of the corporate bodies seeking to influence policy for their own means. It did introduce the problem that non U.S. citizens could influence the outcome of a presidential election, but then since foreign companies had been doing that for centuries anyway, what was the difference? The arguments would rumble on ad infinitum, but then that was politics, the merry-go-round of misdirection on the road to nowhere. Why change a lot when you can change a little? An apt assertion some might say for the ruling class – as legislators liked to think of themselves.

Brett moved to the washbasin and placed her holstered sidearm and badge to one side. She splashed water on her face and gazed into the mirror. Hard eyes looked back at her. Tall, with a wide face, short brown hair and a solid build, she was well suited to her role as an agent of the state, a law enforcer. A sharp mind complemented by a passion for solving crimes, she saw herself as the leading lady in a world dominated by men, a woman who'd show the testosterone-fuelled morons how policing should be done.

A knocking disturbed her. Wiping water away from her mouth and nose, she walked over and opened the door. Sniffing, she looked at the man standing before her.

He peered past her, confused. 'Can I speak to a Brett Taylor, please?'

'I'm she.'

'Sorry, I assumed you were a man. I mean the name, not—'

Brett held up a hand. 'I get it, what do you want?'

'Ms. Taylor, the sentencing is about to begin.'

She looked at her watch. 'They told me it wouldn't take place until this afternoon.'

'It's been brought forward. The situation is unusual, what with the GMRC's involvement.'

Brett grunted an obscurity before her computer phone vibrated. Thanking the administrator, she answered it. 'Yes.'

'FBI Agent Taylor?' a man said, his voice stilted and accent strange.

'Who wants to know?'

'You have a problem, agent; I can help you with it.'

She frowned. 'Who is this?'

'Who I am is of no consequence, it's what I can do that matters.'

'Sorry, I don't do cryptic.' She hung up. Grabbing her suit jacket, she snapped her holster clip onto her belt and put her badge in her pocket. Checking her gun's safety was on, she holstered it and went out into the hall. Around her other people filtered out of rooms, no doubt heading to the same place she was. Striding down the hall, she turned a corner and caught an elevator, stepping between its closing doors just in time.

Her phone rang again.

'Taylor,' she said in answer.

'Agent, it's in your interest to hear what I have—'

She snorted and hung up again. She couldn't stand nuisance calls.

The lift doors opened and people streamed out into a large foyer, the merging of modern and neoclassical architecture of the building a fitting venue for the Supreme Court of California. Moving with the flow of bodies, the chatter of footfalls and murmurings echoing in the halls, she queued up outside courtroom one. Flashing her identity badge at one of the many police officers in attendance, Brett filed past the security checkpoint and moved inside. She took her seat in the front row, just behind the low rail that separated spectators from the trial's current participants. Above, the upper galleries filled, the hubbub of movement swamping the senses.

It had been many days since she'd taken the stand and the

process had left her mentally fatigued, the questioning and cross-examination had been intense. It would have been difficult anyway, what with her involvement being pivotal to the charges brought – she was, after all, the arresting agent – but she'd had an underlying fear that a crucial piece of information might have come to light at any point, be that by a mistake of her own making or the insinuation of another. As luck would have it, her resolve to keep such pertinent and potentially explosive revelations to herself had proved to be the right call, the potential of being exposed unrealised.

At various times throughout the proceedings the court had been conducted behind closed doors, enforced in part by the GMRC officials in attendance. These outsiders couldn't help but infuriate the judiciary, their involvement curtailing normal practice and slowing the process of law to a crawl. The reason for this infringement was the secretive nature of the defendants' work. Both men had high ranking positions within the GMRC's U.S. Programme – whatever that involved – and as such they were privy to an unheard of amount of protection when it came to the withholding of virtually anything and everything to do with their lives; which included their work, where they lived, their ages, their names, heck, even their place of birth. The only things that had been disclosed were that they were both U.S. citizens and worked for the GMRC, and one of them was a Colonel in the U.S. military.

At first the GMRC had tried to cover up the fact the two terrorists had been a part of their staff, but inevitably the information had been leaked. Brett suspected her superior for the infraction, FBI Director Patrick Flynn, who had an axe to grind with one of the GMRC's head honchos, a man called Malcolm Joiner. The fallout from this disclosure had caused a sudden increase in rioting and anti-GMRC demonstrations, but as time passed the protesting lost momentum and some semblance of order returned.

Of course, when it came to identity, Brett knew the details of one of the defendants perhaps better than those in the GMRC who were succeeding in keeping it withheld. The man in question? Colonel Samson, her father.

Since the incident in the prison in which a fire had taken her parent's life, Brett had felt a strange kind of detachment. It had taken her a few days to realise what that feeling had been. It was relief, sheer unadulterated relief. For so long she'd hidden her memories of her father away. The brutal beast had mistreated her mother and scared Brett so much in her younger years she'd wet the bed until she was thirteen.

That her father had loved her wasn't in question, it was his interpretation of love that was. Whatever twisted upbringing he'd endured, Brett knew his idea of love was skewed from a place of horror, pain and rage. So much so, he'd often given her a split lip or black eye, only to get angry when she'd cried or refused to kiss him goodnight.

Now he was dead she felt free, stronger.

A weight had been lifted and she could breathe again. It was strange as she'd always thought she'd moved on from that part of her life, but its poisonous echoes had still lurked in the recesses of her mind, torturing her soul with vicious claws and strangling her from within.

When Colonel Samson, or Major Samson as she'd known him, had abducted Brett from her place of work in the FBI's LA field office weeks before, her life had descended into one of nightmares. After wreaking havoc across the city of Los Angeles, killing dozens of her colleagues and over thirty police officers, plus a host of innocent civilians, Samson had taken refuge in an abandoned warehouse, rejoined by his partner in crime, an old man whose demeanour smacked of power and influence. As a profiler she could tell things about people they didn't know themselves. Sadly she didn't seem able to translate this skill to herself; her personal life was a shambles of iconic proportions. Sober, she sought out kind, gentle souls, men who were the opposite of her father, but these men were never enough, always falling short of expectations physically and emotionally. When such affairs had broken down, she often found herself drunk, craving the company of the cruel and brutal. In the morning when she'd awoken, hung-over and wretched, she'd often thrown up, not through the after-effects of excessive alcohol consumption – although this was sometimes the case – but because she'd seen she'd chosen to sleep with the darkness that her father had so embodied. She felt cursed to walk the same path over and over again, never finding peace and never feeling the virtue of another for longer than it was to be disappointed or revolted in equal measure. Despite her training and intuition, the reasons for her father's actions had eluded her. Why had he tracked her down? She had no idea. The thought of his words returned to her, words she'd ignored at the time, thinking them lies. But she should have remembered her father, while capable of misdirection, refrained from doing so unless it was a necessity.

You're making a mistake, he'd said, *your life – in danger*. What danger had he been speaking of? It made no sense, he was the one who'd put her in danger, no one else. What was she missing? She'd been unable to gain access to him in prison, so the questions she had for him remained unanswered, and now he was dead he'd taken his secrets to the grave. There was the old man, of course, who looked like a school teacher but carried himself with the authority of a just king. She still wanted to know what *he* had meant when she'd overheard him talking with her father. The words still kept her awake at night even now.

'You don't care about anything, that's the problem,' the old man had said. 'You murder innocent people like slaughtering cattle and disobey my direct orders, effectively condemning hundreds of thousands of civilians to a premature death!'

It made no sense, none of it. Why had the old man been so concerned about saving lives when he'd helped her father take so many in his depraved rampage? And if he were capable of giving orders to a serving colonel in the United States armed forces, then he must have been powerful indeed. A GMRC official, obviously, but doing what? And trying to protect whom? Where were these hundreds of thousands of people who needed saving, and what did they need saving from? Just thinking about it drove her crazy.

A vibration against her leg drew Brett back to the present, the tumultuous chatter of the hundreds gathered in the courtroom drowning out her ringtone. She withdrew the phone to see the caller was unknown. She switched it off.

Angry mutterings built and Brett looked up as the lone defendant entered the room behind a frosted, glass panel, his orange jumpsuit standing out for all to see while his identity remained concealed. Surrounded by four armed GMRC soldiers, the old man kept his head down, the chains around his ankles and wrists clinking in time with his movement.

A door opening to the right drew Brett's attention and the Supreme Court Marshal appeared. 'All rise!' Silence fell and people rose as his voice boomed out. 'Hear ye, hear ye, hear ye! The Supreme Court of the great state of California is now in session. All who have cause to plea, draw near, give attention and you shall be heard. God save these United States, the great state of California and this honourable court!'

◆

Professor Steiner stood waiting to face those who sat in judgement. He adjusted his stance and the bonds that bound him clinked in response, but no matter how he moved, the restraints continued to rub against the bruises inflicted by his jailors. To take his mind off the pain his thoughts turned to the recent past.

Since Colonel Samson's fiery demise, Steiner had been submitted to further interrogations by various factions trying to get to the bottom of the murder inside the supermax prison. It seemed to Steiner an odd paradox whereby the people seeking to end Samson's life by legal means should then be upset when his time had been cut prematurely short. However, despite his best efforts to aid their investigations, following the colonel's passing Steiner had become the last man standing and, inevitably, all attention had descended on him. He alone bore the burden of the murders committed by the colonel, who had escaped justice in the eyes of the law. Steiner now stood as the sole focus of hate for the many that saw him as the epitome of evil.

The Chief Justice and her Associate Justices filed in from the rear of the courtroom, their black robes whispering round them like the cloak of death. Six more similarly dressed individuals joined them soon after. Steiner knew them to be U.S. GMRC attorneys who were ready and willing to advise the court on matters of national and international security pertaining to the case.

A GMRC soldier nudged Steiner in the back, forcing him forwards.

The Chief Justice cleared her voice. 'Defendant B, you have been given the opportunity to be heard and show cause why judgement should not be imposed and offer matters of mitigation. This court has considered the extenuating and aggravated circumstances presented as available, and has prepared a sentencing decree which is on file with the staff attorney. No legal cause has been shown to disqualify the imposition of this sentence and our judgement.'

The woman peered at Steiner as though he were the lowest of the low, the filth of humanity she knew him to be. 'This case involves a horrific act of terrorism,' she continued, 'that resulted in the murder of fifty-six federal agents, thirty-two Los Angeles police officers and twenty-five U.S. citizens, all of whom were living out their daily lives as valuable members of society. It has been determined the defendant had ample opportunity to prevent further loss of life during the time of the incident. It has also been determined the defendant willingly assisted Defendant A, now deceased, in planning his acts of murder.

Due to the unusual nature of this case the public will be dissatisfied with the information disclosed; however, they can rest assured that the evidence submitted for consideration has been significant, detailed and without flaw. While motivations for these senseless acts of violence have not been forthcoming, it can be said this court's decision has been based on facts that cannot be disputed.'

The woman paused and Steiner's heartbeat felt like a drum, the thump thump thump of blood pumping through his veins filling his ears as his verdict neared. He closed his eyes and prayed.

'Hence,' the Chief Justice said, 'this court has found that the mitigating factors do not outweigh the aggravated circumstances beyond a reasonable doubt and therefore finds that the sentence of death shall be imposed upon Defendant B with immediate effect.'

Cheering and applause erupted from all sides and Steiner's focus narrowed to a point as the reality of his situation crushed down onto him. His vision faded. The sound of joy and laughter filled his ears and the room around him whirled and spun. Steiner stumbled back as his legs buckled and he toppled to the floor and into darkness.

◆

Brett Taylor left the courtroom, pleased with the verdict but concerned that her many questions would now remain unanswered. While she wanted the man to pay for his crimes, she also wanted to find out about the secrets he held, secrets she knew would continue to eat away at her day and night.

Leaving the courthouse behind, Brett turned her phone back on and went outside into the freezing air of the impact winter. Above, the dark skies remained in a state of flux, the dust cloud from the asteroid impact the year before continuing to rule the lives of every living thing on the planet. Floodlights lined the streets, creating a false daytime light and a barrier held back the waiting media scrum and the heave of people trying to catch a glimpse of the man who'd become the nation's number one figure of hate. Even with the GMRC's media blackout, blurred images of him still circulated, fuelling speculation as to his identity like never before. When her father met his grizzly end, the public had accepted it as poetic justice. But that sentiment had quickly been forgotten as their attention switched to his accomplice.

Yet again her phone rang and she gave a growl of annoyance before answering it. 'What?!'

'You had your chance, Ms. Taylor; we've had to force your hand.'

'Who the hell are you? Where did you get this number?'

'I'm someone who can help.'

'I don't need any damn help.'

'I thought you wanted to find out about your father's companion?'

Brett's blood ran cold and she looked around in fear. 'What did you just say?'

The caller didn't reply.

How had someone found out about Samson being her father? She felt sick. 'I don't know what you're talking about.'

'I think you do, Brett Samson.'

Brett's hand shook, the sound of her old name sparking childhood memories.

'Are you still there, Agent?'

She turned away from the media cameras. 'I don't know who the fuck you are, but you're messing with the wrong person. I can have a hundred agents hunt you down in a heartbeat.'

The person on the other end laughed. 'I don't think so, Ms. Taylor. You look quite alone at the moment.'

Realising the implication, Brett whirled around, her eyes darting over the crowded scene, searching for someone on a phone. *There!* A man glanced her way, his hand to his ear. But no, there was a woman fifty feet to his left, her eyes passing Brett's. The more she looked, the more people seemed to be staring at her and any number of them could have had a communication device at their fingertips.

Her brow furrowed as she continued to look for this hidden intruder. 'What do you want?'

'The question is what do *you* want? We can help you find the answers you seek.'

'And what answers are they?'

'The name of the man who has just been sentenced to death.'

'What is it, then?' Brett tapped away at a device inside her jacket pocket, the keypad just visible enough to use.

'His name is Professor George Steiner.'

'How do I know you're not making that up?'

'You don't. But if you want to know more you need to do exactly as I say.'

'And what do you want me to do, *exactly*?'

'You need to resign your tenure as an FBI agent.'

It was Brett's turn to laugh. 'And why would I do that?' She looked at the response coming back on her device. It read:

Trace complete
Source coordinates attached

'You must resign as that is the only way you will find out the truth.'

'What truth?' Taylor said, trying not to sound distracted as she opened the file to see a map of her location. A red pulsating dot indicated the caller's position and she held the device in front of her in an attempt to pinpoint its location.

'The truth about the GMRC and the threat to mankind.'

Brett closed in on their position. 'Go on.' She flashed her badge and pushed past the police and on into the crowd.

'I'll tell you more when you are no longer a federal agent.'

'Come on,' – Brett approached the media crews from the rear, homing in on a van that stood apart from the rest – 'just a little more and I'll do as you say.'

The caller didn't reply.

Brett yanked open the doors to the back of the van, gun in hand. No one was inside, but through the windscreen she glimpsed a person wearing a baseball cap running away. Brett dodged round the vehicle and set off in pursuit.

The suspect dived into the passenger side of another unmarked news van as Brett closed in. The vehicle's wheels spun, then screeched as it gained traction and sped away, and Brett ran flat out in pursuit before stopping to train her gun on it. The van wove into traffic and Brett swore. She lowered her weapon and put the phone back to her ear. 'Hey,' she said, out of breath, 'didn't you want to say hi?'

'That was unwise, Agent Taylor.'

'I haven't upset you, have I?'

'This will go badly for you, Agent,' the man said and hung up.

Brett shook her head and slid her pistol back into its holster. So, someone knew her secret and claimed to know much more besides. This turn of events left her feeling vulnerable, and if there was one thing she hated, it was to be weak. She dialled her LA office to request a drone be tasked to her location and all local traffic cameras be consulted for a match to the van.

'Agent Taylor?'

Brett turned to see two of the FBI Director's Washington agents striding towards her.

'You need to come with us,' one of the men said.

Brett looked at their grim faces. 'I'm in the middle of an investigation; can't it wait?'

The other man shook his head. 'Director Flynn has requested your presence.'

Brett fell into step beside them as they led her back to the court house. 'Any idea what this is about?'

Neither man answered; instead they guided her back into the now empty courtroom that had housed the trial.

At the front of the spectator area stood the Director of the FBI, Patrick Flynn. By his side were a cluster of Brett's colleagues from the LA field office, including the new Assistant Director in Charge, Donald Anderson. The Chief of Police for the Los Angeles Police Department also stood close by. All turned as she approached.

Brett stopped in front of her director. 'You wanted to see me, sir?'

'We've received some news from the military's medical examiner,' Flynn said.

'Regarding?'

'Regarding the federal autopsy of Defendant A.'

Brett waited for the news, wondering what this was all about.

Anderson passed Brett some images. 'It seems the man who died in the fire was not Defendant A, but an impostor.'

'What?!' Brett sifted through the photos, trying to discern with her own eyes the unfathomable results. 'That can't be.' She looked at Anderson and then to Flynn.

'It can be and it is,' Flynn said. 'The man who died in the fire was a foreign national, a murderer who'd secured release on appeal due to a technicality. While his teeth failed to reveal his identity, enough DNA could be retrieved from inside the body for a definite ID.'

'Then where's Defendant A?'

'Good question,' said the Chief of Police.

'Shouldn't we be out looking for him?' Brett looked in alarm at the men before her, her stomach turning in knots at the news.

Flynn took the images back from her. 'Even as we speak the Bureau is on full alert, as are all other law enforcement agencies nationwide. But perhaps the most disturbing thing is this.' The FBI Director handed Brett a folder, his look intense.

Brett accepted the file and glanced at Anderson before looking inside to see a picture of a man in a uniform. Underneath, were the words, '*Major Samson*'. Brett turned it over to reveal another photograph. This one made her heart race and her head spin. She'd seen this image before, many years ago. A young Brett sat on her father's knee, looking as scared as she remembered feeling. Flicking through the documents behind revealed the extent of evidence stacked against her. She looked up into a sea of angry eyes, the expressions mixed with hate and betrayal.

'Sir, I can explain.'

Flynn's face was a mask of cold fury as he motioned to the two men who'd led her in. They moved closer and powerful hands grasped her arms.

'Agent Taylor, you are hereby suspended from duty pending a full inquiry.' Anderson reached out and pulled her gun from its holster. He then moved in to check her pockets and extracted her FBI badge and ID card.

'That you knew this man was your father,' Flynn said, 'put this whole trial at risk. But we'll be damned if it prevents the court's decision from being carried out. Breathe a word of this to anyone and it'll be you taking the stand. Now get out of my sight!'

Released, Brett moved in a daze, out of the building and back into the icy cold, her life in ruins, and worse still, her father alive.

CHAPTER THIRTY-TWO

PROFESSOR STEINER SAT in his cell. He'd been aware the death penalty had been reinstated in California a few years before. Ironically it had been the GMRC that had ordered the directive; citing governments needed stronger deterrents when dealing with public disorder before and after the impact of the asteroid AG5. Steiner himself had voted against such a punishment, but the motion had been passed, driven through by others including the man who'd turned on Steiner in USSB Steadfast, an act which had led to his current circumstances. That man was Malcolm Joiner.

Waiving his right to a last meal, Steiner sat alone contemplating his failure at saving the men and women who still remained trapped in the aforementioned subterranean base. The military, controlled by Joiner, would ensure their chances of reaching the surface were slim to none.

The image of his friend, Nathan Bryant, came to mind. His kind face and supportive words would have gone down well round about now, although it would take nothing short of a miracle to boost his current state.

Steiner had tried to speak to those GMRC officials that had come to see him during his incarceration, pleading with them to speak to the Directorate about Joiner's duplicity and the plight of those trapped underground. He'd even disclosed information about the next wave of meteors, in particular the one destined to destroy USSB Steadfast in 2042. Unfortunately such claims fell on deaf ears; all of the officials were already under the influence of the intelligence director. Joiner had even given Steiner a message: '*Try to tell any more people about the coming events and I'll make sure USSB Steadfast won't be the only base to suffer a cataclysm.*'

Since that time Steiner had kept his thoughts to himself, not that he'd been given much opportunity to speak to anyone other than the GMRC puppets who'd been responsible for his defence. These traitorous individuals had also ensured his continued seclusion, creating an impenetrable barrier between him and the FBI, police and judiciary. The only people he'd been left alone with were the guards at the prison, who had been too busy beating him to pay any attention to anything he had to say.

The clang of an iron gate made Steiner look up. Standing before his cell and accompanied by a guard was an elderly Catholic priest.

The man of the cloth entered and Steiner stood.

The guard, however, remained and the priest hesitated. 'I'd like time alone with this man if I may.'

The guard shook his head. 'I'm sorry, father, all prisoners are deemed too dangerous for you to be left alone with, no matter their size or appearance.'

The priest sighed. 'At least give us a little more privacy.'

The guard moved away as far as he could, but still close enough to return if the clergyman required assistance.

The priest laid a hand on Steiner's arm making him flinch in pain; blotchy bruises still covered his body like a maroon blanket.

The priest held up a hand in apology while Steiner sat.

'Father, forgive me for I have sinned.'

'How long has it been since last your last confession, my son?'

Steiner took the priest's hand. 'Many, many years. I lost faith ... in everything.'

'God never leaves us,' the priest said, 'but acts of the Devil may make us think we are so forsaken. Confess and find redemption.'

Steiner looked into his eyes and nodded. 'Where do I start?'

The priest smiled and patted his hand. 'At the beginning, my son, at the beginning.'

◆

Brett Taylor arrived outside the supermax prison where the death sentence of Defendant B was to be carried out in less than an hour. The traffic on the surrounding roads was nose to tail and it took a few minutes to find a place to park her car. When she finally found somewhere, she got out and made her way towards the main gates, where a large crowd had gathered.

Some of those that had travelled had done so to be close to the justice they sought for loved ones killed in the LA massacre, others for the occasion, a sick form of entertainment that made Brett's skin crawl.

As she pushed through the crowds she caught a glimpse of her FBI colleagues entering the prison, preparing to bear witness to the justice of the state. And between her and them, a wall of police separated those protesting against the death penalty as they hurled abuse at those who supported it with equal ferocity.

Brett stopped at the fence, the way forward barred. Her suspension as a federal agent prevented her from seeing first hand the justice she still craved. It had been her testimony and actions that had caught the people responsible for her colleagues' deaths, so she felt bitter that her relationship to one of the perpetrators meant she'd been forced to watch from afar. Some would say the crimes would never have been committed had she not been there, which was a fair assumption; however, how could Brett be responsible for the actions of another, related or not? The answer: she couldn't.

Someone pushed past her and she felt fingers slip into her back pocket. Spinning round, she saw a small figure vanish into the throng. She attempted to follow, but found the press of human bodies too dense. Searching, she thought she spotted the pickpocket further ahead, slight of size, a youth maybe, the nimblest of fingers a perfect companion to the art of close quarters theft.

Brett touched her pocket out of instinct and felt something there. She pulled out a scrap of paper. Scribbled words read:

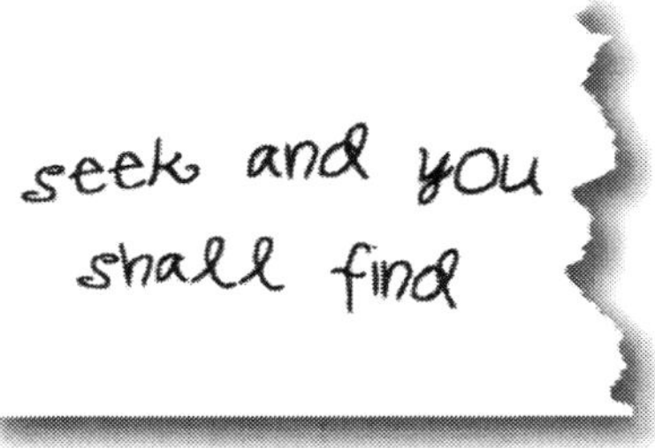

She looked up in consternation. Someone was playing games and she didn't like it. She bent down, removed the gun from her ankle holster and slipped the small sidearm into her belt before pulling her shirt back over it. Exhaling into the cold air, her breath winding up in tiny trails, she forced her way back through the crowd.

♦

Professor Steiner sat on his bed while the guard attached chains to his ankles and wrists. His thoughts lingered on the words spoken by the priest, *God never leaves us*. They were wise words, words he hoped were true. A host of other phrases sprang to mind: *you are what you think, you will become what you imagine, positive thoughts end in positive results*; except most of his life had been blessed with positive thoughts, propelling him through each day in relative happiness. The result of this attitude? Death row, awaiting execution. *So much for positive thoughts attracting positive energy,* he thought with bitter irony. *But then that's where faith comes in*, his other self reasoned.

However, the main agency that disturbed his inner calm was an overactive imagination and the thoughts that went with it. *What if nothing awaits after death?* He couldn't help but let fear consume him, the fear of not being, of ceasing to exist. *What if 'nothing' is all there is?* An upsurge of terror sought to overwhelm him and he fought back the panic by breathing deep and slow in an attempt to clear his mind. His chaotic thoughts turned to his work and his many accomplishments. *Has my life been worthwhile?* he wondered. He thought it had. He'd helped mankind to continue its battle for life and to prepare for its long journey into the unknown. Every manmade subterranean base utilised his designs, the cascading chambers, the revolutionary earthquake-proof foundations. These things would help extend human existence, not just for the millions living underground, but for many generations to come, perhaps for thousands of generations. Without the underground bases humanity would be wiped out in a matter of years, every advance lost to the whim of chance – and the asteroids were just one threat of many. A super volcano, comets, solar flares, nuclear war, environmental collapse, climate change, plague, the list went on. Only multiple underground complexes, completely independent from the surface, could hope to protect against all of these horrors of nature. And, despite what anyone thought, whatever man created was by definition natural, as man was from nature. Everything was natural; it just might not fall into the category of what people perceived as *normal*.

He also knew the bases would give people more time to populate space, as it was clear as time went by that transitioning to the realm of other planets, moons or the vacuum of the universe would be a long and difficult road. If the visions of space travel into the solar system and beyond were to reach fruition then humans needed time, and lots of it. And since some of the cataclysms that awaited were inevitable, then only a fool would risk the advances of its entire species to chance. Steiner relaxed at the thought, before rough hands hauled him to his feet.

Shoved out of his cell, Steiner shuffled forward with his last moments on Earth burning bright and his senses on overload. The smell of bleach tasted sweet on his tongue. The sound of the guard's keys jangled like Beethoven's fifth symphony and the colour of his orange jumpsuit was beautiful to the eye, its rough texture glorious on the skin. Even his bruises and the pain they induced made him feel alive. He moved down the long corridor with a guard on either side of him. A glimmer of light through a window made him glance up to see the small form of a creature he'd come to cherish. The bird he'd first seen from his cell had continued to visit him day in and day out during the latter part of his captivity. And even now it perched on a ledge with its tiny eyes peering into Steiner's own. *Does it know my fate? Does it care? Does anyone?*

One of the guards followed Steiner's gaze and banged the window with his extendable stick, and the bird fluttered away in distress.

Soon after, they entered the execution chamber and Steiner's stomach cramped tight as he laid eyes on the table he would be strapped to and the cylinders of lethal fluid that stood close by. It was all he could do to keep moving.

In front, a mechanical blind blocked the view beyond and the warden entered to check over the systems, accompanied by a GMRC official.

The guards removed Steiner's chains and helped him onto the table, where they strapped him down. Steiner lay back and looked up into the bright lights on the ceiling.

'Time to die,' one of the men whispered in his ear. 'My cousin was one of the police officers killed by your friend. I hope you burn in hell.'

Steiner looked at the hate in his eyes and clenched his left hand where his thumb rubbed his gold wedding band.

The other guard must have seen the movement and pointed to his colleague. 'Take the ring.'

Steiner's eyes widened. 'NO!'

He clamped his fingers tight as the guard fought to prise it open. Steiner gritted his teeth before the man cracked his baton down, once, twice, three times until Steiner cried out in pain. With help from his partner, the guard tore the ring from his finger and then removed Steiner's glasses and spat on him. Steiner winced and turned his head away as the spittle ran down the side of his face.

A siren sounded and the table beneath him rose to vertical, while the blind retracted to reveal a window and a room less than half full. The few that had been allowed access watched with grim expressions.

Steiner searched for someone he might know, but only strangers met his gaze.

Thinking of Amelia, his thumb sought the ring that was no longer there. Only then did he feel truly alone, as if his one true love had left when he needed her most. He imagined her eyes and found his turmoil prevented the visualisation from appearing.

The warden stepped forward to press a button, his shadowy form in the darkened room beyond seeming like the cast of death himself. 'Do you have any last words, prisoner?'

Steiner gathered himself and cleared his throat. 'May God grant me forgiveness for my crimes as I forgive those who've wronged me. For those among you who may know, as I do, remain steadfast that sanctuary may not be waiting for us all.' He let his words sink in, hoping his cryptic message might fall on friendly ears. 'I also ask that I be laid to rest by my wife, Amelia. May life continue for you all. God bless.'

The warden released the button and gave a signal with his hand. Steiner heard a hiss of sound and turned to see the first plunger sink to the bottom of its cylinder. He rested his head back and his eyes focused on the dark glass and the reflection of a skylight from above.

On the ledge of this window sat his feathered friend, its tiny beak ruffling feathers. His wife had always liked birds.

Steiner concentrated on this sight of life as the sensation of warmth swept through his veins. A tear rolled down his cheek. 'I'm coming home, Amelia,' he whispered. 'I'm coming home.'

CHAPTER THIRTY-THREE

Outside the Pelican Bay Supermax State Prison, Brett Taylor, alongside thousands of others, watched the image of her father's accomplice dying on the big screens. While his face had been blurred out to preserve his identity, the vision gave those present closure, along with the millions who tuned in to the macabre broadcast from around the world via the mass media. Brett herself felt satisfied, but she knew, unlike those around her, that the man responsible for pulling the trigger remained at large, her father having been spirited away by people unknown posing as GMRC employees. At least that seemed the most likely scenario, but since this was the GMRC they were talking about, anything was possible.

That her father had escaped from his crimes bit deep into Brett's core, her quest for justice as tainted as her familial bond. The release she'd experienced at the news of her father's death had felt like a great weight had been lifted, her past wiped clean and her future fresh with possibility. Now, however, the status quo had resumed and his shadow hovered at the periphery like a stain on her soul.

The noise of the crowd roused her from her melancholy. Despite the event they'd come to see being over, the people around her continued their vigil. News crews also remained, the correspondents speaking into cameras under floodlit glows in the dark.

Brett looked again at the piece of paper that had been slipped into her trouser pocket.

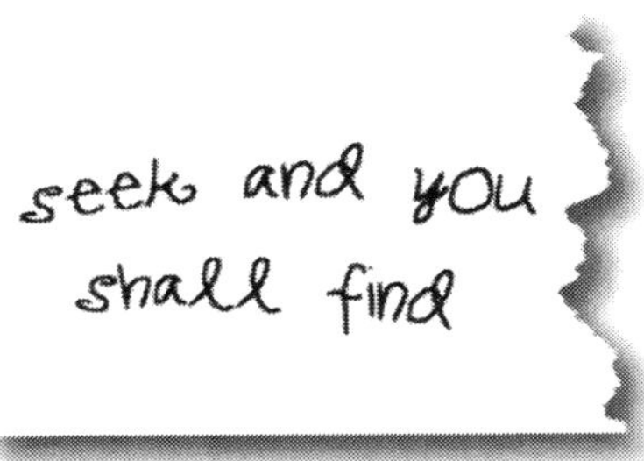

What do I want to find? she asked herself. *My father.* The thought struck her like a stone to the temple. What if the person who'd given her this message knew where her father was? She looked around. The prison's floodlights shone in all directions, their rays highlighting the dying trees that lined the road behind. Working her way to the street, she walked along through shadows, searching for something, anything, she knew not what.

Perhaps her father had come to save his friend. No, she thought, he had no love for the old man. And besides, if he was here to save him he was too late. Unless the accomplice wasn't his target. The colonel's words came to mind once more. You're making a mistake, your life – in danger. Her hand strayed to the gun concealed beneath her shirt. Perhaps he's come back for me, to finish what he'd started, saving me from whatever madness he's conjured from the hell he calls a mind.

The idea was a frightening one, but she wasn't about to turn tail and run, and after half an hour of *seeking*, Brett had found nothing in the vicinity of the prison that looked suspicious or resembled anything like a clue. She decided to head back to the motel where she'd been staying, but as she made her way to her car she spied something out of place. A white news van stood parked amongst a host of its fellows, but this vehicle had no markings or plates. It was the same one that had fled from outside the courthouse earlier that day.

She removed her pistol from her belt and approached the rear of the van. Reaching out to one of two doors, she grasped its handle and yanked it open.

Dark emptiness greeted her.

Brett stowed her weapon and got in to search the detritus on the floor, and then slid into the driver's seat. Feeling under the passenger side dash, she opened the glove box and found it empty save for another piece of paper.

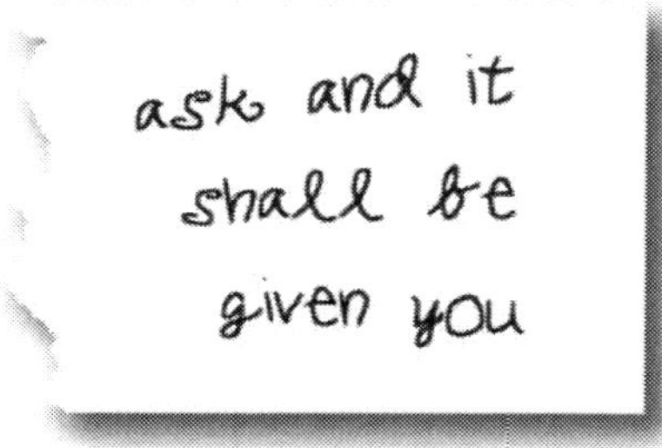

Ask who? She turned the paper over to see it was blank.

A prison security officer approached and tapped on the window. 'Ma'am?'

She opened the door and got out.

'Are you the owner of this vehicle?' he said.

'No, I'm a federal agent.' She reached for her badge and realised her mistake. 'Why, is there a problem?'

He hesitated and she hoped her appearance and confident manner ensured he wouldn't want to see ID.

'Someone said this van was causing an obstruction.'

Brett looked and saw it was doing no such thing. She frowned. 'Who told you that?'

'Some kid.' He held his hand out around waist height. 'He was hanging around the rear of the compound.'

'Show me.'

The man nodded and led her back into the crowd before skirting the perimeter of the prison's fence. A minute later they emerged into an emptier area.

The security man looked around. 'He was right here.'

'What did he look like?'

His radio crackled. 'Disturbance at gate two, Andy, can you assist?'

He grasped the handset. 'Copy, Control, on my way.' He looked to Brett. 'Not sure, short dark hair, Asian looking? I have to go.'

The man jogged away and disappeared back into the melee.

Apart from a small access road and a high fence, all Brett could see were three tall guard towers and their searchlights raking the compound's interior.

Movement inside caught her eye and she raised her computer phone and zoomed in to get a better look. A large blue and white truck stood parked behind a mass of security fencing and on its side were the words:

COUNTY OF LOS ANGELES DEPARTMENT OF
CORONER
SPECIAL OPERATIONS RESPONSE TEAM

Brett could just make out two people dressed in black uniforms with matching caps getting out of the back of the vehicle. They pulled a collapsible gurney with them and its legs unfolded to the ground, enabling them to wheel it into the prison's main building.

A couple of minutes later the two state employees re-emerged, but this time an ominous body bag lay on the trolley, its shape leaving little doubt that its function had been fulfilled.

When the grisly cargo had been loaded, the prison warden, accompanied by two of his guards, came to sign off the undertaking and waited as the two death dealers slammed shut the rear doors before climbing into the cab.

Something about the scene niggled at her, but she couldn't put her finger on it. The body language of the two coroners seemed tense, almost rushed – *but no, that isn't it*. Brett zoomed further in on the image.

The driver was a woman, her features hidden in shadow and Brett was hit by a flash of recognition; she'd seen this person before! An image of a figure running away from her back at the court house sprang to mind. She looked again and tried to visualise the two together.

The truck moved forward and the first set of gates opened to allow them through. Then another set opened and the vehicle crept along toward the rear exit as two police patrol cars moved in to escort the coroner to the final gate.

Lights from the guardhouse homed in on the truck. Passes were shown and words exchanged before a siren wailed once and the final barriers lifted. The patrol cars lit up their light bars and the truck's red and white LEDs also blazed to life.

The small convoy rolled out down the service road and Brett turned and ran.

Pushing into the protestors, she thrust people aside and glanced left, keeping the coroner's truck in sight. Legs pumping, she collided with a man and stumbled before regaining momentum. A moment later she burst free of the masses and rushed to her car. The hybrid engine whirred to life as her quarry gained speed and turned onto the main highway. Wheels spinning on the grass, Brett bounced her blue sedan onto the asphalt and gunned the accelerator. The back of the car slid out before snapping back as Brett sped to catch up to the flashing lights ahead.

She went to phone her office to call in support and then swore. She'd have to do this on her own.

Weaving in and out of traffic, she worked her way closer to her target, which turned off Lake Earl Drive and toward the I-101 interstate. After a minute the flashing lights stopped and the two patrol cars peeled off onto a side road, leaving the coroner's truck to continue its journey alone. At an intersection Brett drew up alongside and peered at the passenger. The young, clean-shaven man shot her a sideways look and tugged his cap lower to hide his face.

The truck pulled away and crossed over the I-101 and on into the darkness.

Brett waited before following at a distance.

The coroner's truck took a left onto the Redwood Highway soon after and Brett found herself driving through a forest of trees. But the journey didn't last long, as after a few miles she pursued the truck to a small camping ground. She switched off her headlights and drew to a halt at the side of the road.

The twin beams from the coroner's vehicle highlighted the forms of giant redwoods before its taillights glowed red as it pulled into a parking bay. Brett touched her computer to activate a low glow by which to see. Taking out her weapon, she chambered a round and got out of the car.

The cold night closed in around her and she approached the rear of the vehicle.

The gas guzzler's engine continued to burble and Brett switched off her gun's safety as she crept up to the driver's window.

She paused ... and then darted forward to aim her pistol into an empty cabin. A twig cracked behind her, she whirled round and something cracked across her head. A gunshot rang out and a flock of birds flew up, screeching into the night.

CHAPTER THIRTY-FOUR

'Is she dead?'

'Of course not, look, she's breathing.'

'So who is she?'

'How do I know?'

Brett lay on a cold floor, pretending to be unconscious. She'd been aware of her surroundings ever since she'd felt herself being manhandled by the two people she now listened to.

The woman who'd just spoken had to be the driver of the coroner's truck and the voice of a young man, who she assumed to be the passenger, spoke again.

'Didn't he say?'

'What do you think?' the woman said.

'No?'

'Correct. As usual he wants to keep us guessing.'

'According to this she's called Brett Taylor. Weird, eh?'

'I'm more concerned she had a gun.'

Brett heard the floor creak as someone moved closer.

'What are we going to do with her?' the young man said.

'Don't look at me. This wasn't my plan.'

'Shouldn't we tie her up?'

Silence ensued before the woman spoke again. 'Okay, you do it and I'll cover you.'

Brett felt hands on her arms and she cracked open an eye to see a youth bending over her with a gun in his hand. She grabbed his wrist and twisted. He cried out in pain, dropped the weapon and Brett surged to her feet.

'Stop or I'll shoot!'

Brett froze as she looked down the barrel of a revolver. She held up her hands. The female driver stood before her with a shaky finger on the trigger of her weapon. They were in the back of the coroner's truck. Brett dropped her hands back down and made to pick up the gun that the young man had been holding.

The woman moved forward. 'I said stop!'

Brett looked at her. 'You're not going to shoot me.'

A look of fear crossed her assailant's face.

Brett reached down and picked up the gun, *her* gun. Checking it she turned it on the driver and her partner. 'Now, *you* put down the gun or I'll shoot *you*.'

The woman's hand shook and Brett feared she'd misjudged her.

'I'll lower mine if you lower yours.'

'What is this, kindergarten? Lower your damn gun, I'm a federal agent!'

'Then where's your badge?' the young man said, his accent strange.

'In my car.' She cocked the hammer and advanced. 'Now lower your weapon!'

The woman stood her ground, forcing Brett to re-evaluate her position. Seeing her opponent was caught in two minds, reluctant to shoot but unwilling to cede control, she made a bold decision and released the trigger, then held up her gun side on.

The woman, English by her accent, saw sense and lowered her revolver.

'Who are you?' the lad said.

Brett, keeping her eyes on the armed female, gestured at her wallet on the floor. 'You already know.'

He screwed up his face. 'That's not what I meant. Did *he* send you?'

Brett flicked her gaze to him and then looked back at the woman. 'Who hit me?' The back of her head throbbed with a dull ache.

The young man pointed at his friend, who gave her a nervous smile. 'Sorry, I saw your gun and panicked.'

'You're lucky I didn't shoot you.'

Silence ensued as they considered one another.

Brett frowned and looked back to the youth. 'Did *who* send me?'

He and the woman swapped a look of concern.

'You were the ones that called me, remember?' Brett rubbed the back of her head. 'And then you ran from me.' She pointed at the woman. 'You ran from me.'

'That was you?'

'You said things will go badly for me.' Anger flared when realisation dawned. 'You're the ones who cost me my job!' Brett moved forward, brandishing her gun.

They backed away and the driver scrabbled for her revolver, but Brett reached out and snatched it from her grasp. 'How did you know who my father was? What the fuck is going on?'

The youth's eyes strayed to the body bag that rested on the trolley.

Catching his mistake, Brett held her gun on them and grasped the bag's zipper. She pulled it back to reveal the body of the man she'd just seen executed. Her eyes widened and she swung back onto them. 'Who the hell are you people?'

CHAPTER THIRTY-FIVE

A FEW MILES from the Pelican Bay Supermax State Prison in California, a figure crept through the misty woods. While the forest floor was littered with the decay of leaf and branch, the man made no noise in his passage, slipping amongst the tall trunks of giant redwoods as silent as a predator stalking its prey.

A wolf howled in the distance, sending its eerie cry shivering through the trees and the man paused. Seconds later an answering call confirmed his fears and intensified the need for haste. Moving forward, stealth transformed into a loping run, the terrain slipping past like a forbidden dream. On and on he ran until a clearing appeared out of the gloom, the lights of a vehicle an oasis of bright in an otherwise pitch-black wilderness. Slowing to a stop, his breathing laboured, the man searched heavenward for celestial guidance, only to remember the dust cloud still thwarted such starry shepherds from delivering their earthly divination.

Muttering a prayer to his forefathers, he stepped from his place of hiding and approached the truck, the word *CORONER* on its side just discernable to straining eyes. Careful to keep his presence undetected, he pressed his ear up against the vehicle's cold metal skin and waited for his cue.

CHAPTER THIRTY-SIX

Jessica Klein stared at the gun-toting woman before her, unsure what to say. From what they'd gleaned up to now this was the person they'd been told could help them, but so far she seemed like a dangerous liability. She said she was an FBI agent and Jessica had to admit she did fit the profile. Tall, long overcoat, smart shirt, tailored trousers, and an athletic build more like a man than a woman. She glanced at her young German friend, Eric, who had eyes only for the gun pointed in their direction.

The self-proclaimed government agent swore. 'If someone doesn't start talking, I'm gonna start cracking heads.'

'Jessica?' Eric said, sounding worried.

The agent smiled at the disclosure of the name and then blinked as if seeing Jessica for the first time. Her expression turned into one of conflict as the usual computations took hold. 'Do I know you?'

Jessica sighed. *There goes my anonymity*, she thought, *might as well get it over with*. 'I work – did work – in television.'

The woman's eyebrows rose as recognition slapped her round the face. 'Holy shit, you're that English newsreader, Jessica Klein, the one that got fired for working with terrorists.'

'That was a lie, the GMRC set me up, and besides it was a right-wing group with terrorist ties, not terrorists per se.'

'And I'm supposed to believe that, after you knock me out and pull a gun on me?'

Jessica blinked, she had a point. 'Believe what you like, it's the truth. Are you going to keep waving that thing about or can we call a truce?'

The agent looked at Eric's scared face. 'Fine,' – she made her gun safe and tucked it into her belt – 'but I'm keeping this.' She dropped Jessica's revolver into her coat's inside pocket.

Jessica breathed an internal sigh of relief. Sometimes celebrity status had its plus side, people tended to believe what you said. 'So, Brett, is it? I guess you're confused.'

'You could say that, and pissed. Do you know the punishment for assaulting a federal agent? The only reason I'm not hauling your asses in is because I wanna know whatever *this* is. And what the hell are you doing with this body?'

'I thought you said we cost you your job?' Eric said, looking nervous. 'That means you're no longer an agent, no?'

A strange glint appeared in Brett Taylor's eyes and Jessica sensed danger. She held up a hand to regain the agent's attention. 'Look, we don't know anything about you losing your job, but I can tell you what I know.' *This is going to get complicated*, she thought as Brett turned to regard her with steely eyes. 'Okay,' Jessica continued, 'we were told to go to the courthouse and wait for further instructions. That's all. We didn't call you.'

'Then how come I traced the signal to the van?'

'*Aus diesem Grund*,' Eric said and held up a holographic touch-screen device.

Brett glared at Jessica in consternation.

'Pardon my German friend, when people make him nervous he forgets his English.'

Eric shot her a look of admonishment.

'He said,' – Jessica pointed to the device – 'that's what you traced. But we never spoke to you, we weren't controlling it.'

'So someone else was. Who?'

Jessica groaned. Here came the hard bit. It would have been easier had the woman not been in law enforcement, but it seemed their mysterious puppetmaster continued to pull their strings with a sadistic flare.

'He's our friend,' Eric said butting in. 'A hacker.'

Jessica gave him a look of warning.

Brett sat down next to the body bag. 'You might as well tell me, Ms. Klein, or we can all go to LA and speak to the director of the FBI and see what he has to say.'

Jessica sighed. 'Fine, his name is *Da Muss Ich*, roughly translated, "Because I Can". You've probably heard of him, he was—'

Brett swore. 'Responsible for some of the worst cyber attacks in U.S. history, for stealing millions of dollars and national secrets, which included exposing undercover federal agents.' She bore down on Jessica, pistol raised. 'You said you didn't work with terrorists, B.I.C. is the biggest terrorist there is!'

Jessica shrunk from the agent's ferocity. The petite newsreader could handle herself, but without her gun this woman frightened her. There was something about her eyes, something not quite right. She put her hands up in supplication. 'Calm down, okay, he's a bad guy, I get it—'

'That's a fucking understatement!'

'—but you need to hear what I have to say.'

'Do I? B.I.C. is the most wanted criminal in the United States, probably the world. I should report you right now.' Brett took out her phone. 'In fact, I will.'

Jessica felt her anger rise and she knocked the phone from Brett's hand.

The agent's eyes flared and she grabbed Jessica's throat and thrust her gun forward.

'*Scheisse, stoppen*!' Eric moved to intervene, but Brett turned the gun on him while glaring at Jessica and he backed off.

Jessica lifted a hand to pry the agent's thick fingers away from her neck and Brett seemed to regain her composure and let go. She then took a backward step and crouched down to pick up her phone.

'Look,' Jessica said, as the agent put the device back to her ear, 'I've had a bad couple of months; I've been imprisoned, assaulted, kidnapped and drugged—'

'Taylor, Brett, secure code in, put me through to my nearest field office.'

'—if I'd have known who he was I'd never have got involved with him. He's manipulated me from the outset. I trust him about as far as I could throw this van—'

'Yes, I know, I'm on suspension,' Brett said into the phone, still looking at Jessica.

'—but if you turn us in now you could be condemning millions, perhaps billions, to their death.'

'FBI Sacramento, how may I direct your call?'

Brett paused as the operator spoke again. 'Hello ... Agent Taylor?'

Jessica saw the sincerity of her words had hit home. 'Please, we need you, trust us, trust me.'

Brett held her gaze, considering her plea. 'I'll phone you back,' she said and ended the call.

Jessica let go of her breath. 'Thank you.'

'Don't thank me yet, if I don't like what I hear I'm getting right back on this,' she brandished her phone, 'and I'll have this place crawling with agents quicker than you can blink.'

Jessica gave a nod, her palms sweaty. Usually nothing fazed her. Having worked as a television news anchor for the BBC over many years and as a war correspondent before that, amongst other duties, she had grown a thick skin. Add to that her recent experiences with B.I.C., the hacker extraordinaire who courted worldwide condemnation, and almost anything seemed possible. But she also knew she had to save her family from what she and Eric had discovered with B.I.C.'s help, and she couldn't afford to get locked up – all their lives depended on it.

'*Da Muss Ich*, B.I.C., or Bic, as I call him,' Jessica said, beginning her explanation, 'contacted me after I was fired from my job back in

London. He told me that my friend and colleague who'd been investigating the GMRC had been murdered, and that if I wanted to find out what they were willing to kill for, then I had to go to Germany.'

'And you went, just like that, on his say so?'

Jessica shook her head. 'For years my colleagues have been disappearing without trace or dying in freak accidents with increasing frequency, and not just in the UK but all over the world. Martin's death was one in a long line and I had to make a stand. The media is being controlled like never before and now I know the reason why.'

Brett sat back down. 'Which is?'

'The fallout from the asteroid impact is worse than they're telling us.'

'I could have told you that.'

'No, the food shortages, the water rationing, the dying eco systems, it's not going to get better.'

'That's not what they're saying on the news.'

'I know, because they're told what to say! They always have been. I always have been. Our producers watch us like hawks; any word or report is vetted by the GMRC and UK government. The same goes for your networks, Fox, CNN, they're all controlled, all censored. You're told what they want you to hear so you think what they want you to think. But I know what they've been hiding, at least in part. The GMRC and the world's most powerful nations put by stockpiles for when the impact winter hit, correct?'

'Yeah,' Brett said, 'everyone knows that. They've been telling us for years the impact winter and dust cloud would really slow food production, and it has, just as they predicted.'

'Yes,' Jessica said, 'but why are the shortages getting worse? They had decades to prepare and it's only been a year since the dust cloud formed.'

'They're just making sure we have enough for the future.' Brett folded her arms. 'If this is your argument it's not very convincing.'

Jessica suppressed an angry retort and continued. 'The reason they are getting worse is because all the food is being siphoned off, and the water, too. And that's not all, every resource, every material is being moved and more is taken each day until nothing will be left. We're on the edge of a precipice, the end of the world as we know it.'

'And where is all this mysteriously disappearing food and water going? The man on the moon?'

'Underground bases, massive subterranean complexes, bigger than anything ever built before. I've seen one first-hand on the German-Austrian border. Its size, it's unbelievable, it's—'

Brett chuckled. 'You're serious, aren't you? This Bic has you running in so many circles you'll believe anything he says. I thought journalists looked for truth, not fantasy.'

She picked up her phone again and Jessica got to her feet. 'Wait, it's true! I've seen it, we can prove it. Eric, show her.'

◆

The words Jessica Klein had uttered echoed in Brett's mind ... *if you turn us in now you could be condemning millions, perhaps billions, to their death.* The gravity of the warning mirrored those spoken by the man who now lay dead beside her; could she afford to ignore them again? *Can I just sit here and do nothing? Underground bases, are they insane?* These thoughts and more swirled around her like a toxic shroud.

The young German unfolded his touchscreen's big display and tapped a button to bring up an image on-screen.

Brett felt her stomach churn. She'd seen the emblem before.

Eric, perhaps seeing the impact it had on her, switched to another image. 'And there's more, look.' He pressed play and the picture turned into a video stream.

Brett looked at them in fury. 'Is this some kind of sick joke?'

'What do you mean?' Eric said. 'Look at him, that badge is on his shoulder.' He pointed at the video of a man in an armoured suit, his camouflage glinting in the bright light of a drone that followed him across the top of a building. The soldier returned fire at those who chased him, an FBI S.W.A.T. team.

'That man works in one of these underground bases,' Jessica Klein said, 'USSB Steadfast, a United States Subterranean Base.'

Brett knew this man all too well; the same man who'd kidnapped her and held her hostage. The armour had been close enough to touch, the action a vivid nightmare that had gone on forever.

Eric paused the footage as the fearsome warrior looked up at the camera, green eyes glowing in the dark.

Brett tore her gaze from the image to look at Jessica. 'You don't know, do you?'

'Know what?'

Brett rested an elbow on her knee, *I might as well tell them, everyone else who matters in my life already knows, so why not a couple more?* 'Your friend knows – your terrorist. He set me up. That man,' – she pointed at the image of Colonel Samson – 'is my father.'

'What?!' The newsreader looked at her in shock while the German let out a string of foreign expletives.

Brett turned back to the image and touched the screen to bring up the emblem again. One part of the puzzle dropped into place and then another. *That's why the GMRC wouldn't allow the defendant's jobs to be divulged during the trial, they were working in one of these bases.*

'You were the hostage?' Jessica Klein said. 'Oh my God, and he was your father, that's awful. I'm so sorry.'

Brett stood up, her emotions in turmoil. 'Don't be, he's a monster.' She gestured at the prone body of the old man. 'Much like him.'

Jessica indicated for Eric to put the screen away. 'Yes, but we don't think Professor Steiner, him,' – she nodded to the body – 'just worked in one of these bases, or even ran one. We think – no, we know – he had a seat on the GMRC Directorate itself, he probably controlled them all.'

Brett gazed at the old man's face, the pale sheen on his skin detracting from the expression of peace that had settled upon him. *Perhaps the death penalty gave him a release he didn't deserve.* The thought depressed her. *Those that welcome death should be left to suffer in torment; this murdering bastard has escaped while my father lives, where is the justice in that?* 'It explains his demeanour,' she said, 'he smacked of power.'

'You spoke to him?' Eric said.

Brett nodded.

Jessica touched her arm. 'You believe us, then?

'Do I believe they work for some secret collaboration run by the government and the GMRC? Yes. Do I believe the world is at an end? No.'

'What?' Jessica said, shocked. 'How can you not, after what we've shown and told you?'

'Quite easily. One, most of your information comes from a known criminal. Two, despite what you've seen, or think you've seen, the government doesn't go about starving its citizens to death; if anything was going on, I'd have heard about it. And three, if you want to hear it enough, you can convince yourself of anything, and you seem like someone who believes anything she's told. In fact, you admitted as much – how long did you spew out the BBC's lies for?'

'What? That's tosh! Just because I read it doesn't mean I believed it, it was my job. I see that now.'

'Now being the operative word.'

Jessica scowled at her, but Brett knew she had her; there was no arguing with logic. A noise outside the truck made her tense. 'Did you hear that?'

'Hear what?' The newsreader, still fuming, glanced at Eric, who gave a shrug.

'Wait here.' Brett opened the rear doors and stepped out into the dark, gun in hand. She peered around both sides of the vehicle, but nothing stirred.

Moments ticked by before a mournful cry sent the skin on her arms to tingling. She climbed back into the interior and slammed shut the doors. 'Damn wolves.'

'Agent – Brett – please,' Jessica said, moving towards her, 'you have to believe us. If Bic wants you working with us he did it for a reason. We need you, I need you. I have to protect my family and get them into one of those bases.'

'Good luck with that.' Brett activated her phone and redialled the previous number.

NO SIGNAL

She swore and opened the doors again to hold her phone aloft. The dust cloud was playing havoc with the satellite replacement relays again. *The sooner they get more drones in the sky, the better.*

Jessica followed her out into the open. 'Please, I'm begging you, reconsider.'

Brett ignored her. She knew if she could provide a lead that could catch the Notorious B.I.C., as she'd heard him called, then she could use it as leverage to get her job back, or at least find work in another agency. This was her ticket back into the game; if she threw it away she'd regret it for the rest of her life. *Still no signal. I'll have to take them in myself.* And for that she'd need the spare handcuffs from the trunk of her car. 'Okay, I'll give you another chance, but I'll need to speak directly with Bic or no deal.'

'Can we do that?' Jessica turned to Eric, who appeared sceptical. 'Yes,' she said, 'we can do that.'

'Good, you contact him and I'll bring my car round.'

'You won't regret this, Agent, thank you!'

No, but you will, Brett thought, *dumb bitch. And I thought the British were supposed to be intelligent, so much for girl power.* As she walked to her car she almost felt sorry for them. And she might have if it hadn't been for their involvement with the biggest terrorist known to man. Instead they'd get what was coming to them, a pair of cuffs and a nice cosy interrogation room. And while they gave up their secrets, Brett would be taken in from the cold, a just reprieve for hard work rendered. Everyone was a winner; well, nearly everyone. She smiled to herself before the lights to her car bloomed into life. Brett ran forwards, but it was too late. The car's wheels kicked up a cloud of dust into her face and sped off down the road. Brett fired off three shots, taking out the rear screen, but the vehicle continued on without deviation.

She looked up at the sky. 'Fuck!'

CHAPTER THIRTY-SEVEN

THE TAILLIGHTS of Brett's stolen car disappeared round a bend in the road and she wondered if anything else could go wrong. Hanging her head, she sighed, and then returned to the truck. The rear doors stood closed, but it was what was written on them that confounded her. In the dirt, someone had used their finger to scrawl eight words:

Knock
and it shall
be opened
unto you

Yanking on the handles revealed Jessica and her cohort, Eric, looking fearful inside.

'What happened?' Jessica said.

'It doesn't matter. I want to speak to your friend, Bic, right now!'

Brett stood with hands on hips, her mood sour, while Jessica tried to get in touch with their *friend* via the touchscreen device.

As she waited, Brett looked around for suitable cabling with which to secure her prisoners-to-be.

After some moments a bleep from the portable computer brought a jubilant raised fist from the young German. '*Ja, er ist hier!*'

Brett moved closer.

'He's replied,' Jessica said and handed her the display.

The screen had two lines of text on it and the second ended with a flashing cursor.

Bic, where are you? We need your help. We've made contact with an FBI Agent called Brett Taylor. I assume you meant for us to meet, however she doesn't believe what we say. She needs convincing! Jessica

I am here, Jessica Klein. Tell her to speak into the device _

Brett glanced at Jessica and Eric, who watched her in anticipation. She knew she had to choose her words with care; this individual was dangerous and highly intelligent. From what she'd read about him in the past, he could lead those that followed his demands on a merry dance; and it was assumed B.I.C. was a *him* from profiling carried out by the NSA and FBI.

She cleared her throat. 'B.I.C., Bic, what is it you want from me?'

Eric has shown you the footage of your father? _

. . .

'Yes. Why did you send those files to my boss?' she said, failing to keep the anger from her voice. 'And where did you get them from?'

Forgive me, Brett Taylor, but I did warn you of the consequences of ignoring my request _

'That's bullshit and you know it. How could you ever expect me to resign on the back of a phone call from a stranger? In fact, you knew that, didn't you? You were going to sell me out regardless.'

The terrorist failed to respond. Then letters appeared, chasing the cursor across the screen.

I see there is no fooling you, Brett Taylor. You are correct. That is why I was left with no choice. You are crucial to our plans; the preservation of the species is at stake _

Brett glanced at her audience of two. 'So they tell me. Why me *exactly*?'

Why? Because you are a fully qualified and experienced FBI agent, and also because you saw your father's armour. You interacted both with him and his superior, Professor George Steiner; this makes you much more able to accept the truth we tell you. You may also have vital information that can help us. Anything they said to you, or to each other, could be priceless clues as to the secrets they hold _

'Hang on; I thought you knew their secrets? The stockpiles are depleted, underground bases, death to us all.'

. . .

You don't sound convinced, Brett Taylor _

'I am,' – she berated herself for her lapse; she had to try and keep up the pretence of belief – 'but I'm still sceptical, I admit. That's why I wanted to speak to you, to improve my understanding. The more I learn, the more I can accept. So, what other information is the government and GMRC hiding from us?'

I am unsure. I only know my computations do not add up. Something is missing. We need to know more so we can act appropriately. Jessica Klein needs to save her family, she must have the full knowledge of the GMRC's cover-up otherwise she may put her family in greater risk than they are now, her daughters Daniela and Victoria are counting on her, as is her husband, Evan _

Photos of the disgraced BBC newsreader and her family scrolled across the screen, and Brett looked at Jessica. She knew what Bic was trying to do, elicit sympathy and make Jessica's plight more real. It would have worked had Brett not been trained to be emotionally detached, to inspect the facts as they presented themselves. It also helped that she could be a cold-hearted bitch, or so she'd been told by some of her old partners, both romantic *and* professional.

'They did say something that made me think,' Brett said, knowing truth mixed with lies strengthened her hand.

And what was that, Brett Taylor? _

'There were actually two things. One must relate to your theory on the resources. Colonel Samson, my dear father, told me I was making a mistake; he said my life was in danger.' Brett gauged the expressions of Jessica and Eric as she spoke. 'And I believe your two colleagues here think the colonel is dead, but you and I know differently, don't we, Bic?'

Jessica and Eric looked stunned by the news and Bic's response took some time to appear.

You are sharper than I thought, Brett Taylor. What gave me away? _

It was just a hunch on Brett's part, but she wasn't going to tell Bic that. *Let him stew*, she thought. It would also sow seeds of discontent between him and his two followers. 'I'll leave that for you to work out.'

And the second thing they said? _

'This is what the old man – Professor Steiner, as you call him – said. He and Samson were arguing and he said, 'You don't care about anything, that's the problem. You murder innocent people like slaughtering cattle and disobey my direct orders, effectively condemning hundreds of thousands of civilians to a premature death.'

Interesting. Hundreds of thousands, not millions, or billions, you are sure that is what he said? _

'Yes, that's exactly as he said it. Is it helpful?'

Perhaps _

. . .

Brett took that as a yes. 'So, Bic, how are we supposed to find out what else the GMRC is up to? My father has been spirited away. Unless you know where he is?' Her heart raced as she waited to see if her second hunch paid off.

I do not, Brett Taylor. However, we do not need your father _

'And why's that?'

Why interrogate the pawn when you can petition the king? _

'What?'

I must go, Brett Taylor. I look forward to speaking to you again _

'What? No, wait!' The screen went dark and Brett swore.

Eric accepted the device back off her and Brett pondered the cyber terrorist's final words.

Jessica moved closer. 'What do you think now?'

'I don't know, but—' A thought struck her and she turned to face the corpse that lay unmoving in its black bag.

Jessica came to stand by her side and looked down at the old man. 'All our questions will soon be within reach.'

'The king—' Brett whispered.

'—was dead,' Jessica said, 'long live the king.'

TERMINOLOGY / MAP

USSB – United States Subterranean Base
GMRC – Global Meteor Response Council
Darklight – World's largest private security contractor
SFSD – Special Forces Subterranean Detachment (*Terra Force*)
SED – Sanctuary Exploration Division
Deep Reach – Special survey team working within the SED
S.I.L.V.E.R. – An elite military unit available to the highest bidder
Sanctuary Proper – Ancient underground structure built by an extinct species of Hominid, Homo giganthropsis (the Anakim)

USSB
STEADFAST
NEVADA
UTAH
COLORADO
CALIFORNIA
Las Vegas
USA
Los Angeles
ARIZONA
NEW
MEXICO
TEXAS
MEXICO
USSB
SANCTUARY

CHAPTER THIRTY-EIGHT

DEEP in the bowels of the Earth the Anakim creation sprawled, layer upon layer of chambers, tunnels, caves, cliffs and crevasses. So vast was this underground world, the surface area of its many levels was said to equal half that of all the land mass on Earth. Stretching for hundreds of miles north to south and east to west, Sanctuary also cut a swathe into the Earth's crust thirty miles straight down, its lowest fringes rubbing shoulders with the molten rock of the mantle itself.

Nestling in one of the largest chambers, small in comparison to the whole, but immense in its own right, was a hidden city that comprised hundreds of soaring towers that stood silent and still in the pitch-black. To the east of this abandoned dwelling full of long forgotten ghosts, the surface of a deep, cold subterranean lake rippled as something briefly broke its calm. Fanning out in procession from this disturbance, telltale expanding circles announced the presence of something lurking beneath to anyone or anything that had borne witness. A mile away at the shore's distant edge, a few thousand men and women toiled under floodlights powered by high-tech, water fuelled generators. The sound of shouting and chatter created by teamwork filled the air as the desperate refugees from

Steadfast sought to feed themselves and their brethren from the plentiful fish stocks of Sanctuary seeded millennia past. To the south of this hive of activity, separated by a dark void of featureless ground, was a makeshift camp that had become home to the thirty thousand people that had found themselves trapped inside Sanctuary Proper.

Amongst the scarce lighting rigs and small tents, a central command post had been erected, its fabric construction now a permanent structure as necessity dictated. Above this material that undulated against a silent breeze, flew the proud sigil of the world's largest private security firm:

Inside the shelter a number of armoured, black clad soldiers carried out their duties which included the day to day running of the site. Food and water had to be allocated and dispensed while the mounting medical woes of the residents required careful maintenance. Such was their isolation from civilisation – be that from the seemingly unobtainable location of the USSB, or the surface itself – supplies had all but run dry.

A soldier walked into the outpost and approached the small form of a woman who stood poring over a computer screen and a set of complicated looking graphs. He handed her a document. Glancing at its contents she looked up in alarm. 'That's the second person this week.'

'Yes, ma'am, he had a rare heart condition and his drug supply ran out a month back.'

'And there was nothing we could do?'

'Not with the resources we have.'

Dr. Kara Vandervoort sighed and looked back at the image of the person who had died. Arnold McIntyre, the name read underneath, a twenty-four year old civilian who'd worked in the command centre back at USSB Steadfast. She wondered if he'd left any family behind on the surface prior to his inclusion in the GMRC's Subterranean Programme. Was there someone waiting for Arnold to return to them? Was his disappearance from their life as unexplained as the work he'd been tasked to carry out?

Cover stories for all personnel inducted into any USSB had always been part of the transition from the surface; however, some people suited the upheaval more than others. Due to the nature and location of their work, civilians and U.S. military personnel alike had to pass rigorous physical, medical and physiological tests in order to enter the Subterranean Programme, but some, due to the nature of the skills they could bring to the table, had been given special dispensation for the good of the project. And it was these unfortunate souls who were the first to pay the price for their underground marooning.

It was at these low moments that Kara wished her doctorate wasn't in biomechanical engineering, the science of her learning of no help to those that suffered. All she could do was concentrate on what she was good at, which was the management of others and the analysis of data, providing those that battled on with the most efficient means by which to live.

She ran a hand through her browning locks, the blond dye all but grown out. 'Does Richard know?'

'The Director is still in the city,' the soldier said.

Kara muttered a curse. Ever since the *light creature*, or *entity* as some called it, had killed three Darklight soldiers and spirited away one of their number – a young disabled woman – the man she'd grown to love had succumbed to a malady of his mind's own creation. The warnings had been there in the past that he was susceptible to such a collapse in reasoning, but she had thought they were minor aberrations despite his protestations to the contrary. Now, though, she saw his tenure in the dark abyss had finally taken its toll as he'd once prophesied, the trauma of recent events driving him over the edge. He still claimed to be rational, but Kara could see through the illusion of purpose he'd created for himself.

Unable to help find the vulnerable woman who'd been taken from them while under his care, he had taken to roaming the Anakim city in search of answers, accompanied as ever by the dark skinned African, Major Offiah, who now led the Darklight forces in his leader's absence.

'How long has he been gone?' Kara said, her South African accent strained.

The soldier consulted with a colleague. 'He left with a team early yesterday morning. They're scheduled to return in three days.'

'Three days!'

'That's what we were told.'

'And where's the Major,' she said, 'still running around after him?'

The Darklight man looked uncomfortable. 'The Major is in the field, ensuring our perimeter is secure.'

'But he'll be back with Richard as soon as he's done?'

'I believe his route will intersect with the Director's at certain intervals, yes.'

Kara frowned. Since the Darklight leader Commander Hilt had left with his best soldiers in search of Susan and the thing that had taken her, the camp and everyone in it felt exposed. However, the absence of the warrior who'd been Richard's right hand man during their time in Sanctuary Proper wasn't the only reason for their perceived vulnerability. The knowledge that something else roamed the darkness alongside them, something terrible and capable of taking out heavily armed mercenaries was more than something to fear, it was a monster come to life, a terror in the deep that seemed capable of disappearing at will and formulating devious plans of attack. If there was a time when they should be sticking together it was now, but it seemed like she'd been left holding the reigns of power while people looked to others for guidance. In charge of the ecosystem back in Steadfast she had been responsible for a lot of people, but here things were entirely different. Not only were they fighting for survival in an alien world, it felt like they were fighting each other as they stumbled from one crisis to another.

'Have the new sanitation trenches been dug?' Kara asked another operative.

The woman glanced up and shook her head. 'They'll take another week.'

'What about the water stocks, have we met the quotas?'

'No, since the attack from the ... entity, we've had to limit the number of teams leaving the campsite.'

'There's also been an incident at the lake,' the first soldier said, 'four people were attacked, all have multiple lacerations.'

Kara felt her stomach churn. 'The light?'

'No, it sounded like it was some kind of eel.'

She heaved a sigh, but her disquiet remained.

The Darklight operative cleared his throat to regain her attention. 'There's more ma'am, there's been an outbreak of an unknown illness in the south eastern section of the camp.'

'Illness?'

'Vomiting and diarrhoea. It might be a batch of bad fish, or—'

'Or what?'

'Cholera.'

'What about the purifiers?'

'We only brought a few from the surface; we never thought we'd be down here this long and it takes teams of people working round the clock to keep everyone watered. Due to this some of the civilians have taken to boiling their water and we suspect, if it is Cholera, this could be the cause.'

'Do we have any antibiotics left?'

'No, none.'

Kara felt despair rising, nothing seemed to be going right, something needed to change. 'Can you get a message to Richard for me?'

'We'll try, ma'am, but it may take a few hours if they're out of direct transmission range.'

'Okay, tell him we've lost someone else and he's needed back at camp – I need him back at camp, and not in three days, but *now*.'

The soldier gave a nod and got on the radio.

Kara went back to poring over the data but her focus remained on the problems at hand and their missing leader. *Where are you, Richard?* she thought. *I can't do this without you.*

CHAPTER THIRTY-NINE

RICHARD GOODWIN, the exiled civilian director of USSB Steadfast, ran his hands over the dry, dusty soil to reveal the faint outline of ancient inscriptions. He bent low to inspect it and then blew along stone channels to chase away the dirt. On his hands and knees, Goodwin picked up a brush and swept the area clean until the pattern he'd found emerged in its entirety.

'It looks like the ones we found earlier.'

The voice made Goodwin start; immersed in his investigation he'd forgotten he was not alone. He looked up into the eyes of the woman who'd spoken. 'I think you're right.' He got to his feet and stood by her side to view his latest discovery. 'Do the symbols look familiar to you?'

Rebecca shook her head.

Goodwin was sure he'd seen something similar on the surface, although how that could be he wasn't sure because – as far as he was aware – human and Anakim cultures were mutually exclusive. 'I know someone who'd know.'

'Kara?' Rebecca said.

'Sadly, no; his name is Professor Steiner.'

'The man who told you to leave USSB Steadfast?'

'The same. If he hadn't done so we'd still be there, trapped underground.'

'Like we are here?'

Goodwin grimaced. Rebecca had a point, but those left in Steadfast beneath the New Mexican and Colorado border faced – as hard as it was to believe – a much more immediate threat than they did in Sanctuary Proper. Now they at least had water and a food source, and while the mysterious light had transformed their dark tomb into a nightmare, those in Steadfast faced annihilation by an asteroid, one of four due to arrive in 2042.

As ever, Goodwin kept the information about these approaching destroyers of Earth's surface to himself, that and the knowledge that two more much larger ones would follow in their wake in 2045. His decision to tell only the Darklight leader, Commander Hilt, about the coming apocalypse had been a difficult one, but he'd felt more bad news for anyone else would foster despair when they needed hope.

'I have every faith the commander will find a way through to USSB Sanctuary,' Goodwin said, making sure to avoid the sensitive subject of Susan, the mentally handicapped woman taken by the light from under their noses, the same woman Hilt had promised to Goodwin he would return to safety.

Rebecca didn't reply; instead her gaze strayed to the figure of her ward, Joseph, who suffered from an acute learning disability. The young man, who had the intelligence and behaviour patterns of a toddler, was busy entertaining some of the Darklight troops who protected Goodwin's party from the threat of the elusive light.

Major Offiah had insisted on no fewer than a hundred bodyguards for any excursions into the city, the soldiers all fully suited in their black armour and sporting an array of armaments suitable for war. So far, no further sightings of the creature that shimmered in the dark had been made, although that might have been because all reconnaissance teams had been recalled in order to protect those at the lake and camp. Their primary mission – escape from the enormous chamber they found themselves trapped in – had taken a back seat to the immediate safety of its reluctant citizens.

Ever since Hilt had left on his mission over a week before, Goodwin had resolved to do everything he could to unravel the riddle of the light, to find out what it was and what it wanted. Those in the camp had voiced their opposition to his new focus, and that included both Major Offiah and Goodwin's partner, Kara. However, Goodwin knew his efforts took precedence, how could they not? He also knew that Kara thought him obsessed, and perhaps she was right. He needed something to occupy his mind and the day to day management of the camp wasn't enough to fulfil that duty; he was used to managing a base of half a million people. But that wasn't the only reason he lusted after a complex challenge; he needed a change of scene. Back in USSB Steadfast he'd employed a variety of measures to curtail the chronic and sometimes acute depression he experienced due to his sustained underground existence. A powerful 3D screen had been fitted to his office to recreate the surface and he'd also been able to visit the bio-chambers in order to soak up the rays from Steadfast's sunlight generators. Compare that to the eternal dark of Sanctuary and he'd done well to fight off the desolation for as long as he had.

'How is Joseph?' Goodwin said, forgetting he was trying to avoid the subject of Susan.

Rebecca glanced over to where the young man played. 'He's okay.'

Joseph held a transparent bottle above his head and tilted it this way and that. Every now and then he showed it to his Darklight minders, before laughing in pure, unadulterated joy.

'What's he doing?' Goodwin said. 'He's been messing about with that water for hours.'

'He can't understand how the fluid stays level inside the bottle when he moves it,' Rebecca said. 'He has no concept of what gravity is, for him it's like magic or an impossible puzzle.'

'He seems to be enjoying himself.'

'Yes, I suppose. He's fine during the day; it's the sleeping that's the problem.'

'Nightmares?'

'Sometimes he screams so loud it feels like he could wake the dead.'

'I didn't hear him last night.'

'He seems much better here. I think you're the cause.'

'Me?'

Joseph saw them looking over at him and he waved in an exuberant fashion, eliciting a smile from Rebecca and a return wave from Goodwin.

'You know how he dotes on you,' she said, 'he always goes on about his Winnie.'

Goodwin smiled at his nickname, the feeling odd due to his current low mood, like the expression of humour was disconnected from his face somehow.

'That's why I wanted to be here,' Rebecca continued, 'with you. He seems to calm down when you're around.'

'I'm glad someone feels that way. Normally when I'm like this people want to get as far away from me as possible.'

Rebecca gave him an odd look. 'I haven't noticed any difference.'

'Then you're the only one.'

Rebecca stayed silent for a moment before removing something from her pocket and handing it to him.

Goodwin flicked through the thin sheaves of paper which had been scrawled upon with black charcoal. 'Joseph's handiwork?'

She smiled. 'Yes, he wanted you to have them. He was quite insistent.'

He turned one of them round. 'What are they of?'

'I have no idea. He spent hours on them, though, and got quite angry when I tried to get him to stop for meals.'

Goodwin folded them up and slid them into his back pocket before an itchy tingle on his wrist made him scratch at it.

Rebecca saw the movement and pulled up his sleeve to reveal a red rash. 'You should have that looked at.'

Goodwin glanced down at the angry mark. 'It's nothing.'

'You've been scratching at it all day.'

'Have I?' He turned his focus back to the image on the floor. He was sure the symbols looked like something he'd seen before ... or was it the lines that accompanied them that sparked the sense of familiarity? He withdrew his mobile computer and took a photo. *Perhaps Kara or someone else at the camp will know.*

'You do know the dangers of being out here, don't you?' he said. 'You'd be safer back at camp.'

'Helping you keeps our mind off things.' Rebecca looked around at the shadowy forms of their armed escort, who stood alert in the gloom. 'And besides, if these soldiers can't protect us then I doubt the camp would be much safer, do you?'

Goodwin gave a downturn of his mouth. He'd spoken out of habit rather than genuine concern, trying to keep up the pretence of a humanity he supposedly possessed. He moved to stand beneath a portable floodlight to bathe in its glow and closed his eyes to imagine its heat came from the sun.

'Director, sir.'

Goodwin looked around to see the svelte figure of Lieutenant Gabriela Manaus, the Darklight officer in charge of his protection.

She hesitated as he gazed at her, perhaps unused to his dour demeanour and lack of manners – *like I care*, he thought.

'Recon Alpha has located something of interest to the west,' the lieutenant told him.

'Such as?'

'I'm not sure, an artefact, but you said you wanted them to look for anything unusual, something that might help us understand the entity, and the Anakim themselves.'

A deep rumble of noise drew everyone's attention to the enormous tower that stood at the centre of the metropolis a mere hundred yards away.

'Cover your eyes!' Manaus shouted.

A roar of sound and a flash of light erupted into being. Goodwin closed his eyes before a powerful purple radiance tore up the side of the two mile high, crystalline edifice. Moments later, another wave of energy pulsed forth, sending Goodwin's skin to tingling. He shielded his eyes and craned his neck to see the electricity fire up to the ceiling of the chamber a further mile above the spire's summit, the branches of lightning fanning out in all directions before dying back to black.

It was this very phenomenon that had drawn Goodwin to the centre of the city. It was no coincidence that this process had started when the entity had revealed itself to them. Goodwin himself had been one of the first people to see the ethereal light creature. Unaware of what they pursued, he and Kara had followed it into the city on their own. Only when it had turned on them did they realise the threat it posed, and only after it had taken Susan and killed three Darklight soldiers did it become universally accepted that the shimmering light had to be stopped. Of course, the prodigious Darklight leader, Commander Hilt, had proven up to the task, setting off to hunt it down, or to die trying. This act of valour, while admirable, had condemned Goodwin to a condition of perpetual torment, his remaining calm eaten away by worry for the welfare of those around him, and for poor Susan, who'd been abducted by the monstrosity. Unable to bear the mundanity of running the camp – and to escape his impotency to ease their suffering – he'd set off in search of answers, any answers.

After Hilt left it had dawned on Goodwin how much he'd been relying on the Darklight leader. Just his brooding presence was enough to make it seem like the impossible was possible. He was also the only person who he felt he could speak openly to, free from the fear of disclosing the surface apocalypse to come. Major Offiah was a competent leader, but he wasn't Hilt, *but then who is?* Goodwin reasoned. And then there was Kara, the South African beauty who'd made life in the black abyss almost bearable. He relied on her, too, but he'd failed to confide in her as he had with Hilt. He couldn't bring himself to destroy the optimism that seemed to exude from her tanned skin like an invisible glow. Kara's ability to lift his mood had been the one thing that had been keeping his depression at bay, to destroy that would be to destroy himself. He knew that such a secret could end their relationship, but he'd tried to deny such thoughts, concentrating on the far more urgent need to get everyone to the safety of Sanctuary's elusive USSB.

Still shielding his eyes from the blaze of light wreathed around the tower's base, Goodwin watched the remarkable sight as the energy rippled up the tower once more.

Lieutenant Manaus moved closer. 'Sir, we should move. We still don't know what effect this energy could have on us.'

Goodwin stayed bathing in the dazzling light, his mood lifting.

'Richard,' Rebecca said, touching his arm.

Reluctantly he turned away and followed the two women as they rejoined the bulk of their force. At the same time, Joseph came wandering over to hold Rebecca's hand, his attention fixed on the awe-inspiring tower behind.

Moving off at a brisk walk, the black clad mercenaries formed a roving perimeter around them, weapons at the ready and visors lowered, their combat systems glowing blue in the dark like the eyes of demons.

'And we still don't know what causes it?' Rebecca said to the lieutenant.

'No, it seems the source of the tower's power is located underground.'

A thought struck Goodwin. 'Have you tried tapping into it?'

Manaus raised her visor, her expression surprised and a little concerned. 'No, sir. You asked us to do that a few days ago. Don't you remember?'

Goodwin waved a dismissive hand. 'Yes, yes, of course.' *Did I?* he thought as they continued on in silence. Thinking back, he couldn't recall asking any such thing. *That's because I had more important things to do*, he told himself.

'Why couldn't you tap into it, Lieutenant?' Rebecca said, breaking the awkward moment. 'What was the reason?'

'We determined it was too risky and the sporadic nature of the event made it an unreliable power source.'

Rebecca and the Darklight officer continued to talk and a minute later the tower's light show ceased, plunging them back into darkness and eliciting a grunt of displeasure from Joseph. Goodwin knew how he felt, he could have done with soaking up the precious rays for longer and his mood plummeted as they made their way through the forbidding city, their path now lit by the dim glow of the soldiers' in-built helmet torches. Unlike before, his fear of the creature that stalked the blackness was numbed, like the rest of his senses. He could tell, however, that the men and women around him didn't feel such calm; their movements sharp and alert, ready for the unexpected. *Ready for death*, his mind taunted him.

After a two hour trek through the city's silent avenues they joined up with another substantial force of Darklight mercenaries, their number greater than Goodwin had been expecting. At their head stood the form of Major Offiah, the newly crowned Darklight leader, his black armour glinting alongside the three hundred men at his back.

'What news, Major?' Goodwin said, as the two forces became one.

Manaus saluted her superior and made way for Offiah, who fell into step alongside Goodwin. 'May we speak in private, sir?' the major said.

Goodwin sighed and the two men moved out of earshot of those around them.

'So, what's with the cloak and dagger?' Goodwin said.

'Sir?'

'Nothing, just get on with it, man.'

A flicker of unease crossed the soldier's features. 'We've still had no contact from the commander, but there's been no sign of the entity. It seems our fears of there being more than one were unfounded.'

'And you think such news should be kept private, do you, Major?'

Offiah glanced back at Rebecca and the lieutenant. 'Yes, sir, don't you? We need to keep the civilians calm. If they thought we suspected there might be more than one of those things out there, we could have a panic on our hands.'

Goodwin rubbed his eyes while a headache throbbed through his temple. 'So it's good news for a change; that's something, I suppose.'

'It's more than something, sir. One of those things could be enough to take out – well – it could decimate our whole force, for all we know. Its capabilities are untested. We know very little.'

'We know it's attracted to the glowing blue stones,' Goodwin said.

'That's true, although the hypothesis is still relatively untested.'

'Hilt seemed to feel otherwise.'

Offiah remained silent, perhaps unwilling to criticise his absent leader.

'And it's capable of withstanding direct gunfire,' Goodwin continued. 'It can manipulate our technology and apparently outsmart us, too. It can appear and vanish at will. It breathes, from what I remember; it can move quickly and can at the very least submerge in water. It's able to corral a defenceless person and take out a forty strong survey team, along with military support in the form of highly trained, well-armed Special Forces commandos. Have I missed anything?'

Offiah shook his head.

'Then to say we know very little is not accurate and I intend to find out more. If it comes back we'll be ready, do you hear me, Major?'

'Yes, sir.'

'Good. Now, is there anything else, or can I actually look at what I've just walked miles to see?'

Offiah stepped aside and Goodwin moved back to the rest of the company.

'And they still haven't found any more of the glowing stones, Major?' Rebecca said after the Darklight man had rejoined them.

'No, ma'am. The location at the lakeshore where you originally found them was searched with a fine toothcomb, as was the surrounding area. All civilian personnel have also been told to stay vigilant for any sightings, but as yet nothing.'

The conversation continued and Goodwin tuned out until he was shown the object they'd come to see.

'We found it by chance,' a Darklight recon leader was saying, 'one of our men literally tripped over it.'

Goodwin bent down to inspect it. Measuring ten metres long and five high it appeared to be made of granite, its dark, dusty surface smooth to the touch. A jagged outline had been uncovered from the compacted earth and strange carvings adorned its interior.

'I need more light.' Goodwin waved a hand and moments later the scene illuminated. He stood up. Curious creatures lined the outer edge while the upper left quadrant depicted a cluster of symbols arranged in two sweeping arcs, one following behind the other with a space in-between.

'This is what you brought me here to see?' Goodwin looked at Lieutenant Manaus and then Offiah, his eyes demanding an answer.

The recon leader moved past Manaus and pointed at the symbols. 'Can't you see it, sir?' he said. 'Look, they're part of a map.'

'A map of what?'

The soldier looked at his major, uncertain.

'A map of the city,' Offiah said, intervening, 'at least the centre of the city.'

'I don't see it,' Goodwin said.

'It's a radial pattern. They are two of its arms. It's as I told you the other day, the centre of the city is laid out in the form of a spiral.'

Goodwin remained pensive. What is he talking about? I don't remember him telling me anything of the sort. Are they testing me, he wondered, or worse, trying to make me look incompetent?

'So it's a map?' Rebecca said.

Goodwin's interest refocused. A map, this is what he was searching for. Something like this may lead them to the USSB. He crouched back down. 'Where's the rest of it?'

'This seems to be it,' the recon leader said.

Goodwin ran his hands around the edge, searching beneath the thick slab by touch, and everyone else watched as he worked his way round.

'They've already looked, Richard,' Rebecca said.

Goodwin glanced up at her and she gave him a small smile.

'Someone give me something to dig with.' He held out his hand and a soldier passed him a collapsible shovel. Unhinging it, Goodwin dug into the hard earth to the left of the stone slab. Minutes passed and the Darklight contingent filtered away, leaving him to his work while Rebecca stayed nearby. The sound of more digging made him pause. Looking round he saw Joseph had also sourced a shovel and now moved to work alongside him. The young man gave him a broad grin and Goodwin gave him a nod of recognition. It seemed someone still believed in him.

Side by side, the two men tore at the ground until Joseph's tool clanked down onto something hard. He froze, eyes round in wonder and shock and Goodwin eased him aside to see what he'd found.

'What is it, Richard? Has he found something?'

'I'm not sure.'

Piece by piece and chunk by chunk, another section of the map appeared. It was deeper down than the first, but still very much in existence.

Goodwin looked up at her. 'Get the Major, we need help.'

Excited, Rebecca hurried away.

◆

Hours later, and with a workforce numbering two hundred, the men and women of Darklight aided Goodwin, Joseph and Rebecca in exposing the hidden monument that lay up to two feet below the surface. At the edge of vision, the remaining soldiers stood guarding them, guns at the ready, while four Anakim towers beyond formed the boundary to the square plaza buried beneath their feet. With an array of lighting rigs set up, the monstrous size of the structure that had lain hidden for what could have been a thousand generations or longer emerged from the dry earth.

Goodwin's arms ached as he continued to toil while others flagged. Sweat dripped from his brow and soaked his dirt-covered shirt, but he couldn't stop now; this could be the answer to their prayers.

He dumped another shovel full of soil onto a growing mound as Rebecca held out a canteen to him. 'You better have some water,' she said in concern, 'you haven't had a break in hours.'

Goodwin shook his head and increased his work rate until a hand on his arm made him pause. Joseph passed him a bottle of water and Goodwin – unable to refuse his loyal assistant – accepted the offering and drank long and deep. The cool liquid felt good, as did the cease in movement. He looked around at what they'd achieved. The sparkling granite plaque stretched away in all directions, some sections glistening with the sheen of pristine metal.

'It's a bit like the Elgin Marbles don't you think?' Rebecca said. 'Like a horizontal frieze.'

She was right; the high relief design resembled the marbles that had once adorned the Parthenon of Greece, except these were on a different scale. The shapes of various Anakim figures dwarfed those that worked to uncover them, and while the full spiral map had long since been revealed, Goodwin had pressed on, insisting further detail could be found that would help them in their quest for knowledge. As time went by, however, it had become apparent that no further depictions of the city or of the surrounding area would be forthcoming, the relief favouring the ornate rather than the factual.

Major Offiah approached. 'Sir, we've had an urgent message from Dr. Vandervoort, she's requesting your immediate return to camp.'

Goodwin walked away to look at the spiral carving of the city and Offiah followed. 'Director, did you hear me? We need to go back. Someone has died, and a variety of issues need your attention.'

'Died? Was it the light?'

'No, a lack of medication.'

'Then there's nothing to be done.' He traced the spiral arms of the map with a finger, the shapes comprised of symbols denoting the surrounding structures.

'Sir, I have to insist—'

'Insist, Major?' Goodwin said, continuing his inspection. 'I think you'll find I'm the only director here, or hadn't you noticed?'

'Sir, I know that, but—'

'No buts, ifs or maybes, Major. We stay. There's too much at stake to do otherwise.'

'Director, forgive me, but there's nothing here to help us.'

Goodwin stood up. 'Did I just hear a "but" in there, Major?'

'It's just some old relic,' Offiah said, 'even the map is useless to us. We must return—'

'Must?'

'We *should* return. Dr. Vandervoort—'

'Is not in charge, I am. And what I say goes. If you feel you need to return to camp to help, then by all means do so, but you'll leave me with the force I was allocated and I'll return as scheduled. Is that clear, Major?'

Offiah glanced at Rebecca, who looked shocked by Goodwin's words. 'Clear as crystal, sir.'

The Darklight major strode away, issuing orders as he went.

'I don't think Kara would say it was urgent if it wasn't,' Rebecca said, watching as the majority of the mercenaries assembled to leave.

'Kara can deal with the camp; she's more than capable, as are those by her side. This is more important.' Goodwin returned his attention to the frieze, now notably devoid of workers. The unearthing process had increased the visible area to a large square about half the size of a football pitch, but the enormity of the designs made it difficult to resolve from up close.

Goodwin looked around and spied a cluster of fallen statues next to one of the towers and a large, barren plinth that had once supported them. Dropping his shovel, he walked over to it and Rebecca and Joseph followed.

Lieutenant Manaus joined them while the plaza emptied of most of her comrades, who returned with Offiah to camp. 'I hear you've decided to stay, sir.'

'Give me a hand up will you, Lieutenant?'

Manaus interlaced her hands and boosted her director up the side of the platform. Goodwin grasped the ledge and hauled himself onto it. Joseph, not one to be left behind, held up his hands from below and Goodwin reached down to him.

Anxious, Rebecca stepped forward. 'Be careful, Joseph.'

Stronger than he looked, the tall form of the young mentally handicapped man scrambled up alongside Goodwin, before turning to look down at his carer. 'Come, Becca.'

Rebecca looked uncertain, but when the lieutenant offered her a boost she accepted and let out a small shriek as Goodwin and Joseph hauled her up.

The Darklight officer followed and the four of them worked their way further up the oblong construction. At its peak they stopped atop the bases of the statues whose smashed remnants lay forty feet down on the ground below. Rebecca held tight to Goodwin's arm while the dim beam from his torch and the lights from the lieutenant's helmet left large patches of shadow around their feet.

They gazed out at their handiwork, but since Offiah had left most of the portable lighting had gone, too, leaving swathes of the design in deep shadow. Manaus pressed a button on her helmet. 'Corporal, I need some more light on the artefact.'

Goodwin heard a faint reply and Manaus swore. 'Hang on, sir, I'll go down and sort it out.'

The lieutenant clambered back down and Joseph decided to go with her.

A few moments later they'd made it to ground level and moved in tandem to rearrange the lights, although Joseph seemed to hinder the process rather than assisting it.

With the frieze illuminated, Goodwin felt a tingle of excitement. To think, they were the first people to behold this fabulous creation for millennia, and more than likely the first humans ever to do so. He wondered how much an archaeologist would pay to be in his shoes right now. *Not much*, he thought, *considering the precarious nature of our existence.*

Taking in the scene, his heart dropped. While the figures of the Anakim crafted into the granite were amazing, they revealed no further insight into their surroundings or bore any relevance to the spiral map of the city's interior, which was positioned in the relief's far corner. Goodwin felt another headache coming on; all their work had been for nothing.

'We might as well carry on,' he said, making his way down, 'there's still more to uncover.'

Rebecca remained where she was, muttering to herself and staring with intensity at the scene below. 'Do you read the scriptures, Richard?'

He hesitated. 'You mean the Bible?'

'Yes.'

'No, not since I was a child.'

She continued to gaze at the Anakim frieze, and when she failed to say anything else he returned to her side.

'What is it?' he said. 'Have you seen something?'

'I'm not sure.' She pointed to shapes of the Anakim at the bottom of the scene, their faces not quite human.

Goodwin followed the direction of her finger and saw the naked forms of ancient men and women reaching up, their faces contorted in fear and wonder.

Her finger rose to larger figures above, their denuded forms carved in lewd, explicit detail, mouths agape in expressions of bestial lust and horror. Thick chains bound these fearsome visions of antiquity to a platform made up of the dead.

'It's a bit gruesome,' Goodwin said, 'but then it doesn't seem too different from anything we humans call art.'

'That's the point. It's not that different.' She paused as if recalling something. 'And the angels who did not stay within their own position of authority, but left their proper dwelling, he has kept in eternal chains under gloomy darkness until the judgement of the great day—'

'What's that?'

'Jude 1:6. You said Homo gigan ... how do you say it?'

'Homo giganthropsis, according to Corporal Walker, anyway.'

'The man from Sanctuary's USSB?'

'Yes, part of the U.S. Army decontamination team. He said that's the scientific name for them.'

'Did he say who called them the Anakim?'

Goodwin thought for a moment. 'No, and neither did the Professor in his message. Why?'

She frowned. 'There's two more passages I remember—'

'Go on,' he said, when she didn't continue.

'Genesis 6:4. The Nephilim were on the earth in those days, when the sons of God came in to the daughters of man and they bore children to them. These were the mighty men who were of old, the men of renown.'

'And the second?'

'Deuteronomy 1:28. The people are greater and taller than we. The cities are great and fortified up to heaven. And besides, we have seen the sons of the Anakim there.'

Goodwin didn't know what to say, but the words stirred him. He ran his eyes over the sculpture below. 'You think the beings at the top are the Nephilim?'

She looked around her. 'This is a city fortified up to heaven, man never created towers as high as these. And the Anakim lived here. Also, the figures at the top are chained, and if this isn't gloomy darkness I don't know what is.'

Goodwin could see where she was coming from, but it was a stretch of the imagination by anyone's book – including God's.

'Although,' she said, seeing his scepticism, 'it's not like the world is ending; this isn't the great day of judgement.' She sighed. 'I just got carried away, what with the meteorite on the surface, it's a little like the end of days, don't you think?'

'What was the first one you said again?'

She took a breath. 'And the angels who did not stay within their own position of authority, but left their proper dwelling, he has kept in eternal chains under gloomy darkness until the judgement of the great day—'

Rebecca's words echoed in his mind, *it's not like the world is ending.* That was the problem, the world was ending, the surface world anyway. Soon only ash and darkness would remain, *fire and brimstone.* Unless, of course, the GMRC's Space Programme accomplished what it had failed to do so far – avert the approaching asteroids. He ran his eyes over the frieze, its representation taking on a whole new light, the message a sinister prophetic warning from the past and the ancients that crafted it.

'It's funny, though,' she continued, 'it looks like a symbol runs through the whole image.'

'I don't see anything.'

She drew him closer and he glanced at her face so near to his before following her finger as she traced the path of metallic lines hidden beneath the sculptures.

He squinted, concentrating, before he realised what it was. 'A pentagram.'

'That's weird, isn't it?'

'Is it?'

'You don't know, do you?'

'Apparently not.'

'It used to be used as the symbol for Christ the Saviour,' she said, 'the five wounds of Christ, although it's now looked upon as pagan or satanic by pretty much all Christian churches.'

'How do you know all this?'

'I go to church; plus, I'm a live-in carer, I watch a lot of television. Didn't you have the Discovery channel in your USSB Steadfast?'

Goodwin thought he might smile, but instead he just shook his head, his thoughts returning to the biblical verses. 'So you think they could have predicted AG5 impacting Earth?'

Rebecca made a face. 'Why not? You said the Anakim civilisation went on for hundreds of thousands of years, didn't you?'

'According to Corporal Walker – yes. He says they've got a museum in the base dedicated to the Anakim and Sanctuary itself.'

'And they were more advanced than us.'

'Supposedly.'

'Why supposedly? They built this place, didn't they?'

Goodwin looked up at the enormous tower next to them, its dark bulk disappearing into the pitch black. 'Yes, but they still died out.'

'True, but that doesn't mean they didn't possess knowledge. The

Mayans had a prophecy for the end of the world, didn't they? So why not the Anakim?'

'Well, for one the world didn't end in 2012, so the prophecy didn't work, and for two, wasn't it all a misnomer anyway? The Mayans predicted a new age rather than the end of the world.'

Rebecca shrugged. 'I suppose, although the Anakim were far more advanced than the Mayans.'

'Exactly, so if they were so powerful they'd just blow the asteroid out of the sky.'

'Like we did, you mean?'

Goodwin gave a wry smile. 'We tried, didn't we? All those missions by NASA and the GMRC ... but they just kept falling short of diverting it, and the rockets they fired didn't even dent it.'

'Perhaps they didn't have any space technology at all,' Rebecca said, 'or they wanted the asteroid to destroy the surface when it arrived and that's why they built this underground world.'

Goodwin could see she had a point. The GMRC Subterranean Programme could just be a much later version than one devised by the Anakim before them. He shook his head. 'No, why would anyone want to destroy the surface? It would make no sense.'

'It would if you lived underground.'

Goodwin pondered the answer. It was a good one, but also moot. They could never hope to understand their long dead cousins anymore than they could the minds of the dinosaurs before them. He also had more important things to think about, like how to get everyone out of this godforsaken place. They couldn't rely on Hilt finding a way to the USSB, or – as much as he hated to think it – of returning at all. It was up to him to find a solution. He needed to act, not to procrastinate. Taking some video footage of the frieze, their conversation over, Goodwin and Rebecca returned to the ground and the task of trying to discover a glimmer of hope amongst the ruins of the past.

CHAPTER FORTY

ANOTHER TWO DAYS drifted by and the excavation of the giant granite sculpture revealed no further insight into the layout of the chamber, the underground city loath to release Steadfast's refugees from its mighty grasp. It seemed the only way out had been the way they'd entered over half a year before. *If only the earthquake hadn't triggered a collapse to the cave system*, Goodwin thought, *we'd all be safely tucked up inside the USSB.* He thrust such pitiful thoughts from his mind, his brain forever tricking him into reliving the same mistakes, the same tragedies, over and over in a game of mental self-flagellation.

And yet despite his best efforts to free himself from these negative processes, they persisted, and Goodwin's enthusiasm for the frieze waned; and it wasn't long before he, Rebecca and Joseph, accompanied by Lieutenant Manaus and her one hundred Darklight soldiers, made their way back through the city.

After they'd passed the final tower, a faint halo of light could be seen in the distance, the glow hovering in the black like the lights of an alien craft.

On their way in a fifty strong Darklight patrol hailed them in greeting, the reacquainted men and women of the multicultural security firm exchanging pleasantries and banter in a state of camaraderie. Goodwin felt his spirits lift a little as they entered the campsite; the unease of being away from a large body of people had been eating away at him without him realising. This feeling, he knew, also had a lot to do with safety in numbers. Despite having a large, well-trained and well-armed entourage for company, the city had still felt sinister in its isolation.

As they walked towards the central command post, a group of civilians rushed past and Lieutenant Manaus collared one of them as they ran by. 'What's going on?'

The man looked distraught. 'Two rafts didn't return from the lake, twenty people are missing.' He shrugged off her grasp. 'I have to go, we're assembling search parties!'

Manaus swore. 'Sorry, sir, we'll have to leave you here.'

Goodwin nodded.

'Recon Alpha, with me!'

The officer ran off, followed by her troops, leaving Goodwin, Rebecca and Joseph on their own.

'So much for the relaxation of camp,' Goodwin said, as another mass of people ran by ahead of them.

Rebecca drew Joseph to her. 'Should we go and help, too?'

Goodwin shook his head. 'No, you get back to your tent. I'll go and see what's happening.'

Joseph gave him a hug in parting and Rebecca followed suit. 'Thanks for letting us go with you into the city. If you need any help with anything just let me know, I'll,' – she glanced at Joseph – 'we'll, be happy to help.'

Joseph grinned at him.

'I may take you up on that.' Goodwin waved them goodbye and a short walk later found himself entering the Darklight command post.

'Well, how am I supposed to know?!' Kara glanced at Goodwin as he entered, a communication device held to one ear. She turned away and paused before shouting. 'Just do it!'

Throwing the earpiece onto the desk in front of her, she moved to have a heated discussion with two other civilians who then rushed out of the tent to carry out their respective orders.

'Problems?' Goodwin said.

Kara snorted. 'Like you care.'

'They say we're missing two rafts.'

Kara ignored him and brushed past to collect some maps of the shoreline.

Major Offiah arrived. 'Sir,' he said, acknowledging Goodwin, his tone curt.

'Any survivors?' Kara asked the officer.

Offiah shook his head. 'We've pulled three bodies from the water on the south east quadrant. We're getting reports of a lot of activity near the surface.'

'Which means?'

'The predators are feeding,' Goodwin said.

Kara kept her eyes on the major.

'The director's correct,' Offiah said. 'If they smelled blood a feeding frenzy would be the likely outcome. We may not find the other crew members.'

'At least not alive,' Goodwin said.

Kara's eyes blazed. 'What! What is wrong with you, Richard?! People are dying and all you can do is make useless comments! Is there anyone left in there capable of feeling anything?'

'I don't know what you mean.' He looked to Offiah, whose angry expression provided no answers. 'I've been in the city trying to get us out of this place, what more can I do?'

'You can help me run this camp, that's what you could be doing, instead of running around looking for nonexistent maps!'

'You haven't heard? We found a map. Did the major not tell you?'

'Oh, he told me. He also told me it was next to useless. You better get a grip, people are beginning to question whether you should remain in charge.'

'Are you one of them?'

Kara drew a breath, seeking calm. 'Not yet, but if you don't drop this crazy crusade ...'

Goodwin put down his rucksack. 'I'm trying my best, but all this,' he gestured around him, 'is pointless if we can't find the subterranean base.'

'And the USSB is pointless if there's no one left to find it.' Kara held his gaze until the buzz of an incoming radio message drew her back to the desk.

Goodwin knew she needed him, but he had to take a stand. Not against her, but *for* her – for everyone. *When I find a way out*, he thought, *they'll see I was right*. He picked up his bag and left them to it, but his departure didn't go unnoticed, a look of fury on Kara's face switching to one of deep concern as she exchanged a meaningful look with Major Offiah.

◆

It had been a few hours since Goodwin had left the command post and he'd returned to the white tent he and Kara called home. A dim light cast deep shadows as he sat cross-legged on the rickety, lightweight portable bed that dominated the sparse interior, the single piece of furniture one of many brought with them inside the five thousand strong Darklight contingent's ample backpacks.

Spread out before him on the thin sleeping bag lay the printouts of the photos he'd taken of the frieze, and the numerous inscriptions and carvings he'd discovered on the ground around the city's eastern quarter. As with everything else in their camp, such things as printers were scarce and the ink and paper to go with them scarcer still. However, being the director had its privileges and he'd been able to convince one of the civilians to let him utilise their precious kit. Now with time to spare, he'd been able to study the images in detail and he jotted down notes on anything he found that might aid them in their plight. So far such writings had been unrelated observations, and yet he felt some had merit.

A large photo of the frieze had proven the most useful. From what

Goodwin could see the pentagram in its centre, while missing a couple of its points, was the structure upon which the sculpture had been based. Everything seemed to revolve around it. The passages Rebecca had quoted from the Bible also weaved their magic around his mind like the murmurings of messages through time. Did the Anakim have links to human culture? Did the creatures depicted portray the fallen angels of God, the Nephilim? And if they did, how did that help him?

His eyes strayed to a separate photo of the spiral map of the city's centre. It covered a massive area and each spiral arm encompassed some of the largest towers, its middle dominated by the massive structure that continued to amaze with its purple light show. He'd been told, however, the unusual phenomenon was winding down. Each time the energy flowed up its great bulk to discharge into the sparkling ceiling of the chamber beyond, its duration diminished. When they'd first witnessed it, the event had lasted for nearly twenty minutes. Since that time it had reduced to only a few, its decline estimated to reach non-existence within the week.

He wondered for the hundredth time if they were missing anything. Should they be doing something to use this resource?

Goodwin's frustration mounted and more time passed as he struggled to pluck meaning from obscurity before Kara appeared, pushing aside the tent flap to enter.

She looked down at the images on the bed. 'Wasting more resources, I see.'

Goodwin hastily swept the photos aside as she sat down. 'I'm not wasting anything. There's something here, I know it.'

Kara eyed him, her expression unfathomable, and Goodwin reached out a hand. 'Please,' – he touched her arm – 'will you take a look for me?'

She gave a weary shake of her head and picked up some photos. 'Do you want to know about the search?' she said, flicking through the images.

Not really, he thought. 'Have they found anyone else?'

'Two more bodies washed up. They're still looking for the others.'

'It's not looking good, then.'

'They tell me if the fish haven't finished them off, the cold water will have done.'

Goodwin sought the words to say, but feeling sympathy when depressed was like trying to grab an eel in oil. Instead he pointed to the corner of one of the photos. 'Those symbols keep appearing all over the city.'

Kara paused and gazed at the carved lines he'd indicated:

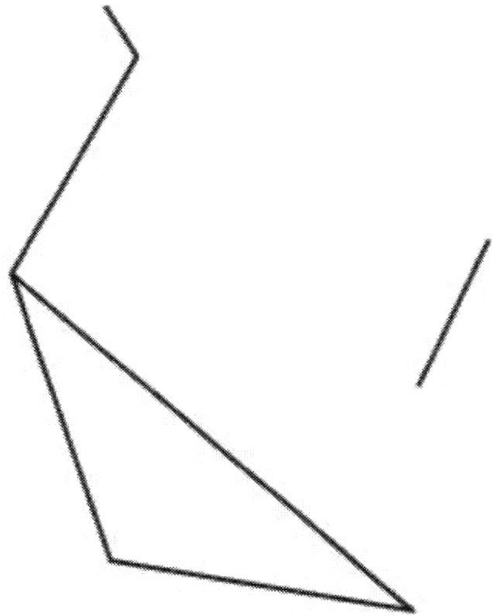

She handed them back to him. 'They're meaningless.'

Goodwin went back to his analysis and rearranged his media while Kara undressed for bed. Putting a foot into the sleeping bag, she stopped to look over his shoulder at the images of the symbol and spiral map he now held. Goodwin saw her brow furrow.

He moved the photos closer to her. 'You see something, don't you?'

She squirmed under the cover. 'It's nothing.'

'Tell me.'

'I told you, it's nothing.'

She tried to roll away from him, but he held onto her shoulder. 'Kara, if you've seen something it could be important. Just because you're angry with me, don't punish everyone else.'

She sat up. 'Angry? No. Furious? Yes. But I'm also worried out of my mind. In almost a matter of days you've lost touch with reality, chasing after shadows and ignoring your responsibilities.'

'So you don't want to encourage me, is that it?'

'That's not what I said. Are you even listening to what I'm saying?'

'For God's sake, Kara, JUST TELL ME!'

She blinked at his ferocity, her eyes brimming in distress and turned away to hide under the covers once more.

He looked heavenward, cursing himself. *She'll never tell me now.*

Deep within he wanted to snap out of his malady, to be who he was, to be the man she wanted, not the morose, ill-tempered monster he felt himself becoming. He lay down beside her, his thoughts in turmoil. Mistakes past and present ran through his mind, tormenting him. Everything seemed too much. Everything was too much. Whatever he did turned to pain and darkness. *People are dying and I don't even care.* The thought horrified him and it was all he could think about until morning.

CHAPTER FORTY-ONE

AN ALARM WOKE Goodwin from his shallow slumber, his cumulative hours of sleep numbering just one. Kara was already up and dressed.

She switched off the buzzer and gazed down at his bleary eyes before moving to the tent's exit.

'Kara—'

'It's a constellation.'

He propped himself up on an elbow. 'What?'

'The symbols on your Anakim carvings, they match the constellation of Libra.'

He leant over and peered at one of the photos he'd left on the floor. 'Are you sure?'

'Pretty sure, and the map spiral, it looks—'

He blinked back his tiredness, trying to concentrate. 'Looks like what?'

'The Milky Way, the spiral arms match our galaxy.'

Stunned, Goodwin could see she still held more information back. 'There's something else, isn't there?'

Her expression turned pensive. 'If the carvings are truly ancient, then the stars would have altered positions. The constellation should look ... different.'

'How different?'

'I don't know. I'm not an astrophysicist and I have work to do, look it up.'

The tent flap rustled and she was gone.

He rolled out of bed, his fatigue forgotten and neurons firing.

Fifteen minutes later Goodwin entered the civilian computer centre on the other side of the camp.

A man with long hair and a beard shuffled around a desk towards him. 'Director, we don't normally see you in these parts.'

'I need to use your netcube.'

'Haven't your Darklight chaps got one?'

'They have, but it's integrated into their control setup and I need it mobile.'

The man grimaced and picked up a large square device by its carry handle. 'People won't be happy if you take away their only source of reference.'

'I'll get it back to you as soon as I can,' Goodwin said, accepting the heavy computer, 'I promise.'

'I'll hold you to that, Director!' the man called after him as he left to return to his tent.

By the time Goodwin reached his spartan dwelling, he'd had to swap the device from one hand to the other numerous times and his shoulders and arms ached with pain. He set the box down with relief and connected it to a power supply from the small water-powered generator Darklight had set up nearby. He then unfolded his mobile computer's large screen and synced the netcube to it.

A wonder of the modern age, even ten years ago the capacity of storage drives would have been nowhere capable of holding the vast amount of data of a modern day netcube. But when humanity had neared the fourth decade of the twenty-first century, the power of fluid drives had taken a leap forward and the possibility of storing – not the entire World Wide Web, but the majority of its mainstream data – had become a reality. Of course, the company that provided the *webinabox*, as they'd become known, could be told what sites and files to omit so valuable space for knowledge wasn't taken up by videos of amusing kittens or unforeseen accidents starring the unfortunate.

A search box popped up on-screen and Goodwin entered the term *Libra Constellation*. A myriad of entries spooled up, and he clicked on the first. The image shown was indeed similar to the stone carvings he'd found dotted around the city, except the carvings had one line omitted from the image. Unable to think of any reason why the Anakim had failed to link all the points, he switched his attention to the image of the galaxy. According to the sites he read, it seemed the actual number of major and minor arms in the Milky Way's spiral – and their positions – had been hotly contested by the scientific community for decades. That was until more advanced deep space telescopes, probably designed with tracking the approaching asteroids in mind, had cleared up the ambiguities; which meant the Anakim had possessed technology sophisticated enough to realise complex cosmological structures.

Kara was correct in her assumptions, however. It seemed – given a long enough period in time, say fifty thousand years – the constellations in the night sky would alter, which meant something was amiss if the symbols matched the current position of stars for the Libra collective. Unless, he reasoned, the symbols were carved much later. Although according to Corporal Walker, Sanctuary has been abandoned too long for that to be an option. So what does it mean? It means, he realised, that the Anakim designed the symbols to coincide with the position of the stars as they are today, or at least during the current duration of human civilisation.

Rebecca's biblical prophecy, Jude 1:6, once more came to the forefront of his mind ... *kept in eternal chains under gloomy darkness until the judgment of the great day*. His eyes strayed to the photo of the unearthed frieze and the demonic nature of its sculpture. He shuddered and thought of the creature that roamed the darkness. *It could easily be classed as some kind of ethereal being, but a fallen angel?*

He typed in the word Nephilim and read on. It seemed the term could mean a number of things, depending on what source of reference you listened to. The Bible indicated they were the offspring of the sons of God and female humans, as per Rebecca's quotation from

Genesis 6:4, although, according to other sources, specifically another passage from the Bible, Numbers 13:30-33, the Nephilim were giants who lived in a place called Canaan.

But Caleb quieted the people before Moses and said, 'Let us go up at once and occupy it, for we are well able to overcome it.' Then the men who had gone up with him said, 'We are not able to go up against the people, for they are stronger than we are.' So they brought to the people of Israel a bad report of the land that they had spied out, saying, 'The land, through which we have gone to spy it out, is a land that devours its inhabitants, and all the people that we saw in it are of great height. And there we saw the Nephilim (the sons of Anak, who come from the Nephilim), and we seemed to ourselves like grasshoppers, and so we seemed to them.'

So, the Nephilim were not as he'd initially thought, fallen angels, but their half-human offspring, half human, half demon. More investigation revealed they could also be the children of Seth, the brother to Cain and Abel and the third son of Adam and Eve. Goodwin sipped some water, his lack of sleep catching up with him. This was confusing stuff in itself, but to then try and link that with far older Anakim sculptures made for a powerful headache. He needed some help. Collecting his photos, he stowed his personal computer, picked up the netcube and left his tent.

A few minutes later he'd worked his way across the floor of the dark chamber and followed the camp's sparse lighting rigs to Rebecca's sprawling tent.

He ducked his head inside to see all was quiet. Rebecca and the two other mental health carers, Julie and Arianna, sat on the ground in muted conversation, while their brood, including Joseph, slept in a mass huddle near the back of the tent. A pang of guilt for bringing these people here lanced through him. He'd saved them from the rioting after the asteroid had hit, the streets of Albuquerque having turned to chaos, but he'd brought them here, to a pit of despair as barren as his own mind.

Julie saw him and nudged Rebecca, who turned round to wave him over.

'Richard, what brings you here?'

He sat down opposite her while Julie and Arianna went to make themselves busy elsewhere.

Rebecca caught his look. 'It's nothing personal; they needed to get the noon meal ready anyway.'

'I need your help,' – he held up the netcube – 'I've had a breakthrough.'

◆

'So, let me get this straight,' Rebecca said, 'the symbols are the Libra constellation, the spiral is the galaxy, and the frieze has a pentagram, which we also think mirrors, tenuously, passages from the Bible.'

'Correct.'

'And Kara says the constellation should be different if it's as old as we think it is?

'Yes.'

She looked thoughtful. 'Then we should go through it methodically; perhaps we need to find more links between the Anakim and the Nephilim.'

Goodwin gave a nod, he was glad she could be rational, just having someone lay it out in simple terms was enough to get him back on track. He typed in the two words and looked at the results thrown up by the netcube.

Rebecca touched a link and it popped up on-screen. 'Deuteronomy 2:10,' she said. 'The Emim formerly lived there, a people great and many, and tall as the Anakim.' She scrolled down the page and then went back to the first set of results.

Time passed as she continued to sift through page after page of text. She went back over the same scripture, flicked through the same photos, and then went back to the beginning and started all over again. She asked him variations on questions he'd already answered and when she put to him another such ambiguity Goodwin slapped his knee in frustration. 'This is getting us nowhere!'

Rebecca glanced round to see her patients still slept.

'Sorry,' he said, dejected.

She patted his leg and looked at the notes she'd been taking. 'Don't worry about it. And I disagree. It seems to me the Nephilim were one of four things: the children of fallen angels and human women, fallen angels who possessed men, the descendents of Adam who followed false gods, or ordinary men who rejected God and chose to be wicked. And what's more the Bible and other ancient texts tell us giants were commonplace all over the world in the days before the great flood, although according to other scholars the term *Nephilim* literally means *giants*, a derivative of the Hebrew word *naphil*. And some say the giants referenced were just tall peoples from Africa or other distant states.'

Goodwin rubbed his temples. 'Didn't mankind start in Africa?'

Rebecca shrugged before looking it up. 'Yes, South Africa. Bones of our distant ancestors were dug up in a place called the Cradle of Humanity.'

'Then it stands to reason the Anakim could have evolved from there, too.'

'Maybe.'

Goodwin stared at the screen, wishing for something to jump out at him and make sense. Nothing did.

Rebecca yawned. 'Perhaps the flood drove the Anakim underground.'

'What did you just say?'

'The flood, perhaps the water drove them down here.'

'Maybe. But—' he gave a groan.

'What's wrong?'

'All this, we're beneath Mexico, none of this can be related. The Anakim from the Bible would have lived thousands of miles away.'

'So?'

He shoved the screen away. 'So this is all pointless.'

'How do you know there's not another Sanctuary over there?'

He blinked and then shook his head. 'Corporal Walker said this is the only one.'

'As far as they know. Maybe they just haven't found it yet.'

The idea made him feel dizzy and he bent his head.

'Are you okay?'

'Yes, I'm—' A figure on the frieze stared back him, its photo on top of the pile. He picked it up and then sorted through the rest with increasing speed. Behind all the figures, as clear as day, the forms of giant waves reared up to create the background. How could he have missed it? Then something else caught his eye. Two of the photos containing the Libra carvings had fallen one across the other. He picked them up. Each photo had been taken at a different location in the city and consisted of various carved lines and the constellation itself, and they matched up, the designs flowing seamlessly from one to the other. He spread the remaining photographs out on the floor and moved those of the frieze to one side.

'What is it, Richard? Have you found something?'

Goodwin didn't reply. He scanned through the designs as he sought to match them together. One looked like it would connect to the first two. He folded it in half and the designs merged.

Rebecca moved away and returned with some scissors and Goodwin cut up the first three photos, which enabled him to lay them down flat next to each other on the ground. In silence, they continued to find more photos which flowed on from the first three until the pattern ceased, with two thirds of the photos left over. An hour passed and they found that some of the remaining images also matched up to one another – two here, and three there – but none to the ten images they'd already aligned into a single whole.

Sitting back, they assessed their handiwork.

Rebecca prodded at a couple of the photos to move them closer together. 'It doesn't look like much.'

Goodwin wasn't so sure. He moved some of the smaller sections around the larger group, which he left in the centre. 'I think the constellation is the key. Look,' – he pointed to the corner of each image – 'each depiction of Libra coincides with the corresponding piece next to it, creating a spiral pattern of the same symbol.'

'Like the galaxy map?'

'Exactly! And each representation of the constellation is just how it looks at different places in the night sky when viewed from Earth, at various locations and times of the year.'

'Then it might be telling us how to get to the surface,' she said.

Goodwin's eyes grew bright, but something else nagged at him. *I'm missing something.* He picked up his handheld computer and turned the large screen transparent, then held it over their newly created mosaic and took a photo. Not sure what to do next, he used the touchscreen to remove parts of the image he didn't want, including all of the inscriptions and elaborate pictograms.

He showed the image to Rebecca. 'What does that look like to you?'

'A bunch of squiggles?'

'Look again.'

She did so, but her expression remained confounded.

'It's the lake,' he said, 'the shoreline!'

'Are you sure?'

Goodwin was positive. He'd been in Hilt's command post for months on end, watching as the Darklight reconnaissance teams pieced together a map of their surroundings, metre by metre and mile by mile. Even though it was incomplete and only showing the southern portion, there was no doubt in his mind it was the outline of the ancient aquifer that sustained them with both food and water. Knowing things always came in threes, he believed this revelation indicated a third resource lurked in its inky depths – a way out of Sanctuary itself!

CHAPTER FORTY-TWO

Despite Goodwin's excitement at cracking the code of the carvings and the possibility of a route to the surface, Rebecca had soon pointed out that they were unable to enter the lake to find out what lay within. Not only were there fierce, sharp-toothed creatures swimming in its near bottomless expanse, the twenty-seven square miles of surface might as well have been on the moon as they had no equipment with which to dive. And not only that, where in such a large body of water were they supposed to look? It could take years, decades, to locate something they knew not what.

Now back in his own tent, Goodwin pondered on the tantalising nature of his discovery and ground his teeth in frustrated distraction. Getting to the surface of course would be second to finding the USSB. But even though the next wave of asteroids would soon be arriving, they would have time a plenty to relocate to another base – if, that was, Goodwin could contact the GMRC Directorate without Malcolm Joiner finding out about it first. No small feat, but one he felt he might be able to pull off, given the chance. He still had contacts he could call upon if needed, notably the Director of USSB Pelagic down in South America. If he'd have known the consequences of trying to enter Sanctuary at the time, he'd have continued their journey south.

Full of expectation, later that evening Goodwin decided to raise his findings with Kara, who sat on the bed in subdued silence while reading a report on projected food stocks for the camp.

Kara held his photographic collage and listened as Goodwin gave her his theory about a way to the surface.

'And Rebecca's been helping you with this?'

'Yes.' He pointed at the line that represented the lake's edge. 'Do you see it?'

'And what *else* has *she* helped you discover?'

Goodwin failed to notice the edge to his partner's voice as he regaled her with their observations about the frieze and its connection to the Anakim, the Bible and even the Great Flood.

Kara massaged her eyes. 'Richard, can you hear yourself?'

He didn't understand what she meant and his wrist had started itching again. He scratched at it. 'What do you mean?'

'You're quoting passages from the Bible, for God's sake! The Nephilim, the apocalypse, the flood, this is all fantasy, don't you see? Rebecca is a sweet woman, but she believes everything the book says is real, she's detached from reality and she's dragging you down with her. You're vulnerable, willing to accept fiction as fact and fact as inconsequential.'

'But the map of the lake, look!' He pointed at it again and then showed her the photo of the frieze. 'Can you see the waves in the background? It's a foretelling of the great flood. I looked it up; every nation in the world has the same stories, passed down from generation to generation. It can't be a coincidence.'

'It can, and it is.' Kara came to him and held his hands in hers. 'Calm down and think. None of this makes sense. The Anakim are far older than the biblical tales. You know this. They aren't related in any way. If you look for something long enough, if you want it badly enough, you'll find it. You've altered the answers to fit the question. Science is littered with people who searched for something and lo and behold they found it, justifying their miraculous findings with facts that couldn't be verified one way or the other. It's like the Higgs boson; they pumped billions of dollars into Cern's Large Hadron

Collider and surprise, surprise, they found what they were looking for, the so-called God particle. Who could verify it was as they said it was? No one, as no one knows what it really is – something that exists for a fraction of a second and which the scientists themselves admit cannot be given a hundred per cent guarantee of being the theorised particle at all. Just because people say it's true doesn't mean it is. What would you do if you had a set of results that cost billions to achieve? Would you go, "Sorry, folks, we've wasted your time and money," or would you do everything in your power to make it fit, to get the answer that validated your career, your life, your very existence?'

Goodwin frowned. 'Coming from a scientist that seems like a funny way of looking at things. You think we shouldn't even bother with trying to advance ourselves?'

'No, not at all. What I'm saying is, belief is a powerful thing. It can create as well as destroy. It can also blind those behind it to the starkness of reality. Add a powerful motivator to the mix, like money, or a way out of Sanctuary—'

He held up the photos. 'This is not fiction. It's real. The map of the lake is real. The constellation symbols that match up – *are real.* You just refuse to believe it because you lack faith.'

Her face blanched. 'What?! Unlike your precious Rebecca?'

'That's not what I meant, but now that you put it that way, yes. At least Rebecca trusts my judgement and respects what I have to say.'

Kara slapped him round the face.

Shocked, Goodwin gaped at her in hurt confusion.

'Get out!' Kara thrust a finger at the tent's entrance.

Goodwin bent down and collected his photos from the floor.

'I said, get out!' Kara hurled a shoe at his head.

Goodwin made a hasty retreat and ducked out into the darkness, his bridges burnt and sanity questioned.

◆

Kara stood in her tent, her breathing shallow and hands clenched. She let out a shriek of fury and kicked out at the bed, sending its frame skittering across the room.

Pain throbbed in her foot at the site of impact, stifling her anger, and she limped to the tent flap and peered out to see Goodwin's form disappearing into the gloom. Her expression turned to one of despair. 'Richard,' she whispered, 'come back to me.'

CHAPTER FORTY-THREE

California, USA

Cold winds blew through the creaking limbs of the dead and dying carcasses of the majestic old-growth trees that covered the flowing plain of the Jedediah Smith Redwoods State Park. Brown leaves, whipped up by swirling vortices, tumbled through the air alongside the pervasive dust particles that sifted down to the ground from the heavens above; these tiny pieces of pulverised rock an ever-present reminder of the devastating and distant impact of the asteroid impact a year previous.

A darkened campsite lay amongst the giant columns of bark and wood, its facilities empty except for a blue and white coroner's truck which stood parked in quiet isolation.

Inside this large vehicle, two women, one large and one small, stood next to one another in quiet contemplation.

The disgraced BBC newsreader, Jessica Klein, stared into the face of peace that was Professor Steiner, lost in his own mind to death's eternal embrace. Dark welts that scarred his pale skin drew her eyes down, their blood red striations creeping over his exposed chest and neck in equal measure. A well of pity and sorrow grasped her heart. *What suffering has this poor man endured? Beaten and abused by those that sought their own justice. And what does he know that can help my family? And why did he help the man known as Colonel Samson to commit such atrocious crimes?* Soon, all would become clear, or so she hoped.

Special Agent Brett Taylor shook her head. 'No, he can't be—'

Jessica looked up at the newest recruit to their company. 'He can and he is, although he should have woken up by now.'

'How? How did you do it?'

'With great difficulty. Bic helped with most of it, passes, clearance and the like. Coroners can get into places you wouldn't believe. The hardest part was sourcing the serums.'

In a dream-like trance, Brett withdrew her pistol and turned it on the professor.

'No!' Jessica threw herself over the comatose man.

'He deserves to die!'

'He's our only chance of finding out the truth!'

Brett tried to throw Jessica aside, but she clung on to the gurney for grim life. 'Eric!'

Her German friend ran to her aid, but Brett knocked him down with a crunching blow to the jaw. Jessica leapt and grabbed onto the gun, but Brett swung her round, lifting her off the floor before slamming her into the side of the truck. Pain exploded down her back, but she maintained her grip on the gun. Eric scrambled back to his feet only for Brett to land him a vicious head-butt.

The German dropped unconscious to the floor.

Jessica let out a screech of fury and plunged her teeth into the agent's hand, biting down with all her force. Blood gushed; Brett screamed and released one hand on the pistol only to grab a handful of Jessica's hair and ram her head into an up rushing knee. Light exploded before Jessica's eyes and she fell back, dazed. Vision clearing, she saw Brett press her gun to the professor's forehead.

'Killing him will make you a murderer, just like your father!' Jessica said. 'Is that what you want, to be a killer?'

Brett didn't look at her, but Jessica could tell she listened.

'Do this and you not only condemn my family to death,' Jessica said, 'but everyone else's, too. This man is the key to everything, do you understand me, EVERYTHING!'

Brett's fierce eyes glared at her from beneath furrowed brows.

Jessica, breathing hard, got to her feet. 'You know I'm right or you would have already pulled the trigger. Help us, help yourself. Help your countrymen. You swore an oath to defend the United States against all enemies, foreign and domestic. Every action in your life has led you to this moment, this point in time, don't throw it all away for the illusion of revenge. You're more than that, we all are.'

Brett lowered her weapon and stared at her hand where Jessica had bitten her before looking back at the prone form in the body bag, her expression fraught.

Jessica brushed past to help Eric, who'd risen into a sitting position.

A laceration across the bridge of his nose dripped blood. '*Autsch!*' he said, holding his head. 'That hurt.'

Jessica helped the young German to his feet.

He leaned against her, mumbled something and moved a couple of shuffling steps to pick up a mask attached to a canister of laughing gas.

Jessica plucked the apparatus from his grasp. 'That's for serious injuries.'

Eric looked like he was about to argue, but a beep from the touch-screen told them Bic had sent them a message. She bent down and picked up the device.

Is everything okay, Jessica Klein? _

She looked over at Brett who still gazed at the professor, lost in thought. 'Yes, you were listening?'

. . .

I was. Turn on the speaker so I can speak to you all _

Jessica did so, as Brett came out of her trance and began attending to her bite wound.

'You might need a tetanus shot for that.'

Brett ignored her and cleaned her injury with some antiseptic before placing a plaster over it.

'Eric,' Bic said via the device, 'are you there?'

Brett's face changed when she heard the new voice, her attention refocused.

'Yes, *Da Muss Ich*,' Eric said, 'I'm here.'

'Does Professor Steiner still sleep?'

'He does.'

'He shouldn't be. Connect the electrodes as you practised; we need to check his vital signs.'

'Okay.'

While Eric carried out his duties, Jessica considered the voice – not the words – of the international cyber terrorist in their midst. Bic, or *Da Muss Ich* as he was known in Germany, didn't sound German at all, but American, although there was a strange inflection to his words that she couldn't quite place. Of course an American accent didn't mean that person came from America, far from it. She'd met some Russians in media circles who sounded more American than some Americans did, so Bic could have gained his distinctive twang having learnt English in America, or from an American source. Whoever he was, she still didn't like the fact that he continued to call the shots, especially after he'd deceived them previously. Eric still trusted him implicitly, unable to see the duplicity within – unlike Brett Taylor, who appeared not to trust anyone. *Although*, Jessica reasoned, *she was willing to listen to what Bic had to say. She also admitted she believed her father and Professor Steiner had worked for a secret government project* – Jessica eyed the large figure of the FBI agent *– but she's undecided on our theory that the impact winter is worse than* *the GMRC says it is, and that the world's resources are being siphoned off into underground bases.*

Such thoughts turned Jessica's mind onto her family. The memory of her two girls leaving with her husband, Evan, back in England, drove a spike of fear into her heart.

'Are the electrodes attached, Eric?' Bic said.

'*Ja*, and the machine is on.'

'Sync the results to my device.'

Eric did as he was bid.

Moments passed as Bic digested the data fed to him. 'Something is wrong, his brainwaves are too weak. We must act quickly. Jessica Klein, administer the injections, hurry!'

Jessica rushed to a nearby cabinet and extracted the pre-prepared syringes. Returning to the body, she placed a hand on cold skin and rested the needle against the man's throat.

Her hand shook and a spot of blood appeared as she pricked the skin.

Eric moved closer. 'What are you doing? Inject him!'

She breathed deep, trying to calm herself, but the shaking continued. 'I'm trying!'

A hand grasped hers and she looked into Brett's face.

'Give it here.'

Jessica hesitated.

A bleeping sound came from the machine. 'He is dying, Jessica Klein,' Bic said, 'do it now!'

'You can trust me,' Brett said.

Jessica stared into her eyes.

The beeping turned into a continuous drawn out sound.

Jessica ceded control and Brett grasped the professor's neck and punctured the skin with the syringe. She glanced up at Jessica, who nodded and Brett depressed the plunger.

The machine's output returned to a slow beep.

Brett held out her hand and Jessica passed her the next injection, its thick needle twice as long as the first.

'Where does this one go?'

Jessica pointed a shaky finger at his chest. 'In his heart.'

'Insert the needle between the fourth intercostal space in the ribs,' Bic said.

Brett blew out her cheeks and put the point in place.

A diagram appeared on the touchscreen, which Jessica had placed next to the body.

'Down a bit,' Eric said.

Brett adjusted its position and pushed it home, making Jessica wince.

An instant later Brett sent the liquid payload into its target and withdrew the needle.

Nothing happened. The machine that monitored the man's vital signs continued to bleep and beep at irregular intervals.

'What's happening?' Eric looked at Jessica. 'Why isn't he waking up?'

She shook her head, fearing the worst.

Eric jabbed a finger at Brett. 'You did something, you switched the needles!'

Jessica looked at the agent's nonplussed expression.

'She didn't have time,' Jessica said. 'Besides, we'd have seen her do it.'

Eric remained glaring at Brett.

'This doesn't make sense,' Bic said, his voice emanating from the touchscreen.

Jessica picked up the device. 'Did we do something wrong?'

'No, but I must check some things.'

The screen went dark as Bic went off to God knows where.

Jessica felt dizzy and she put a hand against a wall to steady herself. 'I don't know what happened. This is my fault, I delayed too long.'

'You thought your family's life was on the line,' Brett said, 'you panicked.'

Jessica shook her head. 'That doesn't happen to me.'

'It has now.'

'A few seconds wouldn't have made any difference,' Eric said, shooting Brett a look of angry distrust. 'If anyone's to blame, it's her.'

'How do you figure, little man?'

'Because you distracted us. This is your fault, you killed him.'

Brett snorted. 'I won't lose any sleep over it.'

Eric sent a string of German curses her way before a hand from Jessica calmed him.

A sick feeling rose like bile in Jessica's throat, she'd just condemned her family to death. It had been down to her and she'd failed.

A roar of noise outside the truck made Jessica start and dazzling light lit up the cabin.

'*Was ist das*?!' Eric said, scared.

Jessica shielded her eyes and moved to peer out of the driver's window.

A loudspeaker blared out a computer-generated voice. 'ATTENTION! Occupants of vehicle registration, 1558674, this is a restricted area. GMRC curfew is in effect in the state of California. You have exceeded this curfew. Please step out of the vehicle and await the relevant authorities.'

Eric grabbed his head in distress. 'What're they going on about? We're in a federal vehicle!'

Jessica switched on the touchscreen. 'Bic! What's happening? There's a GMRC drone saying we've broken curfew!'

'Perhaps your terrorist isn't as good as he says he is,' Brett said.

Jessica pushed past her to check on the professor. She still couldn't feel a pulse. 'Eric, start the truck!'

Eric jumped into the driver's seat and started the engine.

'ATTENTION! Occupants of vehicle registration 1558674! Failure to comply with GMRC protocols is a federal offence. Turn off your engine and step out of the vehicle, or suppression measures will be utilised.'

Eric's face creased in concern. 'Measures?'

'I've had enough of this,' Brett said.

Jessica waited for Bic to reply before a rush of cold air made her turn to see Brett opening the rear doors.

'What is she doing?!' Eric said.

Jessica had no idea.

◆

Brett Taylor emerged from the back of the coroner's van. Like all federal agents, she knew the facial recognition software in the GRMC drone would flag up her official record. Even though she was suspended, it would be enough to alert the nearest FBI field office to her whereabouts. She'd have these two idiots and their dead friend wrapped up in a nice little parcel by the time her colleagues arrived, and she'd be able to provide hard intelligence on the Bureau's number one terrorist target. Surely that would be enough to get her reinstated, or at the very least, it was a strong hand to lever her way back into the game. Even if she lost the direct lead, no agent had ever got close enough to speak to B.I.C.'s informants, let alone the terrorist himself. Plus she had two of his accomplices in the palm of her hand. She smiled to herself in satisfaction; the tide was turning in her favour.

'CITIZEN, identify yourself!' The drone moved to the back of the truck to turn its lights on her, the roar of its turbine rotors blowing up dust and debris from the ground.

Brett held up her hands and shouted, 'Special Agent Brett Taylor, FBI!'

The drone flew lower and a grid of blue lasers appeared on the ground before flowing up Brett's body and over her head. 'Brett Taylor, you are in violation of GMRC curfew, remain where you are.'

Brett lowered her arms.

'CITIZEN, drop your weapon and keep your hands up!'

Brett swore and took a step forward. 'Secure code in, 986523.'

'Unrecognised. Drop your weapon and put your hands up, this is your final warning!'

The truck's doors slammed shut behind her and she turned to see the vehicle driving off.

The drone blared out a deafening noise. A small gun turret on the machine's underbelly swivelled into action. 'DRIVER, cease movement or you will be fired upon!'

Brett swore and ran to catch up.

'Driver, you have violated a GMRC directive. This asset is authorised to engage!' A burst of gunfire erupted into the night.

♦

'Eric!' Jessica dived for cover as bullets tore into the side of the vehicle.

Somehow the ageing truck kept moving and the gunfire stopped. The young German reappeared in the driver's seat, nervous eyes peering over the wheel. The light stayed with them as they moved out onto the highway and one of the rear doors opened.

Out of breath, Brett re-entered the truck. 'Jesus, what are you doing?!'

'We can't afford to be captured,' Jessica said, staying low.

Brett heaved the door closed. 'Well you're going a funny way about it. When a drone opens fire it brings in five more for support.'

'We thought it was going to kill you.'

'So you thought you'd leave me; thanks.'

'What else could we do?'

'Waited for the police and I would have talked our way out of it.'

Jessica didn't think that was likely, but she had more pressing issues to worry about. 'Why has it stopped shooting?'

'This is a remote location; sometimes they reduce the ammo so they can take on more fuel.'

'Lucky us.' Jessica picked up the touchscreen and Eric increased their speed as they headed along the highway.

The light from the drone dimmed as it fell behind, although Eric said he could still see it in his mirrors, following at a distance.

'You won't outrun it,' Brett said, 'you might as well give up now.'

A ping of noise announced Bic's return.

What is happening, Jessica Klein? _

'We've been shot at by a GMRC drone. Sound familiar?'

Is it still following you? _

'Yes.' Jessica lowered her voice as Brett rummaged around at the rear of the truck. 'This better not have been you, Bic, or so help me God—'

It was not me. I would not try to kill you or Eric, you know that. When I hacked into the drone in Germany I saved your life with it, remember? _

Jessica did remember. She also remembered Bic admitting to calling the GMRC in the first place to get her moving in the direction he wanted. Sometimes she didn't know what to think. He had her right where he wanted her and there was nothing she could do about it except tag along for the sake of her family. She looked back at the unmoving form of the man on whom so much rested. 'The professor still hasn't woken up. What did you find out?'

I am worried. I have found something ... odd _

'Odd , how?'

The dosages administered back at the prison should have worn off without the need for injections, but with them he should have regained consciousness almost immediately. I checked the records in the prison and it seems our replacement vials were never used _

'Then why isn't he dead?'

Because neither were the prison's fatal drugs _

'Then what was he given? If they didn't use our replacements, and they didn't use their own, what *did* they use?'

I am unsure. It is strange, but the only explanation is that someone else ensured his survival _

'What?! Like who?'

Who indeed, Jessica Klein, who indeed _

. . .

'What can we do?'

'We wait.'

Jessica jumped at the sound of Brett's voice, the FBI agent reading the screen over her shoulder.

Brett Taylor is correct. We wait and hope _

CHAPTER FORTY-FOUR

RED and white pulsing lights lit up the dying tree line along Route 199. One – two – three police cars whooshed past, dry grasses bending as they sped on into the night, sirens wailing. It wasn't long until their target came into view, a large blue and white truck with its own lightbar flickering in the dark. Above and just behind it, a cluster of black GMRC drones cut through the air, shepherding the vehicle like a swarm of flies.

The lead patrol car drew closer, its driver resuming manual control. 'Dispatch, I have suspect vehicle in sight.'

'Copy, Officer. What's your twenty?'

'Still eastbound on 199. Speed in excess of one hundred miles an hour, suspect's driving is erratic, holy—'

'Say again, Officer?'

'The truck just forced a car off the road. I'm going to make a PIT manoeuvre.'

'Copy that, ambulance services are en route.'

The police car accelerated.

◆

'He's going to kill us!' Brett said.

'Not helping!' Eric swerved the truck back onto the road.

'Eric, let me take the wheel.' Jessica grabbed onto the dashboard as they swept past another intersection.

The young German computer hacker shifted over and Jessica grasped the steering wheel and slid in to take his place.

From her position in the passenger seat, Brett pointed ahead in alarm. 'CAR!'

Jessica let out a shriek and hit the brakes. All four wheels locked up before regaining traction. Engine roaring, obstacle missed, the truck sped on.

Behind, tyre smoke covered the highway and in her door mirror Jessica saw a police car draw closer.

◆

Eric fell backwards into the rear of the truck and let out a string of curses. *And they thought I was a bad driver*?!

He held onto the gurney, the dead body rolling towards him as the vehicle swayed again; pushing it back, he heard Jessica shout a warning.

'Hang on!'

BANG! The truck shuddered. Tyres squealed and Eric flew sideways and smashed into a cupboard. Debris flew everywhere and something hit him in the head. Pain exploded and Eric found himself lying on the floor in a daze as he slid from one side of the truck to the other, along with the gurney and everything else not tied down.

A canister rolled toward him and big letters on its side read: *NITRONOX*. He grabbed its transparent mask, put it to his face and breathed deep.

◆

Jessica held onto the wheel, hair streaming out behind her in slow motion. Mouth agape, she made eye contact with the officer in the patrol car that had rammed them. A screech of tyres, a shout from Brett and the truck continued on its three hundred and sixty degree spin. A fleeting vision of the road behind merged into a streak of trees before their vehicle resumed its forward motion.

Jessica slammed her foot back on the accelerator and they surged forward once more. Another police car attempted the same tactic, but Jessica braked and swerved into them, forcing them back.

'You won't be able to keep this up!' Brett said.

Jessica's knuckles whitened as she grasped the wheel tighter. She glanced at Brett, stuck the manual transmission down a gear and floored the pedal, and the truck leapt forward in response.

◆

Eric lay on the floor in a daze. The vehicle rocked and rolled this way and that as they careered down the highway. In tune with its movements, the youthful hacker rolled over to his front and then back again. Something soft and heavy fell on him. Focusing, he saw the pallid features of the professor an inch away. A machine hit the floor with a crash near his head, its beeping suddenly increased and the old man's eyes flared open. Eric's own eyes widened in shock and horror, and he let out a scream and kicked out.

◆

Thump, thump, thump. He could feel his heart beating, his mind racing, his body aching. *Where am I? Am I dead? Is this heaven? I can't move!* A loud crash sent a shockwave through his mind. Professor Steiner opened his eyes to a fearful mask. He wanted to scream, but couldn't. A second later he was flying through the air. Something hit his head and everything went dark.

... beep ... beep ... beeeeeeeep ...

A flash of light.

'You need to shock him again, Eric.'

'*Da Muss Ich*, where are you?'

'Eric, you need to concentrate or he will die.'

Someone giggled. 'I am concentrating, centrating, *konzentrieren*.'

'Eric, listen to me!'

'Charging! Clear!'

Thwump.

Noise roared and a burst of chaos.

'Again!'

... beeeeeeeeep ...

Thwump.

... beep ... beep ... beeeeeeeeep ...

. . .

'One more!'

'Charging, *klar*!'

Thwump.

... beep ... beep ... beep ...

A roar of noise and Steiner opened his eyes to gut-churning mayhem. Debris clattered in all directions. Sirens wailed. Things screeched and loudspeakers blared. A strange face leant over him and laughed.

'Professor Steiner, you're alive!'

Steiner couldn't move and he eyed the stranger with trepidation as he danced a jig above him. The man leant down to him, his face going from distant to massive in a heartbeat.

'I know who you are, GMRC man!' He shoved a mask on Steiner's face. 'Have some of this, it's really good!'

Steiner sucked in the gas.

'*Aussehen*!' The man whisked the mask away, turned round and pulled down his trousers.

Steiner's eyebrows raised in alarm. Perhaps I'm in hell? If it is, it isn't at all what I'd envisaged.

The man looked back and slapped his left buttock. 'I was injected like you! Terrorists!' He laughed merrily and lowered his bum closer. 'If you look close you can see the puncture wound, look!'

'Eric!' a woman called out, 'what the hell are you doing?!'

Another person appeared, someone he thought he recognised.

'The old man's awake!' she said, then bent down to pick him up from the floor.

Steiner felt himself strapped to a table and he tried to raise his head.

A firm hand pushed him back down. 'You're a tough bastard,' the woman said.

Steiner frowned. *That voice*. 'Agent Taylor?'

The young man's face reappeared inches from his. '*Ja! Ich bin Eric!*'

Steiner's heart raced at the sight of him, a beeping machine nearby replicating the rhythm.

Brett Taylor yanked him away. 'What's the matter with you?'

The person identified as Eric grinned at her. He held up a canister. 'It is good, no?'

Brett snatched the Nitronox from him and put the mask over Steiner's face. 'Stay alive, old man, I want to hear what you have to say.'

The FBI agent disappeared again and Steiner looked up at a strange ceiling and realised he was in a moving vehicle. The gurney rolled across the floor and Steiner closed his eyes as sleep took him. He'd been wrenched from the arms of his wife, Amelia, for this. *Why can't they just leave me be? All I want to do is rest, that's all I want.*

◆

Brett returned to the cabin and shoved Eric into the passenger seat.

Jessica checked her mirrors. 'They've dropped back.'

'They're regrouping,' Brett said, 'or there's a roadblock ahead.'

Eric chuckled to himself and a tear rolled down his face.

Jessica frowned at him. 'What's going on? Is the Professor alive?'

'Seems laughing boy here saved his life,' Brett said.

Eric let out of whoop. '*Das Gespenst* to the rescue!'

'He's also been helping himself to the gas you saved for the old man's revival.'

'Eric did well, Jessica Klein,' Bic said, as Brett placed the cyber criminal's touchscreen device on the dashboard.

Jessica switched off the truck's flashing light bar. 'It will have been for nothing if we all get caught.

A GMRC drone flew over them, its cameras aimed in their direction, and Brett moved back into the truck, staying out of sight.

'*Hallo*!' Eric waved at the UAV.

Speeding along, they rounded a long bend and Jessica let out a curse. Two miles ahead a massive roadblock spanned the next junction with lights and police galore. 'Bic, now would be the time to do your stuff.'

Silence.

No answer, wonderful, Jessica thought and slowed their travel.

'Ram them,' Eric said. 'Big truck, small cars, *das ist einfach*.'

'That's not simple,' Jessica said, 'that's crazy.'

'Do you have a better idea?'

It looked like a fairground in her mirrors, so many lights. More patrol cars had joined the party. They were trapped.

The hacker's device beeped. 'Eric,' Bic said, 'show me the road ahead.'

Eric picked up the touchscreen and pointed it forward.

'Eric is right; you must smash your way through. The vehicle you're driving weighs four point two tonnes. At a velocity of ninety-five miles an hour, the energy created will carry you through this section of the barrier.'

Eric turned the screen to show Jessica an image of the roadblock. Bic had placed an arrow on it where they needed to break through.

She frowned. 'How did you work that out?'

'Software is a powerful thing, Jessica Klein.'

'They'll shoot at us.'

'Correct, but not to kill you. They believe an FBI agent is on board, they will attempt to take out the tyres, but all federal vehicles are fitted with run flat–inflate mechanisms. Also—'

'Also what?'

'You have no other choice.'

'Ride or die,' Eric said, 'like the films. Sweet!'

Jessica rubbed her temples. What do I do? I'm no use to Evan and the girls dead, but if we're caught I'd be equally useless. She sucked in a breath. 'Buckle up.'

Eric punched the air. 'Go, Jessica!'

♦

'Everyone fan out!' Police Chief Denton cocked his rifle. 'We stop them here!'

A collective preparation of weapons greeted his order as the blue and white truck picked up speed. Behind it, the patrol cars dropped back and stopped.

Denton picked his spot. 'Concentrate on taking out the tyres and front grille!'

Faster and faster the vehicle barrelled towards them and then a thunderous horn sounded from behind.

The police chief looked round to see lights blazing.

A massive articulated lorry bore down on them. Its horns sounded again and he dived out of the way as the enormous vehicle ploughed through their barricade.

Patrol cars flew into the air, tossed aside like matchsticks, and moments later the coroner's truck shot past in the opposite direction, powering through the fiery carnage without slowing. Denton caught sight of someone laughing and waving at him through the passenger side window. Bewildered, the police officers around him managed to get off a couple of wayward shots.

'What now, sir?'

He looked at one of his men and at the wrecked patrol cars scattered around them. He gestured at a single GMRC drone that shot past in pursuit of the federal vehicle. 'It's the GMRC's problem now; get me whoever's in that semi-truck.' In the distance the lorry had come to a stop. 'I want their head on a fucking stick!'

CHAPTER FORTY-FIVE

'I don't see it anywhere.'

'That doesn't mean anything, it could be shadowing us.'

'She'll know.'

Jessica turned to Brett. 'What do you think?'

Brett's expression was noncommittal.

Eric made a noise of displeasure. 'What's the point of her if she isn't going to help us?'

'Bic, are you there?' Jessica said.

'I am.'

'Have we lost the drone?'

'I believe you have. They can travel far, but they have their limits like anything else and you've followed my directions to the letter.'

'But you can't be sure?'

'Nothing is certain, Jessica Klein.'

Jessica sighed. 'It looks like this is as good a place as any, then.'

'About time.' Brett moved into the rear of truck.

Let the inquisition begin, Jessica thought, and switched off the engine.

◆

Inside the back of the coroner's truck FBI Agent Brett Taylor eyed their captive with apprehensive expectation. What is this man willing to reveal now he's endured his ordeal, now he's facing civilians without power or influence? Can anything he says be trusted? Only time will tell, but one thing is sure, I'm not going to let him deny me again. He'll give up his secrets if I have to pry them out of his mind with a crowbar myself.

The man known as Professor Steiner sat propped up on his gurney, wearing the clothes he'd been provided. His tired eyes left Brett's and surveyed his two saviours, Eric, and the newsreader, Jessica Klein.

No one said a word for some time as each considered the other.

'I have your glasses,' the German said, stepping forward to hand the old man his spectacles.

The professor managed a small smile in gratitude. He put his eyewear on and cleared his throat. 'There was a ring—'

Eric dug a hand in his pocket, rummaged around and produced a gold wedding band which the old man accepted with reverence, his bruised hand clasping the shiny object tight.

Jessica moved to the fore. 'We've come a long way to speak to you, Professor, are you feeling up to talking?'

His eyes flicked towards Brett.

'I'm no longer with the FBI, I'm suspended awaiting dismissal.'

He raised a questioning eyebrow.

Images from multiple funerals flashed into Brett's mind and she suppressed the urge to wrap her hands around his scrawny neck. 'It seems my director doesn't appreciate his agents being related to mass murderers,' she said, 'especially those responsible for killing his colleagues.'

'I'm sorry; that must be difficult for you.'

'Save it. Tell us what you know and maybe I won't put a bullet in you.'

Jessica gave Brett a stern stare before continuing. 'Professor, my name's Jessica and this is my friend Eric. We know who you are; you were on the GMRC Directorate, weren't you?'

He sighed. 'Who I was doesn't matter. Whatever it is you think I know, I can't help you. I'm sorry, you've wasted your time.'

Eric looked shocked. 'But we saved your life!'

The professor hung his head. 'And I should thank you for that?' He looked up. 'I was ready. I've served my country, my planet. Haven't I done enough? Didn't I deserve to rest in peace with my wife?'

'We're sorry, but we needed your help. The world needs your help.' Jessica laid a hand on his leg, which made him flinch.

Brett quelled the sympathy that tugged at her deepest depths. She remembered too well the fear induced by a beating and this man had endured more than she had at the hands of the tormented devil that was her father.

'We know the world's stockpiles are being taken into the subterranean bases,' Eric said, 'and the surface is doomed.'

Brett saw a brief look of shock on Steiner's face. A sense of unease descended on her. *Had these two fools been telling the truth after all?* 'So it's true?' She took a step forward and Steiner cowered from her like a wounded animal.

A hand on Brett's arm halted her advance and Jessica moved past. 'I've seen one of these bases, been inside one, EUSB Deutschland.' She pointed at Brett. 'Her father worked in one, USSB Steadfast. You were his superior, you know all there is to know.' She took out a photo of her family to show him. 'I need to know, I need to save my daughters, my husband. Don't they deserve to live? Don't they deserve a chance? Please, Professor, I need to get them into one of these bases, I will do anything, just help us.'

'I'm sorry; I don't know what you're talking about. I worked for the GMRC's Public Relations Division.'

'Bull!' Brett pushed Jessica aside and grasped his shirt.

Trembling, the old man turned his head away.

'Let him go!' Eric said, grabbing her wrists.

Shaking with anger, Brett released the old man and Jessica

squared up to her. 'You're not helping. Go and get some air!' The tiny newsreader thrust a finger at the rear of the truck.

Brett scowled at the professor, her heart beating ten to the dozen. *I might have known he'd tell us squat. What was I thinking?* Stifling a sneer of contempt, she pushed open the doors and dropped down to stalk away into the dark.

♦

Jessica Klein watched the FBI agent come to a stop twenty feet away from the truck, her breath curling up into the freezing air. She closed the doors and turned back to Steiner. 'I'm sorry, our friend, she's—'

The professor wasn't listening. He faced the wall, blocking out sight and sound.

Jessica laid a tentative hand on his shoulder.

He twitched at her touch and turned to face her, his expression one of sorrow and defeat. 'It's understandable – she hates me, and with good reason.'

'Why did you help that man, Colonel Samson? Why did you help him do what he did?'

'I don't know anymore, everything's a blur, but I feel responsible for all those poor people he killed. I deserve to die, I accept that now.'

'I don't believe that.'

Steiner remained silent and Jessica gestured for Eric to join her outside.

Closing the doors behind them, they moved a few paces from the truck to afford themselves some privacy.

Eric blew into his hands to warm them. 'That's the man we came all this way to rescue? He can't save himself, let alone the world.'

'He's clearly traumatised, beaten black and blue. I think he's lost the will to live.'

'Which means he's no use to anyone,' Brett said, rejoining them. 'You've risked everything for nothing.'

'No.' Jessica shook her head. 'I won't accept that. He just needs more time.'

'According to you, time is exactly what we don't have. It could take weeks for him to come round, if at all.'

'The stockpiles are going fast,' Eric said. 'Brett is right, time is running out.'

Jessica thought for a moment. 'Perhaps we should up the ante.' She withdrew the touchscreen device. 'Bic, the professor isn't opening up to us and he may never tell us what he knows. Any ideas?'

The computer gave a bleep. 'We always knew this might happen, Jessica Klein. Take me to him.'

'But you said if he knew you were behind his release he'd be reluctant to talk.'

'That is correct, but we have little option if what you say is true. It is time for him to know. It's time for us to talk.'

CHAPTER FORTY-SIX

Professor Steiner leaned his head back against the wall. He ached all over and his skin felt like it was on fire. Whatever they'd injected into him back at the prison hadn't killed him, but its after-effects lingered on. The smell of chemicals hung in the air and he could hear the muffled voices of his captors outside. How they had found out who he was he didn't know, but that they knew about the Subterranean Programme was bad – very bad. There was still time to disrupt the GMRC's carefully laid plans, if word got out.

The doors to the back of the truck opened and the Englishwoman and the German entered, followed by Samson's daughter. The doors slammed shut and Steiner jumped at the sound, startled.

The woman who called herself Jessica handed him a small computer. 'We have someone we want you to speak to.'

Steiner looked at her expectant expression and then glanced at Agent Taylor, who gazed at him with analytical eyes.

The screen lit up, beeped, and a flashing cursor danced across the screen.

Professor Steiner, I have been waiting a long time to speak to you _

. . .

Steiner sat looking at the message unsure what kind of torment he was to be subjected to next.

The young German came to peer at the screen. 'You can speak into it.'

Steiner couldn't have cared less. He dropped the device to his lap and shut his eyes.

Another beep sounded and a new voice spoke. 'Professor Steiner, you will be interested in what I have to say.'

'Will I,' Steiner said, his eyelids remaining closed.

'It has taken me many, many years to reach this point in time. To be speaking to you now is a culmination of unspeakable commitment. You are probably wondering who I am. But we have met on occasion, at least indirectly. You have proven quite a resilient adversary.'

Steiner remained still, but his mind had tuned into the voice, the formulation of its words spoken with a tone that captivated the senses.

'I have seen your work in the raw when you helped Brett Taylor's father in Los Angeles,' the voice continued. 'That was quite the hack, Professor Steiner. Utilising GMRC servers to infiltrate the FBI's mainframe: impressive. But without your inside knowledge of the GMRC's systems you would have found it far harder to achieve.'

Steiner felt a desire to respond, but once more he held his tongue.

'So, by now you are wondering who I am. And I shall tell you. I go by many names, but you, I think, will know me best as B.I.C. or Bic.'

Steiner cracked open a weary eye.

'Or perhaps you know me as *Da Muss Ich*, D.M.I. or Deforcement Insidious?'

'I know who you are,' Steiner said. 'Because I Can, the international terrorist. The hacker idolised by his peers. A man without a code. A man without morals.'

Brett Taylor gave a snort of derision.

'It seems others think the same of you, Professor Steiner,' Bic said. 'Times change, people change—'

'But the game always remains.'

Bic chuckled. 'Ah, you know me well, do you not?'

'I know you seek to manipulate me. That's all you know.'

'Is saving the world such an evil, Professor Steiner?'

'Is that what you think you're doing?'

'I – like those standing before you now – wonder where the governments of the world are taking our food and water, and all our other resources. You think someone wouldn't notice, Professor Steiner? You think just because you have the power of the GMRC controlling the masses with your big data servers, population control and all-seeing eyes that you are gods?' Bic laughed, the sound disingenuous. 'Your arrogance is monumental.'

Steiner took a breath. 'And yours isn't? You think your attacks are justified, that you know better than those that lead?'

'Ah, so you don't deny the resources are being taken?'

'That's not what I said.'

'But it is inferred. But then I do not need you to confirm what I already know. We know there are underground bases. We know the resources of the world are being taken to these bases. And we know there is something you are not telling us.'

Steiner searched the faces of the three people before him. He was getting pulled into a debate he did not care for.

B.I.C. – the great hacker. Steiner had battled against his attacks for decades, working with those across multiple GMRC divisions to protect their secrets for the good of the species. This man was a menace like no other. No one else had caused them more problems or wasted more of their time, and no one else had the skills he possessed. Steiner had often thought the name to be a cover for a group of people, but over the years it had become apparent, through their interactions with him, that B.I.C. was indeed one individual. It had amazed everyone that someone so incredibly gifted had flown under their radar because, like it or not, B.I.C. was by far the most talented, elusive, resourceful and motivated criminal of the twenty-first century, perhaps of all time. Some theorised his IQ was off the scale. Steiner was himself regarded as something of a genius in certain circles, not that he courted such accolades, but even he struggled to comprehend the abilities B.I.C. wielded during his infiltrations. Genius was not the word; his coding – sections that they'd managed to find – was something else. Computer experts still pored over it today. A special team had even been set up to track him down, but to no avail.

'Conspiracy theories have been around since the beginning of time,' Steiner said, his need to speak unfathomable. It felt like this man knew him better than he did.

Bic's device let out a bleep. 'What is a conspiracy theory except the truth wrapped in a lie, wrapped within truth? People scoff and mock conspiracy theories as they're not willing to see a world as it can be, horrific and dark, and yet if you can recognise the dark you can also see the light posing as dark, or dark posing as light. *In Veritate Scientia*.'

Steiner knew those words. *In truth, knowledge*. The motto of the GMRC Directorate.

'Just because it's a theory doesn't mean it's not true,' Bic continued, 'in fact the media's propaganda can be full of lies and the conspiracy theory full of truth. You should know that, Professor Steiner. Ignore the words of compulsive liars. The politicians say what they have to, they say what they're told to say. You say what you're told to say. You think how they tell you to think. Actions always – without fail – speak louder than any words.'

Steiner heaved a sigh. 'If you think you know so much, why do you need me?'

'Because a half-truth can be as dangerous as a lie. Brett Taylor needs evidence and justice, Jessica Klein must save her family, and Eric Wolf wants to save the world.'

'And what about you?'

'I, Professor Steiner, seek only one thing – understanding.'

Something Bic had just said sought to awaken an elusive memory from Steiner's subconscious mind. He tried to focus, but the last few days had left him weak and befuddled. The thought slipped away, lost, and he ran his parched tongue over cracked lips.

Eric noticed his discomfort and handed him a bottle of water, which Steiner accepted with gratitude.

'Who are the hundreds of thousands of civilians condemned to a premature death, Professor Steiner?' Bic said.

Steiner looked at Brett as he sipped his water.

'Is a city in danger?' Bic continued, 'or one of your underground bases, perhaps?'

Steiner didn't reply.

'Come now, Professor, we could help you save these people. Do you not see the opportunity we provide? You have been deposed from power, forced into a criminal act against your will. You have no direct power, no influence, and yet you still have the one thing that can shape the world.'

Steiner couldn't understand how Bic seemed to know so much about him. And yet he couldn't describe how little he cared. 'And that is?'

'Knowledge. The secrets you hold could save billions of lives, or at least millions. Is that not a worthy cause?'

'Not if it endangers millions more.' Steiner had a sudden thought, recalling what had previously eluded him. He looked at the slender figure of the woman from England. 'Jessica Klein, the BBC newsreader. I thought I recognised the name.'

'Former newsreader,' she said, her tone bitter. 'Your people at the GMRC saw fit to frame me.'

Steiner held Bic's device before him. 'And that's your grand plan, to find out what I know and relay it around the world for all to see? Using this woman you've conned into your service as your conduit.'

'I've conned no one, Professor Steiner. I leave that up to the GMRC.'

Steiner held Jessica Klein's gaze. He could see doubt behind those eyes. 'And yet it seems Ms. Klein feels otherwise.'

'I said no such thing,' the newsreader said.

Bic gave a chortle. 'Ah, Professor Steiner, your quick wit is returning. Good. We will need you at your best in the days and weeks ahead.'

'There is no "*we*". If there's one thing you should know about me, *Bic*, it's that I never make the same mistake twice. I've already helped one terrorist; I won't aid another, no matter what you say or do.'

'Is that right, Professor Steiner?'

Steiner held his tongue again. He knew his time at the GMRC had ended as soon as Colonel Samson had fired his first shot in the FBI stronghold back in LA. Or was it when Joiner turned on me back in USSB Steadfast? he wondered. Either way, his power had gone, and with it his ability to influence anything in the grand scheme of humanity's future. I've done my part and I'm satisfied – no – proud. I can help no one now. Anything I do will lead to further loss of life. I have to accept saving those in USSB Steadfast is beyond my control, anything I do to bring attention to their plight would expose everything, would threaten all the plans I've worked half my life to achieve. They will have to find their own way and I'm so tired, so very tired.

'What if I told you I intercepted a military communiqué yesterday,' Bic said, 'a message that indicated a massive field of space debris had been tracked entering Earth's atmosphere? What if I told you I have unearthed other such communications, all of which confirm the destruction of all four space stations that were orbiting the globe?'

Steiner felt his chest tighten. The GMRC's Space Programme was the last hope the surface had. A slim chance of survival, considering their past attempts had failed so spectacularly, but still a chance, nonetheless, or perhaps a chance for billions to survive for a few years longer. He had always seen NASA's effort to stem the flow of the approaching asteroids as a shot in the dark, a throw of the cosmic dice, a toss of the galactic coin – heads you win, tails you lose. But as all had come to accept, only a network of underground bases could guarantee humanity's survival.

'Are you still there, Professor Steiner?'

'He's listening,' Brett said, 'we all are.'

'Yes,' Bic continued, 'this information will be of interest to you all. Do you know what else I found, Professor?'

Steiner watched the expression of Eric, eager to hear what this terrorist had to say. Jessica Klein looked wary but equally enrapt, while the FBI agent stood, arms folded, phone in hand, her face one of guarded hostility. 'I'm all ears,' he said.

'I found a hidden message buried in the jumble of data that managed to penetrate the dust cloud.'

'What did it say?' Eric said, unable to contain himself.

'It is too weak to comprehend in its entirety, but it's a distress signal, of that I am certain. The curious thing is the process and frequencies used are quite old, in fact they predate the GMRC era by three decades, a twentieth century relic in analogue form. The sender has gone to a lot of trouble to hide their identity and location.'

'Why is that weird?' Jessica said.

Eric shot her a look of disbelief. 'Because why would you want to hide a distress call?'

'Eric is correct, Jessica Klein. The only reason I could discern for such a move would be to avoid detection by the GMRC itself, or those government agencies that work alongside it. It is a cry for help and we need to respond. If Professor Steiner is unwilling to help us, then perhaps whoever is behind this message will.'

Steiner knew the hacker could be making this up. In fact, it was more than likely a ruse to pressure him into spilling his secrets. A pity for them he was in no mood to comply. He closed his eyes, rested his head back and retreated into his battered body. *Bic can play all he likes; I'm not even in the game.*

♦

The GMRC man shut his eyes and leaned back against the truck's interior while Jessica contemplated the hacker's words. 'How can we speak to them if the signal is so weak?' she said.

'There is one place that will be capable of retrieving the full message,' Bic replied, 'enough, anyway, that it can be pieced together.'

'And where's that?' Jessica said.

'It is a large cluster of radio telescope antennas called ALMA. The Atacama Large Millimeter/submillimeter Array in Chile, South America.'

Brett snorted. 'And how you do you expect us to get there?'

'There is an aircraft waiting for you on a runway two miles from your current location.'

'Why am I not surprised?' Jessica shook her head.

'Because you know me too well, Jessica Klein.'

'I think you're missing something, Bic,' Steiner said, his eyes remaining closed.

'And what is that, Professor Steiner?'

'No one is going to be able to reach your plane.'

Silence ensued before Bic spoke again. 'Elaborate.'

'How long since you called them?' Steiner said.

There was no answer.

Eric looked at Jessica. 'What's he talking about?'

Steiner opened his eyes and looked at Brett.

The FBI agent considered him. 'I didn't think you were awake.'

Eric grasped Jessica's arm. 'What are they talking about?'

Jessica saw the phone in Brett's hand. 'You didn't?!'

'I did. The FBI has heard everything. Bic's transmission will have been traced and you'll all be going to prison for a very long time.' Brett looked at her phone. 'And according to this, they're almost here.'

CHAPTER FORTY-SEVEN

'You bitch!'

'What can I say?' Brett said. 'I want my job back.'

Jessica rushed to the front of the truck, heart racing. In the distance the lights of a vehicular convoy approached at speed. Turning the key failed to start the engine and she tried again.

Nothing!

Brett appeared behind her. 'Having trouble?'

Jessica turned the key again and the engine spluttered to life.

Something cold pressed against the back of Jessica's head and she turned to see the barrel of a gun an inch from her eye.

'I can't let you go, I'm afraid,' Brett said, as Eric approached the FBI agent from behind, the heavy canister of laughing gas raised to strike.

'Take another step, *mein capitan*,' Brett said, 'and she's dead and you're next.'

Eric froze mid-step.

The lights drew closer before a roar of noise shot past overhead, closely followed by two more, the sound rattling the truck's panels.

'I didn't know the FBI had fighter jets,' Jessica said.

An oscillating ringtone emanated from Brett's phone and she

frowned. Keeping her gun trained on Jessica, she accepted an incoming video call.

A face appeared, one Jessica didn't recognise, but judging by Brett's expression, one she did.

'Ah, Agent Taylor, isn't it?'

'What do *you* want?'

'My my, agent – or should that be ex-agent? – I expected a less frosty welcome than this. I am in a position, after all, to restore your privileges and more besides.'

'I don't want anything from the likes of you.'

The angular face turned towards Jessica. 'Ms. Klein, we meet again.'

'I don't believe we've had the pleasure.'

The man's mouth contorted into a repulsive smile. 'Forgive me. My name is Malcolm Joiner, I'm the GMRC Director of Intelligence. I have to admit, I had hoped you were dead, but it seems you just keep coming back – like a bad penny.'

'My director will have your job for this,' Brett said.

Joiner laughed. 'FBI Director Flynn can't tie his own shoes without help. And besides, you'll all soon be six foot under and you've given me the greatest prizes of all, the cyber terrorist, and another chance to say goodbye to an old friend.'

A bullet tore through the windscreen to punch into Brett's chest. Her gun fell to the floor and she slumped sideways.

Jessica slammed the truck into reverse and hit the accelerator. 'Eric, grab Bic's console!'

More bullets peppered the truck as they reversed at high speed. Keeping low, Jessica swung the truck round and floored it.

Eric returned to her side, device in hand, and Jessica glanced in her mirrors to see military humvees bearing down on them. 'Bic, we need you!'

He didn't answer.

'Jesus Christ, where is he?!'

Eric pulled aside Brett's shirt to reveal a bullet-proof vest. 'She's alive.'

The agent's eyes blinked open.

'And what were you thinking?' Jessica said to Brett. She saw a sign with a picture of a plane on it and made a sharp right turn. The truck leaned and wheels screeched.

Brett winced and struggled into a sitting position. 'You're all terrorists, I was doing my duty.'

'And look where that got you!'

A bright light appeared in the sky ahead.

Jessica slammed on the brakes and something hit them from behind, throwing them all forward.

'Take a left turn!' Bic's voice said.

Jessica heaved on the wheel and the truck lifted onto two wheels. Moments later it dropped back down with a jolt.

'Where have you been?!' Jessica said.

The noise of helicopters above drowned out Bic's reply. Blinding lights suddenly illuminated the brush and trees outside and a message appeared on Bic's screen.

I've been preparing, Jessica Klein. Keep going straight, you're almost there _

An explosion in the air turned into a fireball, followed by another. Black GMRC drones shot past overhead.

'What's happening?!' Eric shouted.

Jessica didn't know; scared out of her wits, she kept her foot to the floor.

Closed gates appeared ahead. Smashing through them, the coroner's truck careered into the airport.

'Where's our plane?!' Jessica said.

Straight in front of you _

. . .

'You're kidding, right?'

A sleek military jet waited on the dark runway.

It's a hypersonic VIP drone transport. Hurry, you don't have much time! _

Jessica drove up to the aircraft, slammed on the brakes and jumped out. Behind, five GMRC drones hovered in the air by the gates, guns blazing. The military that had been in pursuit took evasive action and returned fire. Bic had done it again, hijacking more UAVs to buy them time.

Running to the back of the truck, Jessica threw open the doors and jumped inside. Grabbing the disorientated professor, she helped him to the floor.

He grabbed her arm. 'Leave me, save yourself.'

'Don't be stupid.' She half-dragged him onto the tarmac. 'Besides, you're too valuable.'

He grimaced in pain. 'I'm touched.'

'Eric, get Bic's device!'

With the old man leaning on her shoulder, Jessica stumbled toward the plane, the noise of the firefight driving her on. Eric appeared alongside with Brett following.

'Where do you think you're going?!' Jessica shouted at the FBI agent.

'With you.'

'Like hell you are!'

Brett ran ahead to the plane and Jessica cursed.

A massive explosion shattered the air.

The coroner's truck disappeared in a ball of flame, followed by the thunderous roar of a fighter overhead.

Their transport drone hummed to life, its engines whining to a crescendo.

No sooner had they hurried up its ramp than its hatch closed behind them. Sealed inside the cramped area, red lighting all around, the jet blasted forward and Jessica fell back against a wall.

Deafening noise made her ears ring while g-force pinned her arms to her sides. She gritted her teeth as the sensation increased. Her body felt like a five tonne elephant.

Seconds later the discomfort lifted and Jessica retrieved Bic's console and, leaving the professor with Eric, went to seek out Brett. Squeezing past a bulkhead, she found herself in the craft's cockpit. The duplicitous FBI Agent sat in one of the seats with a mind-boggling array of holographic screens all around her and a large head-up-display in the centre.

'Who's flying?' Jessica said.

Brett looked round and pointed at Bic's console in Jessica's hand.

A message appeared on the cockpit screen.

You may want to sit down, Jessica Klein. We have company _

Three dots appeared on the screen's radar image, closing fast. Jessica scrambled into one of the pilot seats and struggled into its harness. 'I thought this was a drone?' she said, seeing a joystick before her and a black-visored high-tech helmet suspended above.

It's a dual system. Hang on. This may get bumpy _

A beeping alarm sounded and Jessica saw six more dots materialise from the first three. A message flashed on-screen.

WARNING!
MISSILE LOCK
WARNING!

Jessica heard Brett swear. Flying close to the ground, their plane rolled right and up and Jessica felt her stomach leave her.

The flashing warnings continued and their aircraft released a spray of blazing flares.

Two explosions rocked Jessica in her seat. The four remaining dots closed on their position and Bic banked the aircraft up and then dived down. The horizon line on the HUD spun as the plane ducked and weaved. More flares were released and three more explosions buffeted them.

Skyscrapers of a floodlit city appeared ahead and Jessica's eyes widened.

Engines screaming, the aircraft tore through the narrow streets at low level, shattering glass with its passing. The final rocket closed before the aircraft turned at the last minute, dodging a building.

The missile on the radar disappeared and Jessica fought down the urge to vomit. 'Bic, never do that again!'

'I'm afraid I can't comply with your request, Jessica Klein.'

The three fighter jets chasing them reappeared ahead. Rockets fired and their plane angled up. The same warning message appeared as six more rockets homed in on them.

A new alarm buzzed in the cockpit and a sheath of material curled over Jessica's legs and waist. The helmet that had hung above her lowered to muffle her ears and the dials in its visor blazed to life. A single message appeared before her eyes:

SABRE ENGINE ACTIVATION IMMINENT

The missiles drew closer.

'Have you ever wanted to be a record-breaker, Jessica Klein?' Bic said.

Jessica's fingers dug into her seat. 'Not really!'

The plane levelled out. 'That's a shame, as you're about to become one.'

'What!?'

Another message appeared:

SABRE ENGINE ... ENGAGED

A deep rumble exploded into deafening noise. A flash of light, and the aircraft went hypersonic.

◆

The lights from roads and towns flashed past, faster and faster, blurring into lines. Behind, the missiles fell back as their drone passed Mach 6.

A host of systems tracked their craft as it shot south across the continental United States. Missile batteries on the ground fired and tracer rounds lit up the air.

Bic angled the plane left, right and into a series of heart-stopping barrel rolls. Teeth rattling, Jessica clung to consciousness as the world span out of control, upside down and inside out. They levelled out and soon after they were over the black swell of the Pacific Ocean, which tore past below. The drone dropped lower and calm waters exploded upwards in their wake. Another alarm sounded. The United States North Pacific Fleet unleashed its weaponry, lighting up tranquil seas in a blaze of fire.

Bic banked the plane up, while multiple rockets chased them through dark skies.

Jessica closed her eyes. 'I thought planes couldn't fly through the dust cloud!'

'We're about to test that theory,' Bic said.

A blaze of light, a sound like thunder, and the craft thrust forward. Jessica thought of her family as they entered the upper atmosphere to disappear into the great cloud.

♦

Some time later Jessica opened her eyes. *I must have passed out*, she thought. Ahead the dust cloud thinned and a shimmer of light exploded into a blaze of glory. The sun's rays bathed the cockpit of the military drone before its engine stuttered to silence.

Jessica's body felt light. 'Are we in space?'

'Just brushing its fringes,' Bic said.

The sensation continued a while longer before gravity returned and the plane sank back into dark swirling obscurity. Warning messages and symbols covered the displays.

'The craft's engines are no longer in operation,' Bic said, 'I'll have to glide you down.'

'Have we dodged the missiles?'

'Yes, their tracking systems would have been disrupted by the dust and this craft's defensive technology. We will have to hope the military units in South America are too occupied in their civil wars to worry about one lone plane entering their airspace.'

Skimming down through the heavens, the streamlined craft plummeted back to Earth.

Lightning dazzled as they passed through an enormous storm. Dust and rain battered them while thunder cracked the sky open like the hammer of God.

A bolt of lightning struck a wing, plunging the plane into a flat spin. Warnings sounded and lights flashed red.

Jessica's breathing sounded ragged to her ears as they dropped like a stone. Sounds and lights swamped her senses. Unable to move, she managed to say one word: 'BIC!'

The plane continued to fall out of control. The cyber terrorist didn't reply and Jessica felt consciousness slip into the abyss of nothing.

CHAPTER FORTY-EIGHT

'JESSICA.'

'Hmmm?'

Hands shook her shoulders. 'Jessica, wake up.'

Jessica opened her eyes to see the face of Eric peering at her. 'What's going on? Did we make it?'

Eric gave a nervous laugh and looked around the cockpit of the military aircraft. 'It looks that way.'

'Where are we?'

'I have no idea.' Eric helped her up from her seat.

'Where's Brett?'

'She took the professor into the building.'

'Building?'

Eric led Jessica out of the plane and pointed to a large structure nearby. Shrouded in darkness, a single light emanated from one of its many ground-floor windows.

They moved towards the glow.

'This way,' said a disembodied voice.

Jessica adjusted course to find the shadowy form of Brett holding a door open for them.

They entered and the FBI agent pushed past to lead them down a dim corridor and on into a brightly lit room. Jessica looked around what appeared to be some kind of operations hub. Long, curved desks stood spaced out in rows before a large wallscreen, each one sporting a host of computers and banks of intriguing electrical equipment.

The still form of Professor Steiner lay on one of the desks.

'Is he okay?' Jessica said.

Brett followed her gaze. 'He's alive, if that's what you mean.'

'He must have passed out like the rest of us.' Jessica walked over to see that his chest rose and fell in the rhythm of life. Nearby a printer lay idle, a continuous sheet of paper hanging down from it in folds. Jessica studied the data that had printed out. It was a mass of meaningless numbers and graphs. 'What is this place?'

'We're at the radio telescope array,' Brett said.

'We made it to Chile?'

Brett moved to a window and pulled up a blind. Outside, sat the grey bulk of the military drone, its shape just discernable in the lights of the building they now inhabited.

Eric rubbed a shoulder. 'I thought we were goners.'

'Me, too,' Jessica said. 'Bic must have regained control somehow.'

The pocket of her coroner's uniform vibrated and she withdrew Bic's console.

'You are correct, Jessica Klein,' Bic said. 'But it was touch and go, you are all lucky to be alive.'

'No thanks to her.' Eric gestured at Brett.

'I was doing my duty.'

Jessica ground her teeth. 'Did you believe anything we said?'

'You're convincing,' Brett said, 'I give you that. But whatever is true, it doesn't change the fact you've committed multiple crimes.'

'And your career comes first, is that it?'

'Of course. I'm not about to let a bunch of terrorists determine my future.'

Jessica bunched her fists. 'You don't have a future, none of us do!'

'According to you.'

Jessica let out a screech of frustration. She'd never met anyone so pig-headed.

Brett leant against the window. 'I don't know why you're so surprised.' She pointed at Steiner, who stirred awake. 'He's told us nothing. You really expect me to let him go? That my father escaped justice is bad enough, but for them *both* to get away with mass murder – no way. I can't let that happen.'

'And so you decided to offer us up,' Jessica said, 'just like that?'

'Pretty much.'

'Didn't work out though, did it?

Brett ignored the comment and returned her gaze to the darkness outside.

'Who the hell was that man, anyway?' Jessica said. 'What did he call himself?'

'Malcolm Joiner.' Brett glanced back. 'He's on the GMRC Directorate.'

Jessica thought back to his words. *I had hoped you were dead.* He obviously knew her. He must have been the person behind her fall from grace. It made sense. Her on-air rant about the GMRC back in New York would have ruffled more than a few feathers. That it attracted the attention of the Directorate should be no surprise. But now he knew she was working with Bic, she'd become the terrorist, fighting against the system she'd once enabled. She massaged her face, trying to make sense of it all. *One thing is certain*; *Bic has taken me even further into the rabbit hole.*

Professor Steiner groaned and sat up.

'Are you okay, Professor?' Eric helped him to his feet.

'Apart from a blazing headache, it seems so.'

'So, what happens now?' Eric said.

Brett faced them. 'Well, it looks like your theories are out of the window.'

'How do you figure?' Jessica said.

'The skies are clearing.'

'What?'

Brett pointed outside. 'Look for yourself. The dust cloud is lifting, light is filtering through.'

'Where?' Jessica moved to the window.

The twenty-four hour night they'd been enduring had shifted to a darker shade of brown and a flat desert landscape was just visible, as if illuminated by the dying embers of dawn.

Brett stared out at the concave dish of a nearby radio telescope. 'So much for your doomsday theory, they said as soon as the light reappears the dust will disappear exponentially.'

'And who told us that?' Jessica said. 'The GMRC. I'd rather trust you.'

Brett scowled at the inference before Bic's console beeped. 'I'm picking up a signal, Jessica Klein.'

'The one you told us about?'

'No,' he said, 'it seems to be GMRC in origin.'

'What does it say?'

'Is there a wallscreen in the room?'

She turned round to look. 'Yes.'

'Put my device against its induction pad.'

Jessica walked over to it and attached the console to the magnetic area designed for high speed data transfer.

The wallscreen powered up at Bic's command and its image coalesced into a mass of black and white pixels. With a fuzz of sound a picture emerged from the ether, depicting a scene of pure beauty. Sunlight glinted on a distant horizon. Blue skies shone above a lush green forest and a flock of red and green macaws flew past a tribe of howler monkeys foraging in the trees.

The sounds of nature came through the room's speakers to further immerse them in the lustrous vision before a shadow moved across the screen and a tall figure appeared.

Jessica recognised the man from Brett's video call.

Malcolm Joiner held his hands behind his back and faced the camera that filmed him. 'Ah, there you all are. I feared you for dead.'

No one spoke and Jessica moved to the fore. 'What do you want from us?'

'Ms. Klein. It seems you and your merry band lead a charmed life. Your escape from U.S. airspace was nothing short of miraculous, although I believe that was down to your hacker friend more than anything else. Is he there, by chance?'

'I am here,' Bic said, his voice also coming via the room's speakers.

'Excellent,' Joiner said. 'Your acquisition of our drone was – well – *unexpected* shall we say? You'll have to let us know how you keep managing to access our systems so freely.'

'That is for you to find out, Malcolm Joiner. I would have thought, however, with the resources at your disposal you would have figured it out by now. Clearly your intelligence is as lacking as your power.'

The half-smile fell from Joiner's face. 'You think that because you continue to elude us you have power? You have none. Your attempts to disrupt GMRC protocols have all failed. The information you think you have is worthless and whatever plans you've devised will never reach fruition. Time is running out for you, B.I.C., running out for you all.'

'You didn't answer my question,' Jessica said. 'What do you want from us?'

'Do you know the worst thing about a traitor, Ms. Klein? They forget on which side their bread has been buttered.' The intelligence director moved to his screen, where a graphical box appeared at a touch of his hand.

Jessica's eyes grew wide with fear.

'This is your family, is it not?' Joiner paused the footage of her husband and two daughters. 'The young are so precious, aren't they? And so fragile, unable to defend themselves against the terrors of the world.'

Jessica felt panic rising.

'It would be a shame for them to meet a premature end, would it not?'

Jessica didn't know what to say. What could she do? She was helpless and he knew it. She would do anything to protect her children, anything.

Malcolm Joiner failed to hide a smile of pleasure. 'And you, Agent

Taylor. I've spoken to the relevant departments and it seems we have a position available for you here at the GMRC. It would be a massive pay increase, of course, and you would be operating outside the limited reach of the United States government. Is that something that would interest you?'

Brett glanced at Jessica. 'I don't work well with people who threaten the lives of innocents.'

'Pity,' Joiner said. 'Your father will be loath to hear of your death when the time comes.'

'You know where he is?'

'Oh, yes. I was the one who ordered his release.'

'He wasn't released, he was broken out, and you've just admitted a federal offence to an agent of the state.'

'A suspended agent, Ms. Taylor. And one who'll be lucky to stay alive, let alone step foot back in the United States and bring charges against a man who's above the law.'

'No one is above the law.'

Joiner chuckled. 'Ah, dear me, you really don't know how the world works, do you, child? You see, when you have power such as I wield, the rules of the masses don't apply. The higher up you go, the more power you have, the less rules you have until, finally, you realise, the rules are as you make them. For those on the outside, who've lived their lives chained by these laws, I can see how that can be hard to comprehend.' He leaned toward the screen as if taking them into his confidence. 'I can tell you, though, the experience is quite liberating.'

'Malcolm Joiner,' Bic said, 'we know the world's resources are being taken into your subterranean bases. Your secrets are unravelling and soon I will have them all.'

The intelligence director appeared unaffected by the hacker's admission.

'I have already located USSB Steadfast and EUSB Deutschland,' Bic continued. 'It is only a matter of time before we uncover the rest. And when that happens I will disclose the information worldwide.'

'Considering your current company,' Joiner said, 'I thought your knowledge would have been far greater. Isn't that so, Professor?'

Jessica turned to see Professor Steiner staring down at his clasped hands while his body trembled.

'Come, Professor, I would have thought you of all people would have something to say to me.'

The professor didn't respond, failing even to look up.

Malcolm Joiner laughed. 'Oh, how the mighty fall. I'm sure, no, I know, the company you're keeping must boil your blood – Professor Steiner working with the terrorist he so despises. The irony!'

Jessica saw the old man's jaw clench in anger as he shook and twitched with increasing violence.

'Your position really is between a rock and a hard place, isn't it, Professor? You're powerless. How does it feel to be so impotent? I find it hard to imagine. I guess Nathan Bryant could tell you, or should that be *could have* told you.'

Professor Steiner remained in a state of tremorous flux, immobilised.

'Did you hear about the explosion on the news, Professor?' Joiner continued. 'Although how could you, you were in prison. Some said it measured over six on the Richter scale. They said it was strange as the epicentre of the quake was located on the Colorado and New Mexican border, near a town called Dulce. Ring any bells?' Joiner paused, waiting for a response. When none came he resumed his monologue. 'When those in Steadfast tried to fight their way out I had to take steps. You understand? They were a diversion I could no longer afford. The nuclear bomb we dropped on them wasn't that large, although I heard it created quite a substantial crater on the surface.'

Professor Steiner was looking up now, his eyes ablaze with fury and hate.

'There he is,' Joiner said. 'I thought that might get your attention. I guess you're wondering why? Why sacrifice such a significant investment? There were a variety of reasons, most of which I'd have thought you'd have worked out by now with that big brain of yours. I suppose I might as well tell you, what harm can it do? If the truth you unearthed had come out, Steadfast's half a million residents would have been moved to another base, a base we both know is too valuable to become overcrowded. Secondly, there were—'

'I know what you're doing, Malcolm Joiner,' Bic said, 'but your efforts will be in vain.'

'Will they now; our trace is almost complete.'

'And yet so is mine.'

A smile crept across Joiner's face. 'Is it? Tell me where I am and I'll let you know if you're getting warm.'

'You are in the state of New York – no – wait, Washington ... or—'

'You don't sound too sure.'

'Jessica,' Bic said, 'you must leave. They've found you!'

Joiner approached the camera until his face filled the screen. 'You're wrong, hacker, I've found you all!'

CHAPTER FORTY-NINE

THE IMAGE of Malcolm Joiner disappeared to be replaced by a stream of coding.

'Eric,' Bic said, 'they've overcome my defences. I need your help, we need to divert their trace. Quickly!'

Eric rushed forward and pulled a keyboard from the wall. He looked at the code. 'What do you want me to do?!'

'Follow my lead on-screen; I need you to work fast.'

Eric gazed ahead, fingers tapping at the keys.

'But you told us to get out?!' Jessica said.

'He hasn't found you yet, Jessica Klein,' Bic said, 'but soon, very soon.'

Jessica watched in frustrated fear, unable to help her young German friend with his task.

Malcolm Joiner's image reappeared in the corner of the wall display. 'You might as well give up; I know you're in Chile,' Joiner put a finger to his ear as if listening to instruction, 'in the north east. The Pacific Fleet already has bombers in the air.'

'You need to work faster, Eric,' Bic said, his tone urgent.

'Ich kann es nicht, ich bin zu langsam!'

'You can do it, Eric,' Bic said, 'concentrate.'

An alarm sounded on the screen.

'*Scheisse*!' Eric raised his hands in anguish. 'It's no good, there's too much!'

A calloused hand grasped his shoulder and Eric looked up into the face of Professor Steiner.

'Four hands are better than two.' The professor sat down next to him with another keyboard and joined their defence, his fingers a blur as they flew over the user interface.

The clatter of keys filled the air and Jessica held her breath.

Seconds dragged by like minutes, then the code vanished and Joiner's image filled the screen once more. He smiled at them. 'Time's up.'

Another image appeared – grey footage of the ground from high above. In two of the corners numerical values fluctuated in value, while crosshairs in the middle traced the surface as it flowed past beneath.

'We need to move!' Brett shouted.

Professor Steiner turned round to meet Jessica's eyes, his expression one of despair. 'I'm sorry, it's too late.'

A massive cluster of radio telescope dishes came into view on-screen.

The missile homed in on its target and everything went black.

CHAPTER FIFTY

'IS HE STILL AWAKE?'

Rebecca lifted her head. 'I think so.'

'And Kara kicked him out?'

'That's what he said.'

'Sounds serious.'

Rebecca thought so too.

Julie snuggled back under her cover. 'Poor guy, you'd think with his depression she'd give him a break.'

'Yeah, you would.' Rebecca lay back down, wondering if there was something she could say that could ease Richard's suffering. Unable to think of anything, she closed her eyes and let the sounds of those that slept around her ease her back into the land of dreams.

◆

Richard Goodwin sat on the floor of Rebecca's tent, a tiny light by his side enabling him to view the photographs laid out in front of him. His confusion and frustration at Kara's actions had long since left him; now he only had time for the problem in hand – how to help those in camp escape from their infernal underground tomb. And to do that, he had to solve the riddle before him. He turned his attention back to the photo of the Anakim frieze. Picking it up, his eyes followed the line of the metallic pentagram that had been woven into the granite sculpture.

On instinct he removed a marker pen from his shirt pocket and traced red lines over the image to fill in the symbol's missing gaps and render the pentagram complete. *What had Kara said? If you look for something long enough, you'll find it.* Perhaps her words hadn't been a coincidence. Perhaps it was a message for him to follow.

He stared at the picture a while longer, then switched to his compilation of photographs of the constellation carvings. He saw something that looked familiar and picked up the frieze photo again. His brows furrowed before a spark of recognition sent his heart racing. He picked up his portable computer and expanded its screen. Bringing up the image of the lake's outline he'd discovered hidden in the carvings compilation, he inserted all the inscriptions, lines and pictograms back into the photographic mosaic. And then, one by one, he removed them again, leaving in any straight lines and the outline of the lake itself, which he'd compared to the Darklight version to produce a solid line.

He gazed at the image he'd created:

The shape surrounded by the lake's outline had segments missing, just like the missing segment in the Anakim's Libra constellation. *Another clue, perhaps, or just a coincidence?*

He returned his attention to the photo of the frieze and the Nephilim, with the great flood depicted behind and the map of the galaxy in the corner. The pentagram that he'd previously traced in red pen leapt out at him. This was no coincidence. Powering up the netcube, which he'd managed to grab before Kara chucked anything else at him, he typed in the term *pentagon*. Selecting the first result, he found what he was looking for. A regular pentagon was made up of five equal sides.

He turned back to his computer's screen and switched his pen round to use the digital scribe on the other end and filled in the gaps to get another image.

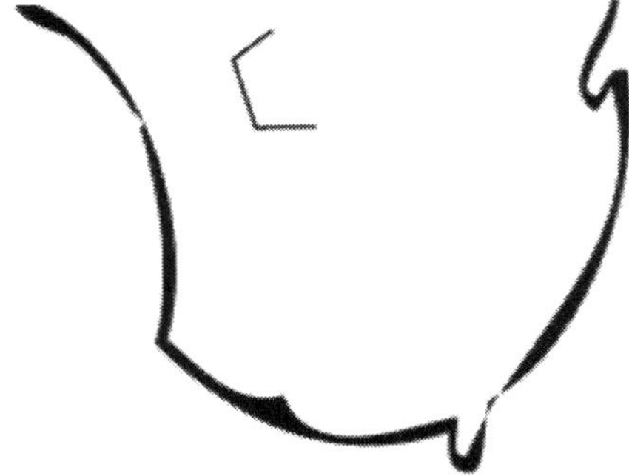

He activated the measuring tool and, using the length of the first edge as a guide, extended the other two lines to match. Referring back to the results from his net search, he saw that all regular pentagons had the same interior angle between each edge, one hundred and eight degrees. Creating the correct angle, he then added the final two sides.

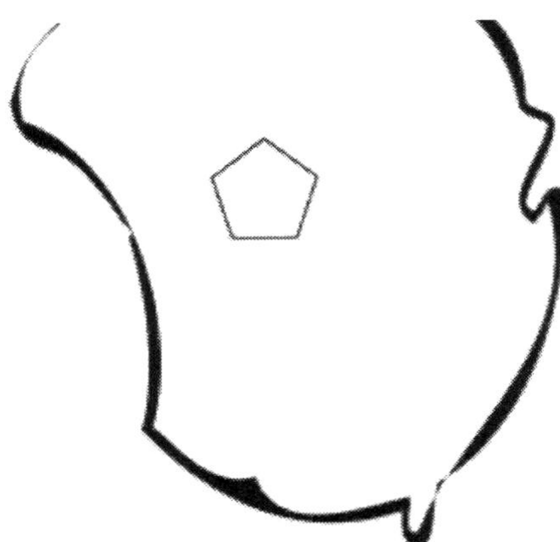

Believing he was on to something, he snatched up the photo of the frieze and turned it upside down. The same regular shaped pentagon made up the centre of the pentagram:

'This is beyond coincidence,' Goodwin murmured. 'Something is in the lake.'

CHAPTER FIFTY-ONE

A RIPPLE of water lapped over the edge of the raft, sending rivers of dark liquid running between black timbers. The long dead trees that had once populated the Anakim chamber had proved their worth time and again, and yet even their usefulness had its limits.

A full day of searching the lake had come and gone and Goodwin found himself returning to shore, where he could see Rebecca waiting for him. Earlier that day he'd arranged for five teams of civilian fishermen to comb the waters around the area depicted by the pentagon. Since the recent loss of two rafts was fresh in the crew's minds they'd been reluctant, but when Goodwin had explained it could see them freed from Sanctuary it was decided the risk was worth it and many had volunteered. Sadly, however, they'd failed to find anything of note, just an empty expanse of calm water, devoid of anything except the craft that sailed upon it. Goodwin knew, however, that more investigation was needed. He'd go back a thousand times if he had to; there was something out there waiting to be found.

As they approached the crowds that laboured on land his mood fell hard. Out in the stillness of the lake Goodwin had felt at peace, his mind occupied, but now he descended back into misery.

The raft beached on shore and he jumped down to help the men and women who'd toiled by his side all day. Hands raw from paddling with crude oars, he noticed little pain as he heaved on the rope to draw the craft to higher ground. His work done, he made his farewells to those around him and made his way beyond the stench of fish and on to Rebecca, further up the shingle beach.

'You didn't find anything?' she said, standing.

He shook his head and rubbed at the rash on his wrist in distraction.

'Haven't you sorted that yet?' Rebecca indicated the inflamed skin.

He stopped touching it and shook his head again.

She gave his arm a consolatory pat and accompanied him in silence as they walked back to camp, their respective torches clicking on. The noise of people and the buzz of water generators faded to nothing as they left the bright lights of the beach behind.

The black void closed in around them, but ever since the light creature had attacked a Darklight reconnaissance team, security had taken precedence and now armed patrols roamed the narrow corridor that connected the camp to the lake's shore.

Usually Goodwin would have felt nervous out in the open, having experienced the terror of meeting the entity face-to-face, but now – as he was – he felt nothing, only the bitter taste of failure. He'd been so sure they'd find something on the water, or just beneath its inky surface. Torchlight had revealed the odd glimpse of a scaly hide, but that was it.

A noise made Goodwin glance at his companion, it sounded like she was crying. He touched her arm. 'Rebecca?'

'I'm sorry, walking through here reminds me that Susan is out there on her own, with that ... that *thing*.'

Goodwin didn't know what to say. He willed himself to feel, and a spark of compassion forced its way through. He found her hand in the dark and her fingers wrapped around his. They continued on hand in hand while Goodwin felt his own despair rising, as if Rebecca's emotions flowed into him unimpeded.

'Sometimes,' he said, 'it feels like I'm losing my mind.'

The silence after his words hung heavy until Rebecca eventually replied. 'You've been under a lot of pressure. Everyone gets overwhelmed at some point in their lives, you're only human.'

'I don't feel human; I have terrible ... frightening thoughts.'

Her hand tightened around his. 'Everyone experiences such feelings. I have in the past. Just remember the thoughts aren't you, they're your mind trying to make you anxious. Remember that and they'll lose their power.'

'But I—'

'What?'

He couldn't bring himself to say it.

They approached the camp and its illumination.

'What, Richard? You can tell me, you know that. I won't judge.'

'When those people died—'

'On the lake?'

'Yes, when I found out, I ... it felt – it felt like I didn't care, I felt nothing, part of me almost felt relieved, a few more people not to worry about.' He hung his head in shame. 'What kind of person does that make me?'

Rebecca stopped walking and pulled Goodwin to a halt. She put her hands to his face. 'You look at me, Richard. You're a good man, one bad thought doesn't change who you are. A thousand bad thoughts won't change who you are. Thoughts are just thoughts, depression, anxiety, it makes you stronger, it's your body's way of telling you things need to change, and if you don't change it'll keep telling you they need to until you do something about it.'

She drew him into a hug.

'I'm trying to change, to find a way out.' He buried his head in her shoulder and her soft hair covered his face. He felt like he could cry, but no tears came.

'I might have known I'd find you with *her*!'

Goodwin looked up to see Kara standing nearby, her eyes full of cold fury.

Goodwin didn't know what to say.

'Kara,' – Rebecca took a step forward – 'it's not what it looks like.'

'I don't care what you think, little miss perfect. But I do care when you put things in his head,' – she turned on Goodwin – 'and encourage him to go chasing after miracles. Jesus wept, quoting the damn Bible, for pity's sake! Are you trying to get us all killed? Without your help we're struggling, or hadn't you noticed? People are dying and you two carry on like it's a game, looking for clues, searching for God knows what, God knows where!'

Kara paused for a breath and Goodwin went to speak.

She held up a hand. 'I don't want to hear it. You know full well we just lost two crews on the lake, and you go and take five more out into its furthest reaches. I have people coming up to me asking what route out of Sanctuary you've found, and how long will it take to reach the surface. False hope, Richard, really?! I thought you were suffering from depression, but it looks like you really have lost your damn mind!'

'Kara, he needs your help, not your anger.'

Kara glared at Rebecca. 'I thought I told you, I don't care what you think.'

'But I have found a way to the surface,' Goodwin said, 'it's in the lake.'

'Just stop, stop it!'

Rebecca tugged on Goodwin's hand. 'Perhaps you'd better go.'

'Perhaps you'd better both go.' Kara stood aside.

Rebecca moved past her and Goodwin followed, before pausing to look Kara in the eye. 'I'm doing my best, that's all I can do.'

'I don't know who you are anymore.' She turned her head away and Goodwin sighed and followed Rebecca into camp.

◆

Kara watched Goodwin go, her fury simmering above a sea of loss. A part of her felt relief at what had to come next, but another part felt a deep sense of fear and woe. She took a deep breath and pressed a button on her walkie talkie.

'Ma'am?'

'Put me through to the major.'

She waited before another voice responded. 'This is Offiah.'

'Major, it's far worse than we thought.'

'What's happened?'

'Richard has become a liability; as of this moment he's no longer in charge of this camp.'

'How should we proceed?'

'As planned. Until he returns to sound mind he is a danger to himself and everyone around him.'

'I'll issue the arrest order.'

'Fine, but do it with as few witnesses as possible. We don't want to cause a scene; we need to preserve the integrity of command for the sake of the camp.'

'Very good, I'll see it's done.'

'Oh, and Major—'

'Yes?'

'Make sure he's secure, and administer the drugs as discussed. We need him back to normal as soon as possible.'

'Yes, ma'am.'

Offiah hung up the com and Kara let out a sigh of her own. It was done.

CHAPTER FIFTY-TWO

RICHARD GOODWIN STARED in disbelief at the three soldiers before him. 'Under whose authority?'

'Major Offiah, sir.'

'There must be some mistake, let me speak to him.'

'I'm sorry, sir, we were told to take you straight into detention.'

Goodwin found himself being relieved of his possessions and another soldier secured handcuffs to his wrists.

'Is that necessary, soldier?'

Goodwin turned to see the form of Lieutenant Manaus approach, her amour glinting in the dim floodlights.

'Orders are orders, Lieutenant.'

'Where are you taking him?'

'North side, he's to be held along with the U.S. Army decontamination team.'

Manaus turned to Goodwin. 'I'm sorry about this, Director. I'll speak to the major for you and see what can be done.'

Goodwin felt disorientated and gave her a nod as he was led away.

♦

'And you both think having him locked up is going to help this camp?'

'You forget yourself, Lieutenant, this is a command decision.'

Dr. Kara Vandervoort held up a hand to Major Offiah. 'No, wait, let's hear her out.'

'Thank you, ma'am,' Manaus said. 'What I'm saying is, even if Director Goodwin has taken leave of his senses, surely locking him up won't help anyone. Or am I missing something?'

Vandervoort shifted her stance. 'You're quite right, spouting religious scripture and jumping to ridiculous conclusions isn't an arrestable offence. But when that person is in charge, and is capable of making decisions that affect us all, he needs to be removed from office. If he's left to his own devices there's no knowing what chaos he could cause. He would still have great influence over the civilians and he won't let go of his crusade. More lives could be lost.'

'I still don't like it,' Manaus said. 'Word will get out.'

'And we'll let everyone know Richard is sick and is being properly cared for. In the meantime we'll continue as we were and wait for news from Commander Hilt.'

Lieutenant Manaus knew she could say no more without crossing the line.

'If that's all, Lieutenant,' Vandervoort said, 'we have work to do.'

Manaus bobbed her head and gave a crisp salute before leaving the command tent behind. Walking through the camp, her thoughts swirled with a myriad of concerns, while instinct screamed its warning that there would be trouble ahead.

CHAPTER FIFTY-THREE

Corporal Adam Walker sat in his fabric prison, a large black tent provided and administered by the heavy hand of his jailers, Commander Hilt and his mewling pet, Major Offiah. As the ranking non-commissioned officer of his U.S. Army decontamination unit, Walker was in charge of the twenty-seven other soldiers who had also been put under house arrest at Hilt's behest. After the hulking Darklight Commander left on his quest to hunt down the creature, Walker had hoped Offiah would see fit to release him and his men from their invisible bonds, but it seemed Walker's deceased sergeant – Alvarez, who'd been killed by the entity – had given Offiah cause to feel only distrust and thinly veiled contempt for all those that wore the baggy green uniform of the United States Army.

Walker watched as one of the armoured Darklight mercenaries strolled past the tent, the visor of their helmet lowered and blue eyes aglow in the darkness, while their assault rifle remained in hand, at the ready.

Walker's eye twitched. He rubbed a hand over his goatee beard and returned his attention to the newest member of their motley crew. Director Goodwin sat apart from everyone else, fiddling with his shirt sleeve while staring into space. How the leader of the camp had fallen so low as to become imprisoned by his own people, Walker couldn't imagine, but he intended to find out. He got up, exchanged a few light-hearted insults with some of his men, and made his way over to the dishevelled form that had been deposited in their midst.

'Director,' he said.

'Corporal.'

'You look the worse for wear.'

Goodwin glanced in his direction. 'You don't look so hot yourself.'

Walker chuckled. 'That's what happens when discipline goes out the window. Most of us joined the army for a sense of control and purpose. It's funny, I thought once I made it into USSB Sanctuary my chances of becoming some bum rotting away in a prison cell somewhere had all but gone. But here I am, locked up, rotting away in the biggest prison cell on Earth.'

Goodwin failed to respond, his expression unchanging.

Walker leant closer to him. 'So, Director, why are you here?'

Nothing.

Walker tried a different tack. 'Come on, sir – Richard – we're all comrades in this tent, your secret's safe with me, I swear it.'

'On what?'

'Eh?'

'You said you'd swear it; swear on what?'

'On my mother's life.'

'Not good enough.'

'On my daughter's life, then.'

'Do you have one?'

Walker pointed a finger at him. 'Aha, you're quick. So what's the word then?'

Goodwin remained silent.

'You still want me to swear, eh?' Walker scratched his head. 'Oi, Priest!'

A balding soldier at the rear of the tent turned round.

'Loan me your book.'

'No chance.'

Walker grunted, got up and went over to the man's bunk, which consisted of a rolled up decontamination suit at the end of a piece of ground that had been fashioned into a body sized dip. Walker snatched the book from under the makeshift pillow and waggled it in its owner's direction.

'You ruin it,' the man said, 'and I'll cut your balls off and stuff 'em down your throat!'

Walker laughed before sitting down next to Goodwin again. He placed his hand on the Bible. 'I swear whatever you tell me is in strictest confidence, so help me God.'

Goodwin's expression changed and he snatched the book from his grasp.

Walker's cheek trembled and his eye twitched in response; he rubbed it with the palm of his hand.

The director flicked through the book's pages as if searching for something. 'So you want to know why I'm here?'

Walker nodded.

Goodwin stopped reading and looked him in the eye. 'I'm here,' he said, keeping his voice low, 'because I've found something they don't want anyone else to know about.'

Walker frowned. 'And what's that?'

'I'll tell you if you promise to help me.'

'Help you do what?'

Goodwin nodded to the guards outside the tent, a feverish look in his eyes. 'Escape from them.'

Walker followed his gaze. 'And what's in it for me?'

Goodwin chuckled, the sound hollow and unnerving. 'How about getting out of here?'

'To the USSB?'

Goodwin shook his head. 'No, better.' He leaned toward him and whispered, 'I've found a way out, a way to the surface.'

'And why wouldn't they want anyone else to know that?'

Goodwin dropped his voice further. 'Because it's the end of the world, the asteroid, the dust cloud.' He held up the Bible. 'The Apocalypse is nigh!'

CHAPTER FIFTY-FOUR

Walker eyed Goodwin with apprehension; the man looked to be out of his mind. He'd been babbling on about biblical tales, some weird sculpture they'd found in the city and a map of the lake. Leaving the director to his ramblings, he got up to see two Darklight soldiers talking outside. One of them, a female officer, handed her weapons to the other, and headed towards the tent. The soldier she'd left behind blew out his cheeks and bent his head to one side to drink in his colleague's seductive form. Ducking inside, she removed her helmet and dark hair fell in waves down her back.

She moved toward the director, but Walker barred her way. 'What brings you here—' he looked down at her chest armour, '—Lieutenant Manaus?'

'I've bought Director Goodwin some of his possessions.'

'I'll take them to him.'

'I don't think so.'

He held his ground. 'What's with him, anyway? He's acting odd.'

Manaus hesitated. 'He's been medicated for his condition.'

'If that's medicated I'd hate to see what he was like before.'

She peered over his shoulder. 'And why's that?'

'Because he's lost the plot, raving on about signs on the ground, angels from heaven and the end of the world.'

Manaus searched his face with her eyes. 'And yet you believe him, don't you?'

He laughed. 'Don't be stupid. Why; do you?'

'I saw a frieze in the ground. It was ... interesting.'

Walker felt his eye twitch. 'Interesting or not, the man's not well.'

'Hmm, I was afraid the drugs might make him worse, but they wouldn't listen to me.' She handed Walker what she held, some photos and a portable computer. 'Give him these; tell him I've arranged for visitors tomorrow.' She went to leave and stopped by the tent entrance. 'Corporal Walker, isn't it?'

'It is.'

'Look after him and I'll see about getting you some more freedom.'

His expression turned serious. 'You have my word.'

She gave him a nod and left.

Walker looked down at the cluster of objects in his hands and then over at Goodwin. So, someone else thinks there might be something to the director's theories. Has he really found a way to the surface? Either way, he thought, things are looking up.

◆

Goodwin woke late the next day, his mind still foggy from the drugs given to him by the Darklight medic over eighteen hours before. They said it was some kind of tranquiliser, but he felt awful, like he had the hangover from hell. Why they'd had to drug him in the first place was a mystery, he felt fine apart from his low mood, but to keep the peace with Kara he promised them he'd try his best to get better from the illness from which they believed he suffered. His reasons for this were many, but he'd come to realise if he wanted to pursue his search of the lake he would need his freedom, and that meant toeing the line.

At least I have my photos back, he thought, as he gazed at the images before him. But despite what he'd already discovered he still had the niggling feeling that he was missing something. He picked up the photo of the Anakim frieze, which contained the pentagram and the five-sided regular pentagon in its centre. He then unfurled his mobile computer's big screen and looked at the image of the lake he'd uncovered, and the pentagon near its centre:

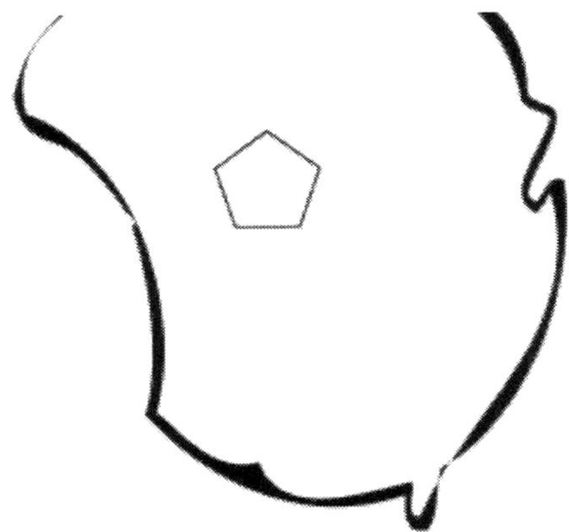

After an hour or three of contemplation an idea struck him.

'Corporal?'

Walker sat by his side, engrossed in photos of the constellation carvings. He glanced up.

'Do you have a marker pen?'

With a bob of his head, Walker scurried away and returned a moment later with a selection.

Thanking him, Goodwin uncapped one of the pens and used it as a stylus to draw on the digital image. First of all he went over the central pentagon, redefining its borders, and then he drew a series of five straight lines, using each side of the same pentagon as a starting reference. Each of these lines extended out to intersect with one of its counterparts to create a five pointed star.

Walker sat back down, intrigued. 'What's that?'

'A message.' Goodwin looked at the corporal, but his eyes were drawn to a badge on his shoulder:

He lifted his screen and took an image of it. 'Do you remember why they call Homo giganthropsis the Anakim, Corporal?' Goodwin manipulated the emblem's image.

'No,' Walker said, watching, 'no one ever said. Why?'

'It's funny, don't you think?'

'What?'

'That the emblem for USSB Sanctuary has not one, but two pentagons hidden in its design.' Goodwin removed all the text from the emblem, the central map and the middle rings, along with the coded base identification bars located at the bottom. This left the outer circle and ten small triangles in its centre, five of them small and five slightly larger.

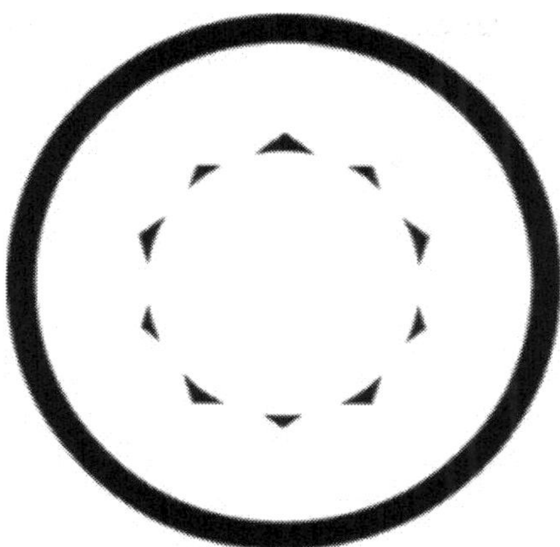

Goodwin then drew five straight lines, linking the five largest triangles together.

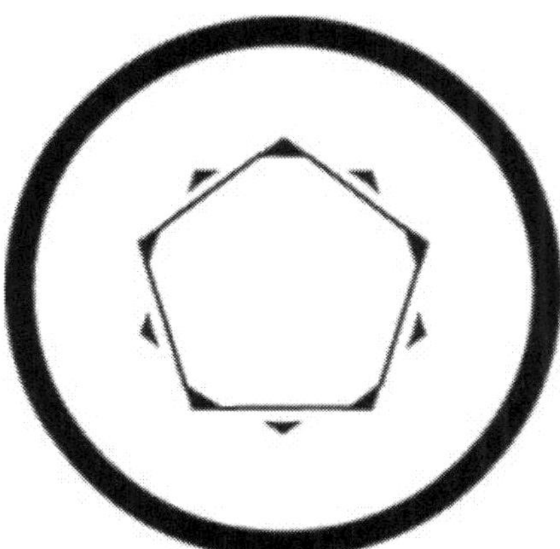

'I see one pentagon,' Walker said.

'Look again; the smaller black triangles are the corners of another, only it's upside down.'

'Is that significant?'

Goodwin gave a shrug, but he looked at the single circle surrounding his latest image and returned to the map of the lake. Selecting another digital tool, he laid a circle over the five pointed star.

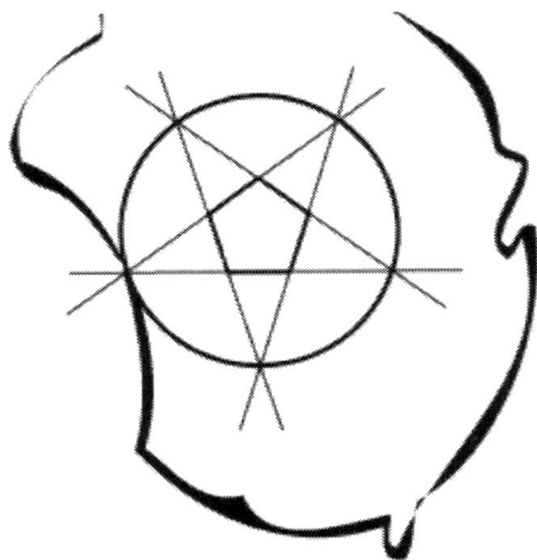

And there it was, as plain as the nose on his face: a pentagram – a pentagram which pointed the way to the shoreline, not only by the point of its star, but by the circle that intersected the land in the exact same place. It was a sign, a hidden message from the Anakim, and a way to access the secret protected by the lake that enveloped it. All he had to do now was get there.

'What do you think?' Goodwin said.

Walker's eyes glittered with fervent fascination. 'I think you've just made me a believer, Director.'

CHAPTER FIFTY-FIVE

Two days had passed since Goodwin had discovered the Anakim's hidden message and almost ever since he'd been waiting for the opportunity to speak to the woman who currently sat on the ground opposite him. Rebecca had been allowed in as a visitor and he held her gaze, his eyes imploring her to reconsider.

'Richard,' she said, I'd love to help you, but I can't.'

Goodwin held up the screen. 'But, look!'

Some of Walker's men glanced round, the corporal having gathered them together at the back of the tent.

Goodwin lowered his voice. 'Just look, it's amazing. It points the way, there's something there. All you have to do is what I just said, simple.'

Rebecca grasped his hand. 'I believe you, but I'm scared. What if they lock me up, too? I have to look after Joseph.'

'They won't, trust me. When we find what's at the lake they'll realise I was right all along.'

She shook her head. 'I can't—'

'What if I told you there was more truth to the frieze than you know? What if I told you the words you quoted were right?'

'What do you mean?'

He looked around to make sure they weren't overheard, then flicked through the pages of the Bible. He held it up for her to read.

'And the angels who did not stay within their own position of authority,' he said in quotation, 'but left their proper dwelling, he has kept in eternal chains under gloomy darkness until the judgement of the great day. Jude 1:6. Your words, yes? Do you remember when you said, it's not like it's the end of the world?'

She nodded, captivated by Goodwin's intensity.

'Well, it is. There are six more asteroids heading for Earth right now and only a miracle will stop them all.'

She shook her head and half stood. 'Six more? That can't be.'

Goodwin pulled her back down, glancing back to make sure they hadn't been overheard. 'Professor Steiner told me in his message. The world really is at an end and only the GMRC's Space Programme has a chance of saving us, and so far their efforts have apparently all been in vain. They failed with AG5. They are likely to fail with the rest. The asteroids will hit, and the surface will burn. Nothing will be left.'

'Oh my G—' Wild-eyed, Rebecca looked like she was going to be sick.

'Please, Rebecca,' he grabbed her hands, 'the fish stocks won't last forever, the light could come back, Hilt may never return. But I *can* get us to the surface and into another subterranean base, but I need your help and I need it now. Are you with me?'

The dilemma in her eyes gave way to a weak smile. 'How can I say no?'

A fleeting ray of hope laid a hand on his heart. 'Thank you,' – he kissed her cheek – 'thank you.'

♦

Darklight operative Zack Michaels waved to his comrade sixty feet away. The soldier acknowledged him with a nod before moving back out of sight around the perimeter of the small enclave that held the U.S. Army decontamination team. As ever, Zack had landed the nightshift. He couldn't believe it, twelve days in a row, it was unheard of. His captain, Winter, had just waved away his complaints when he'd raised the issue, which was typical; the man had had it in for him ever since Zack had slept with his cousin, who held a position in one of Hilt's reconnaissance units. How was he to know the two were related? Women shouldn't have to change their surnames when they married, it made things too complicated. He couldn't help but smile at the memories, though; he'd had some fun and so had she, so what was the harm? He never said the relationship was monogamous; he wasn't a damn mind reader.

His thoughts turned to Lieutenant Manaus, the buxom, long-legged seductress he'd seen the day before. He'd heard she was a tiger in the sack, but also choosy. He'd have to play the long game if he was to land her, but he'd get there in the end ... he always did. There was one big problem, however; if his captain had been pissed about his cousin, he'd be spitting feathers if Zack had his way with his sister. A half-sister, granted, but a sister nonetheless. *Darklight should introduce a law against nepotism, although,* he quickly decided, *that would limit my supply of—* A noise nearby made him focus.

Rifle raised, he scanned the area with his visor. A woman approached. It was the young carer who'd visited the director earlier. She looked nervous, and he found his eyes drawn to her shapely figure and ample bosom.

He lowered his gun. 'Hi there, miss, are you lost?'

She gave him a grimace of a smile and moved closer. 'Yes, I think I am.' She got out a map. 'I thought I was heading back to my tent, but I got turned around.'

'Here, let me take a look.' He propped his rifle up against his leg and took the map from her. She moved to his side and his eyes dropped to her cleavage, and he had to remember what he was supposed to be looking at. He held up the map and turned around. 'I think you need to go that way—' He lowered the sheet of paper to see a man standing before him, grinning, and the last thing Zack remembered was a fist flying toward his face.

CHAPTER FIFTY-SIX

'WHAT DO YOU MEAN, GONE?'

Captain Winter hung his head. 'They managed to overpower the sentries.'

Offiah swore. 'And Director Goodwin is with them?'

'He's not in the tent and no one else has seen him, so, yes, it's a fair assumption.'

Kara muttered a curse of her own. 'And they haven't been picked up by any of the patrols?'

'They would have reported in,' Offiah said, giving Winter a stern stare.

Kara checked the time. 'And why are we only finding out about this now, Captain?'

'Corporal Walker and his men secured our personnel and took their weapons and helmets, ma'am,' Winter said. 'We think they've been listening in to our coms for some time as they called in the correct codes at the right intervals.'

'So where are they?'

'We don't know, ma'am.'

'The lake?' Kara looked to Offiah.

The major shook his head. 'They'd have been seen.'

Kara felt sick. How has this happened? she asked herself. Because Richard is no fool, her mind answered. He may have become detached from reality, but he is nothing but persistent. If he believes something is in the lake, he won't stop until he finds it. 'We need to check all the rafts are accounted for,' she said, 'and send out teams to scour the shoreline.'

'We can check the rafts at the beach in case they sneaked past us,' Offiah said, 'but if we release personnel to roam the rest of the water's edge we'll weaken the security of the camp. The entity could return at any moment.'

Kara feared for Goodwin's safety, but she couldn't risk the lives of others to ensure his return. She didn't know what to do.

Captain Winter turned to Offiah. 'Let me take my team, sir. We're redundant now anyway.'

The major looked uncertain.

'How many are in your unit, Captain?' Kara said.

'Twenty, and we can get more gear from the central cache.'

'I'm willing to reassign a single operative from daytime patrols,' Offiah told her. 'One won't make much difference and it'll boost Winter's force to forty-five.'

'Do it,' Kara said, 'but keep it peaceful, I don't want Richard killed in some kind of firefight.'

'If we're fired upon we'll have to defend ourselves,' Winter said, incredulous.

'No,' – she gave a shake of her head – 'just use warning shots, or retreat if you have to.'

The Darklight officer didn't respond.

'Do I make myself clear, Captain?' Kara said, her tone like iron. 'Warning shots only.'

Winter nodded and Kara moved away to speak to the communications team at the rear of the command post.

♦

Captain Winter moved closer to Major Offiah, his voice low. 'Sir, with all due respect, I'm not going out there if we can't engage. They'd soon realise we didn't want to hurt the director, we'd be sitting ducks.'

Offiah made sure Vandervoort was still out of earshot. 'The doctor is making a decision based on emotion, we know that, and on this occasion she's made the wrong call. We can't allow Walker and his men to be on the loose, it compromises the integrity of this entire camp.'

'So you sanction return fire?'

Offiah rubbed the back of his head where Sergeant Alvarez had knocked him unconscious a couple of weeks before. He'd had just about all he could take from the U.S. Army decontamination team and their games; they'd been a thorn in everyone's side from day one and this was the final straw. 'It's time to stop playing games with these people. Hilt was always too lenient. I'm in charge now, and I say this ends.'

Winter's eyes lit up. 'Attack and extract?'

'You do what you have to do, Captain, just bring Goodwin home.'

Captain Winter gave a crisp salute and left the tent.

Major Offiah gazed after him, hoping, praying, he'd made the right call.

CHAPTER FIFTY-SEVEN

'Look, Goodwin, I like you, you're an okay guy. You've looked out for us in the past when you didn't need to, I see that. But, don't mistake me for a fool. Alvarez may have been my superior, but he was a racist, hot-headed idiot who didn't know his ass from his elbow.' Walker hefted his rifle. 'I'm the leader of this little excursion, and what I say goes. And right now I'm saying she stays.'

Rebecca moved forward. 'I won't say anything, I promise!'

Walker grabbed her arm and yanked her close. He drew a knife from his belt and Rebecca went stock still as he put the blade to her throat; he looked at Goodwin over her shoulder, his eyes calm and calculating.

'Harm a hair on her head, Corporal,' Goodwin said, struggling against the men that held him, 'and I'll see you hang!'

Walker ran a finger down Rebecca's face and down the side of her neck to her top which he teased out with a finger. 'Very nice,' he said.

Rebecca cringed away from him and Goodwin felt his rage surge. 'Let her go or I swear to God you'll never see the surface. You'll be stuck down here forever!'

Walker hesitated and then pushed Rebecca from him. 'Do you know how long it is since some of these men have had a woman,

Director?' Walker moved amongst his unit. 'Do you know how long it is since *I've* had a woman?'

Goodwin said nothing, his eyes holding onto Rebecca's. She stood on her own, exposed and terrified. He couldn't let her suffer the same fate again, he'd rather die.

'I heard she likes it rough,' Walker said, 'but this time Hilt's not around to protect anyone, so this is how it's going to be, Director – *Richard*. You'll find this entrance, exit, or whatever it is you've located, lead us out of here, and I'll promise not to take this tender morsel and pass her round so we can all get our fun on. How about that?'

'Yes, YES! Just leave her alone!'

Walker gestured to his men and Goodwin fell forward, released. He ran to Rebecca who clung to him like a vice.

Walker pulled on his stolen Darklight helmet and switched on the visor to assess their position in relation to Goodwin's map. 'It's two clicks, north west.' He put his hand out in the direction. 'Let's move.'

The small party of thirty moved off, Walker in the lead with Goodwin and Rebecca ushered along behind, at gunpoint, the secret of the lake beckoning them onward.

◆

A few minutes later a small light appeared where Walker's unit had stood. A shimmering form reached out to touch the soil, the tracks in the dirt a giveaway to everything that had just transpired. The illumination blinked out and darkness resumed. The chase was on.

CHAPTER FIFTY-EIGHT

'WHAT LIGHT?'

'I saw a light behind us.'

'If you're screwing me about—'

'No, seriously, I saw it.'

Walker's eye twitched, his nervous tic forcing his cheek into a rhythmic jig. He wiped a hand over his face. 'Everyone take defensive positions. If something moves, shoot it. Fuck!'

'We could call it in.'

'What, and have Offiah come down on us like a ton of bricks? No chance. We're safer out here with weapons than back there without, and if I'm going out it's under my own terms, not waiting to die like a caged animal. Now shut up, secure silencers and get eyes on!'

A ripple of fear swept through the group of men. They fanned out, weapons made ready, eyes scanning the pitch black that pinned them against the cold of the lake at their backs.

Walker turned to Goodwin, who examined a small, rune-encrusted obelisk. 'Right, Director. We're at the coordinates you found. It's time for you to try out our equipment.'

Goodwin looked down at the decontamination suit he wore. 'And you kept this a secret why?'

'Because they're not meant for diving,' Walker said. 'Alvarez didn't even know they can be taken underwater, and when Hilt wanted to explore the submerged caves he found with his scanners, these suits would have been useless. They can only go down forty metres and the self-contained air breathers only last for ten minutes in liquid. I didn't say anything as—'

'As you're a conniving bastard who also knew about the entity, but failed to tell anyone until it was too late.'

Walker sniffed and then a smile creased his rat-like features. 'I like the new you, Goodwin, bluntness suits you. But you're right, why should I have told you anything? We were your prisoners for weeks on end. I didn't trust you, and I still don't.'

Goodwin looked around. 'Then why come out here? Why risk everything?'

'I told you, I believe, like you do. Now stop your chatter and get in there.'

Goodwin stared out at the lake, the dark surface a black calm. He glanced at Rebecca who stood at his side and held out a wadge of paper to her, which she accepted.

'Joseph's drawings and my photos,' he said. 'Keep them safe for me?'

She nodded and he gave her hand a squeeze before moving towards the water's edge.

Torchlight from atop Goodwin's transparent helmet highlighted the hard stony ground that disappeared beneath the glistening liquid. Either side, remnants of ancient stonework marked the fringe of an extensive chain of derelict structures that led off towards the Anakim city behind. The edges of these low-slung creations also sank into the subterranean loch, further cementing Goodwin's belief that they were in the right place.

He adjusted his helmet and removed his shoes and socks. The surface felt cold against the soles of his feet and he quickly pulled on the loose-fitting boots provided. Suppressing a shiver, he paused; about to embark into the unknown he couldn't help but fear – not for himself – but for Rebecca. *If this suit fails and I don't return she'll be left alone with Walker's animals*. The thought made his mind cry out in horror.

Walker drew alongside; he held his knife in one hand while the fingers of his other played with its razor-sharp edge. 'Time to do your stuff, Director. Don't make me ask again.'

'I'll be back,' Goodwin said to Rebecca. 'I promise.'

Rebecca gave him a fearful look. 'Be careful, Richard.'

Goodwin broke eye contact with her, activated his breathing mask and stepped into the water. A shock of sensation swept up his spine. Icy liquid poured into his boots, consuming his feet and ankles, with only his suit preventing further infringement as he waded deeper.

When he was in up to his waist, the sound of sloshing water faded as his motion slowed. He stopped, the impenetrable blackness before him daunting even to *his* numbed mind. If someone had told him just a week before he would willingly walk into the lake's freezing depths, he would have laughed and told them they were mad. But now it was his sanity that was questioned, his leadership doubted. Remembering what was at stake, not just Rebecca's life, but the lives of everyone else back at camp, he pressed on. His next step sent water washing over his shoulders as the lakebed shelved off. His body felt buoyant, but the air canisters and circulation equipment on his back kept him firmly planted. Another step sent him sinking beneath the surface. The lake rushed into his helmet, covering his head in its glacial chill. A thrill of fear and pain sent a flash of light dancing before his eyes.

A voice echoed through the water that burned frigid in his ears. 'Don't forget to breathe, Goodwin,' Walker said via the helmet's communication system, 'the mask is sealed tight on your nose and mouth, the water can't get in.'

Goodwin fought for calm, but found himself unable to open his eyelids against the bitter fluid. 'It hurts!' he said, his voice muffled.

'Suck it up,' Walker told him, 'time's ticking, you've got less than ten minutes.'

Cursing, Goodwin forced open both eyes and pain lanced through them like a spike to the brain. Seconds passed and his vision cleared. A small display encased in the helmet's transparent shield showed him a myriad of warnings and data. Through the blur of fluid he only had eyes for the small timer that signalled the duration of his oxygen levels. *Nine minutes to go.*

Thankfully, the decontamination helmet also boasted a screen that enhanced vision. It was nothing like as sophisticated as Darklight headgear, but in conjunction with its powerful light bar it provided adequate illumination of his surroundings, albeit distorted by the constant ripple of water. Pressing a button, he vented his exhalation and it bubbled up around him. The ground angled down and he took another step, and then another. Down and down he went, into the darkness, searching for something, anything.

After another minute a depth gauge told him he'd passed below twenty metres. Something swam past his face and he cried out.

Walker's voiced warbled in his ear. 'What's happening?'

'I'm fine, it was just a fish.' *Just a fish*, Goodwin thought with an emphasis on the 'just'. He knew full well what sort of animals patrolled these depths. Creatures that could tear flesh and consume bone. He carried on and another ten metres down, the lakebed levelled out. In itself this wasn't a curiosity, but when other parts of the lake had been found to descend beyond their capability to measure, which was well over a mile, it meant to Goodwin only one thing – this was where he'd find their exit to the surface.

He continued forward and the phantom shapes of weed-encrusted Anakim architecture appeared out of the gloom, their alien forms drowned long ago in a foreign past. His expectation grew and he looked at his timer.

Six minutes left.

Speeding up, he passed by these sculptural immensities and soon found himself confronted by a darker darkness, a blacker black than that of the water that pressed in around him. The light from his helmet seemed to die against this wall that shimmered like oil in the night. He reached out a hand and drew his gloved fingers across its surface. A trail briefly appeared before fading back to flat. *Strange*, he thought. He looked left and then right; it was like a liquid within a liquid. He'd heard something about underwater lakes on ocean floors from Kara. A *brine pool* she called them – a dark mass of dense fluid formed underwater. These uncanny pools seemed to defy the laws of nature, appearing as an otherworldly phenomenon, but what stood before him seemed different. For one, it was vertical, and for two – he peered closer and touched it a second time. *Yes*, he thought, *there it is again*. A trace of blue shimmered against the black.

He frowned; it reminded him of the blue stones. The same glowing rocks that had attracted the light creature, or so Hilt had theorised. An alarm beeped in his helmet.

Half his air had gone.

'How's it going, Director?' Walker said.

'There's some kind of thick liquid down here, like a barrier.'

'I don't know how far out you are, but if you want to return to shore you should do so soon; either that or return to the surface and fill up your tanks.'

'Roger that,' Goodwin said and turned to follow the dark wall's perimeter. 'I'll go to the surface and then dive back down.'

By means of a digital tracker on his helmet's screen, Goodwin realised the wall traced the path of a circle. He couldn't tell by vision alone, but it was definitely an arc, at least, and considering the pentagram he'd decoded within the lake's boundaries, this could be significant indeed.

Treading through the water like an astronaut on another planet, Goodwin reached a section where the ground fell away, the vertical drop followed down by the strange black obstruction. Unable to go any further, he decided to test the wall's resistance. Sliding his fingers across its surface, deep swirls eddied out. He pushed into it and his hand disappeared inside its blackness. For a moment nothing happened and then an image of horror flashed before his eyes and fear tore through him. Something grasped his hand and dragged him deeper. Terrified, Goodwin pulled back as hard as he could. His arm came free and he glided back in the water.

Something touched his leg and he jerked round. A scaled tail vanished into the abyss and Goodwin scoured the dark before his helmet was knocked sideways.

A massive catfish sailed past overhead, long barbels flowing from beneath its giant mouth. The creature swam back towards him, black eyes distracted by his light.

Goodwin's breathing sounded loud in his ears, his chest rising and falling in quick succession.

The fish turned away, but as it departed it twitched and thrashed as a monstrous reptilian eel cut across it, its tooth-ridden maw severing the catfish's head from its body. Blood flowed into the water and more armoured fish appeared to feast in a frenzied mass of tails, fins and gaping mouths. The first animal consumed the head in a few bone crunching bites before spying Goodwin watching it. The creature reared in the water, its flared head waving from side to side like a snake.

Plate-sized eyes locked in on its prey and Goodwin took a step back before the beast dived straight at him. With no time to think, he launched himself into the wall of black.

Thick viscous fluid engulfed him, swallowing him into its density. Pure terror descended, eviscerating all calm. He felt his throat collapse and horrific images attacked his mind, strobe-like and intense. Black oil seeped into his helmet, forcing the clear water out. Soon it would cover his eyes and clog his equipment. He thrust out with his legs, seeking the surface, but he could no longer tell up from down. Drifting in the oozing oil, fear constricted his chest and pierced his stomach. A sense of death clamped down on his mind.

I'm going to die.

As the thought formed Goodwin felt a presence at his side, a presence so real he could almost touch it. *Is this my guide into the afterlife, the angel of my death*? The being at his side – unseen, but tangible – turned his mind tranquil. His throat released and he swam forward, trusting in this source of serenity. No matter where it led him, it had already saved him from fear. Moving as if in a dream, Goodwin saw tiny branches of electricity ripple toward him through the oil, which had grown semi-transparent. Sparking tendrils passed over his body like a wave and an abstract vision of Joseph tilting his bottle of water flared into remembrance. Goodwin realised the dark liquid that pooled inside his helmet created a flat plane as it rose, indicating the pull of gravity and the direction of down. Using this reference he struck out for up.

Warning symbols flashed on his helmet's screen before a single message appeared:

System Failure

The air from his mask ceased and the black ooze crept over his eyes, which he was unable to close. His arms and legs twitched into inactivity and a spark of light ignited his optic nerves, searing a vision into his brain. A face, a tower, a planet. The smoke trail of a blazing comet as it impacted the Earth. Images of a strange world cascaded across his mind's eye, of peoples transported to distant lands. A beautiful Anakim woman opened her mouth and spoke to him without words. Goodwin didn't understand her meaning, only the feeling of welcome induced. He felt enriched in soul before the face changed into one of horrific fury. Goodwin felt his pulse quicken before the scene filled his mind, sharp teeth and a roar of sound blinding him in a burst of light.

A shimmer of tiny blue atoms coalesced around his spasming body in the dark liquid that had claimed him for its own. Richard Goodwin floated adrift in unconscious rotation. His quest had found its end.

CHAPTER FIFTY-NINE

'WHY AREN'T WE DEAD?'

Eric looked confused. Jessica was too. She looked at the wallscreen and its static fuzz. There were no two ways about it, they should be scattered across the Chilean desert in a thousand pieces. She'd just seen the rocket sent to kill them destroy its target – at least that's how it had appeared – and yet they all still lived. How?

'Unless we *are* dead.' Eric pinched himself. 'Ow.'

With some effort, Professor Steiner stood up. 'I believe your friend was playing Joiner for a fool. Isn't that right, Bic?'

'To have reached a position of such import and power,' Bic said via the room's speakers, 'Malcolm Joiner is no fool, Professor Steiner, as you must know. He is a great adversary, although, he has revealed himself and now I know who is pulling the strings behind this part of the veil.'

'And you think that will help you?' Steiner said. 'Joiner has influence no one man should have. I know that to my cost. If you think you can outsmart him and the tens of thousands of GMRC and government personnel under his control, then you're mistaken.'

'I have just demonstrated I can outsmart him, Professor Steiner. I will do as I must, as must you, as must we all.'

'So he hasn't found us?' Eric said.

'No,' Bic replied, 'but I found him.'

Jessica saw the professor's expression change to one of concern. The ex-GMRC man's body no longer shook from trauma, but his hands still quivered a little and Jessica laid a compassionate hand on his arm in an attempt to still his distress.

Steiner gave her an appreciative smile in response.

'Where is he?' Eric asked Bic.

'All in good time, Eric. For now we should rejoice that he believes you no longer live.'

'And why's that?' Jessica said.

No sound came from the speakers and then Bic spoke again. 'The dead do not pose a threat, Jessica Klein.'

Jessica looked out of the window. 'So where are we, then?'

'You *are* in South America, but Peru rather than Chile.'

Brett pointed at the military drone outside. 'How did you manage to stop them seeing the plane? It's not exactly small.'

'The aircraft came replete with a remote UAV,' Bic said, 'designed specifically to replicate the radar signature of the larger craft. Without satellite telemetry due to the dust cloud the military's powers of tracking their enemies has been reduced. I managed to fly the smaller craft to a hangar near the Atacama telescope array in Chile and left its systems active to draw attention. Combine that with the trace they thought they'd executed and you have a convincing target.'

Jessica could tell Brett was impressed, despite her misgivings about the terrorist himself.

'But if they blew up ALMA, how can we track this mysterious signal?' Eric said.

A blind on the far side of the room whirred into life and another set of windows appeared. 'Observe,' Bic said, 'the Two Square Kilometre Array. The TSKA.'

Jessica moved to the window and looked out into near total darkness. Slowly her eyes adjusted to the faint sunlight that penetrated the dense shroud above. Beyond, vast numbers of radio telescopes loomed, their massive concave dishes angled up to the heavens like the heads of giant flowers with a single petal.

Jessica gazed up, envisioning the smoke trail from a missile that headed straight for them. 'Won't they realise their mistake and find us here?'

'They may well do, Jessica Klein, which is why you must not delay for too long. Professor Steiner,' Bic said, 'things have changed, loyalties are warped and motives skewed, are you willing to help us now that Malcolm Joiner has admitted to the mass murder of your friends and colleagues?'

◆

Professor Steiner wrung his hands to quell his trembling as he pondered the question. His fury at Joiner for killing those in Steadfast had created a well of interminable rage which had infused his being and reignited the fire in his soul. As he'd sat listening to Joiner's words, his whole body had shook. It was as if the malicious words had sparked something within him. It had felt like coming out of a dream into a nightmare. Terrifying fear had filled him, rendering him incapable of speech or deed. As he'd sat, incapacitated, a flood of images had bombarded his mind. Scenes from his time in prison, his beatings, the horrifying sensations he'd suppressed, all rushed back to torment him. But this time, rather than fleeing to another time and place in his imagination, he'd held on, anchoring himself to the present and Joiner's goading, while at the same time imagining the safest place on heaven and Earth, a summer's eve and the loving embrace of his wife, Amelia.

Even now the energy that had been trapped in his system released, sending fresh shivers coursing through his system. As the shaking decreased, he felt the renewal of mental and physical acuity bringing his body back into realignment. He felt strength coursing through his veins and yet for all this, and despite the loss of Steadfast, he still refused to jeopardise the Subterranean Programme. Joiner may have destroyed one base for reasons still best known to himself, but no matter how evil that act was, it would not break Steiner's last resolve. 'How do you know they were my friends?' he said in answer to Bic's plea for help.

'Because of the change in your manner,' Bic said. 'You have regained your voice. Power is in your blood, Professor Steiner. You are a leader of men, you cannot let this injustice lie, it is not in your nature.

'And what do you know of my nature? We've only just met.'

'Have we, Professor Steiner?'

Steiner didn't know what to say to that.

'Your voice and actions give you away,' Brett said. 'He's profiling you, don't believe anything he says.'

Steiner glanced in her direction, but Bic's words rang true in his mind. *Have we met before? Do I know this man? It feels like I do.*

'I can tell you still need convincing, Professor Steiner. Perhaps a friendly face will be able to convince you.'

The wallscreen turned black before a window appeared containing an image of a dark skinned man with long black hair, twisted into two plaits that rested on either side of his chest. Steiner recognised the man's weathered features straight away. They'd only met in passing, like ships in the night, but each had felt an affinity with the other; it was as if they'd been friends from another time.

'George Steiner,' the Apache Indian said, 'I fear we have seen better days than these.'

Steiner could hear pain in the man's voice. 'Norroso, it gladdens my heart to see you alive. After we met I wondered if you'd heed my warning.'

'I didn't want to hear your words. Dulce was my home. I left that night with my family, seeking safe harbour in a neighbouring state, believing your pursuers would not follow. I was right. But as the weeks passed I decided to return to my ranch and things returned to normal, or as normal as they could in this life of shadow. But then one day I was out getting supplies when a large earthquake shook the land. I rushed back to find my house had collapsed. My son and wife were both killed that day and ever since I have been a man without hope.'

Steiner felt his heart lurch in sympathy. Kuruk, the young boy he'd saved from Samson's killing spree, had been full of life. His loss was hard to bear for those memories had been fresh in Steiner's mind during his captivity. His thoughts had often turned to the boy and his father, hoping, praying they would follow his advice and flee the state to avoid the arrival of the next asteroid. And yet it had been for nought. The boy and his mother were dead and Steiner knew only too well that Norroso's suffering meant his life was now without meaning or direction.

'Norroso, I don't know what to say, except that you have my deepest sympathies.'

The Native American continued. 'After the tragedy, the depression left in the Earth was large. It confirmed the existence of the underground world that had existed beneath. You warned me of the danger I faced, but I did not listen. I did not want to listen and for that my son and wife are dead. That is when your friend contacted me. He told me the ground had shaken because of a nuclear bomb. He said that I could help you and right the wrongs done against my ancestors' land.'

'You're the man in the truck,' Brett said, stepping forward. 'I saw you as we drove past.'

'I am, daughter of the man of mist. Bic told me you might not make it through. I was there to make sure you did.'

Brett frowned. 'You're the person who stole my car and left me those messages.'

Norroso didn't reply.

'How did you escape the police?' Eric said. 'There were so many.'

'With great difficulty and luck,' the Apache replied, 'and with your friend's help.'

Professor Steiner didn't like the feeling of being manipulated so easily, but it was clear the cyber terrorist was much more than a one trick pony. 'Norroso, how did Bic find you?'

'A vintage red pick-up truck is easy to find, Professor Steiner,' Bic said. 'DMV records are also easy to access.'

Steiner's eyes narrowed. 'You knew Joiner had already destroyed Steadfast and you said nothing?'

'Would you have believed me, Professor Steiner?'

Bic had a point, but it didn't ease Steiner's concern. This hacker was as dangerous as they came. Whatever his end game was, Steiner would have to be very careful he didn't end up as just another one of his pawns.

'So, Professor Steiner,' Bic said, 'your friend has confirmed that USSB Steadfast is no more. This takes away any suspicions you may have had about Malcolm Joiner's claim. Will you help us now? Will you divulge your knowledge to us so we may prepare for events to come?'

Steiner looked at Jessica, and then Eric and Brett, before turning back to Norroso, who remained on-screen. A small part of Steiner had been holding onto the belief that Joiner might have been lying about destroying Steadfast, but Norroso's testimony had removed that shred of doubt. Of course, Steiner could hardly feel aggrieved at Norroso for confirming the worst; the poor man had endured his own horrors.

'I won't stand in your way,' Steiner said, 'and if I can cause Joiner some discomfort, I will. But I cannot, and will not, tell you what I know. I'm sorry.'

Brett shook her head in disgust. 'You sicken me, old man.'

'Leave him alone,' Eric said. 'At least he didn't nearly get us all killed!'

Jessica put out a hand to restrain the angry German.

'Quiet!' Bic said. 'You have company.'

A red light flashed in the corner of the room, indicating an alarm had been tripped.

'Until we meet again, Professor,' Norroso said. His image disappeared as the screen switched off.

'It's likely the Peruvian police have come to investigate,' Bic said, his voice emanating from his console once more, 'or worse, the local militia. If it's the latter they adhere to strict GMRC curfews. If they find you, they will shoot on sight. You must all hide. Quickly!'

◆

Brett Taylor adjusted her bulletproof vest and withdrew the silver revolver she'd confiscated from the newsreader. Checking it was loaded, she placed it on the desk next to her and then slid her own sidearm from its sheath. Professor Steiner and Eric moved to hide behind a desk while the lights in the room dimmed, perhaps at the hacker's instigation. Bathed in shadow, she saw Jessica reach over and swipe her gun from the table.

With no time to reclaim it, Brett gestured to her. 'Stay here, I'll see if I can speak to them.'

Jessica looked scared. 'Be careful.'

Brett thought it an odd comment. *Has she forgotten I ratted them out to the FBI back in the States?* She moved to the door with her gun's safety on; she didn't want to shoot an officer of the law, she was one herself.

The building they were in was a square two-storey affair and consisted of a collection of corridors and interconnecting rooms. They were on the north east corner on ground level. *If it is the police*, she thought, *they'll check the exterior first for signs of forced entry*. That was where the problem came in as, while Bic had been able to partially disable the alarm system, Brett had been required to smash a pane of glass to get them inside.

Creeping down a corridor, Brett heard voices and the tinkle of glass. They'd found the door. Torchlight flashed across a wall and she stopped her advance. As an FBI agent she'd brushed up on her Spanish, but she couldn't remember if all Peruvians spoke it. There was only one way to find out.

She switched on the corridor's lights. 'Hola. Soy un agente federal de los Estados Unidos de América. Estoy investigando la escena del crimen.'

Brett held her breath and heard some muttering before someone said, '*Mana intindinichu.*'

She cursed. That isn't Spanish.

'*¡Hark'ay!*' someone else said. '*¿Imataq sutiyki?*'

She crept closer to the door and held out an open hand.

Gunshots rang out and Brett snatched her hand back. 'Don't shoot; I'm a U.S. federal agent!'

A flurry of furious commands came back in the same obscure language.

'I have three terrorist suspects,' she said, 'please, don't shoot! *¡No disparar!*'

'Show them to us,' a voice said.

At last, she thought, *someone who understands*. 'Okay, stay where you are and I'll bring them out.'

'No tricks, *señorita*.'

Brett ran back down the corridor to find the others. They were nowhere to be seen. Peering back the way she'd come, she saw a man duck his head through the door. He wore a police uniform. Brett held up a hand to him and he gave her a nod in recognition.

More shouting echoed down the corridor and the man disappeared to join in with his colleagues' slanging match. They sounded scared and disorganised and Brett wondered if the policeman's friends weren't police, but militia. If that was the case they could all be in a lot of danger. She'd heard about the corruption and breakdown of law and order in the South American countries. Things could get out of hand very quickly if she wasn't careful. The sound of a rifle being cocked reached her ears.

Brett slipped off her pistol's safety and strode into another hallway, her eyes searching. *Where are they?* Jogging up a flight of stairs, she saw movement and trained her gun.

'It's me!' Jessica said, a hand outstretched.

Brett lowered the gun a fraction. 'Where are the others?'

Before she could answer, torchlight shone up the darkened stairwell and Jessica disappeared from view. Brett swore and followed, but the light behind vanished, forcing her to stop in a doorway. Feeling her way in the black, she found another light switch and turned it on.

♦

Jessica's heart rate quickened. *Brett can't be trusted.* She'd heard the FBI agent speak to one of the policemen, or whoever it was that sought them out. She would turn them over the first chance she got. Now that Brett knew Joiner had been responsible for her father's escape, she would be after blood. The woman was single-minded. Jessica had met people like her before. They refused to bend, unable to let go of years of training and indoctrination.

Another gunshot reverberated through the building and she heard Eric call out. Disorientated in the dark, she found herself running forward.

'Eric, she said, her voice hushed, 'where are you?'

There was no answer.

Eyes straining to see, she bumped into a wall and she stopped to listen.

All was quiet.

The handle on her gun felt slick in her sweating palm and she adjusted her grip before moving on. Senses heightened, Jessica stepped into another corridor.

Powerful arms grabbed her from behind. Jessica screamed and her gun discharged. The dark lit up with a flash and a bang and she was released.

Strip lights blinked on down the corridor and halfway down Brett knelt with her gun trained on Jessica. 'Put it down!' she shouted.

A man in camos appeared beyond the FBI agent at the end of the hall, his assault rifle aimed at her back.

With no time to think, Jessica raised her gun and pulled the trigger.

Brett returned fire. Two shots in quick succession.

Silence followed before the sound of a body hitting the floor made Jessica glance round.

A policeman lay dead behind her, his pistol resting in limp fingers.

Brett turned to see the dead form of the other attacker felled by Jessica moments before. Standing, the FBI agent ran forward and grasped Jessica's shoulders. 'MOVE!'

Jessica felt dazed. I've just killed someone.

Another man appeared at the far end of the hallway. Letting out a cry of anguish, he picked up his dead friend's automatic weapon and bullets flew.

Brett dived forward and propelled Jessica through a doorway. They hit the floor hard and both their guns skittered away into the dark. Brett lurched to her feet, but Jessica remained sitting, frozen in abject terror. The militia man appeared in the doorway, rifle aimed straight at her. He depressed the trigger; the gun clicked but failed to fire. The man struggled with the mechanism and Brett leapt to grab the weapon's barrel. The two of them grappled before the gun discharged. Brett fell back into the corridor and the man unleashed a barrage of shots at point blank range. The FBI agent dropped to the floor and the man turned his gun on Jessica, who rolled aside, chased by bullets. The deafening onslaught stopped as the man's clip emptied. In the half-light Jessica saw a glint of steel and she scrambled towards it. The man advanced, kicking tables and chairs aside as he switched out his magazine for another. He pulled back the cocking leaver and Jessica flipped onto her back and fired her pistol. One – two – three shots rang out. The man's expression turned to surprise as he toppled sideways, blood gushing.

Jessica lay there for a moment in shock, revolver in hand.

'Jessica,' Eric said, appearing from nowhere, 'are you okay?'

Professor Steiner stepped past him and helped her to her feet.

'Are you hurt?' Steiner said, bringing her into the light.

'No, I don't think so.' Then she remembered. 'Brett—'

They turned to the FBI agent who lay in the hallway, unmoving. Blood was everywhere.

'Oh, my God.' Jessica's voice shook.

Professor Steiner put a finger to Brett's throat. 'She has a pulse.'

Brett's eyes fluttered open and she reared up, gasping for air. She tore open her shirt to reveal a cluster of bullets embedded in her protective vest. Her fingers scrabbled at Velcro fasteners and Steiner helped her remove the bulletproof jacket and her breathing eased.

'But the blood,' Eric said.

'It's not hers.' Jessica pointed a shaky finger at the dead body of the policeman Brett had saved her from before.

Waving away their assistance, Brett struggled to her feet and stood bent over with her hands on her knees.

'I owe you my life,' Jessica said, moving closer.

The agent stared up at her before her eyes grew wild. With a snarl, she surged forward and Jessica found herself slammed against a wall with thick fingers crushing her throat.

Before Eric and Steiner could react, Brett hauled her to the prone body of the Peruvian police officer and Jessica was held down to look into the man's unseeing face.

'Look what you made me do,' Brett said, between clenched teeth. 'LOOK!'

Jessica turned her head away, but Brett forced it back. 'I told you to stay where you were, I had it under control!'

'You were going to turn us over to them,' Jessica said, looking into the dead man's eyes. 'I heard you.'

Brett gave the back of her head one last shove and released her. 'You heard shit; you put me in danger, that's what you did, acting the fucking hero.'

All Jessica could see was blood on the floor, on the walls ... on her hands. The taste of bile built at the back of her throat.

'Are there anymore?' Steiner said, his tone urgent.

Brett regained her composure and shook her head. 'That's it. I only heard three voices.'

'You're both lucky to be alive.'

Brett looked down at the man she'd killed. 'I wonder if he had any family.'

'Don't do that to yourself,' Steiner said. 'You did what you had to do.'

'Did I?' she said, eyes fierce. 'And what do you know? This probably makes you happy, makes you think we're the same,' – she prodded him with a finger – 'but I'm nothing like you, do you hear me? Nothing!' She gazed at them all. 'I'm a federal agent and you're wanted criminals, nothing has changed.'

Jessica steadied herself by avoiding looking at the bodies around them. 'Then why did you save me?'

A glimpse of confusion suppressed Brett's anger.

She didn't know.

Jessica could see the tortured expression on Brett's face, an expression that must have mirrored her own. *I've just killed two men. Two people won't get up tomorrow – because of me.* The thought horrified her and she leant against a wall and retched.

♦

Brett Taylor walked over to the police officer and bent down next to him. The smell of blood and the faint whiff of excrement wafted over her, turning her stomach. The collar on his uniform had folded back on itself so she rearranged it back to neatness. Her eyes worked their way up to his face and the blank expression that stared off into the infinity of death. An image of Colonel Samson flashed before her eyes.

'I'm not my father,' she whispered to herself. 'I'm not a killer.'

With a steady hand she closed the man's eyelids and remained by his side as the living moved away, her melancholic thoughts haunted by the whisperings of dread.

◆

Professor Steiner guided the traumatised newsreader away from the scene. 'Let's get back to the control room. We don't want to stay here any longer than we have to.'

The young German gave a nod while Steiner led Jessica back to where they'd been conversing with Bic.

'I don't think she's right in the head,' Eric said when they were out of earshot of the FBI agent.

'Like father, like daughter,' Steiner said.

Eric gave him a look of incomprehension. 'I don't understand this expression.'

'*Der Apfel fällt nicht weit vom Stamm*,' Jessica said in translation, her voice weary.

Eric nodded in understanding. 'Were your parents from Germany, Professor?'

'My great-grandfather, I believe.'

Eric brightened. 'Maybe we're related.'

'Maybe,' Steiner said, leading them on, his thoughts anywhere but in the past.

As they reached their destination, the lights in the room blazed bright and the wallscreen glowed to life.

Steiner's expression turned guarded as he saw a new face on-screen, a dark-haired man of middle years, with intelligent eyes.

'Is everyone okay, Professor Steiner?' the man said.

Steiner sat Jessica down on a chair, removed his jacket and draped it round her shoulders. 'None of us is okay, but we're alive.'

'Alive is better than dead, Professor Steiner.'

'So this is the real you, is it?' Steiner said. 'The elusive B.I.C., in the flesh?'

'It is.' A self-deprecating smile crept across Bic's face. 'Am I such the disappointment?'

'I don't care what you look like. We need to hear this message of yours and get out of here.'

The hacker's expression turned serious. 'You are correct. Time is ticking. I am just finalising the array's realignment coding as we speak.' Bic turned away from the camera and the sound of keystrokes could be heard.

Seconds passed before the noise ceased.

'There,' he said, facing forward again, 'it is done.'

A number of consoles in the room came out of hibernation, their screens blinking on one by one. Data windows cascaded across them while a great metallic groan sent a shudder through the building.

Eric looked around in alarm. 'What's happening?'

Steiner pointed out of the window at the vast array of dishes. 'The radio telescopes are repositioning, along with the one on top of this building.'

Akin to some kind of mechanical ballet, the huge white saucer-like antennas shifted as one, swivelling up and round to face in the opposite direction.

Once their movement ceased, a strange oscillating noise came through the room's speakers.

'Turn it down!' Jessica said, putting her hands to her ears.

The volume decreased before the signal repeated itself.

Steiner moved to look at one of the screens. 'That's the signal?'

'Yes,' Bic said. 'Why? Do you recognise it?'

Steiner wasn't sure. It did seem familiar somehow. He sat down at the console and brought up a piece of software to analyse it. After a minute or so he had it. A message was buried within, waiting to be pieced together from its fractured state. 'I think it's Morse code.'

'Well done, Professor Steiner,' Bic said. 'You are correct.'

'And you're telling me you didn't figure that out?'

'It appears to be a set of co-ordinates in three dimensions,' Bic continued, ignoring the question. 'A trajectory, to be precise.' Bic's image disappeared to be replaced by a graphical representation of the Earth. Above it a small line traced an arc in the black of space. 'Do you still believe the signal is fake, Professor Steiner?'

'I never doubted it for second,' Steiner said, his tone dry.

Bic chuckled. 'You doubt it now, do you not?'

'We'll see,' he said, before noticing something else.

'There seems to be another aspect to the information,' Bic said, seeing it too.

Steiner studied the data and then realised what it represented. 'It's a fourth dimension.'

'Indeed – time.'

'Which allows us to pinpoint the velocity of the source,' Steiner said, 'along with its exact location as it moves through space.'

'Just so, Professor Steiner, just so. I'll enter the new parameters and we will track its flight.' Bic adjusted the input into the room's computer consoles and the information displayed on their screens altered to match.

'Whatever it is,' Steiner said, 'it's in deep orbit.'

The radio dishes in the array shifted a short distance, sending another groan reverberating through the building. Bic then set them to track the signal's source as it moved.

Steiner waited, listening. He glanced at Eric, who sat stock still, ears pricked.

A new sound pulsed through the speaker system.

'It is a live video transmission,' Bic said, sounding excited. 'I'll put it on-screen.'

The trajectory representation shrank to a smaller window while Bic reappeared in another section of the wallscreen. A third window then popped up in the middle with a green progress bar in the centre and a flashing word above it:

PROCESSING SIGNAL

The bar flashed solid green and disappeared to be replaced by a fuzzy image. Lines of static cut across the screen and the occasional flash of grey and white pixels produced a stuttering, disjointed picture.

Steiner could just make out a mass of buttons, dials and switches in the background.

'That looks a bit like the cockpit of our drone,' Jessica said.

A shadow moved across the camera and a man positioned himself in front of it. He reached out to adjust a dial and his image came into focus.

His lips moved as he spoke, but no sound came through.

Jessica moved forward, her arms hugging her body as if cold. 'Can he see us?'

'He can, Jessica Klein,' Bic said.

'This is—' The transmission crackled. '—nusson. Can you ... me?'

Steiner moved to the centre of the room as Brett rejoined them. 'Please repeat your last,' he said, 'your audio is breaking up.'

The man pressed a couple of buttons and turned another dial. 'Can you hear me now, over?'

'Roger that,' Steiner said. 'Five by five.'

A look of relief passed over the man's face. 'Thank the gods. I'd given up hope anyone would answer.'

'You're lucky,' Steiner said, 'your signal was well hidden.'

The man's expression turned guarded. 'Who do you work for? I don't recognise your output.'

'We're civilians.'

'And you're in charge?'

Steiner looked around him. He was so used to authority he'd just assumed control, but no one appeared to mind. 'Of a sort,' he said, realising his hands felt steady and relaxed.

'Do any of you work for the GMRC?'

Steiner shifted his stance. 'I used to, but we had a difference of opinion. Everyone else you see has no affiliation to the GMRC whatsoever. In fact, I'd go as far as to say they are as far from the GRMC as can be.'

The man considered him for a moment. 'What happened to make you leave?'

'It seems certain people thought me an inconvenience, and believed that I'd be of better service dead.'

'What was your position?'

Steiner hesitated. He didn't want to scare the man off, but equally he didn't want to give information away to Bic either. 'I worked on the Subterranean Programme as an engineer.' And it was the truth. That he was also the Director General of the whole division was best left unsaid.

'If that's true you'll know the name of the base in Colorado.'

Steiner grimaced in recollection. 'USSB Steadfast.'

The man nodded in satisfaction.

'Who are you?' Steiner said. 'Why are you trying to hide?'

'My name is Pilot Commander Tyler Magnusson, I'm a NASA astronaut and acting Captain of the United States Space Station Archimedes of which,' he paused, composing himself, 'of which I am the sole survivor.'

Steiner's expression grew grim. Bic hadn't been telling lies, at least in part. The rest had to be confirmed, but Steiner knew the truth when he heard it. 'Commander, what happened up there? What of the other space stations?'

The man shook his head. 'Gone, they're all gone.'

'How?'

The commander hung his head before looking back up. 'The GMRC. They sabotaged the intercept missions. All four space stations had been rafted together. Nothing is left.' He shook his head, his expression one of loss. 'Why would they want to do such a thing?'

The man was clearly in a state of distress. He had no idea Steiner could know about the missions planned to try and divert the next wave of asteroids. But as Steiner was on the Directorate – *had been on the Directorate*, he reminded himself – he was well aware of the plans. His problem now was working out how to prevent the astronaut from revealing to Bic and everyone else information about the asteroids. He cursed himself. His task was almost impossible. Anything the man said could reveal all in an instant. He'd already disclosed that something was to be intercepted, and it wouldn't take a genius to put two and two together and make six, not with Bic around, anyway.

'I don't know why anyone would want to do that, Commander,' Steiner said. 'Are you sure it was intentional and not an accident?'

'Positive. I overheard the leader of the GMRC delegation. They laid explosives, disabled all the escape pods and jammed the hatches. I saw it happen with my own eyes.'

Steiner couldn't believe what he was hearing. 'What was the name of the GMRC delegate?'

'Sylvia Lindegaard. Do you recognise the name?'

Steiner didn't. 'I know people who worked in the GMRC's Space Programme, but I don't recall her.'

'How did you escape?' Jessica said.

'Luck. I should be dead. I thought I was dead. I woke up drifting through space with debris all around me. No one replied to my calls for help. I feared I'd die alone in the cold, in the dark, but not everything was destroyed by the blasts. My momentum carried me to a Sabre space-aircraft and I was able to board it; that's where I am now.'

'Can't you return to Earth?' Steiner said.

The astronaut shook his head. 'Not enough fuel. I'm drifting in deep orbit. It won't be long before I run out of air. I have no food and hardly any water.'

'Could we go up in our drone?' Eric asked.

'No, Eric,' Bic said, 'it was damaged by the dust, and even if it hadn't been, it isn't designed for extended space flight and even I couldn't steal one that is.'

'The duplicity of the GMRC doesn't stop there,' Tyler said. 'They were experimenting with things, unnatural things.'

Steiner didn't like the sound of that. 'What sort of things?'

'I'm not sure. I saw ... something. It was like some kind of plasma, I don't know.' He rubbed his head. 'I've been getting headaches, it's hard to recall.'

Steiner guessed he was concussed. 'Did you hit your head, Commander?'

'I was hit by something; I think it was a solar panel.'

'Try to remember what you saw, Tyler Magnusson,' Bic said. 'It could be important.'

'It's too difficult.' He rubbed an eye. 'I know what it did, though. It caused some of my colleagues to lose their minds. They ended up in quarantine. Some of them died. My captain died just listening to it. Have you heard of Project Ares?'

Steiner thought back. 'I think I have. Wasn't it a collaboration across multiple organisations? I seem to remember it being mentioned, something about satellites and communications.'

'That may have been the official line,' Tyler said, 'but believe me, it's not what they told you it is. It's military, a weapon maybe, I don't know. Whatever it is, it's dangerous. The GMRC made sure it was removed from the Archimedes before they set off their charges. You find out what Ares is and you find out why they did what they did. Something isn't right, something is very, very wrong. The GMRC is not what it appears to be.'

Steiner wanted to say the GMRC was protecting the species and anything they did was for that end, but ever since he'd been outmanoeuvred by Joiner, his doubts had grown. And what with the confirmation of Steadfast's destruction and now the space stations, too, he was no longer sure of anything. *What the hell is happening?* How he wished he still wielded the power he once took for granted. *Perhaps that's why I was removed, to make way for such actions without anyone offering up resistance.* He crushed the assumption. He was by no means the only person in the GMRC with a conscience and the clout to stand up to Joiner and those that sided with him. He knew there were those that had come to covet the power he'd enjoyed, Joiner amongst them. Perhaps it was those people who had decided to take action. These imaginings flashed through his mind like quicksilver, but he'd thought them through before, round and round the theories went until he could see no end and no beginning, like a snake that consumed its own tail.

'Do you see what you were part of now, Professor Steiner?' Bic said. 'The goliath that you helped create.'

'Professor Steiner?' the astronaut said, astonished.

Steiner didn't respond and he gave a nervous glance at Brett, whose brows furrowed in response.

'It is you,' Tyler said, leaning forward, 'you don't remember me, do you?'

Steiner shook his head, fearing the worst.

'We met once, you and I, at a ceremony. You presented me with a GMRC bronze star for services to the planet.'

Steiner didn't recall. He'd been to many such occasions and presented many such medals and awards.

Tyler suddenly looked fearful. 'This is some kind of trick, isn't it? You want to bring me in, you want me dead!'

Steiner stepped forward. 'No! No, of course not.'

'But you're you, you *are* the GMRC.'

Steiner didn't know how he could prove he was no longer part of the organisation the man feared. He had an idea and unbuttoned his shirt. 'Does this look like the body of a man still working as an administrator for the GMRC?' He shrugged off the garment.

The astronaut looked shocked by the extent of Steiner's dark bruises and stitched cuts.

'Professor Steiner is no longer working for the GMRC,' Bic said, 'you have all our words on that, Tyler Magnusson.'

Steiner put his shirt back on, wincing in pain as Eric assisted.

'Commander,' Brett said, 'who is Professor Steiner?'

'You don't know?' Tyler looked confused. 'Surely you must know?'

Brett moved forward, her expression eager. 'Tell us.'

'He's the Director General of the Subterranean Programme, the most powerful man on the GMRC Directorate, the most powerful man on the whole damn planet.'

CHAPTER SIXTY

PROFESSOR STEINER SAW the looks of disbelief on the faces around him, disbelief mixed with fear, shock and awe. He looked away in discomfort. The truth was out and his fall from grace complete. *Perhaps I should put an advert in a national paper*, he thought wryly before the reality of his situation returned to crush his amusement. He was a convicted criminal, sentenced to death by his peers. There was nothing funny here.

'I *was* the most powerful man in the GMRC,' Steiner said, 'there's a big difference. And considering my current position, that power was far more tenuous than I knew.'

The NASA astronaut's expression was one of shock. 'What happened?'

'We don't have time for extended tales, Pilot Commander,' Bic said, 'and considering your dwindling air supply, neither do you.'

'Wait!' Tyler said. 'There's something else.'

Steiner's stomach tightened in anxiety. What else was this man about to disclose? Steiner considered terminating the transmission, but he knew Bic would be able to counteract any attempt to do so.

'We are all ears, Tyler Magnusson,' Bic said.

I bet you are, Steiner thought.

'I've found something.'

'Found what?' Steiner said, wary.

Tyler held up a hand and floated out of shot before reappearing. He leant forward and detached the camera, the picture jolting in response. The NASA astronaut manoeuvred to an oval window and the image he showed them made Steiner catch his breath. The Earth hung in the blackness of space below, its surface hidden by the swirling mass of the all encompassing dust cloud. Since the impact of AG5, Steiner hadn't been in a position to see the extent of the immense shroud. To see the planet so blighted made the fragility of their situation seem even more profound. Nothing could be seen of the great oceans and their dazzling blue greens. The great forests, mountains and deserts, everything had been hidden from the rays of the sun which blazed bright in heaven's endless 'verse.

Even through the video feed, the solar system's yellow star made the eye squint at its majestic power. Steiner's heart glowed with a safety and warmth he'd long forgotten, the starlight beautiful to behold.

'Can you see it?' Tyler said.

Steiner searched the vista with his eyes. 'See what, Commander, the Earth?'

'No.' The astronaut's hand came into view and pointed between the planet and the sun. 'There,' he said, 'against the light.'

Steiner moved his attention to the area Tyler had indicated. He couldn't see anything.

'I see it, Pilot Commander,' Bic said.

Eric moved past Steiner. 'See what? That black speck?'

Steiner looked again. Eric was right; there was something there, a tiny patch of black against the flaring fire of the sun.

'It's hard to see at the moment,' Tyler said.

The scene changed back to the interior of the ship and the astronaut's face reappeared. 'I'm sending you some photos I took of it yesterday. They're the best I could get with the equipment on board.'

The commander disappeared again before a static image popped up on their wallscreen.

Steiner moved closer. The photograph showed the sun rising above the Earth's horizon and, despite the colouration of the dust cloud, the fringes of the planet's atmosphere still reflected light, making it shine white. Framed against this clarity, a black shape could be seen. The image magnified.

'It's a ship,' Eric said.

Steiner adjusted his glasses. 'That's no ship, it's a space station.'

The picture zoomed in further.

'I ran a spectral analysis on it,' Tyler said, coming back on-screen. 'From what I can work out it isn't just black because it's in silhouette, but because it's made up of black panels. Furthermore, its angular design indicates it has stealth capabilities.'

Steiner frowned. 'A stealth space station?'

'It appears so,' Tyler said. 'Have you ever heard of such a thing?'

'Never.'

'The only reason I was able to see it at all is due to the depth of my current orbit. Lower orbits, where all other space stations operate – did operate – would not be aware of its presence, especially as its path seems to be designed to avoid detection. I've seen it change its trajectory multiple times already to avoid the prying eyes of other satellites.'

'Have you been able to see any markings on it?'

'None, but I believe its last manoeuvre will enable me to make a close pass. I may even be able to use my remaining fuel to dock with it.'

'That's good to hear, Tyler Magnusson,' Bic said.

Tyler made a face. 'My chances are slim, but it's all I've got. Although, if I am able to get to it, I might be able to refuel and return to the surface.'

Depending on who's operating it, Steiner thought. He didn't want to bring it up, although he was sure the astronaut must have already considered it, but whoever built and operated this craft had gone to a lot of trouble and expense to keep it hidden. That they'd been able to do so was a monumental feat, meaning only a few culprits could be responsible for its existence. It was either a secret military project devised by the Chinese, the Europeans, the United States or Russia; or – more likely – a collaborative effort between all four. The only other option was one he didn't want to entertain, but considering the accusations Tyler Magnusson had just made, the GMRC could well be behind this craft that drifted unseen in the darkness of space. What it was for, God only knew, but its presence was disturbing on more than one front.

'When will you know whether it's in range, Commander?' Steiner said.

Tyler pressed a button and glanced to his right. 'About seven hours from now. I'll make sure to document what I see on approach and transmit my findings when I'm able.'

The NASA astronaut's image distorted and a crackle came through the speakers.

'Your signal is breaking up, Commander,' Steiner said.

Tyler twisted some dials above him and the picture cleared a little. 'I'm drifting behind the planet, I don't have much time. I've just sent you a recorded message for my wife and children. Did you receive it?'

Steiner looked to Bic who nodded in confirmation. 'We did, Commander, we'll get it to them for you.'

'Thank you. They're due to enter USSB Steadfast in a few months time when the final protocol is enacted. If you can get it to them before then—'

Steiner suppressed a groan. He couldn't bear to tell the man Steadfast was no more and that his family wouldn't be provided with an alternative.

'Pilot Commander,' Bic said, his tone urgent, 'what were the intercept missions you spoke of? What were they to intercept?'

'You haven't told them, Professor?'

Steiner held his breath as the transmission warped again.

'... incoming ... of ...'

'Repeat your last, Commander Magnusson!' Bic said.

The fuzz and crackle of static came through the speakers as the image faded and broke.

Silence followed, before Tyler's final words came through the speaker system like the death knell they proclaimed. '... intercept ... next wave of asteroids heading for Earth.'

CHAPTER SIXTY-ONE

THE FINAL MESSAGE from the NASA astronaut hung in the air. The secret was out and the cyber terrorist had what he'd always wanted, the truth of all truths. Steiner shut his eyes and heaved a sigh. Curiously, the only thing between all out chaos on the surface and a war with those sheltering beneath was the one man who'd been pivotal to Steiner's current nightmare of a reality. Malcolm Joiner and his GMRC Intelligence Division would have to suppress any information Bic managed to release into the public domain. The problem was, the hacker was a law unto himself and there was no telling what plans he had to disseminate the terrible information he now held.

Eric looked around. 'Did he just say *next wave of asteroids*?'

Steiner opened his eyes to see Bic staring at him from the wallscreen.

'That is *exactly* what he said, Eric,' Bic replied. 'Professor Steiner, do you care to elaborate for us? Or should I just go viral with what I have?'

Steiner held Bic's gaze.

'There are more asteroids?!' Jessica said, her expression wild. 'How many? When will they hit?'

Steiner shook his head, sat down and put his head in his hands.

'Bullshit!' Brett said. 'There are no more asteroids.'

Jessica gestured to the wallscreen. 'Are you deaf? We all heard it!'

Brett laughed. 'It's a trick; all of this is a trick. It's just this terrorist playing games with us.'

'Games?' Eric said, fronting up to Brett and tapping his temple. '*DU BIST EIN DUMMKOPF*!'

'What did he just say? What did you just say to me?!'

'He said you're a fool,' Jessica said, 'and he's right.'

Brett grabbed Eric's arm. 'Say it again, you little bastard and I'll knock your teeth out.'

'Du bist der Dorftrottel. Du blöde Kuh!'

Jessica stepped between them as Bic joined in the argument.

Steiner put his hands over his ears. His head pounded with a headache. *This is too much.* The shouting continued until he could stand no more. 'QUIET!'

The room fell silent as he stood. 'Yes, there are more asteroids. Do you want to know how many? Six. There are six more heading for Earth. Four arrive next year and two more in 2045. And the final two are far bigger than the one that's already hit.' He faced Bic. 'Do you know why we kept it a secret? Do you know why no one should know? Because the surface is at an end. Nothing can stop them.'

Bic stared at Steiner, his expression unreadable.

Silence ensued before Eric broke the impasse. 'What about the intercept missions?'

'The Space Programme has tried for decades to land craft on them,' Steiner said, 'or shunt them off course. It started with AG5, but they all failed.'

'Perhaps they didn't fail,' Bic said, 'perhaps whoever destroyed the intercept missions also made sure AG5 would hit.'

Steiner made a despairing gesture. 'Perhaps so, I don't know anything anymore.'

'What happens to everyone on the surface?' Jessica said in a quiet voice.

Bic blinked, stunned. 'They die.'

Jessica looked at Steiner, her eyes begging it wasn't so.

'The Subterranean Programme was only ever designed to take a finite number of people,' Steiner said. 'There is no way we could cater for nine billion souls, no matter how much we wanted to. Hard decisions had to be made. It's not about right or wrong. The future of the species was at stake. Nothing else matters.'

'What a crock of shit!' Brett said. 'This man is a convicted criminal and you're listening to him like he's some kind of prophet. I can't stand any more of this – this lie!' She stormed from the room.

'Some people take the news better than others,' Steiner said, watching her go.

'That's why all the resources are going; you're pulling up the drawbridge.' Jessica slumped down onto a chair. 'Oh, my God, it's going to be anarchy.'

Eric sat down next to her. 'There must be something we can do?'

'There's nothing,' Steiner said. 'What will be, will be.'

'All those people,' Jessica said, 'there must be a way, there must be something—'

'If we could have saved everyone we would have,' Steiner told her, 'but it's not possible. What we've achieved so far, some said couldn't be done, but we did, against the odds. When humanity unites, it can achieve the improbable, but not the impossible.'

'You're responsible for the deaths of my colleagues,' Jessica said. 'Your GMRC, that astronaut said. You helped create it, helped run it. You're responsible for all the deaths of those that sought to expose the lie. You're more of a monster than Brett thinks.'

Steiner shook his head. 'No, you have my word, I had no hand in the ways the Intelligence Division went about their work. I always counselled restraint and voted against such practices. You must believe me. I found a great many things the GMRC did – does – as repugnant as you do. I may have been on the Directorate, but I was still one of many. There were thousands more from around the world, each with as much a say as anyone else.'

Jessica stood to pace around the room. 'The people deserve to know.'

'Do they, Jessica Klein?' Bic said.

'You've changed your mind? After everything you've said in the past? After everything you've done?!'

'If what Professor Steiner says is true, disclosing the truth will cause a catastrophic failure of human civilisation. The GMRC will collapse inside and out and those on the surface will seek to prise open the gates to the safe havens beneath. One by one the bases will be breached and the human race will destroy itself in an attempt to preserve its whole, when only its heart can survive.'

'So you think we should do nothing?' Eric said, appalled.

Steiner's hopes rose; was the hacker having a dramatic change of heart?

'I didn't say that, Eric,' Bic said, 'but I need to rethink my plans. I don't want to be the person responsible for the demise of the human race. Professor Steiner, if the intercept missions were sabotaged, it means there was a chance they'd be successful, don't you agree?'

'Maybe, but even if we could resurrect them – if that's what you're getting at – they were only ever meant to stop four of the six. Two were always destined to impact in 2042 regardless.'

With his image still displayed on the wallscreen, Bic shifted in his seat and frowned. 'I find that hard to believe. If you can stop four, why not all six?'

'I agree, on the face of it, it doesn't make much sense, but there is method to the madness,' Steiner said, his mood grave.

'Go on, Professor,' Eric said when he failed to continue. 'Why would they only stop four?'

'After the Space Programme's many failures,' Steiner continued, 'budgets were redirected to the subterranean response and it was decided only the largest two of the four asteroids due in 2042 would be targeted for deflection. The decision was a difficult one, but it was predicted the Earth could withstand strikes from the smaller two of the approaching rocks.' Steiner paused for breath. 'You asked why, though, and aside from the reasons above, the answer is simple. Because the first asteroid which makes landfall in the United States is half the size of AG5 and, like the second, which will impact in northern Africa, both have thin, elongated profiles, which favour more accurate composition analysis due to the lack of a large core. The density of both and their likelihood of fracturing in the atmosphere appeared to indicate their fallout would be catastrophic for the closest regions, but the impact winter from AG5 would not be significantly extended.'

'Appearances can be deceptive, Professor Steiner,' Bic said. 'What if the analysis is wrong?'

'Then the surface will descend into chaos faster than envisaged.'

Bic's brow furrowed in concentration. 'So even if the intercept missions were successful, the Earth would still experience mass upheaval. But say only the two asteroids impact in 2042; will they destroy civilisation as we know it?'

'Not completely,' Steiner said, 'but the USA will be decimated and Europe will be in a state of total collapse. It will effectively end global cohesion. Only fragmented nations will remain as mass hysteria takes hold.'

'But there will be some functioning states left – China, Russia – is that right?'

'Perhaps. It depends.'

'On?'

'On how ruthlessly they control their populations.'

Bic moved closer to the camera. 'So there would still be a possibility we could resume an assault on the final asteroids due in 2045.'

'There would no point if the four due in 2042 had already impacted,' Steiner said.

'But if they didn't, if only two made it to Earth.'

'It's extremely unlikely that—'

'Unlikely,' Bic said, 'but not impossible. As you have already said, Professor Steiner, humanity can achieve the improbable.'

'And how do you propose this could be done?' Steiner said. 'If there are elements within the GMRC that want the asteroids to hit – as hard as I find that to believe – then there is nothing we can do. The GMRC's power is total.'

'Not quite,' Bic said. 'Just prior to the 2042 impacts I imagine the beast will no longer have its head, am I correct?'

Bic is living up to his billing as a quick thinker, Steiner thought before a disturbing idea shook him. *Is Brett right? Was the footage of the NASA astronaut faked somehow? If that's the case I'm revealing highly sensitive information to the one man who can utilise it to maximum effect. Don't be stupid*, Steiner reasoned with himself, *if that is the case he already knew about the asteroid threat and the intercept missions.* 'The world's leaders,' Steiner said, proceeding with caution, 'those that are aware of the upcoming events, will retreat below ground to continue governing the new civilisation. And yes, before you ask, that will include the GMRC's ruling hierarchies.'

'And so the GMRC personnel remaining on the surface will be left to die like everyone else,' Bic said, 'which means they will experience the same disruption as everyone else. They'll be scared and confused and open to coercion.'

'Possibly,' Steiner conceded, 'but what do you expect me to do about it? I have no power and my criminal conviction put paid to anyone left who would have listened to my counsel.'

'Not you, Professor Steiner, us.' On-screen, Bic stood up and pointed to Jessica. 'We have at our disposal the world's foremost newsreader and journalist,' his finger moved to Steiner, 'and the GMRC's most influential leader. And if you excuse my self-adulation,' he pointed at himself, 'the greatest hacker the world has ever seen.'

'And *Das Gespenst*,' Eric said.

'Forgive me, Eric. And we have Germany's foremost hacker at our disposal, not forgetting a federal agent and a leading NASA astronaut.'

'If he survives,' Steiner said.

'Yes, if he survives. But if I had to assemble a team of six people to save the world, we would be in my top ten. Don't you agree?'

Professor Steiner felt a thrill of belief send tingles up his spine, but the sensation ended as quickly as it began. *Could they really make a difference, so few?* He looked to Eric and Jessica, their expressions full of renewed hope, before his focus switched to Brett, who stood at the back of the room having returned unseen. Arms folded and grim-faced, the FBI agent avoided his gaze.

Steiner returned his attention to the wallscreen and the hacker he'd once proclaimed as '*the single biggest threat to the Subterranean Programme*'.

'It's just over three years until 2045, Professor Steiner,' Bic said with a glint in his eyes. 'What do you say ... shall we save the world?'

MAP

USSB
STEADFAST
CALIFORNIA
NEVADA
UTAH
COLORADO
USA
Las Vegas
Los Angeles
ARIZONA
NEW
MEXICO
TEXAS
MEXICO
USSB
SANCTUARY

CHAPTER SIXTY-TWO

DEEP inside the Anakim creation of Sanctuary Proper, a small light bobbed in the silent ether of the pitch-black. As time passed, the tiny illumination crept forward while the dark, bottomless lake closed in around it on all sides. From afar, the sound of the cold surface being broken could be discerned, the soft splash of water tickling the quiet with a delicate caress. The illumination continued its advance, the flat calm disturbed by the lone swimmer at its heart.

Breathing hard, Corporal Walker trod water while holding onto the limp form of Richard Goodwin. Weighed down by his decontamination suit, it was all he could do to keep the two of them afloat. He searched about for signs of the fearsome creatures he knew lurked in the depths. Sucking in another gulp of air, he struck out again, being careful to keep the sound of his passage to a minimum.

His legs burned with fatigue and the lights on the lake's shore grew ever closer before the voices of his comrades encouraged him onward. Relief flooded his exhausted body as his men waded forward to meet him.

Hands grabbed Walker's aching arms and dragged him to dry land. He dropped to the ground, coughing and gasping, then crawled forward before rolling onto his back as he sought to reclaim his breath.

Torchlight shone in his face, forcing him to shut his eyes.

'Is he dead?' someone said.

A woman shrieked. 'Let me go!'

Still tired, Walker wiped water from his goatee and waited a few more moments before forcing himself into a sitting position. At his side, the exiled Director of USSB Steadfast lay unmoving, his helmet half-filled with some kind of black oil that covered his face.

Rebecca rushed to Goodwin's side and pulled in vain at the suit's mechanisms. She looked round at those gathered. 'Help me!'

The man Walker knew as Priest bent down, unlatched the complex catches and removed the director's helmet. Thick fluid oozed out onto stony ground, accompanied by a foul stench that made Walker gag.

Rebecca scooped away the black slime and removed the breathing mask that covered Goodwin's nose and mouth. She checked for a pulse and then leaned down, listening to see if he breathed. Without hesitation she moved her hands to his breastbone and administered thirty rapid chest compressions before tilting his head back, pinching his nose and blowing two rescue breaths into his mouth. She then switched back to complete another thirty compressions, followed by two more rescue breaths.

Sweat glistened on her brow as she continued to work while Walker's men stood by in silence.

Minutes passed and the rhythm of her compressions slowed. Walker, recovered from his exertions, moved to her side and grasped her arm.

'Let go!' she said, shrugging him off to continue the CPR.

Walker glanced round to see a look of hunger and discontent in the eyes of his ragtag unit. He grabbed Rebecca round the waist and threw her into the waiting arms of Priest.

Rebecca kicked and screamed.

'Hold her!' Walker said before straddling Goodwin's prone form and taking over the resuscitation effort. More time passed in a rhythmic blur and his thirtieth set of compressions came and went before he tired. He sat back, out of breath and gave a shake of his head. 'It's no good, he's gone.'

'NO!' Rebecca struggled against her captor's hold. 'Let me go!'

Walker stood up and gave Priest a gesture to release her.

Rebecca scrambled back to the cold body and restarted the compressions. 'Come back, Richard. Do you hear me?! Come back!!' She struck his chest with her fist, once, twice, three times before collapsing on him in a fit of sobbing.

Walker hung his head. Their mission had failed. Without the director to find his route out of the chamber they remained stuck in their subterranean tomb. But now things were much worse. Major Offiah and the director's bitch, Vandervoort, would blame them for Goodwin's death. *What will they do?* A picture of a noose came to mind. *Either that or a firing squad*, he decided. Walker looked round at the angry, accusing glares his men were giving him.

'What now?' someone said.

Priest picked up his rifle. 'Now we're screwed.'

'Someone else has to go into the lake,' another man said.

'You volunteering?' Priest said.

The man stayed silent and took a step back amongst his fellows.

'Thought not.' Priest turned to Walker. 'I think the man who got us into this mess should be the one to go.'

Walker stared at the rifle now pointed at his chest.

'What do you think, lads?' Priest said.

A murmur of agreement swept through those gathered.

Walker held Priest's gaze. The man was physically larger than him, and had been helpful in cementing Walker's role as leader. But now things had changed and it seemed that if you lived by the sword, you also died by it.

'You really want to do this?' Walker said, his cheek twitching while his hand drifted to the pistol at his belt.

Priest cocked his rifle. 'I really do.'

Walker froze his motion. He smiled and held up his hands as Priest sent someone else to disarm him.

Walker was stripped of his gun and knives before being handed Goodwin's discarded helmet. He looked at the black mess inside the transparent headgear. 'I think I'll use a clean one, if it's all the same to you.'

Priest stood aside to let Walker past.

Moving through the men, now a sheep among wolves, Walker collected the spare helmet and breathing apparatus they'd brought along, and then returned to the water's edge. He looked at Priest. 'You'll be next.'

Priest grunted. 'We'll see.' He gestured for him to move into the water.

Walker turned back to look at the dark and forbidding lake. He attached the breathing mask, lifted his helmet up over his head, secured its fittings and then shouldered the oxygen canisters.

'See you on the other side,' Walker said and stepped into the freezing liquid.

◆

Rebecca wiped the tears from her face with her sleeve and turned away from Goodwin's lifeless body to see Corporal Walker enter the lake. The decontamination team's new leader, the grim-faced Priest, remained at the shoreline as an armed deterrent against any change of mind on the part of his former superior.

Rebecca struggled to her feet, ignored the suggestive calls from some of the soldiers, and moved to Priest's side. 'You know he hasn't got Richard's resolve. He won't make it – that's if there's even anywhere to find.'

'And what would you have me do?' Priest said, keeping his voice low so those behind wouldn't overhear. 'This was his plan, he's put us in the firing line and now he's paying the price. As will you when they realise there's no one stopping them from using you as they want.'

Rebecca felt a shiver of fear ripple through her. 'What about you?'

'What about me?' he said.

Rebecca looked at him as he watched Walker continue his journey into the unknown. *I'll find no help here*, she thought.

She went to say something else, but movement in the water caught her eye. 'What's that?'

A shimmer of light swam below the surface towards an oblivious Walker, who was now waist deep.

Priest swore, took aim and fired.

Walker spun round at the sound just as a translucent form erupted out of the water to carry him under.

Shouts of alarm came from behind and the soldiers moved forward as one, guns raised.

'It's that fucking thing!' a man said, sounding terrified.

'The light,' another said, searching the black with his weapon, 'it's the light!'

Circular ripples expanded out from where Walker had stood, while the thing that had taken him was no longer visible.

Priest pointed. 'There!'

The top of Walker's helmet surfaced six feet from where he'd disappeared and the corporal stood up in the lake's shallows to face them, his hands raised. A translucent form hovered behind him, dripping water and sporting a pair of glowing eyes.

'Hold your fire!' Walker said.

A cascade of white sparks engulfed the being that held Walker in its embrace. Black armour appeared, glinting wet in the torchlight from onshore.

A strong female voice rang out. 'Drop your weapons!'

Rebecca's hopes soared. *Darklight have arrived!*

'Hold fast!' Priest said to his men, keeping his gun trained on Walker and his new found companion.

A gun appeared beside Walker's head. 'I said drop your weapons!' the woman said again.

'I don't think so.' Priest turned his gun on Rebecca. 'I give you to the count of three to let Walker go, or the girl dies.'

Rebecca felt her legs go weak.

'One,' Priest said.

The Darklight operative's gun remained pressed against Walker's helmet.

Priest took aim at Rebecca's head. 'Two!'

'Alright, alright!' The Darklight woman held up her gun and moved past Walker.

The threat of death passed and one of Priest's men waded into the water to take possession of the woman's weaponry.

Walking onto dry land, the soldier removed her helmet and shook out long, raven hair. 'The major will have all your heads for this,' Lieutenant Manaus said, 'you know that don't you?'

Priest remained wary. 'Where's the rest of your team?'

'Close.'

'She's lying,' Walker said, approaching, 'if there was anyone else we'd all be dead by now.'

Shouting erupted in the darkness beyond, where the rest of the twenty-eight strong decontamination unit stood guard.

All the soldiers swung round as one of their number appeared out of the pitch-black, pushing someone before him.

Rebecca's eyes widened in shock. 'Joseph?!' She ran to her ward, who grasped her in a fierce embrace before burrowing his head into her shoulder.

'What's he doing here?' Walker said.

Manaus frowned. 'He must have followed me from camp.'

'He's lucky we didn't shoot him,' said the man who'd escorted him in.

'I'm sorry,' Manaus said to Rebecca, 'I saw him near your tent; I never imagined he would—'

The Darklight lieutenant caught sight of Goodwin's body and gasped. Pushing aside the soldiers, she dropped to his side. 'What happened to him?' She looked from Walker to Priest and then to Rebecca.

Rebecca fought back more tears, while stroking Joseph's hair. 'He drowned in the lake,' she said, keeping the sight of Goodwin's corpse from Joseph.

The lieutenant felt for a pulse.

'We tried CPR,' Walker said, 'for a long time.'

Manaus looked to Rebecca for confirmation and she nodded her head.

The Darklight officer stood up. 'So, what's your plan now, gentlemen? Hide out here until Offiah's teams find you? You won't last a week.'

'There's a way out,' one of the men said.

'And he's going to find it.' Priest pointed at Walker.

Manaus glanced in the corporal's direction and understanding dawned on her. 'So it's everyone for themselves, is that it?'

'Something like that,' Priest said, 'and if he fails, you're next.'

'Is that so?' The lieutenant stood her ground as some of the men closed in around her.

A cry of anguish drew everyone's attention as Joseph squirmed out of Rebecca's grasp. The handicapped man fell to his knees and grabbed Goodwin's shoulders. He shook the lifeless body and his cries of fear and loss increased. Rebecca moved to his side to try and pull him away, but Joseph pushed her off. He drew Goodwin to him and rocked him back and forth like a child with a doll. The director's head lolled to one side and a trickle of black fluid ran from his mouth, and then Lieutenant Manaus was there, pushing Joseph aside.

'Someone take him!' Manaus said, struggling to hold Joseph at bay.

Rebecca grabbed Joseph and hauled him away while the lieutenant rolled Goodwin onto his side and pounded on his back.

A gush of thick ooze burst from his mouth, the inky slime flickering with tiny glimmers of blue lightning.

Manaus lay Goodwin onto his back and opened an eyelid. The same flicker of energy swept across his iris. His dilated pupil contracted and Manaus restarted the chest compressions before breathing two rescue breaths into his mouth.

The director's body spasmed in response.

'Come on, damn it!' Manaus said, restarting the compressions. 'Come back to us, Director!'

CHAPTER SIXTY-THREE

A MILLION FISH swam in the deep blue seas of eternity, tiny minds living and breathing as one. Sweeping arcs of colour shimmered through the ocean blue as the shoal ducked and weaved like a three-dimensional spirograph of life. Patterns infinitesimal and grand merged and exploded into a chaos of nothing while the wonder of the sunlight shone bright through the waves above. The ultimate essence of beauty in a 'verse of dark, the light of a single star pulsed vibrant, a life source of energy unlike any other in the system of creation. Seasons came and went. Stars scudded across changing skies, black to blue, red to black. Plants grew, bloomed and died before the transitions slowed. A summer dawn broke against a beach of universal energy. At its heart a single burning light throbbed with a spark of life like the passion of Christ, the desire for resurrection vast. Unquenched by the fires of dark, the mind returned as the air-filled lungs recovered their might. A steady pulse beating in time to another's. Pulse, pulse, pulse ...

'Come back to us, Director!'

'They're calling you,' said a deep voice that echoed through time and space.

The consciousness that was, felt confused. 'Who are you?'

'Who are you?' his voice echoed. '... are you ... are you ... are you?'

'You know who I am,' the voice said, its rumbling resonance shaking his soul. 'It is you that is without self. Who are you?'

The mind pondered the question, but the answer remained elusive. 'I am no one. I am lost.'

'Lost ... lost ... lost,' said his echo.

The voice boomed out again. 'We are all lost.' It paused. 'None of us is perfect.'

'Except you,' said the mind.

The voice laughed, the pitch turning human. 'So you do remember me.'

A vision of a preening bird flared before him. The animal paused as if listening before using its beak to beat a tap tap tap in rhythm to his thoughts.

'But who am I? Where am I?'

The voice sounded pleased. 'You are nowhere, as am I.'

'Is this real?'

'As real as real is now.'

'That's not an answer.'

The voice chuckled. 'I know, but I cannot answer what I do not know.'

Another voice made the mind twist its perception.

'You should go,' said the voice, 'they're waiting for you.'

'What about you?' The mind felt scared. *I don't want him to go!*

'Don't be frightened,' said the voice as if reading his thoughts. 'We will meet again.'

The sound of fluttering wings resounded in his mind and a small bird flew away into the light.

'Professor, wait!'

A tsunami of light and sound swamped his senses and Richard Goodwin opened his eyes, emerging from the strangest of dreams like a newborn child from the forbidden canal of death.

An angel spoke to him. 'Can you hear me, sir?'

'Richard, can you understand us?' another being said. 'Say something.'

Goodwin reached out and touched the face of a smiling man, the innocence of spirit powerful in its purity.

The man grinned and a flood of memories ignited Goodwin's scrambled mind.

'Joseph,' he said, looking from the young man to Rebecca. 'I had the oddest of dreams.'

'Sir, can you sit up?'

Goodwin switched his attention to Lieutenant Manaus. He gave a nod and the Darklight officer helped him into a sitting position before nausea and coughing doubled him over. A pressure built in his stomach and he retched up a mixture of water and oil. Wiping his mouth, he tried to stand.

'Slowly, sir,' Manaus said, helping him up, 'you've been through quite an ordeal.'

'How long was I out?'

Rebecca held onto his other side. 'You were unresponsive for a long time.'

'How long?'

'Long enough that you shouldn't be walking and talking,' Walker said.

'Which was?'

The corporal shrugged. 'Fifty minutes, maybe longer.'

'Fifty minutes?' Goodwin turned to the Darklight officer. 'But I feel fine, great even.'

'I don't know what to say, sir.' Manaus prodded at the black ooze with a foot. 'Maybe this material had something to do with it. It gave off some sort of electrical charge when it came out of you.'

Goodwin thought back to his time in the lake and the wall of oil beneath the surface, the sea within a sea, and the nightmarish visions that had struck at his sanity, and his fight for life. 'How did I end up here?'

Walker gestured at himself and the suit that mirrored Goodwin's own. 'I came to the rescue.'

'Only because you wanted the director's escape route,' Manaus said, 'otherwise you'd have left him for dead.'

Walker put his hands up to Goodwin. 'She's not wrong. What can I say? I'm a survivor.'

'Where's the rest of your team, Lieutenant?' Goodwin indicated to the two women he was able to stand under his own steam.

'Sorry, sir, I'm on my own.'

Goodwin looked around at the armed men of Walker's decontamination team. 'But they'll be arriving soon?'

'Offiah has despatched a team led by Captain Winter,' Manaus said, 'and yes, they'll be here soon.'

'And if you believe that you'll believe anything,' Walker said, 'isn't that right lads?'

Goodwin saw animosity on the faces surrounding them, with no small amount aimed Corporal Walker's way.

The man Walker referred to as Priest stepped forward. 'It remains to be seen if the rest of Darklight are turning up,' he said, 'but if they do we'll be ready for them and you'll be back in that lake searching for your way out.'

Rebecca grasped Goodwin's arm protectively. 'He can't go back in there; we've only just brought him back!'

Priest glanced around at his men. 'I can't help that, and besides, he said he's fine, feeling great, which means he goes.'

Walker held out his headwear to Goodwin with a smile. 'Godspeed, Director.'

'And that goes for you, too.' Priest tapped the corporal's helmet with the tip of his rifle.

'What?' Walker's smile fell from his face, his nervous tics roaring to the fore. 'You don't need two of us in there; if we both fail then you won't have any more equipment unless you go back to camp.' Walker looked round at the soldiers. 'Surely you can all see that?'

Priest shoved the corporal towards the lake, making him stumble. 'Twice the manpower, twice the chance of success.' He gestured to Goodwin. 'Now suit up, both of you.'

Goodwin hesitated.

'Now,' Priest said, raising his gun.

Goodwin sighed, retrieved his helmet and transparent breathing mask, and joined Walker at the lake's edge. Bending down, he washed out the black filth that had nearly killed him and looked at Walker who was ready for the off. 'Do you ever have bad dreams, Corporal?'

He gave Goodwin a funny look. 'Sometimes, why?'

'Because where we're going your mind will be tested to its limit.'

Walker held his gaze before Manaus moved forward to help Goodwin secure the breathing apparatus and to check all its systems still functioned. While she was doing this Walker used the pause in proceedings as an opportunity to press home his needs to Priest.

'I don't give a damn what's down there,' Priest said, 'you're not having a gun.'

As the two men argued, Manaus helped Goodwin with his mask.

'Does Major Offiah even know you're here?' Goodwin whispered.

The lieutenant gave a small shake of her head. 'No one knows.'

'Why?'

'I saw Walker and his men had taken Darklight kit. I couldn't risk them intercepting the transmission.'

'So they're not coming?'

'They'll find us ... eventually.'

'Why are you helping me?'

'Because I believe—'

Manaus fell silent as Priest approached.

He pushed the Darklight woman aside and finished preparing Goodwin for submersion. When he'd completed the process, clicking the final latches of the helmet into place, he pressed the hilt of a large knife into Goodwin's hand. 'For protection,' he said, standing back.

Walker rejoined him and brandished his own serrated blade. 'Better than nothing, eh, Director?'

Goodwin noted the bitter irony in the corporal's tone. He had to admit he shared his scepticism, especially after seeing what lurked down in the depths. They might as well have given him a toothpick for the good it would do. But, unlike his reluctant companion, Goodwin knew a greater power was at work and a divine mission could not be stopped, no matter what stood in its way.

Stowing the blade, he accepted a fierce embrace from an

emotional Joseph followed by another from Rebecca. 'You don't have to do this, Richard. Please, there must be another way. This isn't worth your life.'

Goodwin placed his hand on hers. 'I have to go, and not just because they say so, but because I must. I've seen what's down there now. I've seen many things. There's a barrier under the water and it's there for a reason.'

Rebecca's expression grew worried. 'Reason?'

Goodwin touched her cheek. 'You'll see.'

His words didn't seem to ease her nerves, but Goodwin had regained his focus. He had a job to do. *She'll soon see. They all will.* He'd been spared and now it was time to repay the debt. God had spoken and he would answer.

CHAPTER SIXTY-FOUR

Rebecca watched Goodwin enter the lake, the pain of desperate emotion an onslaught on her mind, her heart yearning beyond the ties of friendship past. Joseph held her hand tight and waved farewell to the man they'd grown to trust and love.

Step by step the two men waded deeper until they submerged beneath the surface and only the light from their helmets could be seen swimming through the ripples.

Lieutenant Manaus stood tall and strong by Rebecca's side, the Darklight officer a powerful presence with her fierce eyes and black armour. Behind, Priest and the leering beasts that called themselves men skulked in the shadows, prowling the fringes of light. Unlike before, however, this time Rebecca had the lieutenant and Joseph for company during her tense vigil. *Will that deter the soldiers from enacting their base desires?* she wondered. She prayed it was so, for the alternative brought back memories from a time far darker than the world they now inhabited, a time of shame and pain. She recalled the words her friend Julie had said to her on one of the few occasions when she'd been able to bear acknowledging the event. 'They defiled themselves, Becca,' she'd said, 'they embraced the dark. No one can ever take your light, your power. You may think they have, but you need to let your body heal, to feel.'

And her friend was right, when she'd allowed herself to enter her senses to feel the fear, she'd wept until she thought her heart would burst, but afterwards she felt a power unlike anything she'd ever felt before. 'What doesn't kill you makes you stronger,' her dearest pa used to say, and now she knew how true those words were.

The lieutenant broke the silence of Rebecca's introspection.

'I've just realised where we are.'

'Where?' Rebecca said.

'Do you remember before Susan was taken by the light, the entity?'

How can I not? Rebecca thought. 'Yes,' she said.

'This place isn't far from where I saw the light enter the lake,' Manaus said, raising her voice for everyone to hear.

Rebecca looked at her. 'Are you sure?'

'Positive.'

A few of the men swore and Priest approached the Darklight officer. 'If you don't keep your mouth shut, *woman*, I'll shut it for you.'

'I thought you'd like to know.'

Priest glared at her before shoving a communication device into her hands and stalking away to shout out commands for his unit to double the watch.

◆

Moving through dark, misty waters, Goodwin tapped Walker on the arm and pointed in the direction he wanted to go.

Walker gave him the thumbs up. 'Lead on, Director,' he said, his voice distorted by his mask and coms system.

Goodwin continued on his path down into the lake with the corporal following close behind.

Lieutenant Manaus' voice came through his helmet's speakers. 'How are you doing, sir?'

'Okay so far, Lieutenant.'

'Where's Priest?' Walker said.

'Otherwise engaged,' Manaus replied. 'It seems he didn't like the thought that this is near where I saw the entity enter the lake.'

'And is it?' Goodwin said, scouring the water for signs of any movement.

'Is it what?'

'Is it true the light was seen near here?'

'I'd like to say no,' Manaus said, 'but that would be a lie. Be careful down there, Director, it might not be just fish you need to contend with.'

Goodwin felt his sense of invincibility retreat at the news.

'And you didn't think of telling us this before?' Walker said, sounding angry.

There was no response until the lieutenant said, 'I only just realised.'

'Great,' Walker said, 'fan – fucking – tastic.'

Goodwin pressed ahead. 'It changes nothing.' He moved past the ancient water-bound sculptures that rose up around them while Walker muttered curses and objections under his breath in equal measure.

After a few more minutes of traversing the lakebed, the two divers neared their destination as the black wall emerged from the murky gloom like the Devil's shade.

'Is that it?' Walker said, looking up at the forbidding barrier with anxious eyes.

Goodwin didn't reply. He touched the thick, black ooze as he'd done before, sending ripples across its inky surface.

'What's your progress, Director?' Lieutenant Manaus said over the radio.

'We've arrived at the obstruction,' Walker said.

'Any sign of ... anything else?'

'Not so far,' Goodwin said, distracted.

'We have no idea what this is,' Walker said, drifting closer to Goodwin, 'the Anakim could have designed it to kill for all we know.'

Goodwin pondered the corporal's words. *An ancient security measure. Perhaps he's right.* The dark creation could easily be mistaken for being the veil that separated the living from the dead. And such were the terrors it inflicted on those who dared enter its hidden halls anyone could be forgiven for believing it to be the river Styx made real.

Walker touched the oil with tentative fingers before quickly withdrawing them.

'It protects what lies beyond,' Goodwin said, staring into the viscous obscurity.

'A way to the surface?' Walker said.

Goodwin nodded. 'But I know its secret. I know how to defeat it.'

'And how do we do that?'

'I've solved its riddle.'

'Riddle? I thought it was just some weird fluid?'

'No, it's much more than that. It sees into the darkest part of your mind. It turns you inside out and outside in. It's like the ancients told us, as the Bible says, it's a test, a test of faith.'

'Good luck, Director,' Manaus said over the com. 'We'll listen for your radio contact when you reach the other side.'

'If there *is* another side,' Walker murmured.

Goodwin glanced at his companion. 'Are you ready, Corporal?'

Walker looked anything but, fear etched across his features like a gaping chasm.

Knowing what to expect should have made Goodwin's knees tremble and hands shake, but he felt calm, because he knew the truth within.

'May God guide our way.' Goodwin took a deep breath and walked into the black.

CHAPTER SIXTY-FIVE

GOODWIN DISAPPEARED into the rippling wall of darkness and Walker, breathing hard through his mask, checked his air supply. Five minutes remained. Taking one last look around, he made the sign of the cross on his chest, shut his eyes and followed Goodwin into the beyond.

◆

Lightning consumed Goodwin's mind as he swam through thick ooze. Memories of long forgotten childhood events flickered before his eyes in a kaleidoscopic trance and faces and names merged as the black fluid poured into his helmet. Fighting back the terror that devoured his soul, Goodwin felt his forward momentum slow, the liquid solidifying around him. Panic gripped and doubts rose. *Have I made a fatal error?* An invisible force pulled him down and he fought for breath. *What if God spared me so I could find a different path?!*

His speaker system crackled and Walker's screams shocked him into lucidity.

'Corporal,' Goodwin said, realising his mistake, 'swim up!'

Fighting against the strengthening current, Goodwin thrust out for the surface. The fluid thinned, his movements eased and a wave of energy engulfed his body, spinning him round and into Walker who surged up from below.

The corporal grasped Goodwin's suit, his eyes bulging in terror. 'HELP ME!'

The black ooze crept higher and inched over Goodwin's mask. The oxygen supply faltered and his airway constricted.

Choking and wheezing, Walker's grip loosened, his fingers turning claw-like as he hyperventilated.

Neurons fired and synapses activated in a cascade of electricity and a vision tore through Goodwin's neo-cortex. An Anakim warrior spoke in a foreign tongue. A distant star turned supernova. The sun shone bright in space. Two planets swept past, followed by Earth, a blue pearl in a sea of dark. Goodwin floated through the solar system, a cosmic traveller in a terrestrial world. A jolt of clarity and Goodwin teleported into reality. He gasped for air before the vision submerged him again. The red planet reflected large in Goodwin's eyes, rotating in mystery before the asteroid belt gave way to the gas giants. Jupiter, Saturn, Uranus, Neptune. Goodwin's speed through space increased. The dwarf planet Pluto whizzed by before the vision warped. Another planet hove into view. This rocky mass orbited a dark star. The Anakim warrior reappeared, kneeling before an altar covered in blood. A myriad of other scenes flickered into being. Pain burned through Goodwin's lungs and he grabbed Walker's spasming arm. The black oil thinned, turning transparent and a blue glow shone through warm, pristine waters, and Goodwin's mind cleared as his air supply ceased. Above, a ceiling of azure crystal shimmered, iridescent. *There's no way to the surface!* Goodwin did the only thing he could. Jettisoning his helmet and mask, he swam forward, dragging an unconscious Walker with him.

Pain racked Goodwin's body, his lungs fit to burst. Vision failing, he spied a rippling distortion overhead. He aimed for the irregularity and used his last ounce of strength to propel them up through bright waters. With consciousness slipping, Goodwin's momentum carried the two men through a weed-encrusted circle of stone. Air returned and Goodwin gasped loud, sucking in the precious gas like the elixir of life it was. Taking five more thunderous breaths, he filled his lungs like never before, his head dizzy with the rush of oxygen.

Goodwin looked around to see he was inside a strange tunnel that glowed with the same blue hue that had lit the clean waters below. He swam to the edge of the hole, heaved himself out onto dry ground and then turned back to pull Walker's limp form up beside him. Goodwin forced off the corporal's helmet and mask and washed away the stinking gunk that clung to his face before rolling him onto his side. Walker coughed and a gush of water and oil burst forth. The corporal continued to breathe and Goodwin lay back to recover, exhausted.

A minute or two passed before he felt strong enough to sit up.

Walker remained lying where he was. 'Remind me,' he said, his voice rasping, 'never to listen to you ever again.'

Goodwin stood up. He cared nothing for Walker's words, the man had threatened Rebecca with abhorrence and that was something he could never forgive. 'Get up.' He pulled the corporal to his feet, retrieved and washed out his headgear, and then moved off in search of answers.

CHAPTER SIXTY-SIX

SOMEWHERE BENEATH THE surface of the subterranean aquifer, Richard Goodwin walked down a long, dark tunnel. The glow behind had faded and he'd decided to put his diving helmet back on to illuminate the way.

Walker stumbled along at his back, complaining all the while. 'Do you even know what you're looking for?'

Goodwin didn't reply. Instead he searched round for clues, for anything that would aid their escape from Sanctuary.

'You don't, do you?' Walker continued. 'You hadn't solved any riddle; you're out of your damn mind like everyone says. We could have both died back there.'

They reached a large circular chamber and Goodwin slowed to a stop. 'But we didn't, did we?'

Walker grumbled something before wiping some black slime from his face. 'How does that oil penetrate our breathing masks? They're airtight.' He looked around, confused. 'And where the hell are we anyway? Are we still under the lake or what?'

'I don't know about the oil,' Goodwin said, 'but I'm pretty certain we're inside the lake.'

'So what now?'

'Now we activate that.' Goodwin pointed across a small expanse of water that barred their way.

'What is it?'

'I'm not sure, but I feel like I've seen it before.'

Walker pushed Goodwin aside and peered ahead at the construction that stood on a tiny island.

'You've seen it too, haven't you?' Goodwin said.

'I – I don't know, I saw visions, weird visions ...'

'The lake was trying to tell us something, I think it was trying to guide us.'

'Or warn us,' Walker said. 'We don't know what it'll do.'

'There's only one way to find out.' Goodwin lowered himself into the icy water and swam across.

Less than a minute later he emerged next to the strange mechanism. Standing ten feet high, it glistened wet under the light from Goodwin's helmet. Made from grey pockmarked granite, the intricate carvings at its pentagonal base melded into a smooth surface which ended in a singular point at the top. Halfway up the column, five rods of oxidised silver, each positioned at a forty-five degree angle, sprouted from a circular niche, like the handles on some sort of prehistoric, multiplayer slot machine. Goodwin defied anyone who saw them not to feel the urge to pull them down; they were as welcoming as handles on a door.

Unfortunately the device was designed for a being much taller than himself. He looked up at one of the metal levers and gauged the distance. He jumped, grasping for it, but his fingers fell just short.

A splash of water echoed through the cavern and Goodwin glanced back to see Walker swimming across. Moments later he stood by Goodwin's side.

'I don't think that's the right one,' Walker said, walking round the device. 'Try this one.' He pointed at the next one over.

'Are you sure?' Goodwin said.

'It feels ... right.' Walker looked at him. 'Don't ask me why, okay? It just does.'

As Goodwin didn't feel anything at all towards any of the options on offer, he deferred to the corporal's suggestion, even though it went against his better judgement.

Walker gave him a boost up and Goodwin gripped the lever, which had the diameter of a large grapefruit. He tried to pull it down, but it wouldn't budge. He lifted himself into the air, free of Walker's hold and the mechanism gave a creak, but no more.

'Move further along it,' Walker said.

With difficulty, Goodwin manoeuvred up to the very end of the bar, his legs now hanging over the water some six feet below. Another creak and nothing.

'It's no good,' Goodwin said, interlocking his fingers, 'I'm not heavy enough.' He tried pulling himself up and dropping his weight back down, still to no avail.

Walker looked up at him. 'Have you got a good grip?'

'Yes, why?'

'Hold on!' Walker took a few steps back and then ran and leapt into the air to grab on to Goodwin's legs.

With a screech of metal on metal, the handle dropped down with a dull clang.

Goodwin lost his grip, and he and Walker fell with a splash into the water, which now seethed with bubbles. The island that held the mechanism sank beneath the surface.

On instinct Goodwin and Walker swam back to shore, barely getting out before the water sank down into a whirlpool, while above the ceiling retracted and a huge torrent of water flooded down to form a thunderous waterfall. Goodwin took a step back from the wall of liquid that now tore past just a few feet away.

The deafening noise continued before the ground shifted beneath their feet, making them hold onto the wall.

Walker cupped his hands and shouted, 'It's an earthquake!'

Goodwin didn't know what it was, but soon after, the rumbling eased and the cascade ran dry. Drops of water plip-plopped down into the large, cylindrical shaft that had been revealed, its dark interior extending up as far as it descended below. Around its edge a smooth six foot wide sloping walkway spiralled down into the depths and up into its heights.

Goodwin peered over the edge before jumping down onto the path. On a hunch he walked up the incline and Walker followed.

At the top they emerged into fresher air and a pitch-black void. A breeze rustled their decontamination suits and Goodwin angled the torches on his helmet to see they were surrounded by more water.

Leading out into darkness, a causeway cut a path through the inky liquid a mere inch below the surface.

'What's that?!' Walker removed his knife from his belt.

'Turn off your lights,' Goodwin said, as he switched off his own.

Walker did as instructed, plunging them into total darkness.

In the distance a host of lights approached, the eerie procession strung out in a line.

'We should go,' Walker said, sounding terrified.

Goodwin was about to agree until he heard something that made him pause.

'Quickly!' Walker said in a forced whisper, 'it's almost on us.'

A beam of light shone in their direction. 'Who's there?' said a voice. 'Director, is that you?

Goodwin sighed in relief and switched his lights back on.

Lieutenant Manaus strode across the causeway. 'It is you, sir. We were getting worried.'

'This bridge stretches all the way back to shore, I take it?' Goodwin said, shaking the lieutenant's hand.

'It does, but it's not straight. It spirals in to this point and makes landfall along from where you started.' She pointed at her visor. 'Luckily we were able to see the bridge appear, otherwise we would have only heard the water displacement.' She looked around. 'Which I assume came from here?'

Goodwin nodded.

'Richard, you made it!' Rebecca ran forward to embrace him, with Joseph close behind.

Goodwin enjoyed the reunion, but his mood soured when Priest and his men arrived on the scene.

'Well done, Director,' Priest said, 'you're not dead. Congratulations; now what?'

Goodwin released himself from Joseph and motioned to the slope behind. 'Now we go down.'

'I thought he'd found a way to the surface,' one of the soldiers said. 'Shouldn't we be going up?'

'Man's got a point,' Priest said.

Walker stepped forward. 'We've got you this far and risked our lives to do it. Follow me and I'll lead you all out of here.'

'Like you had anything to do with it,' Manaus said, her tone scathing.

'Whose idea was it to help the director?' Walker said, addressing the decontamination team. 'Me. Who helped him find this location? Me. Who went into the lake and discovered this?' He gestured around them. 'Me, again! If any of you want to get out of this place alive then I'm the one you should be listening to.' He pointed at Priest. 'Not him.'

Priest strode forward and Walker slid his knife from his belt before lashing out. Priest dodged a second thrust and knocked the weapon from his attacker's grasp. He slammed the butt of his rifle into Walker's midriff, doubling him over, and some of the men laughed.

'Nice speech, Corporal,' Priest said, 'but your chance at leadership has come and gone.' He turned to Goodwin. 'Lead on, Director.'

Goodwin glanced at Lieutenant Manaus, who gave an imperceptible shake of her head. There was no way they could win this fight. Not in their current position.

Still winded, Walker struggled to pick up his knife and gave a twisted smile full of bitter humiliation as Goodwin moved past him and back to the slope. The Goodwin of old would have almost felt sorry for the man, but now he couldn't have cared less. He had one thing on his mind; find a way to the surface.

CHAPTER SIXTY-SEVEN

THE GAPING shaft in the centre of the Anakim lake carved out a core below the water's surface half a mile deep, and the sloping pathway that clung to its outer wall spiralled down into the depths. Along this ancient, narrow road travelled the thirty-two strong company led by Richard Goodwin, former Director of USSB Steadfast, the prophet of the hour. So far his reasoning had proven sound, his gut instincts serving him well when others had doubted his sanity. Vindicated and driven on by compulsion, he increased his pace as they neared the bottom.

Ahead, a large, crumbling entrance led into blackness.

Someone touched his arm and the Darklight lieutenant drew alongside. 'I'll go first, Director, see if it's safe.'

Goodwin shook his head. 'There's no ... need.'

It was too late; Manaus had already moved past to assess the lay of the land. Reaching the hole, she pressed some buttons on her recon helmet and disappeared into the gloom.

The rest of the party regrouped at the bottom and waited for her return.

A couple of minutes passed before Manaus reappeared. She

waved them forward. 'It's safe, but tread carefully, there's loose rock underfoot.'

'Next time you wait for my orders,' Priest said, 'is that clear, Lieutenant?'

Manaus gave a mocking salute before switching on her headgear's torches to help light their way.

Goodwin followed her in and helped Rebecca and Joseph tackle the awkward terrain before they emerged into another area.

'Are you seeing this?' Manaus said in awe.

Large, stone steps descended into darkness and Goodwin switched on his diving helmet's visual enhancer and gasped. They were in an enormous chamber. A grand hall, higher and longer than anything he could have dreamt of. It was so high that the ceiling appeared only as a darker black. Either side of this mammoth creation stood colossal statues, but unlike human works from the age of the Greeks, these titans were dynamic, built to inspire and shock. They'd been crafted to make those that dared pass them by feel like the tiny insects they were.

'Fan out,' Priest said to his men, 'and keep alert.'

Goodwin walked forward as the armed soldiers spread out around them, guns at the ready. He turned off his visor to look at the sculptures under torchlight. The dark surfaces sparkled like obsidian beneath a slick coating of water.

'What is this place?' Rebecca said, gazing up at the incredible sight.

Goodwin didn't know, but spectacular wasn't the word. The faces of the bipedal figures were without doubt Anakim, their facial features not quite human. Some of the statues stooped so low that their heads almost touched the floor. They passed by one such figure, and while it still remained ten feet from the ground, its snarling features and fearful pose made Joseph bury his face in Rebecca's shoulder. Goodwin knew how he felt as he noted the cluster of crystals inset into each monstrous eye.

A stiff breeze blew through the chamber and a strange noise made everyone freeze.

'What the hell is that?' one of the soldiers said, as the sound continued.

Goodwin held his breath as the note rose and fell, its peculiar whine drifting to silence. Everyone stood where they were before a deeper howl could be heard coming from higher up.

'It's just the wind.' Manaus pointed at the statues. 'It's funnelling through their mouths.'

Four or five of the whistling notes joined together to produce a frightening soundtrack to the already creepy atmosphere.

'Keep moving,' Priest said.

He didn't need to say it twice as everyone hurried to put the dreadful noise behind them.

The further down the hall they went, the more lurid the statues became, and the more gruesome. Protruding bones ruptured the decaying flesh of naked figures positioned in sickening poses of prostration and obscene debauchery. The horrific spectacle would have made even the strongest of stomachs turn and Goodwin averted his gaze from the corruption.

As they neared the end of the massive gallery, an enormous statue of an Anakim woman had been positioned in the centre of the walkway. With a face full of pain and terror, she clung onto the floor tiles on which they trod and fought against clawed hands that dragged her down into the deep.

Splitting into two groups, they circumvented this tormented figure, one on either side, some looking at it and others not. With the chilling sounds propelling them forward, they passed beneath the legs of the final figure. This multi-headed monstrosity grasped the plinth on which it sat, four clawed hands biting into the rock with tarnished talons. On its back two giant wings stretched out on either side, their ends disappearing into darkness.

They moved on through a great arch which gradually narrowed, bunching them together into a tight tunnel twelve feet across. The ancient route, paved with cracked, worn stone, rose and fell, twisted and turned this way and that, creating a sense of disorientation and claustrophobia. An icy chill permeated the air and no one spoke, their footfalls sounding muffled as if they were surrounded by thick snow.

Sinister, carved reliefs lined the tunnel's curved walls while a black substance oozed over them, falling into deep channels at their base. Goodwin thought it similar to the material he'd endured back in the lake, the nauseating smell that accompanied it almost too much to bear.

'What is this place, Director?' Walker said, his tone hushed.

Goodwin didn't know, but whatever it was it wouldn't deter him from his goal.

Walker shone his light over some of the hideous images and shuddered. 'This place is like a nightmare.'

Rebecca touched Goodwin's arm. 'He's right, Richard. Everything here – it feels ...'

He looked at the fear in her eyes. 'Feels what?'

'Evil,' Lieutenant Manaus said.

Rebecca held Joseph closer. 'We shouldn't be here.'

'You can all go back if you want; I've come too far to turn back now.' He squeezed Rebecca's arm. 'I'm sorry; I have to see this through.'

'Then let's be quick about it, Director,' Walker said, speeding up, 'none of us want to stay down here any longer than we have to.'

A murmur of agreement rippled through the rest of the decontamination team as they moved into another area. Wisps of mist swirled around their feet, rising higher and growing thicker with each step.

Still in the lead, Lieutenant Manaus held up her hand in a fist and everyone came to a halt.

'What is it?' Goodwin said, moving to her side.

The Darklight officer scanned the area with her visor. 'I'm not sure. My helmet should be able to process this type of atmosphere, but all spectrums come back blank. It's like a wall. I've never experienced anything like it.'

'How do we proceed?'

'In formation,' Priest said from behind. 'Lieutenant, take point.

Everyone else,' he said, raising his voice, 'form up, two abreast, close quarter advance.'

The soldiers fell into position as ordered, weapons shouldered and trigger fingers poised.

Unarmed, Manaus moved forward and Goodwin followed, with Rebecca and Joseph in close attendance, and Walker and Priest just behind.

If anything the mist grew thicker and Goodwin could hardly see Manaus, who was only a foot away.

Priest shouted out another order. 'Touch advance!'

Each of the soldiers placed a hand on the shoulder of their comrade in front. Rebecca held onto Joseph and placed one hand on Goodwin, while he latched onto the lieutenant.

As they inched their way forward the way ahead finally cleared, the dense vapour dispersing as a swirling breeze penetrated its borders.

Huge rectangular megaliths appeared out of the retreating mist to tower over them, their grey stone glistening with ice. The party passed between two vertical pillars and beneath the giant slab that had been placed on top.

'These look far older than anything else in the city,' Manaus said.

'They look familiar, too,' Goodwin said, observing the weathered runes that had been carved deep into the stone surfaces.

The giant edifices had collapsed in places, but Goodwin could see they formed part of a circle.

'It's like Stonehenge,' Rebecca said, 'the monument in England.'

She's right, Goodwin thought, *that's exactly what they're like, just bigger*. He peered ahead, but the way remained shrouded in darkness as the mist reared up once more.

'If this forms a circle,' Rebecca said, 'it's massive.'

Goodwin gauged the arc created by the standing stones that were visible in the torchlight. He had to agree, it could be a mile in diameter, maybe more.

'Be careful,' Manaus said, 'there's more of that black sludge on the ground.'

Goodwin shone his light down to find he stood in a pool of the stuff.

'It's everywhere,' Walker said.

Goodwin moved on. 'Don't let it touch your skin; if it's the same stuff as in the lake it could be dangerous.'

They continued with care, but avoiding the carpet of thick, black oil was nigh on impossible. Also, the further they went, the deeper the pools became.

A shout came from behind and Goodwin spun round. One of the soldiers had fallen in up to his waist.

The man struggled against the tar-like substance, unable to move. Two other soldiers went to pull him free before he let out an inhuman scream and fell back into the oil. Clawing at his throat, he thrashed wildly as he tore through skin to sink gory fingers into his carotid artery.

Blood flowed and flesh fell before a gunshot rang out and a bloody hole appeared in the soldier's forehead. With a sigh, he slid beneath the dark surface.

Everyone turned to see a wisp of smoke spiralling up from the barrel of Priest's automatic weapon.

'I'd want anyone to do the same for me,' he said.

Silence fell as the shock of what had just happened sank in.

'These pools must contain a hallucinogenic agent,' Goodwin said, in detached horror, 'like the lake, but concentrated.'

'Whatever it is, there's too many of us to get through it without further incident,' Manaus said. 'It's too dangerous.'

Goodwin felt a surge of irritation at the delay. 'What do you suggest?'

'We split up; the majority stays here while a few of us go on.'

'You six,' Priest gestured to some soldiers, 'with me, everyone else, except the Lieutenant and the Director, stay here and wait our return.'

'No!' Rebecca said, hugging a trembling Joseph to her. 'Where Richard goes, we go.'

'And if you think you're leaving me here,' Walker said, 'think again.'

Priest swore, seized Walker and put a gun to his head. 'Very well, but if anyone tries anything they'll wish they hadn't. Understand?'

'You're still in charge,' Manaus said, staying calm, 'we know that.'

Priest released Walker. 'Good, and don't you forget it.'

Walker scowled and then spat on the floor, his eye and cheek twitching in nervous anger.

With the group split in two Goodwin struck out once more, his party now twelve strong, while the remaining soldiers, looking fearful, retreated back to the standing stones to await their return.

The corporal moved closer to Goodwin as they travelled in single file. 'We can take them,' Walker whispered, 'if we get the chance.'

Goodwin glanced back at Priest and his cronies. 'I'm no fighter, Corporal,' Goodwin said, 'and I won't risk Rebecca and Joseph on a roll of the dice.'

'Then it's just as well I don't care what happens to them,' Walker said. 'If I see a chance I'm taking it, I recommend you do the same.'

Goodwin didn't reply. Instead he turned his helmet's visual enhancer back on and moments later he glimpsed something through the mist, which had returned with a vengeance. 'Lieutenant, I see something up ahead.'

Manaus waited for him to catch up. 'Where?'

He pointed up at a forty-five degree angle. The mist parted and a distant structure appeared out of the gloom.

'It's high up,' she said, pressing a button on her helmet, 'perhaps we're nearing your way out at last.'

Goodwin wasn't sure height had anything to do with what he looked for. He wanted to get to the surface, of course, but he knew they must still be beneath the lake and if that was the case the route out would likely be more complex than a simple staircase leading up.

They pressed on before Goodwin, who'd been looking at the ground to ensure he followed in the lieutenant's footsteps, bumped into the Darklight officer's back.

'I think whatever you're looking for,' Manaus said, 'might be in there.'

Goodwin looked up to see an enormous edifice barring their way.

Walker arrived behind them. 'Is that what I think it is?'

'Looks that way,' Goodwin said, not quite believing what he was seeing.

The largest monument he had ever seen – and that included anything in Sanctuary itself – emerged through the swirling mists like a fabled leviathan from the deep. But what was most astounding was the form the ancient sculptors had chosen for this mightiest of works. As with everything else in the Anakim world, when compared to the human equivalent it was immense, dwarfing its counterpart twenty times over. But what Goodwin couldn't understand – couldn't even begin to get his mind round – was how it resembled what it did. His eyes drank in the scene: the giant claws, furled wings, the muscular hindquarters, the long, elegant back and rearing chest. Of course, the face was different, the entire head for that matter, along with the sweeping headdress that hung down to drape over its outstretched forelegs. But one thing was certain; it bore an uncanny resemblance to one of the most well-known sights on the surface, perhaps the greatest architectural mystery of them all, the Great Sphinx of Giza.

CHAPTER SIXTY-EIGHT

'I DON'T UNDERSTAND IT.' Corporal Walker craned his head back as they approached a set of stone steps that led up into the sphinx's mist-wreathed chest. 'How can this be here? Did the Anakim build the one in Egypt, too?'

'More likely humans visited this place and recreated it on the surface,' Goodwin said, 'who knows.'

'The Anakim could have created the one in Giza,' Rebecca said. 'There are theories the sphinx is far older than the pyramids themselves. Some say its erosion indicates weathering that only heavy rainfall could explain, and that amount of rainfall could only have occurred thousands of years before the pyramids were built. Although, saying that, I think that idea is disputed by the wider scientific community.'

'Even the wildest theories can sometimes prove true.' Goodwin looked up at the symmetry of the Anakim face high above. 'How do you know all this?'

'I told you before, the Discovery Channel.'

'So the Egyptian sphinx could be thousands, or even tens of thousands, of years older than they think it is?'

'It could be,' Rebecca said, 'no one knows for sure as you can't carbon date stone. One thing they do know is that a pharaoh found the sphinx hidden in the sand in fourteen hundred B.C., and it was really old then. Sphinxes aren't exclusive to Egypt, though, they've been found elsewhere throughout history.'

'She's got smarts,' Walker said, 'eh, Director?'

Goodwin glared at him. He knew full well what Walker was doing, attempting to ingratiate himself now that he'd become an outcast from his unit. The man was anything but subtle.

Trying to resist the urge to punch Walker in the face, Goodwin helped Rebecca up onto the first step of the staircase. Built by – and for – much larger people, each stair's height was too great for them to walk up with ease and by the time they reached the top Goodwin was breathing heavily.

With torches blazing bright, Lieutenant Manaus led them into the body of the Anakim Sphinx.

More towering statues lined the interior, much like the ones in the hall they'd seen before, although if anything these were bigger.

Less frightening than their counterparts, these works of sublime art were no less dynamic. The ancient artisans had embodied Anakim warriors battling with the beasts of land and air in striking poses, the same animals that must have roamed the wilds alongside Homo giganthropsis at the dawn of their civilisation. Goodwin recognised giant sloths, woolly rhinos, mammoths and sabre-tooth tigers amongst many other weird and wonderful fauna. There were even statues of reptiles that looked curiously like feathered dinosaurs.

Much like everywhere else in the dank, dark underworld they now explored, every surface lit up by their torches glistened with the residue of water.

'Do you think the water is coming in from the lake?' Rebecca said, her voice quavering.

Manaus shone her torch in Rebecca's direction. 'This place could be eons old; it stands to reason it would leak a little.'

Rebecca murmured an agreement while tightening her grip on Joseph, who kept his head bowed.

The party moved on into a network of soaring columns, their

light beams sweeping the surrounding area as each person's torch found its own direction. Revealed in the shadows, Goodwin glimpsed huge tombs and abstract forms.

After a while the way ahead opened out into a great plaza, but rather than relieve the oppressive silence it accentuated it, their intruding footfalls consumed by distant recesses. Either side of this high vaulted expanse stood a single row of Anakim warriors. Male and female alike, side by side they remained at eternal attention, dressed in strange garb and armed with fanciful weapons.

Made of stone, their expressions had long since eroded away, which Goodwin thought was strange. *They're inside a building*, he reasoned, *they should be free from such weathering*.

Walker moved past the lieutenant to take the lead. 'Look here!' he said, his voice echoing back through the great hall.

Goodwin removed his helmet, which had grown heavy, and detached the light bar from the top to use as a handheld torch. He followed the corporal forward, as did everyone else.

A host of ornate thrones, set in pairs, sparkled under illumination and stretched across in front of them between the two sets of statues. The seats were big, but not as massive as everything else they'd seen.

'These aren't decoration,' Goodwin said, walking around one the thrones, 'they were used by whoever ruled.'

Manaus shone her torch at the cracked surface. 'They look transparent.'

'Some kind of crystal,' Walker said, digging at one with his knife, 'very hard crystal.'

Goodwin felt a tingling itch come from his wrist. He put down his helmet and gave the rash a satisfying scratch before resuming his search.

Behind the thrones, a ten foot high wall of un-worked rock had been left to form a natural barrier to a level above, and in the centre of the wall the ancient sediment rose up into a distant peak. Near to this miniature mountain Goodwin thought he could see the glint of gold. Passing his helmet to Rebecca, he called the lieutenant to him. 'Give me a boost, will you?'

Manaus nodded and held out her hands.

Goodwin jumped up and grabbed onto the upper level and hauled himself up, while Priest and his men milled about below.

'What do you see, Director?' Walker said.

Goodwin turned his torch onto a dark mass that sparkled with the sheen of metal ore. *It looks like a meteorite*, he thought, tapping it with his torch to produce a dull ring. Either side of this strange formation, two gigantic statues loomed in the dark, their shape identical to the sphinx's exterior. Beyond these silent guardians the interior of the complex continued on, and he could tell this section was far older than what had come before as cracked and crumbling stone walls ran off into the black, their surfaces adorned with carvings, many barely recognisable in their decay.

Goodwin walked round the tall outcrop of rock and shone his light on something that took his breath away.

Precious metals glittered in the dark as the light reflected from an immense creation that soared above him. A lustrous gold surface shone rich with diamonds of every description and size. It was another throne that merged into the metallic rock behind it, but unlike the grand seats of power below, this mighty singularity was enormous, easily six times bigger and reserved for someone of great import. And that person sat before him now, towering over him like a legendary Greek titan. Wrought entirely from silver, the figure of a beautiful Anakim woman posed in regal majesty, ruling over her subjects, who would have congregated before her. The effect was so lifelike anyone would have been forgiven for thinking the statue could have got up and walked away, or that it was flesh and blood made metal. Whatever the case, the effect was awe-inspiring.

He moved back and leant out over the edge. 'There's more to see up here.'

'We've found an easier way up,' Manaus said, pointing to her left, 'a slope.'

Goodwin nodded and a minute later everyone had joined him, with many unable to take their eyes off the silver woman and her gold and gemstone surround.

Walker, ever the opportunist, tried prising out some of the jewels. 'They're stuck fast,' he said, muttering to himself.

'How has she not tarnished?' Rebecca said, staying close to Goodwin.

He didn't know. 'Nano technology, maybe? The Anakim were really advanced, or so Walker tells us.'

'You only have to see their city to know they were advanced,' Walker said, giving up on his quest for riches. 'And it's not just me, is it? You forget,' he gestured at Priest and the other six soldiers, 'we're all from USSB Sanctuary. Ask any of them, they'll tell you the same.'

Goodwin didn't care what any of them had to say, he just wanted to find a way out. The group moved on, but Goodwin paused as Rebecca remained where she was, holding Joseph's hand and looking down from where they'd come and then back up to the silver statue.

He went back to her side. 'What is it?'

'How many thrones are down there?'

'I'm not sure, twenty, thirty maybe.'

'I need to know exactly.'

Priest turned back and rested his rifle on his shoulder. 'What's the hold up?'

'Why *exactly*?' Goodwin said to Rebecca.

'Just humour me.'

Manaus, overhearing the request, returned to use her helmet's visor to scan the level below.

'There's twenty-four, isn't there,' Rebecca said.

Manaus raised her visor, her expression annoyed. 'If you knew why did you ask?'

'I didn't know, I guessed.'

'What's going on, Rebecca?' Goodwin said. 'What's this about?'

'Do you still have that Bible?'

'My Bible,' Priest said, moving forward to hold out the battered copy.

Rebecca accepted the book without a word, and not for the first time Goodwin thought it strange such a man was religious. *Perhaps he has a lot to repent*, he thought, *or he thinks he can have his sins absolved with a quick prayer.* Whatever his motivations, they didn't seem to stop him from killing.

Walker grumbled at the delay while Goodwin illuminated the pages with his torch.

Rebecca stopped flicking through it and cleared her throat. 'Revelation 11:9. Then God's temple in heaven was opened, and the ark of his covenant was seen within his temple. There were flashes of lightning, rumblings, peals of thunder, an earthquake, and heavy hail.' She glanced at Goodwin and then pointed at the silver statue before continuing. 'Revelation 12:1. And a great sign appeared in heaven: a woman clothed with the sun, with the moon under her feet, and on her head a crown of twelve stars.'

Lieutenant Manaus turned her torches on the statue's head. A silver crown glinted in the light, a crown with twelve points and on top of each of these points was a five pointed star. At the base on the throne, worked into the gold, was the depiction of a crescent moon.

Goodwin peered at the figure's simple attire. 'I don't see any sun on her clothing.'

'They're stars,' Rebecca said, and our sun is—'

'A star.' Goosebumps prickled the skin on Goodwin's arms.

'That's not all.' Rebecca turned back a couple of pages. 'Revelation, Chapter 4. After this I looked, and behold, a door standing open in heaven! And the first voice, which I had heard speaking to me like a trumpet, said, "Come up here, and I will show you what must take place after this." At once I was in the Spirit, and behold, a throne stood in heaven, with one seated on the throne. And he who sat there had the appearance of jasper and carnelian, and around the throne was a rainbow that had the appearance of an emerald. Around the throne were twenty-four thrones, and seated on the thrones were twenty-four elders, clothed in white garments, with golden crowns on their heads. From the throne came flashes of lightning, and rumblings and peals of thunder, and before the throne were burning seven torches of fire, which are the seven spirits of God, and before the throne there was as it were a sea of glass, like crystal.'

Rebecca looked up to see if she still had his attention. 'And around the throne,' she continued, 'on each side of the throne, are four living creatures, full of eyes in front and behind: the first living creature like a lion, the second living creature like an ox, the third living creature with the face of a man, and the fourth living creature like an eagle in flight. And the four creatures, each of them with six wings, are full of eyes all around and within, and day and night they never cease to say, "Holy, holy, holy, is the Lord God Almighty, who was and is and is to come!" And whenever the living creatures give glory and honour and thanks to him who is seated on the throne, who lives forever and ever, the twenty-four elders fall down before him who is seated on the throne and worship him who lives forever and ever. They cast their crowns before the throne, saying, "Worthy are you, our Lord and God, to receive glory and honour and power, for you created all things, and by your will they existed and were created."

Rebecca closed the Bible and returned it to Priest.

'Twenty-four thrones,' Goodwin murmured, looking at the scene in a whole new light.

Walker gave a snort of disdain. 'It didn't say anything about a woman being on the throne.'

'But it did say twenty-four thrones,' Rebecca said, 'and they could also be the crystal mentioned, the sea of glass. They're made of some kind of crystal, aren't they?'

Priest focused the beam on his torch and angled it up to the side of the sphinx's interior wall. 'And around the throne,' he said, 'on each side of the throne, are four living creatures, full of eyes in front and behind: the first living creature like a lion.'

Goodwin looked up to see a massive sculpture of a sabre-toothed tiger fighting three winged Anakim warriors.

'The second living creature like an ox,' Priest continued, switching his torch to another statue of a wild horse, 'the third living creature with the face of a man,' he turned his light to the other side and a winged griffin with the face of an Anakim warrior, 'and the fourth living creature like an eagle in flight. And the four creatures, each of them with six wings, are full of eyes all around and within.' Priest switched his torch to another statue, that of a magnificent griffin in flight.

'What does it mean?' Rebecca said, watching Joseph reach out and touch the silver figure with a gentle caress.

Goodwin looked up into the statue's serene face. 'I think it's a message, passed down through the ages of man.'

Rebecca looked around them. 'You think this is the land of the gods?'

'Not just any gods,' Goodwin said, '*our* gods.'

Walker laughed. 'The Anakim are not God.'

'But they might be the foundation on which our religions are based, at least in part.' Goodwin looked around and felt a shiver of awe, a stirring of antiquity, a feeling of how old this place really was, and who may have trod its great halls. Frustrated there was no one to answer his myriad of questions, his thoughts strayed to his friend, Professor Steiner. *If only I could speak to him now, he would have something enlightening to say, or at least know someone who would.*

'We need to keep moving, Director,' Lieutenant Manaus said.

Goodwin nodded and tore his eyes away from the majestic statue to pursue their exploration deeper into the Anakim Sphinx – or, as some might come to call it, the Temple of the Gods.

CHAPTER SIXTY-NINE

'WHAT DID the book say about a crystal sea?' Manaus said, stopping her advance.

Goodwin drew alongside the Darklight officer. 'Before the throne there was as it were a sea of glass, like crystal.'

The lieutenant crouched down and rapped the floor with her knuckles. It sounded hollow. 'This might not be *right* before the throne, but if this isn't a sea of glass, I don't know what is.'

Goodwin hunkered down next to her and wiped away a thin film that covered the floor's surface. 'It's frost.'

'There must be some sort of thermal exchange occurring,' Manaus said.

Goodwin wiped more away to reveal a crystalline floor and what looked like water flowing beneath. 'Water cooling?'

'Looks that way.'

'But to cool what?'

She shrugged her shoulders.

Standing up, they followed the *sea of glass* left to where it dipped down before curving up to form a high wall interspersed with concave alcoves, which were also frosted over.

Goodwin reached out to touch inside one the misty chambers, but the lieutenant grasped his hand. Goodwin looked at her.

'I don't think that would be wise, sir.'

Goodwin nodded. After what had happened to the soldier in the tar – or whatever that black slime was – caution was advised.

Further ahead, the icy wall of crystal ended and the ground sloped up to another level.

Manaus hesitated before the darkness beyond.

'Lead the way, Lieutenant,' Priest said.

'She's unarmed,' Goodwin said. 'Send two of your men up first, or better yet, go yourself.'

Priest waved Manaus forward. 'Better her than us, Director.'

Goodwin handed the lieutenant his knife.

She gave him a brief nod of thanks before lowering her visor and sealing the lower part of her helmet to fully secure herself inside her armour. Without a backward glance she crept up the slope, alert and ready for anything she might encounter. *Unless that thing is the entity*, Goodwin thought, *then it won't matter if she holds a knife or an assault rifle, we'll all be as good as dead.*

The next area of the sphinx consisted of slick obsidian blocks. Built to last, the black material covered all surfaces, from wall to floor to ceiling, and their torchlight sent reflections bouncing around in all directions. The effect was almost strobe-like and it forced Goodwin to shield his eyes from the visual onslaught.

With the immediate area deemed safe, everyone fanned out to explore.

A minute later Joseph let out a startled cry and Rebecca grabbed Goodwin's arm. 'What's that?!'

'What's what?' Heart pounding, Goodwin pointed his torch in the direction she looked.

'There's someone there!' she said, terrified.

Goodwin searched the area before the shock of her truth made him stumble backwards. A tall figure moved in the dark!

Manaus rushed to their side. 'Sir, what is it?!'

Hand shaking, he aimed his light back in the direction where he'd seen the being.

Rebecca let out another scream when the form emerged from the pitch-black.

'What's happening?!' Priest said from behind.

'It's okay,' Manaus said, 'it's just a statue, three statues, to be precise. Our lights gave them motion.'

Goodwin felt his fear subside, although Rebecca and Joseph still clung to him for dear life.

They edged closer to see the eerie figures were of Anakim women. Such was the detail and fluidity of style they appeared to be real, their final movements frozen in time for all eternity. Their naked forms shone like polished pewter and the floor around their feet looked like static waves from a petrified sea.

'They look so lifelike,' Goodwin said, 'like they were turned to metal while still alive.'

'Perhaps they were.' Walker moved amongst the statues. 'They're tall enough to be real. What would you say, eight feet, nine feet tall?' Walker stood back and whistled in appreciation. 'Now that's a woman.'

Goodwin looked up into the face of one of the statues. He couldn't see any pain in her expression, just serenity.

'Director,' Manaus said, 'over here.'

Goodwin joined the lieutenant beyond the final statue where the pewter sea melded into a huge frieze that covered the entire back wall of the sphinx.

'Are you recording all this?' Goodwin asked her.

Manaus nodded and tapped her helmet. 'It's all stored in here, sir.'

'End of the road,' Priest said, returning with his men. 'There are no more levels; we'll have to go back.'

'Not so fast.' Goodwin shone his torch over the high relief sculpture and then down to the floor, where a four foot high pentagonal altar had been positioned. A circular indent had been inset into the front of its metallic surface. Goodwin touched the circle with his hand and then noticed a familiar symbol in its centre, the constellation of Libra. What this meant he couldn't fathom, but he knew it meant something.

He looked back up at the frieze where winged Anakim acted out a great battle against a sea of larger creatures. These bestial humanoids resembled the beings he'd seen at the top of the frieze back in the city, the Nephilim, God's fallen angels. *They're in the right place,* Goodwin thought, *if what we've seen so far is anything to go by.*

Rebecca pointed to a section higher up. 'Are they meteorites?'

'Either that or comets,' Goodwin said. A memory of his vision beneath the lake reasserted itself. *Have I been shown the past,* he wondered, *or the future? What was the lake trying to tell me, if anything?* He noticed the skies above the meteorites were littered with constellations. Frustrated by the lack of answers, he was about to turn away before spying something else. A channel had been cast into the altar; it ran around the rim and then flowed down to the floor, where it met a silver band. This shiny metal cut a line through the pewter floor. On the way in he'd thought the flat surface was a path through the seascape, but it was more than that. Following it round, he moved past one of the lifelike statues and continued on.

'What is it?' Rebecca said, holding Joseph close.

'Another pentagram.' Goodwin traced the silver inlay with his torch.

She peered at the symbol beneath their feet. 'It's like the one in the city.'

Goodwin nodded.

'You know what that means, don't you?' Priest said, shining his own light at the pentagram.

'Christ the saviour.' Goodwin looked to Rebecca for confirmation. 'Although nowadays the church considers it to be pagan or satanic.'

'You're looking at it the wrong way up,' Priest said. 'If the central point is facing down, it's not *thought* to be pagan or satanic, it *is* satanic. The sign of the Devil, worshipped in secret, behind closed doors.'

'You seem to know a lot about it,' Goodwin said.

'I know what I know.' Priest walked away without further comment and his men followed behind.

'The Devil,' Walker said, patting Goodwin on the back as he passed by, 'great, well done, Director, that's just what we need.'

Rebecca put a consolatory hand on his shoulder.

'What am I missing?' Goodwin said.

Walker laughed as he walked away from them and held his arms aloft. 'This place is a tomb!' His voice echoed out through the halls, the words *tomb ... tomb ... tomb*, ebbing away to nothing.

The Darklight lieutenant stalked towards him. 'Shhh! Are you crazy? You know what could be out there.'

'I don't care,' Walker said. 'Do you hear me?' he shouted, 'I DON'T CARE!'

His voice boomed out again, echoing into the immense structure.

'He wants something to happen,' Goodwin said, jogging after Manaus and ushering Rebecca and Joseph along in front of him. 'He wants to create a diversion so he can escape. Where will you go, Corporal, back to Offiah to plead your innocence?'

Walker turned to face him. 'I can try. It's preferable to chasing shadows. There's nothing here. You were wrong, there's no way to the surface, just old tombs and creepy statues. You might as well ask the sphinx how to get to the surface, the good it will do you.'

Walker turned round to see Priest standing before him. 'What do you want?'

Priest sent a right hook slamming into Walker's jaw, felling him to the floor.

'If you don't keep your big mouth shut,' Priest said, 'we'll tie you up and leave you down here. Understand?'

Walker cleared his dazed mind with a shake of the head and looked up with murderous intent.

Priest cocked his rifle. 'Keep looking at me like that and you'll wish I had tied you up.'

Walker looked away and Priest continued to glare at him, before turning back to rejoin his fellows.

Goodwin, Rebecca and Joseph followed Manaus past the forlorn form of the corporal, who remained sitting on the floor in a pool of his own torchlight.

Returning the way they'd come, Goodwin slowed as they crossed the frost-laden crystal.

'Richard.' Rebecca put a hand on his arm. 'Is something wrong?'

'You might as well ask the sphinx,' he murmured.

'What?'

'Walker said, you might as well ask the sphinx.'

'So?'

'There was no riddle of the lake. The riddle is here.'

'I don't understand.'

'The riddle of the sphinx.'

Rebecca looked confused.

'The riddle of the sphinx,' Goodwin said again. 'What goes on four feet in the morning, two feet at noon, and three feet in the evening?'

'Man,' Manaus said.

'Yes, but what most people don't know is there's a second riddle. There are two sisters: one gives birth to the other and she, in turn, gives birth to the first. Who are the two sisters?'

Walker wandered past massaging his jaw, disinterested, and Goodwin watched him go.

'Richard, what's the answer?' Rebecca said.

'Huh?'

'I said, what's the answer?'

He looked back at her. 'Night and day'

'And that's relevant, how?' Manaus said.

'Night and day,' he said, wondering how they couldn't see it.

He trotted forward towards the silver God and her golden throne. Once they'd caught him up, Goodwin stood before the giant figure. 'Night and day,' he said again, 'what two things make them what they are?'

Manaus gave him an odd look. 'The sun?'

'And the moon!' Rebecca said in realisation.

'Exactly!'

'I don't understand.' The lieutenant looked from Goodwin to Rebecca and back to Goodwin again.

Goodwin pointed at the stars on the silver statue's clothing. 'The sun,' he said, and then pointed down below her feet at the throne and the image they'd seen before, 'and the moon.'

'Revelation 12:1,' Rebecca said in excitement. 'And a great sign appeared in heaven: a woman clothed with the sun, with the moon under her feet, and on her head a crown of twelve stars.'

Goodwin bent down and ran his fingers over the image of the moon. Glancing up at those gathered nearby, he looked back at the throne, positioned both hands over the crescent moon, and pushed.

Nothing happened.

'Wow,' Walker said, 'impressive.'

Goodwin bit back an angry retort. After trying a variety of different techniques to get the image to move he stood up, heavy with disappointment. *I was sure that was going to work*, he thought. *You're grabbing at straws, Richard*, he answered himself, *Walker's right you're chasing shadows, give it up, you're wrong*. He continued to berate himself before something else caught his eye. A series of constellations adorned the throne on either side of the moon, each centred in a circular indent with five small semi-circles cut out of their circumference at equidistant intervals. He hadn't taken much notice of them before. He reached out and touched the representation of Libra and stroked its golden surface. He held up his hand to the five holes. *Could they be finger holes?* On impulse Goodwin spread his fingers wide, but the tips of each digit fell short of the cut-outs by a couple of inches. 'They had bigger hands,' he mumbled.

Priest having rejoined them, moved closer. 'What's he going on about?'

Someone else replied, but Goodwin was too intent on the throne to pay them any heed. Using both hands, he placed his thumbs together and bunched his fingers into pairs and inserted these into the five holes. Having recreated an Anakim appendage, he tried twisting the circle clockwise. It gave a little, and with some effort he managed to twist it round another quarter turn until it matched the position of the image he'd just seen on the altar at the frieze.

A distant noise made everyone look round.

Priest and his men raised their weapons.

'What was that?' Rebecca said in fear.

'It came from back there.' A sullen Walker pointed back to where they'd just been.

'That's what I thought, too,' Goodwin said.

'And Lieutenant Manaus is about to confirm it for us,' Priest said, 'isn't that so, Lieutenant?'

Manaus glowered at him before sealing her helmet and sending the eye-like sculpturing to glowing blue. Everyone followed behind as the Darklight officer led the way back up to the pewter sculptures.

The oppressive darkness closed in around them and Goodwin found himself holding his breath.

'There's nothing,' Manaus called out after she'd swept the area.

Goodwin moved past Priest, who still had his rifle raised as he searched for potential threats with its torch.

They were about to leave when Rebecca pointed at one of the Anakim women. 'The Lieutenant's wrong, there is something; that statue's moved.'

Goodwin looked again at the figure. Where before it had been standing tall, head held high, it now looked down at the ground towards the centre of the pentagram. It was a subtle difference, but a difference nonetheless. On closer inspection nothing else appeared to be out of place, but Goodwin had the distinct impression the woman was trying to tell him something. He looked up at the wall and the giant frieze where the constellations in its skyscape sent understanding coursing through him.

'Lieutenant, are you able to transfer a static image of the frieze to this helmet?' He held up the headgear he'd used for diving in the lake.

'Yes, sir, no problem. Switch it on and I'll send it you.'

Goodwin pulled on the helmet and turned on its computer system. Seconds later he'd received the desired photo. Minimising it, he reattached the light bar onto his helmet and returned to the throne, with everyone trailing behind. Standing in front of the silver God once more, Goodwin superimposed the Anakim frieze onto his helmet's display and compared the constellations to those on the throne. Combining his fingers and thumbs, as he'd done before, Goodwin proceeded to turn each constellation on the throne to match the position depicted on the frieze. After he'd rotated ten of the circles, another sound echoed through the great hall, the noise once again coming from the area that contained the frieze.

'It's a combination lock,' Rebecca said, amazed.

Goodwin didn't stop, but continued to rearrange the constellations until all but one remained. With aching fingers, he dialled in the correct position of the final circle and a flash of light blew through the hall. Pitch-darkness returned before a cool wind whistled past, its invisible hands tugging at clothing and ruffling hair.

With nervous anticipation, Goodwin led them back once more to find all three statues had altered position. Each of the women now knelt on one knee with head bowed. The one directly before the frieze, which faced them, had placed its hands on the shoulders of its two sisters, creating a semi-circle around the silver pentagram's centre.

That the statues had moved so much and yet still retained their smooth surfaces and lifelike form sent shivers down Goodwin's spine. It really was like they were alive, reanimated by an unseen power, their movements hidden in the dark like an elicit meeting in the night. But the statues were not the only things that had altered form; whereas before the pewter seas had washed over and around the pentagram in its entirety, the pentagon in its centre was now a black void of nothing. Goodwin approached the gaping hole, his breathing sounding loud inside his stifling helmet.

Goodwin's eyes grew wide. 'There's stairs,' he said, glancing round before looking back down into the newly revealed passage with renewed hope. *There might be a way out of Sanctuary yet!*

CHAPTER SEVENTY

BACK OUTSIDE THE ANAKIM SPHINX, past the standing stones and beyond the great hall of wailing statues, up the great shaft and across the causeway to the lakeshore, a host of dark forms appeared out of the black. Torchlights bloomed into existence like a host of Will o' the Wisps in the night.

A figure knelt on the water's surface before standing to walk across it like the son of God himself.

'Well?' a man said as he approached.

'Sir, the causeway is secure. It appears to extend into the lake and out to a small island.'

'An island?'

'Yes, sir.'

'So, Goodwin may have been right after all?'

'It looks that way.'

The man sucked on his teeth for a moment, considering his options, and then turned to a woman at his side. 'Get me command.'

'Patching you through, sir.'

A few seconds later she passed him a radio handset.

'Command,' a voice said,

'This is Captain Winter; put me through to the major.'

A pause followed before Offiah spoke, 'Captain, what news?'

'Sir, we've found something. There's a land bridge out to an island in the centre of the lake.'

Silence ensued as Offiah digested what he'd just been told. 'And Goodwin?'

'No sign of him or the decontamination team.'

'The carer and her ward? The Lieutenant?'

'The same, Major. But their tracks tell us they must have crossed onto the island and have yet to return.'

'Then nothing's changed. Hunt them down and flush them out. I want the director back; use all means necessary.'

'What about Manaus and the other two civilians? A full assault, I can't guarantee their safety. The doctor, Vandervoort she won't—'

'Leave her to me. The director is all that matters for the stability of the camp, the rest is collateral damage. If you can keep it to a minimum do so, but the time for caution has passed.'

'Yes, sir.'

'And if Goodwin has found a way out, secure it and await reinforcements.'

'Roger that, sir.

'And Captain.'

'Yes, sir?'

'Consider the director a hostile; if you need to disable him, take the shot.'

The Darklight officer paused as he computed the order. 'Copy that.'

'Keep me updated, Offiah out.'

Winter passed the handset back to the radio operator before turning to face the rest of his Darklight unit. 'Listen up, the mission is still a go. Weapons hot, eyes on. This is virgin territory and we all know what's at stake. Secure the director and nullify U.S. Army personnel; nothing else matters. If it's your life or his, I expect you to take the bullet. If the director resists, shoot to subdue. Do you get me?'

'Sir, yes, sir!' his team said, as one.

Winter nodded in satisfaction and sent his visor down over his eyes before sealing his face inside his helmet with the lower face-plate. Checking his rifle and syncing it to his combat system, he slapped back the bolt and slid a round into the chamber. 'On me!' he said, and ghosted out onto the causeway.

CHAPTER SEVENTY-ONE

THE TICK TICK tick of his antique wristwatch sounded loud to Malcolm Joiner's ears as he watched the second hand complete another minute on its cyclical journey. He'd received a message from the Committee which had told him to expect a video call within the hour. It had been fifty seven minutes and fifteen – sixteen – seventeen – eighteen seconds, and still he waited in his office in USSB Sanctuary. A sense of expectation and dread seeped into his mind, their poisonous talons gnawing at his core and keeping him from his work. He knew this was how the Committee liked to operate, keeping people hanging on their every word, their every command. It was infuriating! Joiner felt a surge of anger quash the fear that tormented him. *What do they want now? Have I not just been successful in taking down two major players, two men that have been a thorn in the Committee's side for decades?*

At first he'd assumed he was to be congratulated for his work, but as time had passed, doubts had risen. He remembered the pendant and the challenge from S.I.L.V.E.R.'s leader, Ophion Nexus, and how he'd been forced to act against the Committee's wishes and install Colonel Samson as the mission commander. *I had to act*, he thought, *I had no choice. I had to preserve my control over the situation. It was the right decision; the only decision ... wasn't it?*

He'd gone against the Committee's orders before, but always to attain a goal, to further their interests beyond their remit. But he'd never confronted them so boldly. He'd never usurped their orders on anything so important. But what choice had they left him? None. They knew the position they'd put him in. Do nothing and he looked weak while his fate was left in the hands of another. Do something and he challenged the Committee's power head on, risking all. But as he knew, it was always better to be strong, to take control, and so that's what he'd done.

A flashing red sign on his computer ended his wait. The incoming message resolved itself onto his 3D wallscreen, covering part of the Brazilian rainforest that hunkered in the shadows of a full moon's light. The graphical window expanded to reveal the tall figure of Selene Dubois.

'Malcolm Joiner, I have heard worrying things.'

'I thought you would be pleased. Professor Steiner is out of the picture, as you desired, and the cyber terrorist has been captured in the Philippines.'

'I was referring to your decision to install a U.S. colonel at the head of our search of Sanctuary Proper,' Selene said, her tone scathing and expression fierce. 'Did you think we would not find out?'

Joiner stood up. 'I did what I thought was best. Colonel Samson is trained in all things subterranean. S.I.L.V.E.R., while more than capable, are not.'

'S.I.L.V.E.R. are trained to operate in all terrains. Your attempt at maintaining control was poorly executed and has put the whole mission in jeopardy.'

'Samson will get results, I have—'

'We are aware of your methods of motivation, Director. Needless to say word has been sent for Ophion Nexus to resume control.'

Joiner went to say something, but Selene held up a hand to silence him. 'The matter is closed. The Committee has spoken.'

Joiner fought down the urge to respond as Selene picked up a piece of paper and perused its contents. 'As to your earlier comments,' she said, 'it seems the information you sent us was premature. Another failure – and upon such precedents difficult decisions are made.'

'Premature?'

'It seems the man arrested, the man you thought to be the international terrorist B.I.C., is nothing of the sort.'

Joiner's mouth ran dry. 'I assure you, we confirmed his identity. The digital fingerprint matched his previous incarnations. His signal was verified and identity revealed. We have finally put a face to the name.' Joiner struggled with his keyboard, his fingers feeling heavy and disjointed. A picture of the terrorist appeared on-screen, a dark-haired, middle-aged man.

'That is not the cyber terrorist,' Selene said, looking at the picture he'd sent to her location.

Joiner shook his head. 'No, that can't be. I spoke to him and he admitted to his crimes on arrest. That is the cyber terrorist, there can be no doubt.'

'And yet there is. When you told us of his capture we instructed our Asian chapter to confirm the authenticity of your claims. It appears the man you have identified is merely an unwilling participant in a mind control programme. The terrorist manipulated and then subverted him and the image he allowed you to see was a digital render of that same man, a human avatar. A puppet controlled by the terrorist from afar. We are no closer to finding him than we have ever been. And if this wasn't enough, it has come to our attention that Professor Steiner may still be alive.'

'Impossible.'

Another image appeared on-screen of a dark grey aircraft parked next to a large array of radio telescopes. 'Do you recognise this drone, Director?'

Joiner sat back down, stunned.

Selene arched a brow. 'I'll take that as a yes.'

'I—' Joiner felt like his world was falling down around his ears.

He'd never made such errors before, and for them to happen now was catastrophic. 'Send me the location and I will make amends.'

'Your time has passed, Malcolm Joiner. We have taken matters into our own hands. Professor Steiner cannot be allowed to align himself with the terrorist, he has had his nine lives, it's time for him to die. As to your performance, consider yourself under evaluation.'

The image of Selene disappeared to be replaced by two words:

Transmission Terminated

Joiner remained stock still, gazing at the second word on-screen, its meaning reflecting the tenuous nature of his position. His chaotic thoughts settled on the man who seemed destined to haunt him forever more. Professor Steiner had evaded him again. *Will you ever stop fighting me*? he thought. He shook himself out of his introspection to see his 3D screen had switched to a real-time view of the surface. He couldn't tell what location was being broadcast, but darkness reigned as lightning lit up the horizon.

Joiner held down his intercom button to speak to his receptionist.

'Yes, sir?'

'Any news from Agent Myers?'

'Not yet, sir. Sorry, sir.'

Joiner paused.

'Is there anything else, sir?'

'Do you ever wonder why things don't work out the way they should?'

'I'm sorry, sir, I don't understand the question.'

'No, why would you?' Joiner released the button in distraction and stared out into the massive thunderstorm that engulfed the dying Amazonian landscape. A flash of lightning lit up his face. 'Why is it,' he murmured as the light died and thunder rumbled, 'some people just don't know when to lie down and die?'

CHAPTER SEVENTY-TWO

A BLACK CLAD U.S. Navy SEAL flipped over the dead body with his foot to reveal the owner's slack-jawed face. Bending down, he rifled through the deceased's pockets. He found a wallet, some money and a packet of cigarettes.

'Anything?' his superior said.

The soldier stood up and threw what he'd found onto the bloody chest of the dead police officer. 'Nothing, sir, just another local.'

The commanding officer pressed a button on his tactical radio. 'All units, spread out and search the area for signs of a vehicle. The building's a bust.' He turned to his subordinate. 'They can't have gone far. Call in air support and get some drones in the air.'

'Do we have authorisation for such a large scale mission, sir? This is sovereign territory.'

'I've been told the Peruvian military are on board. When they found out these people had killed three of their own, they were only too happy to lend a hand.'

'Do we know who they are yet?'

The officer shook his head as he led the way back outside. 'It's a need to know.'

'It's nice to know we're trusted.'

'Get used to it; it's what we do.' He looked round as more helicopters landed and U.S. troops spilled out onto the ground to spread out in all directions. 'Whoever they are they've got the entire Pacific Fleet on their ass. When you mess with the United States you better be prepared for a fight.'

'Or be a fast runner.'

The leader chuckled. 'A real fast runner.'

'I wouldn't like to be in their shoes when they're caught. I heard the CIA want them for interrogation.'

'I heard a lot of things, none of it good. Whatever the case, they won't get far. And if they resist—'

'They're dead.'

The leader scanned the horizon. 'Terrorists – born cowards, all of 'em.'

'They'll get what's coming to them,' the other said, holding up his water canister, 'and God willing we'll be there when it happens.'

The leader took a swig from the offered container and wiped the excess water from his mouth. 'Amen to that,' he said, 'fucking amen to that.'

CHAPTER SEVENTY-THREE

THE FOUR-BY-FOUR POLICE car rocked and rolled as it bounced over the uneven foothills of the Andes mountain range. In the driving seat the young German, Eric, span the wheel left and right as he fought to keep them heading along the dirt track road.

Professor Steiner sat in the passenger seat, while Jessica Klein accompanied Brett in the back.

The FBI agent stared out of the window as the dark terrain drifted by. She couldn't believe what she'd been told. Jessica Klein had said the world's resources were being taken and that everyone would starve in a fight for life, and now she'd learnt six more asteroids were heading for Earth. To try and compute such information was too much for one person to bear.

I don't believe it, Brett said to herself, I refuse to believe it. They must be wrong. They ARE wrong! But what about father? He said I was in danger; this must have been what he meant, he was trying to protect me out of some kind of warped sense of love. And the old man had said hundreds of thousands of people would die and Malcolm Joiner confirmed the destruction of one of these underground bases. NO! she thought, her inner voice screaming its dissent. No, there's no way they could have hidden six more asteroids, astronomers would have seen them – millions of amateurs, the thousands of professionals. No one could hide that kind of information ... could they? The GMRC might be able to, said the traitor within, you know full well the capabilities of government agencies – the NSA, CIA and the FBI's National Security Branch. And these agencies pale into insignificance against the might of the GMRC's Intelligence Division. Plus, she reasoned, it's common knowledge only a handful of telescopes can see into deep space, it would be easy to limit access to them.

Brett squeezed the bridge of her nose. But what about Da Muss Ich, B.I.C., the terrorist renowned for manipulation and misinformation? There is no way he can be trusted and I sense something about him, something not quite right. He's hiding something and whatever it is I need to stay close until I figure it out. The same goes for these fugitives, she thought, assessing the three people with her. They've already made me kill once; they'll pay for making me make that choice. Whatever the truth, I can't allow them free rein. I'll bide my time. I'll watch and wait, and then I'll make my move.

Time reveals all, her mentor used to say, and if what they said was true she wouldn't have long to wait until that time came. She stared at the form of Bic on the touchscreen device resting on the dashboard. *Make your move, hacker,* she thought, *I'm watching you. I'm watching you all!*

◆

Jessica Klein tried to focus on what the professor and Bic were saying, but all she could think about was her family, Evan and the girls. How can I protect them? she wondered, her heart full of woe. How can I save them? Don't worry, she told herself, nothing has changed, the world was dying before you knew about the next wave of asteroids, this has just made the situation more urgent, that's all. Stay calm and concentrate.

Jessica took a breath. 'I'm not helping,' she said. 'I'm not helping to stop the asteroids.'

The conversation in the front ceased. Eric slowed the car to a stop and glanced back, his expression one of concern, while Bic stared out from his screen, unmoved.

'That man, Malcolm Joiner, threatened the lives of my family,' she said. 'We help them first.'

Steiner gave a nod while Eric turned round to place a compassionate hand on her knee. Jessica stiffened at the contact, but relaxed a little at the understanding she saw in the young German's eyes.

'Do not worry, Jessica Klein,' Bic said, 'I've already been working on that issue. I have arranged for their relocation to a secure site. They can wait there for further instructions when we have figured out a way to take them to a permanent shelter from what is to come.'

'How have you managed to secure their relocation when you've been busy here?' Brett said, her tone sceptical.

'While I am loath to keep blowing my own trumpet, Brett Taylor, I am a man of many talents and multi-tasking is one of them.'

The corner of Brett's mouth twitched at the rebuttal, her expression remaining stiff and aloof.

'And that will be a subterranean base, yes?' Jessica said, glad that she'd decided to stick with the cyber terrorist despite his initial duplicitous nature.

'It can only be so, Jessica Klein. Anything else will be tantamount to a death sentence.'

'Unless we're successful.'

'Yes, but even then their lives would be in peril; the world has become a dangerous place.'

'How will we get them inside?' she said. 'Will we use your man in Germany again, Franz Veber?'

'Maybe; although perhaps Professor Steiner can be of assistance in this regard?'

Jessica looked to the bearded face of the ex-Director General as he swivelled round in his seat, his intelligent eyes holding hers from behind the glass of his spectacles.

'I can't promise anything,' Steiner said, adjusting his eyewear, 'but where there's a will there's always a way.'

Jessica let out a gasp of relief. 'Thank you.' She leant forward to bestow a hug and Steiner gave a small yelp of pain as she touched his bruises. Apologising, she withdrew.

'I wouldn't put my faith in any of them,' Brett said, 'if it was my family on the line.'

Jessica ignored her.

'Perhaps you should have more faith, Brett Taylor,' Bic said.

'I do, in myself. You have no way of knowing if you can help her, none of you do.'

'Have you forgotten so soon, Brett Taylor?' Bic said. 'Seek and you shall find. Ask and it shall be given you. Knock and it shall be opened unto you.'

Brett's expression grew darker. 'I'm an atheist; the Bible – like you – is full of lies.'

'And yet those words led you here, did they not? And belief does not matter when the words are true. There are many mysterious things, Brett Taylor; to deny them is to deny yourself.'

Brett muttered something derogatory, but Bic's caveat sparked a vision in Jessica's mind of the three dead bodies that they'd left behind at the telescope array, which they'd vacated hours before. Since that time she'd been trying hard to forget they'd ever existed, but the unwanted memory reminded her of the immediacy of their plight. 'We should keep moving,' she said, her fear returning.

'Jessica Klein, is right,' Bic said, 'time is not on our side.'

Eric restarted the gasoline engine and they moved off once more into the never-ending night.

♦

As they continued their journey through the bumpy Peruvian landscape, Professor Steiner glanced back to see Jessica had fallen asleep while Brett stared out into the night, her face set in dour contemplation.

'Can we talk, Professor Steiner?' Bic said.

Steiner picked up the touchscreen device and stared into the face of the cyber terrorist.

The dark-haired man returned his gaze, unblinking.

'About?' Steiner said.

'Need you ask?'

'You really think we can restart the Space Programme?'

'I would not be talking to you otherwise, Professor Steiner, I would have already disseminated the knowledge I have around the world for others to decide.'

'Even when I tell you all previous missions have failed,' Steiner said, 'and that even if we succeeded in reviving the intercept missions, they may still fall short?'

'And you would risk the life of every living thing on an assumption?' Bic said. 'Not to try would be the sin, would it not?'

Steiner pondered the question. As much as he hated to admit it, the hacker was right. *If there's even the smallest of chances, surely the surface and the lives of the entire animal kingdom are worth the effort? But there are too many obstacles.* He shook his head. 'No, it won't work. With the world's major powers in disarray after the 2042 impacts, the only nations capable of space flight will be Russia and China, and their resources will be depleted, almost non-existent. To produce the ships and space stations needed for the final missions in 2045, we need at least one fully functioning superpower, a country capable of creating new resources from nothing. And that's even if we get that far. Stopping two of the four asteroids next year is our first concern and I still have no idea how we can achieve it. Without the space stations there's no platform from which to operate.'

'But you're forgetting, Professor Steiner, we still have one space station.'

'We don't know what that is, and unless Commander Magnusson gets back to us, we may never know.'

'As I told you previously,' Bic said, 'I have ensured any signal received by the array is forwarded to my location. When I know, you will know, but I have to say, Professor Steiner, I didn't take you for a defeatist.'

'I'm not a defeatist, just a realist. The intercept missions, in my opinion, were never a viable option; only the underground bases will preserve humanity. If just one of the two asteroids we need to stop in 2042 gets through, the world's ecosystems will not recover a second time. Even if we stop all four of the six asteroids, it will take a generation or longer for the Earth to fully regain its plant and animal life. The world's population will die off at alarming rates regardless of what we do. If we fail in 2042 it will be the end of civilisation on the surface, perhaps for hundreds, or even thousands of years. And if the largest asteroid in 2045 impacts, then the surface may never recover, period. With no atmosphere Earth could resemble the surface of Mars in the blink of a cosmic eye.'

'So you think we should do nothing?' Jessica said, woken from her sleep by the discussion. 'Just roll over and let the surface burn?'

'We must do something, Professor,' Eric said, as he continued to drive. 'Can't we just get the resources from one of the bases and ship them to Russia or China?'

'It's not as simple as that,' Steiner said, 'although—'

Jessica leaned forward between the front seats. 'Although what?'

'It's nothing, forget I said anything.'

'But you didn't say anything,' Eric said, aggrieved.

Jessica gave his sleeve a tug. 'What is it, Professor? What can we do?'

Steiner kept his attention on the touchscreen, remembering who he was talking to and what he was disclosing to the world's most wanted terrorist. He hesitated.

'I can see you are still reluctant to trust me, Professor Steiner,' Bic said, 'and with good reason. We have been adversaries for many years; even though we may not have crossed paths directly, the mistrust still remains. But there are some things I can tell you that may ease the tension that persists between us.'

'And why should he believe anything you say, hacker?' Brett said from the back seat, her words voicing Steiner's own fears.

Bic turned his eyes towards the English newsreader. 'Jessica Klein, have you ever wondered why I am able to access GMRC drones so easily?'

'It had crossed my mind, yes.'

'Professor Steiner, do you remember when I infiltrated the GMRC's servers years past?'

'I do, it meant a complete overhaul of our systems and protocols. You'll have to tell me how you did it sometime.'

'Maybe I will. But the point is I never left.'

'What?!' Steiner said, aghast.

'Yes, Professor Steiner, it may disturb you to know I still have access to the GMRC's system. Well, parts of it, anyway. Which is why I can tell you what I am about to tell you now. What you have helped create, Professor Steiner, is a global organisation. A world government. A single institution to control the masses. A Nazi utopia made real.'

Steiner had heard such claims before. 'No, you're wrong. The GMRC will be disbanded when it has served its function.'

'Will it? I think those in power will be thinking otherwise. It is the nature of man to want more, and at the very least to keep what he has. Only the few would give up money and power for the good of the whole, and of those, fewer still make it into a position of power.'

'I would have relinquished my position,' Steiner said, 'without hesitation.'

'And that might well be why you no longer rule. Times are changing, Professor Steiner. Power has shifted. There are those that operate behind the scenes, those groups, factions if you will, that operate outside the laws of the general populace. Their aim? To subvert the majority to their control and rule them as they see fit. Do you know of whom I speak?'

Steiner did. His mind returned to his first meeting with Malcolm Joiner, the then Principal Deputy Director of National Intelligence, back in the year 2017. *What had he said?* Steiner searched the vaults of his memory. That meeting had been indelibly inked upon his soul, as it had changed his life forever. The vision of a younger Joiner appeared before his mind's eye. He had been telling Steiner about how the world's resources would be redirected to the building of the subterranean bases.

'This process,' Joiner had said, 'has inevitably been hindered by the need to ensure that the reason for such large scale unilateral cooperation between nations and private enterprises, initially, is known to only a select few. Fortunately the need for such secrecy has been aided by organisations that have been operating with complete – how should I put it? – un-transparency for generations, operating around the world unseen by the majority of the populace. They have proved very useful in averting suspicions and minimising the potential for mass panic and the breakdown of civilisation.'

'I see a spark of recognition in your eyes, Professor Steiner,' Bic said.

Steiner returned to the present and the rattling bump and roll of the police vehicle as Eric continued to wrestle with the wheel.

'I have tracked the communications between these organisations,' Bic continued, 'which, I'm sad to say, are quite extensive. Where before they operated in secret, they are becoming bolder, more certain in their power. They believe nothing can stop them. They might not be wrong.'

'It's a nice tale,' Steiner said, 'but I'm not a small child to buy into such fanciful stories.'

'Come, Professor Steiner, I hear the denial in your voice. Have you never been approached to enter the service of one of these societies? In all your years they have never come knocking at your door, promising you greater gifts than you already possess? Promises of friendship, a brotherhood, of camaraderie and a chance to further a career, a vision?'

Steiner frowned. He had been courted on many occasions by people he respected and admired, but their secrecy warned him against accepting such offers.

'Your silence speaks volumes,' Bic said. 'These people, much like your Malcolm Joiner, believe they are above the laws of mortal man. In fact, they don't just believe it, they know it. They do what they want, whenever they want, and if they can't do something, they create laws which will enable them to do so. They manipulate, control and plot to further themselves and their brethren. It is all they know.'

'You're talking about the Freemasons, aren't you?' Eric slowed their travel. 'I hear they're Devil worshippers and that members only find out when they get to the higher levels and by then it's too late to go back.'

'The Freemasons are part of the plague of which I speak,' Bic said, 'but they are not the only society. In fact, there are other organisations hidden within the Freemasons themselves. It is whispered some are even set up to subvert Masons to another cause without their knowledge. In nineteenth century America there was even a political party set up called the Anti-Masonic Party; such was the influence of the Freemason elites, many Americans feared they would control and corrupt the nation. We are led to believe that the Freemasons failed, but they did not fail. They won. They control the majority of the world's multinationals, banks and governments. When you hear about these societies in films it is made to appear fanciful, as if the governments are working against them, when in fact they are already controlled by them. Politicians have even come out quoting the famous saying, *new world order*. These leaders don't even bother hiding their affiliations to these secret groups. Many U.S. presidents have belonged to the infamous Skull and Bones, and serving politicians from the majority of the Western powers often frequent the controversial Bilderberg meetings. All secret. All non-democratic. Should any politician be affiliated to such secret groups, beyond the eyes of the rest of humanity? In a totalitarian world, then that answer is yes.

'Whatever you think the GMRC is, or was, Professor Steiner, know that your vision of its future, of its legacy – of your legacy – will not be met. The GMRC is riddled with these secret groups, rotting it from the inside out and from the outside in. Do you want to allow these people to rule without opposition? Do you want to hand over the fate of humanity to them without a fight? Without saying no, not in my name, not while a single breath still rests in my lungs?!'

Steiner felt righteous anger stir at the hacker's words, but still he held back.

'After everything you've seen, Professor Steiner,' Bic said, 'how can you fail to believe what I say is true? The sabotage of the intercept missions and destruction of the space stations. The betrayal by Malcolm Joiner and your enforced expulsion from the GMRC. The destruction of USSB Steadfast. As I have said before, actions speak louder than words, and if these acts do not convince you of my claims then I fear you may never accept the truth, let alone put your trust in me.' The hacker paused for breath. 'I have said my piece, I can say no more. The decision – ultimately – is yours.'

Steiner sighed, lifted his glasses and rubbed his eyes. 'I hear your words, and they scare me. They scare me because I fear they are true. But there is something else you failed to mention: Project Ares. If what Tyler Magnusson said is right, the GMRC, or those operating within it, are experimenting with things beyond their control, things that should never be tampered with.' Steiner pondered his options. He knew that Project Ares could well be based on some kind of Anakim technology; however, he could not reveal that thought to those around him. For one, they would never believe him and for two, the less anyone knew about Sanctuary the better, as it was by far the greatest hope humanity had of living out a long term, even permanent, existence underground.

Eric stopped the car, looking excited. 'So, Professor, what is it we can do? How can we save the world?'

Steiner looked from Eric to Jessica, the newsreader's expression as expectant as that of her young German friend. *What choice do I have?* he mused. *If I do nothing, I allow Joiner, and those with whom he works, free rein. The alternative? I help those that have the potential to put the entire Subterranean Programme in jeopardy. But they can do that anyway,* he reasoned, *with or without me. Better I stay close to them to make sure the underground bases remain secure.* He would have liked to think it was a case of better the devil you know, but considering he knew two devils, Bic and Joiner, the turn of phrase was less than helpful. He made a decision. 'I will help you, on one condition.'

'Name it,' Bic said.

'That when – if – the time comes, you help me remove Malcolm Joiner from power.'

'It will be my pleasure, Professor Steiner,' Bic said, placing one hand on his heart, 'you have my word. As soon as the opportunity arises, Malcolm Joiner will rue the day he crossed you, and with us working together the Space Programme will rise again.'

'I hope you're right,' Steiner said, 'because if we fail, the surface as we know it is lost forever and those that are left underground will be at the mercy of our enemies.'

'Then we shall not fail, Professor Steiner, we shall blaze forth from the ashes like a phoenix in the night. Now,' Bic said, his expression turning serious, 'the moment has come for you to share your knowledge, as one thing is for certain, time waits for no man.'

CHAPTER SEVENTY-FOUR

STEINER TOOK A DEEP BREATH. 'The only way we can revive the Space Programme is with a superpower's resources.'

'You told us that already,' Eric said.

'And not just any superpower,' Steiner continued, unperturbed, 'but one we stand a chance of influencing. Which means we need to stop the first asteroid due in 2042, specifically the one destined to impact the United States. This will also buy us some time and potentially open up a conduit to NASA's Mission Command.' He shook his head. 'Although don't ask me how, this is all hypothetical.'

Jessica looked confused. 'But the Space Programme is the only thing that can stop the asteroids. It's catch twenty-two,' she glanced round at the others, 'isn't it?'

Steiner tapped his nose and smiled. 'You'd think, wouldn't you? But having been with the GMRC from the beginning I have seen and heard all manner of measures proposed to stop these distant threats. Most have been trialled, all have failed. But when I chose to save USSB Steadfast, I had more than one idea up my sleeve. Steadfast is no more,' his expression grew grim, 'but the USA remains and there is a way to extend its lifespan, at least until 2045 when the final two asteroids arrive. Although whether this would be time enough to reinstall the intercept missions to deflect next year's largest asteroids is anyone's guess.' Steiner shifted in his seat to make himself more comfortable. 'Please bear in mind the idea I am about to suggest is fraught with danger and the chance of pulling it off is slim, the chances of it working slimmer still.'

'Just tell us,' Eric said, growing frustrated.

'The theory is that a tactical assault on an asteroid would be able to break it up in low Earth orbit prior to impact.'

'A tactical assault,' Jessica said, 'you're talking about nuclear weapons?'

Steiner nodded. 'Not just nuclear weapons, *all* nuclear weapons. Mathematical models indicated that staged nuclear explosions would be able to create a percussive force that would vibrate and shatter an asteroid to pieces. The warheads would be detonated in such a way to produce shockwave after shockwave, layer after layer of energy; the resulting blasts would literally shake the rock apart. If you can imagine, it would almost be like creating atmospheric density in space, except this density would provide far more resistance than that offered by the Earth's natural shield.'

'It sounds feasible,' Jessica said, 'but why didn't they use this method to stop AG5, or the rest for that matter?'

'It was not considered a viable option for various reasons, a main one being that the world's nuclear arsenal wasn't big enough to cope with more than one asteroid. In fact, many said it wasn't big enough to cope with one. Furthermore, the computer models also indicated the method would not work for six of the seven asteroids, including AG5, which only leaves one, the smallest, AG5–C, the rock due to hit the United States next year. This asteroid is half the size of AG5 itself but, as I've said before, its impact will still be devastating.

'Some scientists also warned the nuclear explosions could affect the space stations and in turn the intercept missions. There was also another problem with the idea, a pretty major one. None of the nations would agree to leaving themselves vulnerable to attack by another power, as for the assault to work the rockets would need to be fired simultaneously. This meant that if one nation held back at the final moment, they would become the only power on the planet with nuclear weapons. And, as has been the case for decades, China and Russia didn't trust the West, and the West didn't trust China or Russia. And no one trusted North Korea.'

'And this is all theory,' Jessica said.

'Yes, but the science is sound.'

Steiner heard Brett give a derisive snort from her seat in the back.

'There's one big problem,' Eric said. 'How the hell are we supposed to get access to all those nuclear weapons?'

Jessica slumped back in her seat. 'We'd have to convince all those nations to help us; it's impossible.'

'It is not impossible, Jessica Klein,' Bic said, 'but you're right in thinking it would not be easy to achieve. Is there no other way, Professor Steiner?'

'No, that's it. If we want to save the surface that's the first thing of many we need to do.'

Silence ensued as everyone computed the information they'd just received.

Steiner had an idea and cleared his throat. 'There might be one way to pull it off.'

'And that is?' Jessica said, when Steiner failed to elaborate.

'You're not going to like it, Brett especially.'

They all looked at the FBI agent.

'I don't give two shits what you're planning. I want no part in it.'

'You're part of this now, Brett Taylor,' Bic said, 'whether you like it or not.'

'So,' Jessica said, turning back to Steiner, 'how are we going to choreograph the world's biggest nuclear attack?'

'If we get to one man we might have a chance.'

'And that man is?'

'The same man that condemned me as a terrorist and a symptom of the GMRC's corruption,' Steiner said. 'A man that said I deserved the death penalty for my crimes, and one of the most protected men on the planet. His name is John Harrison Henry, and he's the next President of the United States.'

CHAPTER SEVENTY-FIVE

JESSICA COULDN'T HELP but laugh, the sound verging on the hysterical. 'This is insanity!'

'I don't think so,' Bic said, 'Professor Steiner may be onto something. The President would have the contacts and the power to launch a nuclear strike, it is not implausible.'

'But why would he listen to us?' Jessica said. 'As far as he's concerned we're a bunch of terrorists led by the world's most wanted and a convicted mass murderer ... no offence, Professor.'

'None taken. But you're right; convincing the man will be difficult. However, if we want this to work we'll need to find a way.'

'Won't the president be in with the GMRC?' Eric said. 'As soon as we get near him he'll rat us out.'

'The man hates the GMRC,' Brett said, stirring from her malaise. 'I saw his speech on TV; he'd do anything to bring them down.'

'Then that's in our favour,' Steiner said, 'as is the fact he is part of the transitional government.'

Eric scratched his head. 'Transitional government?'

'It's the switchover of power,' Steiner said. 'As the old world awaits its fate, the new world and its governments will be starting anew below ground. Those left on the surface will have no knowledge of what is to come, nor of the subterranean bases that shelter those beneath.'

'That's awful,' Jessica said, 'you'll just leave them to fend for themselves, at the time when they need you most?'

'Not me, the GMRC. But yes, to my shame, I agreed it was the only way. In order to protect the underground bases a cut off point had to be made.'

'I thought it was too good to be true,' Brett said.

Jessica glanced at the FBI agent. 'What was?'

'I wondered how an independent managed to get into the White House; now I know.'

'Won't the GMRC be watching him?' Eric asked.

'They will,' Steiner said, 'very closely. He may be a transitional politician, but he will still have power, and both the GMRC and the new – or perhaps that should be *real* – U.S. government that has been installed to manage the U.S. underground bases will continue to manipulate and control him from afar. Unless we are successful, John Henry will be the last president of the United States of America and yet he also represents our best hope of saving the surface. If he invokes his special powers he can seize control of the U.S. military and launch against the asteroid.'

'But that won't be enough, will it?' Jessica said. 'We'll need the other nations to join with us.'

'He never said it would be easy, Jessica Klein,' Bic said.

'That sounds like the tagline of my life.'

Steiner gave her a fatherly smile and put a hand on hers. 'All is not lost, my dear, we may yet find a way.'

Jessica felt her despair lift a little.

The portable touchscreen beeped. 'Eric,' Bic said, 'we need to keep moving, the U.S. military have found the drone, our secret is out.'

Eric swore and got them moving again.

The rattle and squeak of the Peruvian police vehicle returned as they lurched forward over rough terrain. Behind, in the far distance, tiny white lights cleaved through the cold air, the illuminations giving away the position of the UAVs which hunted the ground for signs of their prey.

'I have to leave you for a while,' Bic said. 'I need to manipulate the signals of the drones that are searching for us.' The hacker's image disappeared to be replaced by a map which had a red line marked on it. 'Follow this route; it will lead you to safety.'

'Good luck,' Jessica said, but Bic had already gone.

Some time passed in silence before Steiner said, 'Can he be trusted? He holds the fate of the whole world in his hands.'

Jessica looked at him. 'I would like to say yes, but I don't know, all I know is he's our only hope.'

Steiner nodded and stared out of the window, deep in thought.

Jessica watched him for a moment before sending out a silent prayer to anyone or anything that would listen. *Please keep my family safe and bring them back to me, they're all I have. I'll do anything you ask, just grant me that one wish.* She paused before adding, *and let Bic be the man I pray that he is, for all our sakes, for without him all is lost.* A host of overwhelming emotion sought to break her resolve, but Jessica knew she had to remain strong for those that waited for her return.

It seemed like decades since she'd left her normal life behind. *So much has happened*, she thought as her eyes drifted down to look at her grubby hands. The dirt-encrusted nails were a far cry from the clean, manicured perfection she had once tried so hard to maintain. *I'm not the same woman that left London all those weeks ago, that's for sure.* She gave a rueful smile before a splash of dried blood on her sleeve caught her eye. Jessica frowned and rubbed at the mark. It failed to come off. She licked her finger and rubbed harder, but the stain remained. Harder and faster she scraped at the cloth, her nails digging deep and fingertips burning, but try as she might the discolouration refused to budge.

The four-by-four carried on into the dark, heading towards the mountains beyond, while Jessica's heartfelt plea drifted into the ether of time and space, unheard by those at her side, but perhaps – as some would like to think – acknowledged by a greater power beyond. As the stolen vehicle continued its journey, few could guess at the importance of the passengers within. They were the only people on the planet who could avert the apocalypse to come, and yet amongst them there was one who contemplated treachery. The future of the surface hung in the balance and never had the lives of so many rested on the deeds of so few. The days of reckoning approached like the asteroids in the heavens above, and nothing and no one could stop their advance.

CHAPTER SEVENTY-SIX

THE PRESIDENT-ELECT, John Harrison Henry, stood at the window of his New York apartment and gazed out at the floodlit city skyline. *I've made it*, he thought, *I can't believe I've actually made it. Who said an independent couldn't become president? If my parents could only see me now.* He sighed. *They'd be as condescending and negative as they'd been in life.* A deep sense of loss touched his heart, a yearning for the loving home he'd never had. 'Stop pitying yourself,' he said out loud, 'you've achieved the impossible. You can finally make a difference, a real difference.'

'You know talking to yourself is the first sign of madness, don't you?'

He turned round to see his personal assistant enter the room. She was dressed in only a bathrobe and left a trail of wet footprints on the wooden floor behind her.

He smiled. 'I always thought it represented inner strength.'

The woman walked towards him and into his open arms. Wrapping her in an embrace, he brushed back a lock of her damp hair with a finger.

'So, Mr. President,' she said, 'how are we going to make the world a better place?'

He kissed her neck with soft lips. 'First, I'm going to eject the GMRC from the United States.'

She unbuttoned his shirt. 'And second?'

'Then I'm going to secure our borders.' He tugged loose the knot that held her robe closed.

'And then?' she said, dropping her garment to the floor to reveal her smooth, soft flesh.

'And then I'm going to bring peace and prosperity to the people.' He kissed her shoulder and ran his hands down her back.

She moved her hands lower. 'And then?' she said, biting his lip.

He let out a groan of pleasure. 'And then I'm going to change the world.' Unable to contain himself any longer, he scooped her up and carried her into the adjoining bedroom, the trappings of power and the politics of the day forgotten like the white robe that lay discarded in a crumpled heap on the floor.

◆

A GMRC operative adjusted the camera angle to follow the first couple into their bedroom.

Another man entered the room and placed two cups of steaming coffee on the desk. 'How's she doing?'

'She's with him now.'

'Poor bastard, he has no idea what's to come. He thinks he's going to bring in some kind of revolution.'

The other man gave a sniff as he watched the rise and fall of the entwined lovers. 'He doesn't look that poor to me.'

'She enjoys her work, I give her that.'

'It's a shame she can't come with us, such a waste.'

'She's been well paid to do as instructed. Who are we to question the Directorate?'

The man sipped his drink and his brow furrowed. 'I hate not being allowed outside the building. I think I'm getting cabin fever.'

'That's the price of knowledge, my friend. Would you rather be running around out there when the time comes?'

The man made a face. 'When do we relocate?'

'I got the order yesterday; the tenth protocol is going into effect any day now.'

'Have we found out what it's called yet?'

'USSB New York.'

'Nice, bring on the U.N.Y.'

'Amen to that.'

The two men continued to watch the screen.

'Did you get the donuts?'

Without taking his eyes off the show, the second man held up a paper bag. 'Last batch.'

Ensconced in the GMRC's massive HQ building on Manhattan's Ninth Avenue, the two men munched down on their sugary feast and settled in for the nightshift. Times were changing and excitement was in the air, but there was still much work to be done and the GMRC would continue its duties on schedule as only it knew how. The countdown to zero hour had begun.

MAP

USSB
STEADFAST
NEVADA
UTAH
COLORADO
CALIFORNIA
Las Vegas
USA
Los Angeles
ARIZONA
NEW
MEXICO
TEXAS
MEXICO
USSB
SANCTUARY

CHAPTER SEVENTY-SEVEN

RICHARD GOODWIN STARED into the black, the lights from his diving helmet illuminating shadowy steps that led down into a place so sacrosanct, so gloriously protected, that even the Anakim must have rarely crossed its threshold. When he'd activated the golden throne by aligning the constellations to match the pewter frieze, he couldn't have dreamt of a better result. That the three statues of the Anakim women, who knelt before him now, had moved to their current position was amazing enough. But to reveal this hidden passageway was a true gift from the gods.

The beautiful female sculptures had each settled onto one giant knee, the arms of the central Anakim resting outstretched hands on her two sisters' considerable shoulders. Motionless, heads bowed as if in prayer, the mysterious forms created a semi-circle around the pentagram's central pentagon and the stairwell beneath.

This must be it, Goodwin thought, *the way to the surface is within reach. Everything has led me here. The frieze in the city, the carvings that revealed the lake's secret, the dark abyss beneath the water and then the riddle of the Sphinx. It was almost too good to be true. If it hadn't cost him his freedom, leadership and probably his relationship with Kara, he might have believed it was. But he knew if he could get everyone to the surface it all would have been worth it. I brought everyone here, I put everyone's life in jeopardy, and it is long past time to repay their faith in me.*

'What I don't understand is,' Rebecca said, breaking the silence, 'how can the biblical texts be the key to what's down here?'

Goodwin couldn't tear his gaze away from the entrance before him. 'It just means some of the ancient legends may have more truth to them than we thought.'

'Our myths and tales are the Anakim's reality?'

'Why not?' Goodwin said, turning to face her. 'If they interacted with humans it stands to reason knowledge would have passed from one species to the other.'

'I suppose,' Rebecca said. 'For all we know Neanderthals could have taught humans art, or how to hunt in the colds of the north.'

Goodwin nodded and resumed his study of the Anakim portal. He went to take a step down onto the stairs but Manaus held him back.

'I'll go first, sir.' The Darklight officer moved past without waiting for his reply.

Goodwin felt a rush of anger at her taking the lead, followed by a sense of shame. *The woman isn't trying to steal my limelight; she's trying to protect me from whatever may lurk beneath.* His agitation remained, however, despite this thought. *I found this place; I should be the one to learn its secrets first.* Trying to keep a hold on his impatience, he followed Manaus down into the Anakim passage, while those behind filed in after them.

At the bottom of the oversized stairs, some hundred steps down, the passage levelled out and shallow water lapped at their feet. The surrounding rock changed from smooth, polished stone to a porous substrate full of tiny holes. Goodwin reached out a hand as he splashed through the waterlogged tunnel and touched the pock-marked surface that glistened wet in the light. Despite the fluid running down its walls it felt rough, like sandpaper or stony coral.

Ahead the Darklight lieutenant pressed some buttons on her helmet and then gestured at the passage around them. 'Sir, switch to ultra violet on your helmet, if it has it.'

Goodwin scrolled through the options on his visual display, saw the UV tag and selected it. To his wonder the walls around him glowed bright with strange patterns, pictures and abstract scripts of all shapes and sizes. The further they went the more intricate the images became, dazzling in their majestic beauty. From Anakim warriors to ancient beasts, from scenes of nature to cityscapes beyond compare, the walls hinted at knowledge beyond comprehension.

'What do you see, Richard?' Rebecca said from behind.

'Wonderful things,' he said, 'many wonderful things.'

'I'm still recording ma'am,' Manaus said over her shoulder, 'when we get back to camp remind me and I'll show you.'

Walker's voice echoed down the tunnel, 'If we get back to camp.'

Goodwin grimaced in the dark; he'd momentarily forgotten their current situation. *One thing at a time*, he counselled himself. *Find the way out and everything else will fall into place.*

The water at their feet shallowed and Lieutenant Manaus slowed her advance.

'What is it?' Goodwin said.

She stopped and held up a hand for silence.

'What's the hold up?' Walker said as everyone bunched up.

Manaus turned round and raised her visor. 'There's a light source up ahead.'

A couple of the soldiers swore and Priest pushed past to join the lieutenant.

'Is it moving?' Goodwin said.

Manaus shook her head. 'No, it's not localised.'

'Keep going,' Priest said to the lieutenant, 'we'll cover you.' He called forward two of his men.

Manaus glanced at Goodwin before sealing her face back inside her helmet and moving on.

Goodwin thought she might have been trying to tell him something with her eyes, but if she had, he'd been unable to decipher it.

After a few minutes the light had grown to a steady pervasive glow, bright enough to see by without the aid of spectral enhancement.

The Darklight officer, still proceeding with caution, disappeared up another flight of stairs, followed by Priest and his men, who continued to scan the way ahead with their rifle scopes.

After a while they emerged into fresher air and a swirling mist that hung in dense patches, lit up by the glow in the encompassing gloom.

'We're back outside the sphinx,' Goodwin said.

Looking round, he could just make out the outer ring of megaliths and beyond those a blacker shape in the dark – the massive form of the Anakim Sphinx.

'We must be on the opposite side we entered from,' Rebecca said.

Goodwin adjusted his visor to see a river of black ooze separating them from the mainland, its deadly reach sweeping round on either side to enclose them within its toxic maw. *One way in, one way out*, Goodwin thought, before hurrying to catch up to Manaus and Priest who disappeared into the brightening mist.

Goodwin removed his helmet as he passed between two more megaliths, their rune-encrusted surfaces thick with ice. The reason for the illumination soon became clear when they entered a large, bowl-shaped depression much like a Roman amphitheatre. Unlike the human equivalent, this structure was naturally formed and its crystalline surfaces pulsed bright with a dark blue radiance. A couple of hundred feet across and surrounded by a circle of twelve colossal pillars, the giant terraces shimmered and gleamed in the shadows like a mythical grotto from another world.

The taste of rusting metal lingered in the cold air and water ran in rivulets over every surface; Goodwin licked his lips and stepped onto a translucent stairway that led down to a wide circular basin. Inside this area a large swathe of soil had built up into odd shaped mounds, creating a dark crater amidst its shining blue surround.

'Can you hear that noise?' Rebecca said, as she helped Joseph descend.

Goodwin listened for a moment. 'Like a deep hum?'

'Yes, I can feel it going right through me.'

Goodwin touched a step but felt no vibration. The weird sensation brought with it a sense of disorientation and a dull ache that took up residence at the crown of his head. Trying to work out if the feeling was pleasant or painful, Goodwin reached the bottom and stepped onto sodden dirt, which crunched underfoot.

When everyone had gathered, Priest relaxed his guard and looked at Goodwin. 'So, what now, Director?'

Goodwin gazed around. There was nothing there and no other route out except the one they'd entered by. And apart from the glowing crystal itself, there were no other features of significance. Around the edge of the soil, water collected in a tiny stream that cut a path towards the far side, where it fed a small, clear pool. At the rear of this tiny oasis a narrow fissure carried away any overflow, the unbroken, musical trickle of water transported away in perpetuity.

'He hasn't got a clue,' Walker said, his tone loaded with derision.

'Give me a minute.' Goodwin wandered around the site, looking for something ... anything.

'Perhaps the answers you seek are back in the tunnel,' Manaus said, joining him in his search, 'and the images on the walls.'

Goodwin crouched down and inspected the ground while the soldiers stood guard. After a further five minutes of fruitless observation Goodwin decided to go back to inspect the tunnel as the lieutenant had suggested.

Rebecca followed, but stopped when Joseph failed to accompany her.

'Joseph, come on. What are you doing?'

Halfway up the stairs, Goodwin turned round to see Rebecca heading back to collect her wayward ward. But despite her best efforts, the young man refused to leave his position on the dirt laden ground.

Feeling a sense of urgency, Goodwin trudged back to help her prise Joseph away from his distraction.

'He won't move,' Rebecca said. 'I don't know what's gotten into him.'

Goodwin crouched down and put a hand on the lad's shoulder. 'Joseph, it's time to go.'

Joseph remained staring at the earth.

'The boy's fed up with you, too,' Walker said.

The comment elicited a laugh from a few of the men.

Goodwin cupped the boy's chin in his hand and turned his face towards him. Joseph looked into his eyes and Goodwin let out a shout of alarm and fell back.

'What is it?!' Rebecca dashed to Joseph's side and looked back at Goodwin who stood staring down at the boy in shock. 'Richard, what's wrong?'

Goodwin shook his head, trying to rid it of the vision he'd just seen. The boy's eyes had been bloodshot and glowing with the same hue as the cave around them, but as he looked into them now they were the same innocent brown eyes they'd always been. 'It's nothing, my mind's playing tricks.'

Joseph stood up and wandered away.

'Sir, what did you see?' Manaus said.

'His eyes ... I don't know – nothing, I guess – a reflection of the light.'

A shout of warning made Goodwin spin round to see Joseph grappling with one of Priest's men. The soldier stumbled back and Rebecca screamed as Joseph, his expression blank, held his prize aloft in the air ... a pistol.

Manaus swore and the soldiers ducked as the mentally handicapped man wielded the weapon in random directions.

'Put it down, boy,' Priest said, advancing. 'Put it down or I'll put *you* down!'

Rebecca rushed to intervene, but Walker grabbed her. 'He doesn't understand,' she said, struggling against her captor. 'Richard, do something!'

Goodwin put himself between the array of weapons now trained on Joseph and the young man himself, and held out his hands. 'Joseph, it's Richard, Winnie, put down the gun.'

Lieutenant Manaus moved in from the other side and a look of confusion flitted across the lad's face before he pointed the weapon and fired.

A deafening gunshot echoed out and Joseph dropped the pistol and put his hands over his ears. Manaus took two long strides and snatched the gun from the ground while Rebecca, now released, rushed to his side.

'How the hell did you let him get a hold of that?' Walker said.

One of the soldiers, looking furious, approached Manaus and held out his hand. 'He took me by surprise.'

'Give it to him,' Priest said, his rifle trained on Manaus.

Reluctantly, the lieutenant handed over the weapon.

Goodwin didn't know or particularly care about the whys and wherefores. He approached the ground where Joseph's wild shot had dislodged a piece of the compacted sediment. Bending down, he swept aside the sodden deposits underneath to reveal a shiny, bronze surface. 'Have you got my knife?' he said to Manaus. The lieutenant nodded and handed it to him.

Goodwin took the blade and prised off another chunk of the rocky soil. 'There's something under here,' he said, scooping out the thick mud beneath.

'You,' Priest said, pointing to one of his men, 'keep a watch.' He turned to another man. 'And you, keep an eye on the lieutenant and the boy. Everyone else, get digging.'

Goodwin was joined by Walker, and Priest's four remaining men, while the man himself looked on, a finger never too far from his rifle's trigger.

Not needing any encouragement, Goodwin pounded away at the layer with a ferocity born of months of pent up frustration. Clawing at it with knife, hand and finger, he tore away the surface like a man possessed. Chunks of hard rock, mud and compacted soil disappeared in a flurry of activity. Even Walker seemed to relish the task, the corporal shifting nearly as much earth as Goodwin himself.

After a while a large area had been cleared and Priest called a halt to proceedings.

'No!' Goodwin said, carrying on. 'There's more under here.'

Someone dragged him away and Goodwin looked up into a steely gaze.

'I said, that's enough,' Priest said.

Goodwin, undeterred and breathing hard from his exertion, turned to look at their handiwork.

'What is it?' Rebecca said, moving to inspect the strange object.

Goodwin didn't know. It looked like the top of a giant sphere, its curved surface dipping down into the ground on all sides.

Lieutenant Manaus pushed past one of Priest's men, removed her water casket and poured the contents over the metallic surface. The water sloshed down over the strange artefact, washing away the muddy covering.

'It's the Earth,' Walker said.

'No.' Goodwin stepped forward, pulse racing. 'It's much more than that; it's a globe, a map. This is what I've been looking for; this will lead us out of Sanctuary!'

CHAPTER SEVENTY-EIGHT

'How does it work?' Rebecca said.

Goodwin hadn't thought that far ahead. *I was right all along!* Elation coursed through his veins, his suffocating veil of depression lifting. *I've found it, at last, a way out of this godforsaken hole in the dark!*

Walker leant down to inspect the enormous globe's bronzed surface. 'Perhaps it's not what the director thinks it is.'

'It's exactly what I think it is,' Goodwin said, pushing Walker aside. 'Here,' – he wiped away more dirt – 'there's the Americas, North and South, or at least their western edge.'

'So what?' Walker said. 'It's a globe, how does it help us get to the surface?'

Goodwin didn't know. 'There must be more underneath.' He looked around. 'This whole area needs to be excavated.'

'That could take weeks,' Priest said, 'we don't have weeks.'

'I can't help that,' Goodwin said, not noticing the dangerous tone in Priest's voice. 'Whatever we need is here, I can feel it in my bones. God brought me here for a reason; I was destined to find this place. It was written in the stars.'

'Richard,' Rebecca touched his arm, 'I don't think God's speaking to you. It's not how it works.'

He gave her a strange look. 'I thought you went to church? You of all people should believe. God speaks to us all, we just have to listen for the messages, see the signs he sends us.'

'I know, but God never intervenes directly. It's up to us to find the right path.'

'How do you know he doesn't intervene? You have no idea what I've seen, what I've felt!'

'I'm not trying to belittle your achievements,' Rebecca said, 'I just—'

Goodwin glared at her. 'Just what?'

Rebecca opened her mouth and then closed it again.

'Does anyone else want to criticise me?' Goodwin said, his eyes manic. 'I led you here, to the Temple of the Gods. I solved the riddle of the Sphinx. I found a place lost for millennia and all I get is looks of pity and anger. And from the likes of you.' Goodwin thrust a finger at Priest. 'You judge me, a man who wouldn't think twice about violating another or killing in the name of God?'

Manaus stepped forward. 'Sir, perhaps you should calm down.'

'No, let him finish,' Priest said. 'I always knew he thought he was better than the rest of us, I just never thought I'd hear him say it.'

'Well, get used to it,' Goodwin said fronting up to him, 'because I am better than you. You make me sick! A man who carries the word of God, but who has the morals of a slop-sucking pig!'

Priest's face turned white with anger.

Goodwin leaned in towards him. 'I know what you are; you're the basest denominator, the lowest ebb, a bottom feeder of bottom feeders. God sees you and it turns his stomach.'

Priest let out a roar of fury and surged forward.

Lieutenant Manaus jumped to Goodwin's defence, deflected the blow aimed at his head and threw Priest to the ground.

The burly soldier scrambled for his weapon, but Walker grabbed it first. 'Not a wise move,' he said, 'the director's all we've got.'

Priest stood up, his expression fearful, before relaxing back to relative calm as his men surrounded the corporal with guns raised.

Walker dropped the weapon while Manaus remained guarding

Goodwin. 'Sir,' she said, keeping her voice low, 'don't antagonise them, they're on the edge.'

Goodwin blinked as if seeing her for the first time.

'It's this place,' Rebecca said, 'it's messing with his mind.'

'My mind's fine.' Goodwin pushed past the lieutenant and glared at Priest, who stooped down to retrieve his rifle.

Before Goodwin could form another thought, a vibration rumbled through the ground and a screech of metal forced him to put his hands over his ears. The giant globe shuddered, and further away another mound shook free eons of sediment. The movement petered out to silence, leaving a stone megalith unearthed at the basin's edge.

Goodwin approached the structure, with a curious Joseph close behind. Standing six feet in height and thrice that in length, a layer of ice covered its grey surface which was adorned with a strange configuration of sunken runes and pictograms.

Before Goodwin could stop him, Joseph stepped forward and touched it. A chunk of ice fell to the ground and the symbol beneath rotated out to stop flush with the surface.

Rebecca went to pull Joseph away, but Goodwin put his hand out to stop her. 'Wait, I want to see what happens.'

Joseph continued pressing sections seemingly at random, then he stopped and a ripple of electricity flowed over the monolith's surface in a wave. The remaining slabs of ice splintered and cracked to drop to the ground with dull thuds and Goodwin stepped closer, his eyes alight with the purple glow that pulsed from the strange stone. He reached out to touch the surface and tiny tendrils of electricity bent around his hand, prickling his skin.

Joseph ran his fingers over the megalith in a sequence of arcs and another section of stone shifted.

'How's he doing that?' Walker said.

Priest pushed Walker aside. 'The boy sees something we can't.'

Goodwin looked at Joseph and his blank expression. *Does the lad's mental deficiency enable him to see beyond the obvious?* he wondered. A movement of the young man's arm made Goodwin look down to see his other hand was bunched tight in a fist. Goodwin leant down and lifted Joseph's unresisting arm and prised open his fingers. A cluster of bright blue stones shone bright in the half-light.

Rebecca gasped. 'They're the same as the stones Susan found. The ones that Commander Hilt said attracted that thing, the light.'

'They're similar,' Goodwin said, as he removed the pulsating objects from Joseph's palm. The stones felt hot and he couldn't help but notice the dark red welt on Joseph's skin where the stones had been. The rash on Goodwin's wrist peeked out from beneath the sleeve of his shirt, reminding him of his own experience with the strange phenomena. However, his bracelet, made by Susan, had only glowed in the absence of light; these stones pulsed strong under the glare of their torches.

As if reading his mind, their power waned and the luminescence faded, leaving the stones translucent like crystal clear glass.

'Where did he find them?' Rebecca said, but Goodwin was too enrapt in the mysterious Anakim relic to pay her any heed, as was everyone else, their hushed silence speaking volumes.

What does this thing do? How can I use it to find a way to the surface? Goodwin glanced at Joseph, wishing he could tell him what he wanted to know, wondering if he even knew anything at all.

Rebecca drew Joseph to her and hugged him close. The young man met Goodwin's gaze over her shoulder and he raised his hand to point at a plate-sized circular indent at the far end of the megalith. Goodwin glanced back to see Joseph had snuggled down in Rebecca's embrace, his interest apparently at an end. But unlike Joseph, Goodwin's fascination had only just begun. He moved to the end of the stone façade and touched his fingers to the circle. The electricity here was less than at the centre, where Joseph had worked his magic, and perhaps that was why nothing happened. *Or only the boy's touch has an effect*, Goodwin thought. Then he remembered the stones and Rebecca's words came back to him, *where did he find them?*

Where indeed.

Goodwin looked around the crater. *He must have found them here, surely? There's no other explanation.* Leaving the others to gawp at the spectacle, Goodwin roamed the basin in search of more blue stones.

When he didn't find any he grew frustrated and was just about to give up when he passed by the pool of water that cascaded into the narrow fissure. Beneath its surface he glimpsed the shimmer of blue amongst a sea of brown. He bent down and scooped out a handful of mud and separated out a shining blue stone from the sediment. Excited, he washed off the remaining dirt to reveal a handful of Joseph's stones. *But how did they get there?* His eyes moved up to the glowing crystals above. *Of course!* He mentally slapped his forehead. Water erosion, the stones weren't stones at all, but the crystals that surrounded them now, the same crystals he'd seen in the lake after he survived his ordeal with the black ooze.

He looked around at the glowing arena and a disturbing thought wormed its way into his mind. If the stones attracted the creature, as Commander Hilt had theorised, then they were standing in the beast's all you could eat buffet. Suppressing the urge to run, Goodwin made his way back to the megalith's circular indent, where the others remained arguing over God knows what. Goodwin, however, only had eyes for the job in hand. He reached out and pressed his palm flat to the surface. The stones grew hot in his other hand and electricity converged on his touch, plunging the rest of the megalith into darkness. Everyone turned towards him just as an almighty groan set the ground shaking. Stumbling sideways, Goodwin found his hand held fast to the stone and his arm wrenched round in pain as he tried to keep his feet.

The monolith shuddered and lurched to the right, dragging Goodwin along with it. The ground cracked and split, like a frozen sea buckling under the prow of an icebreaker, as the massive slab ploughed up soil before it to form a growing mound of earth.

'Sir!' Lieutenant Manaus rushed to pull him free.

'Let go, Richard!' Rebecca said.

'I can't!' He tried to open his other hand, which held the stones, but his fingers wouldn't move. The muscles in his arm went into spasm.

The lieutenant heaved on his hand, but it held fast.

Goodwin glanced behind to see the massive stone tracked a path around the rim of the basin with the top of the giant globe at its heart.

Manaus and Rebecca continued in their efforts to free him.

'It's no use,' Goodwin said over the noise, 'let it take its course!'

The megalith kept up its advance for another thirty feet before it slowed and then jarred to a halt.

A rush of energy swept up Goodwin's arm and he fell to his knees and grasped his head in agony. A flash of light sent him slumping to the ground and Rebecca rushed to his side, but Goodwin's eyes had already rolled up into his head, his body caught in a violent fit.

◆

'Help him!' Rebecca screamed.

Manaus grabbed Goodwin's arm and a blast of electricity blew her from her feet. The Darklight officer slid to a halt ten yards away, unmoving, her armour smoking from the discharge of energy.

Horrified and helpless, Rebecca stared into Goodwin's contorted features while Priest and his crew looked on with dispassionate eyes.

'Fight, Richard!' Rebecca hovered beside his writhing form. 'Fight it!'

'So long, Director,' Walker said. 'I'll see you in the land of the Gods.'

CHAPTER SEVENTY-NINE

'How many?'

'Nineteen, all armed. Some of them have Darklight kit.'

'Did they see you?'

The woman shook her head.

'The director?'

'No sign of him, the two civilians or the lieutenant.'

'Corporal Walker?'

'No, sir.'

Captain Winter frowned. 'Nineteen; there should be twenty-eight, where are the other nine?'

'I overheard them talking, sounds like one of them died somehow, which leaves eight other tangos unaccounted for.'

'With the director, no doubt.' Winter pondered their options. 'What's their formation?'

'Twenty yard spread, alert, but undisciplined.'

'Thoughts?'

'We could take most of them alive with minimal casualties.'

'Negative; they could warn Walker, which might jeopardise Goodwin.' Winter made a decision and signalled for his unit to gather round.

He pressed a com button on his helmet. 'Use the mist and standing stones as cover; silencers and camouflage active. Full auto after primary contact on my signal. We are a go for engagement, I say again, we are a go.'

Winter activated his armour and moved into the dark. His team followed, their forms shimmering out of existence as they slipped into the mists of night.

◆

'If they're not back in ten minutes I say we take our chances with Offiah.'

Another soldier snorted up some phlegm and swallowed it down. 'Make it five; this place gives me the creeps.'

'Priest told us to wait here,' said another.

'Priest can go fuck himself. He had plenty of opportunity to give us Goodwin's bit on the side and he kept her for himself.'

'There's always that Darklight whore, Manaus.'

The first soldier who'd spoken grinned. 'Yeah, I wouldn't mind seeing what's under that armour. Although I think she's too good for you; you can have that disabled woman, what's her name? The one that bastard Hilt went to find.'

The man made a face. 'Simple Susan?'

The soldier laughed. 'Yeah, that's the one, although I think you'd do well to get her. Perhaps Walker's more your type? Or Priest?' He reached out a hand and stroked the man's neck. 'What do you say, pretty boy?'

The other men laughed as the man tried to push him away.

'In fact,' the soldier said, 'we could pass you round instead; what do you say?'

His friend glared at him and the soldier laughed at his discomfort before something whizzed past his head, splashing liquid into his eyes.

Blinking it away, he wiped the back of his hand across his face and looked at it under torchlight. It was covered in blood. The man before him toppled to the ground and then everything turned to chaos.

◆

Captain Winter joined his team at the scene of carnage. 'Report.'

'Zero Darklight casualties. All targets nullified.'

A groan nearby made Winter turn in its direction. Walking over, he nudged the body of a man with his foot.

The soldier opened his eyes. 'Please, I need help.' He coughed and a trickle of blood ran down his chin.

'Where's Director Goodwin?'

The man gave a small shake of his head. 'I don't know, gone. Please ... help me.'

'I recognise you,' Winter said, crouching down by his side.

'Yes, yes, I remember.' The man grabbed Winter's leg and tried to smile.

Winter looked at his wounds. 'I think you need a medic.'

'Yes,' the man said in relief, 'yes, thank you.'

'You're the joker, the funny man, aren't you?'

The man nodded, unable to speak as he struggled to breathe.

'And from what I hear you also enjoy sexual assault.' Winter stood up and his expression darkened. 'Any last words?'

Fear crept into the man's dying eyes and Winter pulled out his pistol to wait for an answer that never came. The man had already gone.

Winter stared down at the dead man, his emotions mixed. *One less fucker in the world*, he thought, *fifty million to go.*

'Sir.'

He looked up.

'We've found tracks leading off into the mist. The terrain looks tricky. Some kind of tar pits.'

'Single file,' Winter said, 'stay alert, they could be close.'

The woman saluted and moved away.

Captain Winter raised his visor with the touch of a button and stared out into the gloom. 'Where are you, Director?'

CHAPTER EIGHTY

RICHARD GOODWIN GASPED FOR AIR. His eyes flared open and he heard Rebecca call his name before he was sucked back into nowhere. His thoughts wandered and images flashed in front of his mind's eye like a strobe. Faster and faster the abstractions came, bombarding him, mind, body and soul. Screaming without a voice, Goodwin fled from the onslaught, his spirit lost to insanity's insidious caress.

A figure appeared through the fog of despair – a white light in a dark abyss. The woman held out a hand and the black fled from her presence like insects before a storm. Goodwin remained cowering until her warmth had driven the ice from his heart. He reached out and felt strength flow through his being, filling it with the essence of life. She whispered to him to follow, telling him there was nothing to fear, not here. Knowing she told the truth he let her lead him into safety and ... LIGHT.

Goodwin felt his disconnected form drop into the whirlpool of a black hole, sucked down into a scene from a forgotten past. An Anakim warrior walked straight through Goodwin's translucent, shimmering aura and knelt before the great throne of gold and its titanic, silver God. Two crystalline statues crouched on either side of the golden seat, their sphinx-like shapes shimmering in the shadows. The giant man bowed to the god and placed a silver sword on the floor before retreating. The vision swirled into a chaos of colour and Goodwin found himself before the massive frieze where the same Anakim man lay on the pentagonal altar, his eyes glowing blue in the gloom. He could feel the man's fear and taste his terror – he wanted to run, to flee, but something controlled him, trapping him on the metal plinth, his massive limbs bound by invisible bonds. A procession of robed figures approached, the tallest of which held the same shining weapon the man had just offered up to his God. The blade rose, its tip sparkling like a star. From its zenith the sword fell and blood flowed. The Anakim's life force gushed from his veins, pumped out by his dying heart. The flow of dark red ran around the altar's outer channel and down onto the floor. Fire blazed and Goodwin was transported again, this time to a frozen lake – no – it was the frosted crystal sea behind the great throne. Nothing stirred and Goodwin could feel the cold spreading up his legs and back into his heart. He walked forward, approaching the sunken alcoves in the icy wall. Wisps of super cool air hung in the blue glow that permeated every atom and every direction. Compulsion drove him to wipe away the frost that covered the back of the tomb-like aperture. Cold gripped his fingers as he slid them across the frosted surface to reveal the clear crystal beneath. His eyes drew him inside the hidden chamber beyond. He could feel ... something ... something inside, something that became aware of his intrusion into its domain. Eyes opened and Goodwin screamed.

Horror returned, shimmering and spinning, weaving its web of pain. A black mist seeped into his mind, stalking Goodwin's prone form. It was his body that lay on the altar now, held fast by an unseen force. The shadowy figure approached and Goodwin was unable to move. Gripped by terror, eyes swivelling, he fought back with pure fury. Suddenly the chains released and Goodwin leapt at the shape, wrestling it into the black in a fit of ferocious fear. Straining every sinew, every muscle, he fought the dark being that sought his soul.

Driving it back he fled for the distant light, the dark mist clinging to his spirit with talons of ice.

'Richard!'

Goodwin's eyes flew open and he scrabbled to his feet. Adrenaline and terror coursed through his system like an out of control freight train. He sucked in great gulps of air and stumbled back to the ground, exhausted.

Rebecca grasped his face. 'Speak to me!'

'I'm ... okay,' he said, wheezing. 'I'm okay.'

'That's the second time you've scared me half to death.'

Goodwin looked up into her anxious eyes.

'You've got nine lives, Director,' Walker said, standing close by.

With some semblance of sanity returning, Goodwin struggled to his feet and looked round to see the still form of Lieutenant Manaus on the ground a few yards away. Her helmet had been removed and her eyes were closed as if in prayer.

A look of shock crossed Goodwin's face when he realised she must be dead. 'What happened?'

'She got a shock trying to free you from the stone. I think her heart gave out.' Rebecca wiped a tear from her eye.

Goodwin glanced at the dormant megalith that had trapped him in its electrical grasp. How he'd survived he didn't know, but one thing was for sure, he'd been lucky, very lucky.

A sense of guilt and sadness swept over him as he gazed down at the peaceful features of the Darklight officer. *Another person dead because of me; how many more will it take before the end comes?*

A wave of nausea made him stumble and he grabbed on to Rebecca for support.

'This place is a death trap,' Walker said, 'and unless anyone wants to risk touching that thing again we're no closer to finding a way to the surface than we were before.'

'Someone will try it again,' Priest said, hefting his rifle, 'and soon, I guarantee it.'

Goodwin blocked out their chatter as something tried to push its way to the forefront of his mind, a sensation of remembrance he knew was important – he just couldn't recall it.

'What's wrong?' Rebecca said. 'Do you need to sit down?'

He waved the suggestion away. 'I saw things, real things from their past.'

'Whose past?'

'The Anakims', at least I think they were real. It felt like the truth, like it happened, or was happening. I don't know, it seemed so—'

'So what?'

'So real?' Walker said, his tone sceptical.

Rebecca shot Walker a withering look before turning back to Goodwin. 'What did you see?'

'The throne, a warrior and ...' his eyes grew wide.

'What is it?'

An image of the Anakim warrior returned from memory and Goodwin could see his torment, but most of all he could see the blue glow that flickered over the iris of his eyes.

A sense of dread settled on his heart and Goodwin's eyes darted over the crystalline crater and its soil laden basin. 'Where's Joseph?'

Rebecca spun round.

The lad was nowhere to be seen.

'Joseph?!' Rebecca said. 'JOSEPH!!'

CHAPTER EIGHTY-ONE

'GET OUT OF MY WAY!'

'No.'

Rebecca screamed and attempted to force her way past Priest and his men. A soldier pushed her back and Goodwin tried to help, but Priest slammed the butt of his gun into his head, sending him sprawling to the ground in pain.

Rebecca kept fighting until one of the soldiers backhanded her to the floor.

'Please,' Rebecca said, with tears in her eyes, 'let me find him.'

'The boy's no use to us,' Priest said. 'We need to find a way out, and the clock's ticking.'

Rebecca put her hand to her mouth and a sob escaped her lips. 'Please …'

Priest remained stony-faced, the pleas falling on deaf ears.

Goodwin got back to his feet. 'You must let us go; you don't understand.'

'Enlighten me,' Priest said.

Goodwin wasn't quite sure what he knew himself. 'The boy,' – he shook his head in an attempt to clear it – 'Joseph, he's not himself.'

'If that's your argument,' Walker said, 'it's not very convincing.'

'No, you're not listening to me! It's his eyes; he had the same blue light as the Anakim warrior.' Goodwin's frustration mounted as the answer he sought seemed to stay just out of his grasp. The men before him remained unimpressed and he looked at Rebecca. 'Did you see that the statue had moved, or did Joseph?'

Rebecca stared at him, distraught.

'Rebecca,' – he gave her a shake – 'this is important. Think; after I activated the throne the first time, was it you or Joseph that noticed the statue had moved.'

'I don't know. I saw its head was in a different position.'

'But did Joseph point to it first?'

'No, but ... he does this thing when he wants me to go somewhere, he leans into me to make me go in the direction he wants.'

'So he pushed you towards the statue?'

'Yes, I think so. Why – why does that even matter? He's out there alone!'

Goodwin turned back to Priest. 'Joseph also helped me uncover the frieze in the city. And he fired the gun that uncovered the globe.' Something struck him as the puzzle came together. 'How did he get out of the camp? The lieutenant said he must have followed her. How? He had no spectral enhancement to see in the dark. How did he evade the patrols? How did Manaus, a highly trained reconnaissance operative, not see him following her? A mentally disabled man wandering around in the dark, who just happens to end up with us, you don't think that strange?'

Priest remained impassive.

'For God's sake, man!' Goodwin gestured at the megalith. 'The boy knew how to operate the stone. Can't you see?!' Goodwin felt groggy and he paused for breath.

'So what are you saying?' Walker said.

A recollection of Joseph playing with his transparent bottle of water in the Anakim city bubbled up from Goodwin's past. The lad hadn't been able to comprehend why the level inside stayed on a horizontal plane regardless of how he tilted it. And he'd demonstrated his discovery to Goodwin many times over. *Did he help me get through the challenge in the lake, too?* Goodwin wondered. *Without that knowledge I wouldn't have known which way was up inside the black oil and I would have drowned.*

'I'm saying,' Goodwin said, 'Joseph was the only one left in camp to touch the stones and to see the entity – the light – and live to tell the tale.'

'Apart from you,' Walker said.

'Yes, apart from me.' Goodwin frowned at the thought. 'What if the stones and my discoveries were all designed to bring us here?'

'Richard, you're scaring me,' Rebecca said. 'What are you saying?'

'What if everything the creature has done was for a purpose? Hilt said it had to be highly intelligent to get past our defences, to deceive us as it did. What if it had a plan, an end game, beyond taking Susan?'

Priest's eyes narrowed. 'And what's that?'

Goodwin rubbed his eyes. His head hurt – badly. 'I don't know, but Joseph was with Susan when the light took her. Why did it leave him? Why didn't it take him, or just kill him? Why didn't it kill me when it had the chance?'

It was all making sense to him now – everything that had happened.

'I think the light showed itself to me and Kara that night on purpose,' he continued. 'It wanted to draw attention to itself. I think we've been controlled – manipulated from the start. This thing thinks ten moves ahead, not just five.'

No one spoke while Goodwin paced back and forth in agitation. 'In my dream, the vision, whatever it was, the Anakim man, I could feel his fear. I could sense his thoughts. He couldn't control his own body. They sacrificed him and his own mind held him captive as they did it. I think ...' – he looked at Rebecca in anguish – 'I think the light is controlling Joseph. I think ...' – he looked down at the rash on his wrist, his worst fears becoming a reality – 'I think it's controlling me.'

Rebecca shook her head in dismay. 'No, that can't be.'

'I saw the mark the blue stones left on Joseph's hand. They must be toxic – possess some sort of mind-altering properties.' Goodwin held up his wrist to show them the red inflammation that encircled it.

'This is where I wore the bracelet Susan gave me, made up of the same blue stones.'

'So everything you've done hasn't been you?' Priest said. 'That's what you're saying?'

'If that's the case,' Walker said, 'how can we trust what you're saying now?'

'And even if you're right,' Priest said, 'what can the boy do?'

'Are you not listening to me? Joseph's being controlled! We need to find him – NOW!' Goodwin saw Priest hesitate, but doubt and suspicion remained the dominating power and Goodwin turned away in disgust.

'Richard,' Rebecca said, the tone of her voice drawing his full attention, 'you said Joseph is being controlled.' She held out a wadge of folded paper. 'Do you remember these?'

Goodwin leafed through the pages he'd given to her for safe-keeping before he'd first entered the lake.

'Joseph's drawings,' she said, 'he really wanted you to have them.'

He peered at the crude shapes which had been coloured in with black charcoal on a white background. The abstract forms were each accompanied by meaningless lines that cut across empty spaces. 'I don't understand,' he said, looking at her.

'He did many other drawings,' Rebecca said, 'some he did with Susan. I didn't think anything of them at the time, but now ...'

'Tell me.'

'He was drawing shapes; many were of the same thing. Susan drew them too.'

'What sort of shapes?'

'Pentagrams.'

'What?!'

'I know – I know, I should have said something at the time when we found the one in the city, but I thought it would sound stupid. I thought it must have been a coincidence.'

Goodwin looked again at the pictures, while some of Priest's men edged closer, their curiosity getting the better of them. Laying the papers out on the globe, around two dozen in all, Goodwin noticed a pattern emerge. All the drawings had a single line sandwiched between areas of black. Like he had with the map of the lake, he tried matching one of the drawings to the rest.

'There!' Rebecca said. 'Turn it ninety degrees.'

Goodwin did so and the two pictures aligned perfectly. Repeating the process over and over, with Rebecca's help, a larger picture resolved itself. When the final drawing was inserted, Goodwin stepped back to view it.

The black shapes had formed together to create a stark outline.

'It's the sphinx!' Rebecca said.

Goodwin's eyes were drawn to the centre where another shape had been depicted, a pentagram, inside which was the shape of a man. Beside this figure, within a sea of black charcoal and with straight lines emanating out from it, was a patch of white, like two overlapping stars. And inside this oddity was an indistinct form.

'What is that?' Priest said, peering at it over Goodwin's shoulder. He pointed at two white marks. 'Are those eyes?'

'It's a light,' Rebecca said.

Goodwin shook his head as fear coursed through his veins. 'It's not *a* light; it's *the* light – the entity!' He grasped Priest's shirt with both hands and stared into his eyes. 'This is where the light comes from, why it entered the lake. God didn't lead me here. We've been deceived. This place isn't a way out at all; it's the creature's lair. Are you hearing me?! We have to go!!'

CHAPTER EIGHTY-TWO

PRIEST SWORE and gestured to three of his men. 'Find the boy!'

'Where's Walker?' one of them said.

Goodwin turned to see the corporal was nowhere to be seen.

'Fuck's sake!' Priest grabbed Goodwin's arm. 'This better not be a trick, Director.' He turned to his men. 'Follow me!'

Goodwin found himself running up the crystal stairs and out into the mist. One of the soldiers stumbled and fell into the toxic tar, but Priest kept going.

Goodwin ignored the man's cries for help and grasped Rebecca's hand as they ran. They reached the entrance to the tunnel and clattered down its steps. Water splashed underfoot as they ran on, tearing down the passage at breakneck speed.

Soon after another staircase emerged out of the gloom and, breathing hard, Goodwin pulled Rebecca onwards until they were back at the frieze and the three statues that knelt in situ. Priest slowed as the oppressive silence of the Sphinx's interior reasserted its pitch-black grip.

A strange noise echoed on a breeze. The temperature dropped and Goodwin's breath puffed into the icy air like smoke.

Priest cocked his rifle and his men did likewise. A scream from behind made everyone jump.

'What was that?' Rebecca said, eyes wide.

'Keep moving.' Priest crept forward across the glistening floor and down into the next area.

A blue glow and pulsing hum throbbed through the crystal sea underfoot while a thick mist hung silent over its frosty surface. Moving forward, the cold increased and the water vapour thinned. The silver statue and its golden throne emerged from the gloom and a figure lay sprawled on the floor twenty feet to its right, unmoving.

'Joseph!'

Goodwin grabbed Rebecca's arm. 'It's not him.'

'It's Walker.' Priest edged closer, rifle raised. He nudged the body with a foot. 'He's still breathing.'

'Where's Joseph?' Rebecca said.

Goodwin shivered, he had no idea; he just wanted to get out of there as quickly as possible.

The background hum peaked, the glow vanished and a powerful vibration made the floor shake.

Goodwin experienced a strange sinking sensation and he pointed his torch down at his feet. 'The floor's melting!'

All around the frosted crystal rippled and shook as the hard surface turned to liquid. They shouted in alarm as the viscous fluid sucked them down.

'Get to the throne!' Priest said, wading forward.

The rapidly melting floor flowed up over Goodwin's knees and within a few steps the icy liquid had reached his waist. Rebecca cried out for help and Goodwin dropped his torch and lifted her up just as the vibration ceased.

Rebecca shone her light in front of them. 'We've stopped sinking.'

The pervasive blue glow returned, sending the dark back into retreat. A wave of electricity flickered through the mist behind and a metal structure reared up out of the deep around them. The liquefied crystal poured from its ancient rune-encrusted surface and Priest scrambled up onto it. Goodwin deposited Rebecca on its edge before he felt something move past his legs.

'What the hell?' One of the soldiers pointed his rifle down into the fluid.

A light coalesced around him and he disappeared beneath the surface. Terrified, Goodwin hauled himself out as another man vanished from sight. Priest fired into the crystal sea while the remaining three men scrabbled to safety.

The light ebbed away and the surface calmed.

'Jesus fucking Christ,' one of the soldiers said, 'what was that?!'

'Can anyone see them?' said another, his voice shaking.

The seconds ticked by, but there was no sign of the men resurfacing.

Priest shook his head. 'They're gone.'

'Fuck this shit, so am I,' said the third man.

Pushing past Priest, he disappeared into the dark with his two comrades close behind. Priest glanced back at Goodwin before following suit.

Left alone with Rebecca, unarmed and exposed, Goodwin wanted nothing more than to go with them, but he knew they had to find Joseph first.

Rebecca tugged at his arm. 'Richard, look.'

The mist dissipated to unveil the rest of the platform on which they stood – it was in the shape of a giant pentagram.

Goodwin could now see where the ethereal illumination was coming from. The wall containing the frozen alcoves shone with an eerie pulsating light which was mirrored by an identical structure on the opposite side. Silhouetted against this unreal backdrop, in the centre of the pentagram, stood a familiar figure.

'Joseph,' Rebecca said. 'Joseph!'

The young man didn't respond and Goodwin steered her in the other direction towards the silver statue.

Rebecca resisted. 'What are you doing?!'

'I'll go back for him,' Goodwin said. 'Promise me you'll wait here.'

Rebecca looked like she was about to protest, but instead she nodded. 'Be careful.'

Goodwin let her go and moved with care back over the slick, metal surface.

As he approached, Joseph bent down and hauled the limp form of Corporal Walker into the pentagram's centre, which was raised a couple of feet above the rest of the platform.

'Joseph?' Goodwin said.

The young man didn't look round. Instead, he withdrew the knife from Walker's belt and hunkered down to trace strange shapes on the floor. Symbols in the metal ignited at his touch, blossoming to life like purple fire.

Goodwin edged closer, his heart beating ten to the dozen.

Joseph stood and an altar spiralled up before him, carrying Walker's spread-eagled body along with it.

Goodwin could hear strange sounds in the air – whisperings – like the voices of the dead. He went to touch Joseph's shoulder, but before he could the young man turned to look at him.

Goodwin froze. Joseph's unblinking eyes gleamed with the same blue sheen he'd glimpsed before; the whites shot through with blood.

The tip of a knife rested against Goodwin's chest and he held up his hands and took a slow backward step.

Joseph returned his attention to Walker's prone form, his free hand hovering over the body.

Goodwin knew what was happening – he'd seen it or something similar before in his vision: a blood sacrifice.

A bright light appeared in the liquid ahead. It shone and glimmered with a beautiful iridescence. Goodwin couldn't take his eyes off it and he found himself following it past Joseph, beyond the pentagram and towards one of the wall's glowing alcoves.

Goodwin could hear a woman's voice calling his name, but all he could see – hear, taste, touch – was the light, the wonderful, glorious light. His depression wilted, his anxiety vanished and his fear fled. Goodwin was walking to heaven and God's embrace. He reached out a hand and ran his fingers over the icy interior of the sunken recess. It felt like home, like life itself.

'Richard!' A hand grasped his shoulder and pulled him round, breaking the spell.

'Rebecca?' Goodwin blinked. 'What are you doing? Where's Joseph?'

Rebecca looked back at the altar. 'I don't know, he was right there.'

A glint of steel plunged down. Goodwin pushed Rebecca aside and grabbed Joseph's wrist. Fingers coiled around Goodwin's throat and he was forced back into the freezing alcove. Unable to breathe, Goodwin fought for his life. His fingers dug into Joseph's face and sank into an eye. The grip on Goodwin's throat increased and he was slammed back – once – twice – three times. He felt his strength fading and his vision blurred. Fluid poured in around his feet and out of the corner of his terrified eye he saw a black shape forming in the crystal. Suddenly the pressure released and he stumbled forward.

Regaining his senses, he saw a revived Walker wrestling with Joseph on the floor.

'Don't hurt him!' Rebecca stepped back as they rolled onto the pentagram.

Goodwin knew there was no chance of that happening as Joseph forced Walker's head down into the liquid within. Goodwin ran forward and hauled Joseph away, but a blade lanced out to slice his arm. Rebecca screamed and Walker attacked. The corporal slammed Joseph into the crystal wall, cracking its surface. They struggled for a moment before Walker grunted in pain and staggered back. Joseph's knife glinted red in the shadows and the corporal collapsed to his knees.

He looked up at Goodwin in shock, hands pressed against his neck to try and stem the gushing blood. Walker let out a strangled gurgle and toppled over, the light fading from his eyes.

Goodwin looked up at Joseph, who remained where he was, stock still and watching the floor, his blue irises following the trail of blood as it flowed down a channel and into the alcove.

Walker's life force merged into the crystal wall, flowing up into two opposing channels before branching out into tiny trails, like veins. *No*, Goodwin thought, *not* like *veins, they* are *veins!* The red blood was flowing into something inside the crystal itself, something dormant, and by the size of its partial outline, something definitely not human.

Goodwin pushed Walker's body over the edge and into the liquid and Joseph let out a guttural growl and launched himself forward.

Goodwin ducked a slash of the knife. 'Stop the blood!' he said to Rebecca.

Joseph swung again, narrowly missing his neck.

'What?!' Rebecca said.

Goodwin dodged back. 'The alcove, stop the blood!'

Inside the crystal wall a dark mist coalesced, joining with the blood that fed it.

He fended off another blow, but the attack was a distraction as Joseph grasped Goodwin's forehead to send pain lancing through his skull. Goodwin fell to his knees in agony. Images flashed before his eyes, vivid and powerful, searing into his brain. He cried out and then the sensation vanished. Sitting up, he shook his head.

Joseph stood before him and held the knife out for him to take. Goodwin felt compelled to accept it, even though part of his mind screamed at him not to. He looked at the knife and then – ever so slowly – turned it on himself. His mind shrieked in protest and his hands shook as he tried to resist his own strength. The blade inched round and Goodwin gritted his teeth, trying to fight back at the invisible power that controlled his movements. A gasp of air escaped his mouth as his lips curled back in animalistic self-preservation. The blade was pointing at his stomach now and angled up towards his heart.

A voice in Goodwin's mind whispered its command for him to end his own life. He continued to resist with everything he had. 'No,' he said, 'nooo ...'

Seeing Goodwin's plight, Rebecca spun Joseph round and slapped him hard across the face.

The power that controlled Goodwin released. Weakness flooded over him and he dropped the blade. Overcome, his eyesight dimmed and the world spun.

Moments later his vision cleared and he saw Joseph holding a struggling Rebecca over the liquid, his knife raised.

Goodwin clambered to his feet. 'Joseph, NO!

The blade fell, Rebecca screamed and a gun fired. Joseph stumbled back. Rebecca slipped, cracked her head on the pentagram's edge and disappeared beneath the thick fluid. Goodwin jumped in after her as gunshots echoed again.

He plunged down into the deep. There was no bottom here. Ears rushing with no sound, the viscous liquid clung to his eyes. Rebecca drifted below him, unconscious. He swam down to pull her up as a bright light formed above. Two glowing eyes appeared in its midst and Goodwin's horror turned to terror as something grabbed his shoulder and dragged him to the surface. Air and noise returned in a rush and hands hauled him back onto the pentagram. He gasped, shivering with cold, and looked up into the eyes of a Darklight helmet. The visor rose. 'Are you okay, sir?'

Disorientated, Goodwin was at a loss for words.

'Sir,' the man said in a louder voice, 'do you understand me? My name's Captain Winter, I'm here to take you back to camp.'

Goodwin heard someone coughing and spluttering and he looked round to see Rebecca on her side a few feet away. He nodded and the man helped him to his feet.

Goodwin wiped the transparent substance from his face. 'Where's Joseph?'

The captain pointed at the alcove.

Goodwin pushed past two Darklight soldiers to find Joseph hanging suspended in solid crystal, his face a mask of shock and fear. Frozen in time, blood seeped from a series of gaping wounds in his chest. Further back, the light in the crystal wall faded and whatever had sought to escape from its hidden bonds died with it. The gruesome sight made Goodwin feel sick to his core with despair. He placed his hand against the surface, where Joseph's outstretched palm was encased.

A tear rolled down Goodwin's face. 'I'm sorry,' he whispered. 'I'm so sorry.'

A whimper of anguish made Goodwin turn to see Rebecca had got to her feet.

'Rebecca no,' – he barred her way – 'you don't want to see—'

She screamed and lashed out in a fit of grief, and Goodwin grabbed her wrists and pulled her to him.

Half collapsing, she clung to his chest, wracking sobs stealing away her breath.

'He's gone,' Goodwin said, gently rocking her, 'he's gone.'

A tremble rippled through Rebecca's body and she surged up. 'NO!' Thrusting him away, her eyes fell on the abject vision of her ward. Another cry of loss escaped her lips and she stumbled to the crystal wall as its light dimmed. Goodwin had no words as Rebecca stroked the surface near to Joseph's face, her tender touch mere inches away, but separated by the infinite gulf of death.

The crystal's final glimmer of light ebbed away to nothing and a deep rumble shook the sphinx. The metal pentagram lurched, sinking back beneath the solidifying floor, and in the same moment, Rebecca's arm sank into the transparent wall.

Crying out, she tried to pull herself free and Goodwin made a grab for her other arm, but his fingers closed on solid crystal.

'Richard!' Rebecca stared into his eyes in terror.

Captain Winter rushed to help, but it was too late, the wall had already consumed her entire body.

Her final shriek cut off to silence as the crystal covered her head, its surface creaking and cracking in thickening expansion. Cocooned inside, Rebecca was locked in her final pose, mouth agape in a frozen scream.

The pentagram continued to sink and the captain hauled Goodwin away. 'Director, we need to go!'

'No, I won't leave her!' Goodwin shrugged Winter off and returned to pound at the wall with his fists.

Without hesitation, the captain brought his armoured hand down on the back of Goodwin's head, knocking him unconscious. Hoisting him onto his shoulder, Captain Winter ran back the way he'd come and leapt from the vanishing pentagram. Moving past the golden throne and down into the great plaza, the Darklight officer and his team headed back through the giant sphinx and towards safety.

CHAPTER EIGHTY-THREE

OUT IN THE sea of darkness where only the stars shone, a single craft manoeuvred in the vacuum of space. Jets of gas vented as Tyler Magnusson used his final drops of fuel to bring him closer to his target: a dark space station, which floated just ahead, its five arms spinning in slow rotation.

Tyler's eyes narrowed as he drew nearer. A white emblem adorned the black skin of the mysterious craft:

The space station sported an unusual design. Tyler had seen the concept on paper, but had never imagined it was already operational. The inner core was engineered so it could move independently to its outer arms. This allowed it, when activated, to rotate much faster to produce a strong gravitational effect for those on board. Currently the system was offline and the large central sphere remained in sync with the rest of its structure.

'This is Pilot Commander Magnusson of the U.S.S.S. Archimedes, do you copy? Over.'

No response. He'd been signalling the stealth space station ever since he'd been within range. The sense of relief he'd felt when he realised he had enough fuel to be able to complete a docking run was immense. But as time had passed and only static greeted his radio calls, his elation had turned to concern. That no one was answering was disconcerting and the silence of his solitary confinement only added to the sense of unease that had built within him. Was there anyone aboard this dark craft? Would it hold enough fuel reserves to take him home? Would he even be able to board it? Tyler remembered the disturbing creation he'd witnessed back on Archimedes, remembered watching his captain die only to see him again, comatose and being transported in some kind of quarantine capsule.

Anger rose within him at the memory while he finalised the sequence to bring his Sabre space-aircraft alongside the enormous bulk of the GMRC's secret outpost.

Warning messages appeared on his navigation screen. The clamps had failed to gain full purchase and the airlocks hadn't aligned. He pressed some buttons and overrode the precautions. 'I'll have to make an EVA,' he said to himself. 'Where did I put those mag-boots?' He floated through to the rear of the ship. 'Ah, there you are.' Picking up his boots he pulled them on and activated the mechanism. The electro-magnets sucked his feet onto the floor with a double clunk.

An alarm from the bridge brought him back to the main console. Two words flashed on-screen.

INCOMING MESSAGE

'At last.' He flicked a switch and the screen went black. Seconds later a fuzzy image appeared, accompanied by the crackle of distorted sound.

Tyler stared at the video footage of an empty room before a face appeared and he jerked back, startled.

The man held the camera close, his eyes wild with fear. '... it's too late ... do not ...'

'Say again your last,' Tyler said.

'... if they knew ... never have ...'

'I can't hear you, you're breaking up!' Tyler twisted a dial.

The picture solidified. 'Whatever you do, do not board this ship. Send no rescue team. It can't be allowed to get back to the surface!'

'What can't?' Tyler said, alarmed by the scientist's fervour.

The lights on the space station flickered and died, plunging the man into darkness. 'It's here,' he whispered, his eyes shining silver as the camera adjusted to the dark. He turned round. 'I hear it ... I hear it breathing.'

Horrified, Tyler saw a strange light in the background drift past a doorway. An all too familiar oscillating noise echoed through the speakers and a tingle shot up his spine, causing his hands to shake.

'Did you see it?' the man said. 'The light?'

Tyler put his hands over his ears. 'No, I—' He hesitated as his eyes were drawn to a time stamp in the corner of the screen. The message wasn't live; it had been recorded two weeks before. He reached out a hand and paused the video. His shaking decreased and he breathed deep to try and calm his nerves. *That sound*, he thought, *why did it have to be that sound?* He'd been wondering where the GMRC had taken Project Ares, and now he knew. Not wanting to watch anymore, but knowing he had to, Tyler turned the sound down a fraction and resumed the footage.

'I don't have much time,' the scientist said, 'if anyone sees this; I beg you, do not continue our research. We should have left it buried in the earth. It's not a machine, it's alive. It knows who we are, it—'

A dark figure appeared behind the man, eyes glowing white in the black. Tyler put a hand to his mouth in horror and pointed, but the man was oblivious to the thing behind him. A split second later the video distorted and the apparition vanished. The scientist glanced round before turning back to the camera, his mouth open in a terror-stricken scream. The image flared white and silence fell.

Tyler felt his heart beating loud. The camera adjusted again as the lights in the room powered back up. Nothing could be seen of the man and the rest of the room appeared normal, apart from a few objects that drifted through the craft's microgravity atmosphere.

The recording continued unimpeded until a shadow fell across the camera and a figure floated past heading toward the exit. At first Tyler thought it was the man who'd been speaking, but he realised it was someone else; the hair was close cropped whereas the other man's had been shoulder length. This new person halted by the doorway and Tyler held his breath as they turned to look back at the camera. Shock hit him as he recognised the man on-screen. It was Bo Heidfield, Captain of the U.S.S.S. Archimedes, the dead captain of U.S.S.S Archimedes.

Bo Heidfield moved out of shot, leaving Tyler standing in stunned silence. After a few minutes of recording the empty room, the camera system switched itself off.

Rewinding the footage, Tyler let it play again before freezing it on Bo Heidfield's image. It was his captain, all right, but his eyes shone with a blankness that made Tyler shudder.

Switching off the screen, he considered his options. 'I don't want to go in there,' he murmured. 'If you want to live you're going to have to,' he told himself. He rubbed his face vigorously as various scenarios flashed through his mind. Finally, with a sickening certainty, he realised he had no alternative.

In a daze, Tyler moved aft and went about putting on his space-suit. Once fully attired, he returned to the main console and turned on the ship's video recorder. He lifted the shield on his helmet and looked into the convex lens. 'Professor Steiner, I'm sending you this message as I've been unable to make direct contact with you since we last spoke. I can only hope it reaches you.' He paused to gather his thoughts. 'I have reached the space station, but it seems—' The lights in the ship flickered and went out and the console died. Tyler swore and flipped switches and turned dials to no effect. The torches on his helmet powered on, sending a narrow beam around the dark cabin.

'Warning,' a computer generated voice said, 'life support will fail in sixty seconds. Fifty-nine – fifty-eight – fifty-seven—'

As Tyler lowered his helmet's visor, his suit's systems blazed to life and the self-contained oxygen supply switched on. Releasing his magnetic boots, he floated to the escape hatch and yanked down the red handle. Twisting it sideways, a series of tiny explosions jettisoned the oval panel out into space. He pulled himself through the aperture and looked up to see that the space station had another docking port a hundred feet away. Gauging his trajectory to the ship, he pushed off to glide through the emptiness of space and soon found himself grabbing onto a handrail. He glanced back at his space-aircraft and the dark mass of the Earth and the Sun beyond. There was no going back now. He turned away from the amazing sight to continue his ascent and a minute later he'd reached the airlock.

Like most orbital vehicles, access could be attained via a concealed control panel. Entering a standard NASA access code, Tyler felt panic rise as the words *ACCESS DENIED* appeared on the rectangular display. Trying to think, he recalled another code. Tapping it in resulted in the same message. He tried another and then reverted back to the one he'd tried first. All failed. 'Think, you fool,' he said, 'think!'

A memory from his time on Archimedes popped into his head. He remembered overriding the GMRC's security when he'd entered their deserted laboratories. A number had appeared on the display. What was it? Tyler willed himself to recall it. It had six digits. He knew that much. Closing his eyes he pictured the scene. A five and an eight. *It had started with a five and an eight!* Tyler entered the first two numbers and found the next two followed on as if by magic, a six and a three. But try as he might, the final two numbers failed to reveal themselves from the vaults of his mind. Praying the entry system allowed multiple entries, Tyler went about entering the first four numbers followed by permutations of the digits zero through nine.

After ten minutes a green light indicated he'd found the correct combination. The doors to the airlock slid open and Tyler floated inside before starting the depressurisation procedure.

Sometime later, when the process had completed, all he could think about was what waited for him beyond the door. And the more he delayed, the more horrors his mind conjured up. His whole being screamed at him to flee, but he knew he had nowhere else to go. Taking a deep breath in, Tyler braced himself and opened the inner hatch.

CHAPTER EIGHTY-FOUR

NASA ASTRONAUT TYLER MAGNUSSON entered a dark, silent corridor on board the GMRC's stealth space station. Looking left and then right revealed rows of dim lights that curved out of sight in line with the vessel's hull.

A distant noise echoed through the ship and Tyler froze. Alert, he listened, but nothing further stirred. His breathing sounded like a freight train, ragged and loud. He looked at the readout on his suit. The atmosphere in the ship was intact, but the temperature had dropped below freezing. 'The heating must have failed,' he whispered to himself.

Still feeling terrified and alone, he turned on his suit's cameras. The one inside his helmet filmed his face while the lens mounted on his shoulder took in his external environment. Whatever was going on here, he had to record his findings. Talking to himself would also alleviate his fear, at least in theory. *I'm just doing another survey*, he told himself, *this is Archimedes and I'm running diagnostics, it's just another day in the office*. Memories of thousands of hours of simulations stimulated brain and muscle memory alike, returning a thin semblance of calm over the seething turmoil within.

'This is—' he wetted his dry lips. 'This is Pilot Commander Tyler

Magnusson, conducting a visual sweep of a deep orbit GMRC space station, designation unknown.'

He completed a three hundred and sixty degree rotation to provide the camera with a view of his surroundings. 'I have so far been unable to make contact with any of the crew. From the transmitted video message I received prior to entry it could be that all have perished. However, said video indicated someone may still be alive.' He paused, not wanting to relive what he'd witnessed. *No one would believe me anyway.*

'While here I will also seek to refuel my ship in order to return to Earth, although this may prove difficult and time-consuming as I'm unfamiliar with this space station's configuration. Failing that, there may be an escape pod, or separate module I can utilise to the same end.'

Steeling himself, Tyler used the wall's handrail to propel himself left, the lights brightening as he passed. Reaching an intersection, he could go any one of five ways. He decided to go up, towards where he'd seen the bridge on approach.

As he moved, all was quiet and yet the questions remained. Where was his captain? Where was Bo Heidfield?

Tyler's fear increased its vice-like grip.

He glided past a number of sealed doors, each numbered in sequential order. He halted at one marked:

LAB 5, ROOM 6

The hatch hung ajar. Looking around, he pushed out a tentative hand – a hand, he noticed, that trembled. The door swung inwards to reveal a darkness within.

Tyler chased away the black with his torches, which lit up a number of metal worktops, their shiny surfaces playing with the light. All he could hear was his strained breathing, the whoosh of air as he exhaled, followed by a hiss of inhalation.

Whoosh … …

… … hiss … …

… … whoosh … …

… … hiss … …

'This laboratory appears to be—' He hesitated. 'No, there's something on the slabs.' He put a reluctant foot inside and the automated systems lit up the room in a dazzle of light. Once all the ceiling panels burned with a white intensity, Tyler moved into the room and floated over to the first table. In its centre lay a flat piece of granite. From its appearance it looked old, very old. But despite its cracked and weathered face, the deep carvings adorning it could still be seen with ease. Tyler reached out a hand to trace the outlines of the symbols around its thick edge, before switching his inspection to where more of these obscure writings decorated its top. In the centre of these was a set of lines, connected together to form a single whole. And where each line met a small, five-pointed star had been exquisitely carved.

Having been involved with everything and anything to do with space for his entire career, and for the majority of his school years, too, for that matter, Tyler recognised the shape instantly: it was the constellation Sagittarius. Moving to the next table revealed another stone tablet, twice the size of the first, but with similar inscriptions. In the centre of this monolith lay another constellation. This one was not well known to most; Tyler knew it as the Charioteer, or Auriga to give it its Latin name. He'd always remembered it because of its geometric shape, rather than for the shape of a charioteer's helmet from which it got its name. He traced the outline of the pentagonal design, recalling when he'd gazed at it through his father's telescope as a young boy.

A rumble of sensation swept through the ship and Tyler looked up to listen, his heart beating faster. The ship's engines had fired up. *It's just an automation*, he told himself, *just an automation*. At least he hoped it was. He returned to looking at the artefacts, as that's what they were. Where they were from he didn't know. They could have been Babylonian, Incan or Egyptian for all he knew. Why such objects had been transported to this remotest of locations he could not begin to guess, but their link to the heavens was clear.

The third and final block sat on a slab apart from its siblings. It glinted shiny black, like crude oil made solid. This piece displayed no sign of wear. Its straight edges and pin sharp carvings looked new and, unlike the other two, this object held a glistening liquid in its centre. Tyler reached out his gloved hand and touched the thick fluid. He held his fingers up to the light. Red blood stood out in stark contrast to the white of his suit. A curious vibration swept through the room, sending ripples across the gory pool. The blood drained into the surrounding runes to reveal another constellation. Tyler gave his head a shake as a sibilant whispering entered his mind.

'No, that's nothing to do with me. It's coincidence, nothing more.'

It's all to do with you, Tyler, his mind told him, *it's only ever been you. This place will be your tomb.* He shook his head. 'There's nothing here,' he said, 'I need to keep moving.'

But his eyes felt drawn to the shape in the centre of the obsidian rock; the sign was his own, the seventh astrological sign in the zodiac, the balanced one, the constellation of Libra.

CHAPTER EIGHTY-FIVE

THE SHIP SHUDDERED AGAIN and Tyler found himself looking at his white glove. Blood no longer stained his fingers. He looked down at the black stone to see the besmirched surface was anything but. He screwed up his eyes and blinked, but the scene remained the same, devoid of sanguine fluid and pristine in its sterility.

Distressed and confused, he left the room with the artefacts behind and made his way to the ship's command centre. The twin doors slid aside as he approached and Tyler put his feet to the floor, activated his mag-boots, and walked onto the deserted bridge. Dark screens and hibernating systems covered the walls of the circular room and the main console at its centre.

A light from a single display attracted his attention. Moving to the screen, he saw a scrolling tabular readout alongside the graphical representation of the planet Venus as it orbited the Sun. However, on closer inspection he realised the data wasn't fixed on the planet at all, but on a smaller object following the same trajectory. Frowning, Tyler touched the screen to expand the image. The planet enlarged and now he could see what was being tracked: a large asteroid in orbit around Venus, effectively a small moon.

A noise made him look up. The protective shield that covered the command centre's sweeping window, retracted to reveal the dark of space beyond.

His pulse raced as he searched the room with his eyes.

It remained empty.

Tyler let out a sigh. *Accessing the computer must have activated a latent command – another automation. Is this whole craft run by autonomous computers?* he wondered. With no answer to hand, he returned to analysing the screen. According to the data the space station seemed to be sending out a signal to this distant rock. He tapped the screen again to bring up a new set of scrolling numbers.

'That can't be right.' He stared at the information, but the figures didn't lie. A signal was being sent, but what disturbed him most was that there was a message coming back!

He looked out at the distant stars and the familiar shapes of the constellations. *What is going on here?* Trying a sequence of commands, he tried to access the signal, but the system was encrypted.

He noticed another window on the display operated beneath the rest. Minimising the data streams unveiled a live stream from a laboratory located somewhere on the ship. In the middle of the floor, surrounded by the lifeless forms of what must have been the crew, was the thing he'd seen aboard Archimedes, the same thing that had caused psychosis and fatal symptoms in his colleagues – the beating heart of Project Ares. The plasma bulged and fluctuated as if alive and Tyler couldn't take his eyes off it.

A sudden sound filled his body, causing it to spasm. Forced to his knees, he clutched his helmet as pain lanced through his brain. The sound continued, increasing in pitch. Blood trickled from his nose and he let out a cry of agony. And then the sound stopped. Ears ringing, Tyler tore at his helmet's clasps before pulling it clear. He breathed deep, sucking in great gulps of ice cold air. Feeling light-headed, he touched his glove to his nose and held it up to see the same red blood on white as he'd seen before. *Had it been a vision?*

A murmur of noise made him spin round. Nothing was there. He heard it again, louder this time, like a voice.

His laboured breath hung in the bitter atmosphere like mist.

'Who's there?' He looked round for something he could use as a weapon.

'We've been wait – ing ... Pil – ot ... Com – mander.'

Tyler felt his hackles rise. The voice sounded ... unnatural. He spied an axe in the corner of the room, inside a red cabinet. He went over and smashed the glass with an elbow. The shattered debris floated into the room and he grasped the handle.

'We see ... you, Ty – ler,' the voices whispered.

Tyler's hands shook as he brandished the axe. 'Where are you?'

'Clo – se.'

Sensing something behind, he swung round.

Nothing was there.

'We see ... you, Ty – ler,' the voices said again.

Tyler span round. 'WHERE ARE YOU?!'

Laughter echoed through his mind, the sound like madness.

Tyler put a hand to an eye as pain lanced through it. The voices sounded like they were inside his head. He stumbled towards the control console. *I have to get out of here*. Pressing some buttons, he tried to locate an escape pod.

The voices came again; he felt disorientated, sick, like he was dying from the inside. He screamed out, 'WHAT DO YOU WANT FROM ME!?'

The voices stopped and a shimmering light appeared in the doorway. His stomach clenched in terror. 'It's here,' he whispered, 'I can hear—'

A shadow fell across him and Tyler looked up to see a figure floating near the ceiling.

'Captain?'

The ship shuddered and span, gravity formed and the captain's eyes flared open. His body fell and slammed Tyler into the floor.

Pinned down, Tyler could feel powerful hands digging into his suit. Terrified he tried to move, but he was held fast. He could hear breathing and his eyes strained down to see the top of Bo Heidfield's head creeping up towards him.

Un-dead eyes stared into his and a whimper of fear escaped Tyler's lips.

The captain's face distorted, turning transparent, and a shimmer of light glittered under his flesh.

Tyler saw his own horror reflected in the beast's mask.

The captain's dead flesh ruptured and the thing that possessed him pushed out like a monstrous larva before entering Tyler's face. Skin parted, bone buckled and cracked, and Tyler's terrified screams echoed into the ship.

His body thrashed and writhed before eventually falling still.

Silence fell and the background hum of the space station continued unheard. Pilot Commander Tyler Magnusson, the last surviving crew member of the U.S.S.S. Archimedes, had joined those who'd gone before him in the eternal bond from which there was no return, the eternal bond of death.

CHAPTER EIGHTY-SIX

Richard Goodwin woke to a blazing headache. He groaned and opened his eyes to find himself propped up against a large step on an equally enormous staircase that disappeared into misty darkness below. Looking up, he could just make out the outline of the Anakim Sphinx's massive head high above.

Someone bent down and pulled up one of his eyelids. 'How you feeling, sir?'

Goodwin pushed the man's hand away. 'Like someone just hit me on the head. Where's your captain?'

The Darklight operative stood aside to reveal his superior officer.

Captain Winter, who'd been studying a map, handed it to one of his men and glanced round as Goodwin got to his feet.

'Ah, Director, you're awake, good. I need to ask you some questions.'

'After we free Rebecca.'

'I'm sorry, sir, no can do. We're under strict orders to take you straight to camp. Once you're back safe and sound we'll return and see what can be done about the girl.'

Goodwin shook his head, which made it throb. 'No. We go back for her now. Do you hear me, soldier? That's a direct order.'

'My orders come from the major and Dr. Vandervoort, nothing you say will convince me otherwise, sir. What you can do is tell me the whereabouts of Lieutenant Manaus, Corporal Walker, and his men.'

Goodwin felt his anger rise, before the thought of the lieutenant swamped him with guilt. 'She's dead, Walker too. The rest, I don't know – gone.'

'Gone where?'

Goodwin felt his anger swell once more. 'I said, I don't know, goddamn it!'

Winter grasped his shirt and yanked him forward. 'You think you're the only one with a right to be upset?'

Goodwin stared into the Captain's seething eyes.

'You just tell me my sister's dead and *you're* angry?!'

Goodwin didn't know what to say. He had no idea Winter and Manaus were related. 'I'm sorry, I ... the lieutenant, she was a good woman.'

Winter fought for control, his eyes rich with emotion. 'Yes, she was. The best.'

'Sir?' a Darklight soldier said.

Winter let Goodwin go and turned to his subordinate. 'What is it?'

'I'm not sure; my scans are picking up a strange build-up in static electricity, along with a seismic fluctuation.'

'Earthquake?'

The woman shook her head. 'No, I don't think so; it's more like a resonance.'

The stone under Goodwin's feet trembled and a piece of rock fell bouncing down the staircase, followed by some smaller fragments.

Winter shouldered his rifle. 'Let's move!'

The floor continued to shake as they clattered down the oversized stairs. As they reached the bottom a whoosh of noise made everyone look up. A massive torrent of water exploded from the sphinx's mouth.

Winter pulled Goodwin on as they reached the treacherous pits of black tar. Behind, the flood continued unabated.

Retracing their steps using the software maps in their Darklight helmets, the soldiers quickly worked their way back through the quagmire. Nearing the standing stones, the pools of black ooze bubbled over as if boiling. A jet of tar erupted into the air like a geyser, barely missing Goodwin as he passed. Another spout of black followed, and then another and another.

Goodwin glanced back to see a wall of water rushing across the plain towards them.

'Pick it up!' Winter shouted above the roar.

They were running now, under the stones and beyond into the narrow tunnel.

Goodwin looked back again to see the tsunami break over the stone megaliths. A few more paces and the massive wave rushed into the tunnel to sweep Goodwin from his feet. Carried along in a sea of frothing mayhem, Goodwin was thrown about like a cork in a bottle. And then he was sliding across the floor of the great hall, the space filled with hideous, wailing statues. Regaining his feet, a Darklight woman grabbed his arm and helped him into a run. The water continued to flood in from behind, chasing those before it with the force of mighty Neptune himself. Goodwin reached a set of stairs and the wailing sounds reached fever pitch and then cut off. Jets of black oil burst from the statues' mouths and Goodwin kept climbing. Scaling a crumbling opening, the fleeing group emerged into the giant shaft and headed up its spiral slope. Round and round they ran and Goodwin found himself falling behind the well-conditioned Darklight mercenaries.

Captain Winter dropped back to offer encouragement. 'Not far now, Director!'

A sudden upsurge in water sent Goodwin sprawling. Carried over the edge of the sloping pathway, he was soon joined by everyone else as the column of icy liquid spun them into a seething whirlpool. Without light, Goodwin was tossed around in the dark, his only reference the torches of the Darklight team that bobbed and swirled around him. The upward motion increased and Goodwin was propelled in a great arc out into the lake. Plunging into cold waters, he swam away from the deluge, which continued unabated.

The Darklight unit, encased in their lightweight armour, gathered together to tread water.

'Where's the causeway?' Goodwin said, spitting water from his mouth as he fought to stay afloat.

'Gone,' Winter said from nearby. 'We make for the shore, everybody stay together!'

The soldiers powered forward, arms and legs sending a spray of water into the air. Tired, but still alive, Goodwin kicked for dry land.

After some minutes a cry of alarm went up thirty feet away.

'We're under attack!' someone else shouted.

A woman next to Goodwin disappeared beneath the inky black, dragged down by something unseen.

A shout of fear rang out as scaly hides broke the surface in all directions. Automatic weapons fired, sending flashes of light flickering across the water. Terrified, Goodwin swam through the chaos, the scene lit up by sporadic gunfire.

A man grabbed Goodwin's arm. 'Sir, keep swimming!'

Goodwin was about to reply when a tooth-ridden maw severed the man in two, spraying blood into Goodwin's face.

In shock, Goodwin span round, unsure which way to go.

A light shone in Goodwin's direction. 'Director, over here!'

Goodwin swam forward once more to rejoin Captain Winter.

'Follow me!' The Darklight officer struck out again with Goodwin in tow.

Limbs aching and lungs bursting, it felt like an age before the Captain suddenly stood up and turned back to help Goodwin to his feet.

Stumbling through the shallows, Goodwin was led to dry land where he dropped down, shattered and numb.

Captain Winter detached his rifle from his back, poured out the water, and walked back in up to his waist. Other men and women struggled to shore while their leader fired off rounds into the lake to protect those further out.

Not long after, when everyone had reached the safe haven of terra firma, Goodwin wiped his hands over his face and tried to make sense of everything that had just happened. He couldn't get the image of Joseph's dead body out of his mind. And when respite finally came, it was only to be replaced by the sound of Rebecca's gut-wrenching scream, the noise echoing through his tortured soul like a jagged scythe. He closed his eyes, trying to shut it out, shut it all out.

If only I'd stayed at camp and listened to Kara, Goodwin thought, *none of this would have happened. Joseph and Rebecca would be alive, the lieutenant, Winter's operatives, even Walker and his men. How did I not see what was right in front of me? I was so sure. How could I have been so wrong? How could I have been so blind?* A well of fury and loathing for the entity, the elusive light, the creature – whatever it was – built within him. But as fast as that sensation grew, it was quickly replaced by the shame and guilt of his actions. He knew deep down it was his single-minded determination to take care of those around him that had ended up killing some and hurting many more. It was his desire to escape Sanctuary that had made him the perfect vessel for coercion, be that to his own delusion or something more sinister. But whatever spell he'd been under, if any, only he was to blame for all that had transpired. Only he was culpable for the losses they'd all endured. Goodwin dug his fingers into his eyes to try and dull the pain and continued to remonstrate with himself as Captain Winter counted casualties.

◆

'A third of our force?' Winter shook his head.

'Yes, sir, just under – fourteen in total.'

Another soldier approached. 'Captain, I'm picking up an all-frequency alert.'

'Patch it through to my helmet.' Winter switched to the appropriate channel. 'This is Captain Winter, code in, sigma two seven niner.'

'Captain, Major Offiah, report.'

'Major, we've secured the director. Darklight losses at thirty per cent. Twenty-one hostiles terminated, seven remain unaccounted for. Secondaries ...' he paused, composing himself, 'secondaries expired.'

'My condolences, Captain. Lieutenant Manaus was an outstanding officer, but the time for grieving will have to wait. I want your unit to rendezvous a-sap to the coordinates I've just sent to your system.'

'Trouble, sir?'

'I'm mobilising the entire camp, stay sharp, soldier, there's—'

A fuzz of noise buzzed through his helmet's speakers. 'Sir? Say again, Major.' Winter looked at his radio operator. 'Get them back.'

The Darklight soldier searched the frequencies and gave a shake of the head. 'It's no good, the whole band's down.'

'Jamming?'

'Maybe, but who?'

Winter lowered his visor. 'Or what.'

♦

Goodwin heard Winter end his transmission, but his thoughts were elsewhere. He'd never felt so low – so numb. His spirit was crushed beyond any hope of redemption. *The surface is lost. Joseph and Rebecca are gone. What is the point of going on? I – the destroyer of lives.*

The captain picked up his rifle. 'Listen up! We're moving out, Major's orders. Coms are down, threat level high. Weapons hot, systems primed.' Winter held out his hand. 'Ready for another round, Director?'

Goodwin looked up with weary eyes. 'Will it never end?'

Winter hauled him to his feet. 'Everything ends, sir, its up to us to keep fighting.'

'So what's the emergency this time?'

'That's what we're going to find out.' He helped Goodwin into a jog and the beleaguered Darklight unit moved off into the dark void of the immense underground chamber, situation unknown.

CHAPTER EIGHTY-SEVEN

FOUR MEN CREPT through the ancient halls of the Anakim Sphinx. The roar of noise that had shaken the monument had fallen quiet and their footsteps echoed loud in their ears. Cold water dripped down from above and the lights from their torches sent strange forms leaping out from the dark, the abstract architecture as alien as anything they'd seen so far.

Priest was unsure where they'd made the wrong turn, but make it they had and instead of finding the exit they'd wandered into another area of the sphinx. There was one upside to their remote location; they were far away from Goodwin and the light in the melting floor. Seeing his two friends dragged under by some shimmering apparition had been too much, he'd never been so scared in his life. *To hell with Goodwin and his Anakim god, to hell with the USSB, to hell with it all!* He wished he'd never let Walker convince him about Goodwin's plan. *I should have stayed on the surface*, Priest thought, *man wasn't made to live underground.*

'We're going the wrong way,' one of the soldiers said.

His friend spun round, gun raised. 'Did anyone hear that?'

'We're all gonna die down here,' said another, 'alone in the dark.'

Priest gave a growl. 'Shut the fuck up, all of you. This place isn't infinite, we keep walking until we hit a wall then we follow it out.'

The man who'd heard the noise stopped moving as the others continued. 'There's something back there,' he said, searching the pitch-black with his rifle scope. 'I'm sure of it.'

A whistling wind blew through the hall, ruffling their hair.

Priest stopped and looked back. All four men now pointed weapons and torches back the way they'd come. The air grew still once more, but something had changed and Priest took a step back.

A distant sound sent a strange vibration through the stone floor.

'I told you I heard something,' said the man, glancing round.

Priest took another step back, and another, as the sound grew louder.

'What is that?' said the soldier's friend.

Racing along the floor and closing fast, a dark shadow ate up their light.

Priest's eyes widened in realisation. 'RUN!'

A massive wall of water tore towards them and the first man disappeared in a sea of black.

Priest dodged round a corner and down a narrow passage. A man's scream vanished in a roar of noise, followed by another soon after. On his own, Priest cast aside his weapon and increased his speed. Bursting out into a great hall, he ran for his life as the raging rapids smashed into the bend behind and erupted out.

An orange glow guided Priest onwards and a few paces later he slid to a stop before a sheer drop. A trickle of dust sifted down into a sea of black tar and steaming lava, and he glanced back to see the liquid torrent rearing up into a giant wave.

He turned back to the shimmering magma, the ruddy light reflecting in his eyes. A myriad of images flashed through Priest's mind, some of them good, many of them bad. 'Forgive me, Lord,' he said, 'for I have sinned.'

Washed over the edge, the last member of the USSB decontamination team fell to his death, his terrified heart full of traumatic regret and self deluding lies.

EPILOGUE

The ousted director of USSB Steadfast slowed his pace, his legs aching and mind faltering.

Captain Winter halted his unit's advance and came back to Goodwin's side. 'You okay, sir?'

Goodwin came to a stop, sucked in some air and shook his head. 'Go on without me,' – he bent down and took another breath – 'I'm done.'

'Where you go, we go, Director.'

'Why? Why bother? What's so special about me that you'll risk your lives for mine? All I've brought you people is an endless nightmare of suffering. You'd be better off leaving me out here to die.'

Winter knelt down on one knee in front of him. 'That's quitting talk, sir. I don't listen to quitting talk. And in answer to your question, we risk our lives for yours because that's our job; it's what we're paid to do.'

Goodwin looked at him. 'I thought mercenaries had the luxury of choosing their fights?'

'Yeah, pretty much.'

'Then you haven't answered my question.'

Winter wiped his nose and sniffed. 'You're right, of course. I act out orders because that's what I do; it's my way of life. I follow a chain of command, always have done and probably always will. But unlike me, there are many others that have a greater purpose, a bigger moral compass, if you will. There's still thousands of people down here who need your help; are you going to let them down when they need you the most?'

'How can they trust me when I can't trust myself?' Goodwin said. 'I've been compromised. My decision-making is shot. Kara was right to have me replaced. I would have done the same in her position.'

'And there's part of your answer. That you recognise your mistakes is why you're such a great leader. Your resolve may have led you down the wrong path this time, but that just makes you wiser, stronger. Can you not see? It's not about you; it's about everyone, the collective. You hold us together, the glue in the mix. Without your reasoning, many, if not all of us, would already be six feet under. My unit, my sister, they put their lives on the line because they believed in you. Commander Hilt believed in you. I still believe in you. You just need to believe in yourself. There's always a brighter tomorrow, Director, we don't even need to find it, we just have to try.'

'Beautiful hope,' Goodwin murmured as he considered Winter's words.

A Darklight soldier approached.

'What is it? Winter said, standing.

'I'm picking up a new transmission.'

'The major?'

'I'm not sure, sir. It keeps breaking up.'

'Let me listen.'

The man adjusted his radio and handed Winter the handset.

A rush of static hissed through the com system before a garbled voice stuttered to silence. The message repeated and then another voice answered. 'Target sighted, in pursuit—'

The radio crackled and the communication cut out.

'This is Captain Winter, what is your location? Over.'

They waited for a reply, swapping looks as the seconds ticked by.

'I say again. This is Captain Winter, what is your location? Over.'

'—coordinates, need immediate assistance ... our location.' The signal faded before returning. '—the light's closing on our position, not sure when we can—'

A roar of gunfire echoed through the handset, to be replaced with a steady hiss of white noise.

Everyone waited with bated breath for the voice to speak again.

'Signal's gone,' the soldier said. 'Coordinates appear to originate from the city's centre, in the opposite direction to the major's rendezvous point.'

'And no one else is responding?'

'No, sir.'

'What do you want to do, Director?' Winter turned back to Goodwin. 'Stay here and wallow in self-pity or step back up to the plate? Fight for what's yours, take back control; lead us as only you know how, or accept defeat and ignore this call for help? The choice is yours.'

Put on the spot, Goodwin glanced around at the men and women who waited for his order.

A light has been seen in the city, Goodwin thought. The coms system is down, so no one else is likely to have heard the call for help. Whoever is out there, they're on their own. The problem is, it goes against the major's orders. Goodwin held the Captain's gaze. The man is testing me, trying to pull me back to the land of the living, to make me care. And does it? he asked himself. He didn't know. It was a clever move by Winter, a bold move, forcing Goodwin into making a decision. A fifty-fifty call that could cost the lives of everyone involved.

'Sir?' Winter said.

The clock was ticking and Goodwin didn't know what to do. Meet up with Offiah and leave the people who'd sent the message to fend for themselves, or put those around him back into mortal danger, or stay where they were in blissful solitude, cut off from the horrors unfolding beyond. Only the latter option appealed; it would ensure no one else died on his watch, keeping his conscience clear.

Goodwin stood up. 'Whatever I decide, you'll back my play?'

Winter nodded. 'To the letter.'

'No questions asked? No complaints?'

'Yes, sir, no questions, no complaints.'

'Very well, Captain,' Goodwin said, 'this is what I want you to do …'

TO BE CONTINUED...

Ancient Origins: Genesis
(Book Four of *Ancient Origins*)

https://geni.us/aogenesis

ABOUT THE AUTHOR

Robert Storey began work on what would become the Ancient Origins series in 2013. The series of six novels was completed in 2018.

Robert died a year later in March 2019.

For more information about Robert and his work, please visit:

fuse-books.com/robertstorey

ALSO BY ROBERT STOREY

Ancient Origins: Revelations

(Book One of *Ancient Origins*)

Ancient Origins: Dark Descent

(Book Two of *Ancient Origins*)

Ancient Origins: Let There Be Light

(Book Three of *Ancient Origins*)

Ancient Origins: Genesis

(Book Four of *Ancient Origins*)

Ancient Origins: The Tenth Protocol

(Book Five of *Ancient Origins*)

Ancient Origins: The Lost Prophet

(Book Six of *Ancient Origins*)

https://geni.us/robertstorey

APPENDIX A - GMRC CIVILIAN PERSONNEL

Professor George Steiner
Director General of GMRC Subterranean Programme
Nationality: American
GMRC Clearance – Level 10 Alpha
Designation – Civilian
Deployment: GMRC Directorate (Oversight) / Transient
GMRC Division: Subterranean Programme
Skill set:
Subterranean structural engineering
Management and leadership
Planning, design and development
Mathematical modelling and forecasting
Computer programming and software development

Malcolm Joiner
Director of U.S. and GMRC Intelligence
Nationality: American
GMRC Clearance – Level 10 Alpha
Designation – Civilian
Deployment: GMRC Directorate / Transient

GMRC Division: Intelligence Division
Skill set:
Espionage and covert intervention
Intelligence gathering, restriction and dissemination
Information pathways / Management and leadership
Psychological warfare

Richard Goodwin
GMRC Subterranean Base Director
Nationality: American
GMRC Clearance – Level 9 Alpha
Designation – Civilian
Deployment: U.S.S.B. Steadfast [U.S.S.B. Sanctuary – unofficial]
GMRC Division: Subterranean Programme
Skill set:
Management and leadership / Planning, design and development

Dr. Kara Vandervoort
Ecosystem Director
Nationality: South African
GMRC Clearance – Level 8 Alpha
Designation – Civilian
Deployment: U.S.S.B. Steadfast
GMRC Division: Subterranean Programme
Skill set:
Biomechanical engineering / Management / Data analysis

Special Agent Myers
CIA Agent and GMRC Intelligence Operative
CIA Special Operations Group (SOG)
Nationality: American
GMRC Clearance – Level 9 Delta
Designation – Civilian
Deployment: Transient
GMRC Division: Intelligence Division
Skill set:

Covert military intervention / Leadership / Strategic planning
Close quarters and unarmed combat

Dagmar Sørensen

Director of GMRC Research & Development
Nationality: Norwegian
GMRC Clearance – Level 10 Alpha
Designation – Civilian
Deployment: GMRC Directorate / Transient
GMRC Division: Research and Development
Skill set:
Scientific exploration and advance
Black project development and integration
(Special access programmes: acknowledged and unacknowledged)
Information pathways / Management and leadership

Grant Debden

Primary Aide to Malcolm Joiner
Nationality: American
GMRC Clearance – Level 8 Delta
Designation – Civilian
Deployment: Transient
GMRC Division: Intelligence Division

Ms. Sylvia Lindegaard

GMRC Delegate
Nationality: Danish
GMRC Clearance – Level 10 Alpha
Designation – Civilian
Deployment: U.S.S.S. Archimedes
GMRC Division: Space Programme / Oversight
Skill set:
GMRC integration specialist
Management and leadership / Planning and development

Information pathways

Nathan Bryant

GMRC Subterranean Facility Coordinator
Nationality: American
Global Acquisitions and Intelligence Liaison
GMRC Clearance – Level 10 Beta
Designation – Civilian
Deployment: GMRC Oversight / U.S.S.B. Steadfast
GMRC Division: Subterranean Programme
Skill set:
Logistics / Management / Negotiation, arbitration and presentation
Linguistics, communication and translation
Skill set:
Organisation and presentation / Information pathways
Linguistics, communication and translation
Intelligence gathering, restriction and dissemination

APPENDIX B - S.E.D. PERSONNEL

Deployment: U.S.S.B. Sanctuary
Designation: GMRC Civilian

Dresden Locke
S.E.D. Facility Commander
Nationality: American
Profession: Explorer

Riley Orton
Deep Reach Team Leader
Team: Alpha Six
Nationality: American
Profession: Explorer

Jefferson Church
Deep Reach Team Member
Team: Alpha Six
Nationality: American
Profession: Explorer & Lead Archaeologist

Cora Islanovich (Deceased)

Deep Reach Deputy Team Leader
Team: Alpha Six
Nationality: American
Profession: Explorer

APPENDIX C - U.S. MILITARY PERSONNEL

Colonel Samson

United States Army SFSD Brigade Commander
Special Forces Subterranean Detachment
(Codename: Terra Force)
Nationality: American
GMRC Clearance – Level 8 Alpha
Designation: Military – Special Forces
Deployment: U.S.S.B. Steadfast
Skill set:
Overt military action / Sniper tactics and marksmanship
Covert military intervention and counter-insurgency
Close quarters & unarmed combat / Leadership & strategic planning
Subterranean warfare / Subterranean transit

General Stevens

United States Army Commanding General
Special Operations Command Sanctuary
Nationality: American
GMRC Clearance – Level 10 Beta (Special Access Personnel)

Designation: Military
Deployment: U.S.S.B. Sanctuary
Skill set:
Overt military action and unarmed combat
Leadership, logistics and strategic planning
Subterranean warfare

Corporal Adam Walker
United States Army Decontamination Team
Nationality: American
GMRC Clearance – Level 5 Beta
Designation: Military
Deployment: U.S.S.B. Sanctuary
Skill set:
Overt military action / Unarmed combat

Leon '*Priest*' Cameron
United States Army Decontamination Team
(Private First Class)
Nationality: American
GMRC Clearance – Level 4 Alpha
Designation – Military
Deployment: U.S.S.B. Sanctuary
Skill set:
Overt military action / Unarmed combat

Sergeant Alvarez (Deceased)
United States Army Decontamination Team
(Staff Sergeant)
Nationality: American
GMRC Clearance – Level 5 Alpha
Designation – Military
Deployment: U.S.S.B. Sanctuary
Skill set:
Overt military action / Unarmed combat

Brigadier General Ellwood

United States Army Commanding General
(Division Commander)
Nationality: American
GMRC Clearance – Level 10 Delta
Designation – Military
Deployment: U.S.S.B. Sanctuary
Skill set:
Overt military action / Subterranean warfare
Covert military action and unarmed combat
Leadership, logistics and strategic planning

APPENDIX D - ARCHAEOLOGISTS

Sarah Elizabeth Morgan

Nationality: English
Profession: Archaeologist, Anthropologist
Current location: USSB Sanctuary

Trish Brook

Nationality: English
Profession: Archaeologist
Current location: USSB Sanctuary

Jason Reece

Nationality: Welsh
Profession: Archaeologist
Current location: USSB Sanctuary

APPENDIX E - ALBUQUERQUE RESIDENTS

Rebecca

Nationality: American
Profession: Mental health worker
Current location: Sanctuary Proper

Joseph

Nationality: American
Mentally handicapped man
Current location: Sanctuary Proper

Susan

Nationality: American
Mentally handicapped woman
Current location: Sanctuary Proper

Julie

Nationality: American
Profession: Mental health worker
Current location: Sanctuary Proper

Arianna

Nationality: American
Profession: Mental health worker
Current location: Sanctuary Proper

APPENDIX F - ASTRONAUTS

Tyler Magnusson

Pilot Commander (acting Captain of Archimedes)
Nationality: American
Rank: Commander
NASA Clearance Level: AMBER 1 (Segregated Personnel)
Deployment: U.S.S.S. Archimedes

Astrid-Hélène Pichon

Flight Engineer
Nationality: French
Rank: Mission Specialist
ESA Clearance Level: JADE 1 (Segregated Personnel)
Deployment: International Space Station (I.S.S.)

Alexei Denisov

Pilot Cosmonaut
Nationality: Russian
Rank: Second Officer
RFSA Clearance Level: JADE 1 (Segregated Personnel)

Deployment: International Space Station (I.S.S.)

Bo Heidfield (1990 – 2041)

Space Station Commander
Nationality: American
Rank: Captain (Deceased)

APPENDIX G - DARKLIGHT PERSONNEL

Commander Hilt

Darklight Officer

Nationality: American

GMRC Clearance – Level 8 Delta

Designation – Civilian / Private Contractor

Deployment: Classified

Current location: Sanctuary Proper

Skill set:

Overt military action / Multi terrain warfare

Covert military intervention / Sniper tactics and marksmanship

Hostage retrieval and counter terrorism

Close quarters and unarmed combat

Leadership and management / Strategic planning / Reconnaissance

Major Offiah

Darklight Officer

Nationality: Nigerian

GMRC Clearance – Level 7 Alpha

Designation – Civilian / Private Contractor

Deployment: Classified
Current location: Sanctuary Proper
Skill set:
Overt military action / Multi terrain warfare / Leadership
Covert military intervention / Close quarters and unarmed combat
Hostage retrieval and counter terrorism / Strategic planning

Captain Winter
Darklight Officer
Nationality: American
GMRC Clearance – Level 7 Alpha
Designation – Civilian / Private Contractor
Deployment: Classified
Current location: Sanctuary Proper
Skill set:
Overt military action / Multi terrain warfare / Reconnaissance
Covert military intervention / Close quarters and unarmed combat
Leadership and strategic planning

Lieutenant Gabriela Manaus
Darklight Officer
Nationality: Brazilian
GMRC Clearance – Level 7 Gamma
Designation – Civilian / Private Contractor
Deployment: Classified
Current location: Sanctuary Proper
Skill set:
Overt military action / Multi terrain warfare / Reconnaissance
Covert military intervention / Close quarters and unarmed combat

Private Zack Michaels
Darklight Soldier

Nationality: American
GMRC Clearance – Level 6 Delta
Designation – Civilian / Private Contractor
Deployment: Classified
Current location: Sanctuary Proper
Skill set:
Overt military action / Multi terrain warfare / Reconnaissance

APPENDIX H - OTHER PERSONS

Jessica Klein

BBC Newsreader and TV Presenter
Nationality: English
Profession: Journalist
Relatives: Daniela & Victoria (daughters) / Evan (husband)
(Pseudonym: Eliza Sterling)

Brett Taylor

FBI Special Agent
Nationality: American
Profession: Federal Agent
Relatives: Colonel Samson (father)

Bic / Da Muss Ich

Computer Hacker / Cyber Terrorist
Nationality: Unknown
(Pseudonyms: DMI / *Da Muss Ich* / Because I Can /
Deforcement Insidious / D'Force / Elusive D / Oyakata / B.I.C.)

Eric Wolf

Computer Hacker
Nationality: German
(Pseudonym: *Das Gespenst*, the self-proclaimed Ghost)

Ophion Nexus
S.I.L.V.E.R. Operative (Taskforce Leader)
Nationality: Classified
GMRC Clearance – Classified
Designation – Civilian / Private Contractor
Deployment: Classified
Current location: Transient
Skill set: Classified

Selene Dubois
Deputy Governor (Central Bank - USSB Sanctuary)
Nationality: Unknown
Profession: Banker
GMRC Clearance – Unknown
Designation – Civilian
Deployment: U.S.S.B. Sanctuary
Unofficial occupation: Member of 'The Committee'
Skill set: Unknown

Patrick Flynn
FBI Director
Nationality: American
Profession: Federal Agent
Deployment: Washington D.C.

Donald Anderson
FBI Assistant Director
Nationality: American
Profession: Federal Agent
Deployment: Los Angeles

Norroso

Native American
Nationality: American / Jicarilla Apache
Relative: Kuruk (son)
Profession: Rancher

James Davis Jackson

Chief Administrator (NASA)
Nationality: American
NASA Clearance Level: AMBER 1 Alpha
Deployment: Houston / Mission Command

Police Chief Denton

Yreka Police Department (California, USA)
Nationality: American
Profession: Police Officer
State County: Siskiyou

Jayden '*Jay*' Connor

Prison Guard (Pelican Bay Supermax State Prison)
Nationality: American

Keira Jones

BBC News correspondent
Nationality: English
Profession: Journalist

APPENDIX I - ORGANISATIONS

BBC (British Broadcasting Corporation) – Television, radio and multimedia network broadcaster operating in the United Kingdom and globally / www.bbc.co.uk

CNN (Cable News Network) – American television news channel / www.cnn.com

Fox News Channel (FNC) – American television news channel / www.foxnews.com

CTV News – Division of CTV Television Network, Canadian television news channel / www.ctvnews.ca

CCTV News – Chinese Central Television / Chinese state television broadcaster / www.cntv.cn

NDTV India – New Delhi Television / Leading Indian news channel / www.ndtv.com

United Nations (UN) – International organisation for law, security, human & civil rights, political freedom and world peace / www.un.org

GMRC (Global Meteor Response Council) – International organisation set up by the world's nations for the protection and preservation of humanity, civilisation and all life on Earth. Consisting of twenty-five divisions, the majority of the GMRC's policies and actions are carried out by a core of twelve divisions (see table below). Each of these divisions operates under one or two of the following three criteria:

PUBLIC: Activities disclosed to society

COVERT: Activities not disclosed to society

CLASSIFIED: Existence not disclosed to society

		OPERATIONAL CRITERIA		
		Public	*Covert*	*Classified*
GMRC DIVISON	Subterranean Programme		•	•
	Space Programme	•	•	
	Research & Development		•	•
	Intelligence		•	
	Population Education	•	•	
	Population Control		•	•
	Economic Control	•	•	
	Conservation	•	•	
	Resource Control	•	•	
	Operations & Military	•	•	
	U.N. Integration	•		
	Oversight	•	•	

NASA – The National Aeronautics and Space Administration (civilian space agency of the United States government) / www.nasa.gov

CNSA – The China National Space Administration (civilian space agency of the People's Republic of China) / www.cnsa.gov.cn

ESA – The European Space Agency (civilian space agency of Europe) / www.esa.int

RFSA – The Russian Federal Space Agency (civilian space agency of Russia) / www.federalspace.ru

Smithsonian Institution – World renowned collective of research centres and museums in the United States of America / www.si.edu

[Author note: I always thought the Institution was called the Smithsonian Institute, but apparently this is a common misnomer.]

Smithsonian Museum of Sanctuary (SMS) – Located in USSB Sanctuary and administered by the Smithsonian Institution, the Museum of Sanctuary is a vast resource on the extinct species, Homo giganthropsis (commonly referred to as the Anakim).

The Committee – A secret society of power elites operating outside the law. Little is known about the global organisation, its members, structure or purpose, however, its near limitless wealth and influence hints at a long and illustrious heritage.

Skull & Bones – A secret society founded in 1832 at Yale University, New Haven, Connecticut, USA. Exclusive to undergraduate seniors at the college, its members are called 'Bonesmen'.

Bilderburg Group – With a membership made up of the political elite and leading lights from the worlds of big business, banking, academia and the media, the group holds an annual conference behind closed doors to promote relations between North American and European nations. Founded in 1954, the meetings consist of up to one hundred and fifty members and continue to this day / www.-bilderbergmeetings.org

Freemasons – Perhaps the most well known secret society. The history of freemasonry is long and convoluted, and unfortunately, due to the nature of their clandestine dealings, the organisation leaves itself wide open to numerous accusations and theories of corruption and nefarious works. Whether these have foundation is open to conjecture; however, like any group, they will suffer from exploitation from within, although considering their overriding message of '*brotherhood*', to a greater degree (pardon the pun) from without.

Anti-Masonic Party – As the name suggests, this political party was set up in order to combat the rise of freemasonry amongst the United States establishment in the 1800s. Founded in 1828, it was dissolved in 1838 as public support waned.

APPENDIX J - FACILITIES, UNITS & DESIGNATIONS

U.S.S.B. – United States Subterranean Base

U.S.S.B. Steadfast – A Class subterranean base
Footprint: circa 20 sq. miles (52 sq. km)
Height: 7,500 ft (2.3 km)
Depth from surface: 3,000 ft (0.91 km)
Deepest point from surface: 10,500 ft (2 miles / 3.21 km)
Cubic capacity: 28.7 cubic miles (119.6 km^3)
Year of build: 1996 – 2035
Population: circa 500,000

U.S.S.B. Sanctuary – A Class subterranean base
Footprint: > 314 sq. miles (813 sq. km)
Height: 21,120 ft (6.4 km)
Depth from surface: circa 10,000 ft (1.9 miles / 3.1 km)
Deepest point from surface: 31,120 ft (5.9 miles / 9.5 km)
Cubic capacity: 1,256 cubic miles (5,203 km^3)
Year of build: 2016 – ongoing
Population: circa 20 million
Motto: '*Protegere Et Conservare, Civilitatem, Humanitas Et Omnes*

Vitam In Terra' ('To protect and preserve civilization, humanity and all life on earth').

Sanctuary Proper – Ancient subterranean structure
Footprint: > 20,000 sq. miles (51,800 sq. km)
Height: circa 20 to 30 miles (32km to 48km)
Depth from surface: circa 10,000 ft (1.9 miles / 3.1 km)
Deepest point from surface: circa 22 to 32 miles
Cubic capacity: 400,000 to 600,000 cubic miles
Year of build: circa 900,000 yrs B.C.

E.U.S.B. – European Union Subterranean Base

E.U.S.B. Deutschland – A Class subterranean base
Footprint: circa 40 sq. miles (104 sq. km)
Height: 8,500 ft (2.6 km)
Depth from surface: 2,500 ft (0.76 km)
Deepest point from surface: 11,000 ft (2.1 miles / 3.36 km)
Cubic capacity: 28.7 cubic miles (270.4 km^3)
Year of build: 2015 – ongoing
Population: circa 2,250,000

Darklight – Private security firm operating around the world and utilised by various organisations, corporations and governments. Primary client: Global Meteor Response Council.

SOG – CIA's Special Operations Group

NCO – Non-commissioned officer.

XO – Executive officer.

SFSD – Special Forces Subterranean Detachment
Division of the United States Army
Member of Subterranean Command

Codename: 'Terra Force'
Active: 2013 – present
Type: Infantry / Special Forces Commandos
Motto: 'No Depth Too Difficult, No Height Too Great – Honor and Country!'
Battle cry / affirmation: 'Ooyah!'
Deployment: United States Subterranean Bases

S.E.D. (Sanctuary Exploration Division) – Founded in 1826 by the sixth President of the United States, John Quincy Adams, the SED has a unique position within USSB Sanctuary in that it has a certain amount of autonomy despite its military oversight. The reason for this independence is mainly due to two factors. Fact one, the SED was operational long before the USSB was built or the GMRC ever conceived. Fact two, the SED was also instrumental in helping the United States government and GMRC create USSB Sanctuary, their knowledge of Sanctuary Proper an invaluable resource to the subterranean engineers during the planning, design and development of the enormous multilevel, underground structure / city.

Types of Team: Mapping, Structural, Archaeological, Scientific and Deep Reach.

Motto: 'Into the dark, into the light, pioneers for life.'

Sancturian – name given to residents of USSB Sanctuary.

Project ARES – Unacknowledged Special Access Programme, or black project, utilising ancient Anakim technology. A collaborative venture between the GMRC's R&D Division, United States military and NASA.

GMRC Directorate – Executive body ruling over the GMRC. Comprising Directors from the twelve major divisions within the GMRC, the Directorate helps to shape the council's policies and actions around the world.

Motto: '*In Veritate Scientia*' (In Truth, Knowledge).

Deep Reach – Special unit working within Sanctuary's Exploration Division (S.E.D.).

Team Alpha Six – S.E.D. Deep Reach unit.

U.S.S.S. Orbiter One – United States Space Ship. Co-funded and managed by NASA and the U.S. military. Small, modular craft designed for orbital observation and scientific research.

U.S.S.S. Archimedes – United States Space Station. Co-funded and managed by NASA and the U.S. military. Large, modular craft designed for orbital observation, scientific research and classified military applications.

I.S.S. – International Space Station. Co-funded by the world's major spacefaring nations. Large, modular craft designed for orbital observation, scientific research and classified military applications.

E.S.S. Guardian – European Space Station. Co-funded and managed by the ESA (European Space Agency) and the EU (European Union). Large, modular craft designed for orbital observation, scientific research and classified military applications.

C.S.S. Jiùshìzhǔ – Chinese Space Station. Co-funded and managed by the CNSA (Chinese National Space Administration) and the People's Republic of China. Large, modular craft designed for orbital observation, scientific research and classified military applications. Jiùshìzhǔ translates as '*the Saviour*'.

Three Sisters – A phrase used to describe the collective of the three space stations, Archimedes, Jiùshìzhǔ and Guardian.

S.I.L.V.E.R. – A multidisciplinary elite taskforce comprising twenty-two highly skilled individuals, or operatives, available to the highest bidder. Masters of various styles of combat, each member has access to the best military hardware the world has to offer and can function as a lone agent, or as part of a greater whole. S.I.L.V.E.R. is an acronym for: Stealth, Infiltration, Liquidation, Verification, Extraction and Reconnaissance. Their existence is hidden from public eye and they are regarded as mercenaries by some, assassins by others, and necessary by those who employ them.

APPENDIX K - WORDS, TERMS & PHRASES

Anakim – Ancient and extinct race of Hominids living on Earth circa 1.2 million to 20,000 years before present-day. Scientific name: Homo giganthropsis (unofficial: Homo gigantis). Alternative plural: Anakai.

Nephilim – The word *Nephilim* is found in the Hebrew Bible. Its true meaning, as far as I can tell, still seems to be contested to this day. Some suggest it derives from the word, *nephal* or *naphal*, which can mean 'to fall', which some then interpret as the 'fallen ones'. Another, and perhaps more reasoned argument, is that *Nephilim* is derived from the word *naphil* which means 'giant'. When researching this, I found that Dr. Mike Heiser gave a well-reasoned argument for the latter hypothesis mentioned above.

Mesoamerica – A region in Central America in which pre-Columbian cultures thrived between approx. 10,000 B.C. and 1700 A.D. Modern day countries contained (partly or fully) within the Mesoamerican area include: Mexico, Guatemala, El Salvador, Honduras, Belize, Nicaragua and Costa Rica. The most well known civilisations/tribes in Mesoamerica include: Inca, Aztecs, Maya, Olmecs, Mixtecs and Zapotecs.

Ooyah – SFSD commandos' affirmation / battle cry.

The Deep Web – Term for the part of the World Wide Web not appearing on regular search engines. Unindexed content not seen by regular Internet users who frequent the Surface Web. This content can take many forms; some is benign while other content can be more sinister in origin and use, resulting from illegal activity by individuals, criminal gangs, corrupt organisations, companies and sovereign nations, although the latter may argue this is just offensive national defence conducted in their country's best interests. Also known as: Deep Net, Dark Net, Dark Web, Invisible Web, Under Web, Under Net, Hidden Web etc.

Scheiße – Vulgar German word for shit, faeces or something rubbish / worthless (alternative: *Scheisse*).

The Father of His Country – Phrase used to describe the first U.S. President of the United States of America, George Washington.

CPR – Cardiopulmonary resuscitation.

KIA – Killed in action.

MIA – Missing in action.

River Styx – The boundary between the underworld (the land of the dead) and Earth (the land of the living) in Greek mythology, which takes the form of a river.

Brine Pool – A high salinity body of water found on the seabed of deep oceans which give the impression of an underwater lake or pool.

Intercept missions – Planned missions by the GMRC's Space

Programme to prevent four of six approaching asteroids from impacting planet Earth.

Caste – Word used by *The Committee* to distinguish between the hierarchical ranks of its members. There are thirteen castes within The Committee, and only nine people can hold the top, and thirteenth, caste.

DMV – Department of Motor Vehicles in the United States.

MACH – The Mach number, denoted by M or Ma, is a variable value commonly referred to as the local *speed of sound*.

PIT manoeuvre – Precision immobilization technique. Utilised by a moving vehicle, usually law enforcement, when trying to turn a fleeing vehicle sideways in order to stop its forward motion.

EVA – Extra vehicular activity is a term used by astronauts and cosmonauts when they operate outside of their spacecraft in a pressurised suit when in the vacuum of space or other unpressurised environments.

Navy SEAL – Sea, Air and Land, S.E.A.L., the term used by the United States Navy for their special operations force.

Der Apfel fällt nicht weit vom Stamm – A German phrase also used in English which translates as: The apple does not fall far from the tree. An alternative can be, 'like father, like son', or 'like mother, like daughter', or, in Brett and Samson's case, 'like father, like daughter'.

Obsidian – Is a volcanic glass which has a shiny black appearance and naturally occurs in nature.

Southern Quechua language – Native language spoken by the indigenous Quechua people of Peru and a handful of other South American countries. There are approx. seven million speakers.

Great Flood –There are many tales of great floods throughout history and in all corners of the world. However, a more recent theory suggests the flood mentioned in the Bible may have roots in a far older event which some theorise destroyed an ancient civilisation that spanned the globe.

Das Gespenst – The name used by the computer hacker, Eric Wolf, which translates from German as: 'The Ghost'.

Da Muss Ich – One of many names used by, and assigned to, the cyber terrorist, B.I.C., which translates from German as: 'Because I Must'. Although, the acronym B.I.C. stands for the better known name of: 'Because I Can'.

APPENDIX L - LOCATIONS, BUILDINGS & MONUMENTS

Sanctuary Proper – Ancient underground structure built by an extinct species of Hominid, Homo giganthropsis. Located beneath the deserts and mountains of central and northern Mexico.

Dulce – Small town located in Rio Arriba County, New Mexico, United States.

Ruins of Copán – ancient Mayan city located in the Copán Department of western Honduras.

Teotihuacan – Pre-Columbian Mesoamerican city located near Mexico City, Mexico.

Pyramid of the Sun – Biggest structure in Teotihuacan, Mexico.

Sterkfontein Caves – Also known as the Cradle of Humanity. Located near Johannesburg, South Africa.

FBI Field Office, Los Angeles, California, USA – Located on Wilshire Boulevard.

City of New York, State of New York, USA – Most populous and arguably the most iconic city in the United States.

Smithsonian Vaults – Secure facilities used to store ancient Anakim artefacts and remains. The vaults are located inside USSB Sanctuary and beneath the Smithsonian Institution's sprawling Museum of Sanctuary.

Military Vaults – As above but with extra security and limited access.

U.S.S.B. SANCTUARY United States Military Scientific Laboratory Complex – High security facility run by the U.S. Army. Utilised by NASA and the GMRC'S R&D Division, the complex contains projects and research based on artefacts of Anakim origin.

Shuttle bay – Area inside the S.E.D. from where air-shuttles are launched.

Departure lounge – Nickname given to the staging area in the S.E.D. used by teams prior to launch.

S.E.D. Control Station – Area inside the S.E.D. Command Centre that controls the launch and return of air-shuttles into Sanctuary Proper.

S.E.D. Command Centre – Area inside the S.E.D. complex that houses the Control Station (see above), shuttle bay and the offices for high ranking S.E.D. personnel.

Tower central – Is an ancient Anakim tower located at the heart of U.S.S.B. Sanctuary. At three miles high the spectacular structure was built to last and it was decided – for reasons both structural and aesthetic – to construct the human subterranean base around it.

Dome Level – The topmost level of U.S.S.B. Sanctuary and the most exclusive, due to the health benefits (both mental and physical) of living, and/or working, in a more open and natural environment.

New Park District – Located on the Dome level (see above), the New Park District is as the name suggests, an area within U.S.S.B. Sanctuary that is filled with various picturesque parks and forests; it also contains within its borders the subterranean base's museum complex

GMRC Command Complex – A large office complex with a central skyscraper (or domescraper) located on the Dome level of U.S.S.B. Sanctuary

Brecon Beacons National park – An Area of Outstanding Natural Beauty (AONB) located in the country of Wales, which itself is a part of the United Kingdom. There are three other countries in the union: England, Scotland and Northern Ireland.

Supreme Court of California – The highest court in the state of California, USA.

Pelican Bay State Prison – A supermax correctional facility located in Crescent City, California, USA.

Mission Control Center (NASA) – Located in the Lyndon B. Johnson Space Center, Houston, Texas, USA, the Control Center acts as the hub of operations conducted by NASA.

The Auditorium – The largest space module ever built, prefabricated on the surface in the year 2032, and assembled in space a year later, it acts as the central node of the International Space Station (ISS). It has multiple uses including: a mission centre, conference room and viewing gallery.

ALMA – The Atacama Large Millimeter/submillimeter Array in Chile, South America. The array consists of sixty-six radio telescopes which have two sizes of dish, twelve and seven metres in diameter. ALMA has many uses, once of which is the study of comets.

TSKA – The Two Square Kilometre Array. Built in the year 2025 in Peru. An array of radio telescopes spread out over two square kilometres.

Redwood Highway – Is a road that straddles two U.S. states, California and Oregon. The northern part of the highway consists of Route 199, while the southern portion connects with Route 101.

Jedediah Smith Redwoods State Park – A preservation area for old-growth redwood trees. Designated as a Californian state park, it surrounds part of the Redwood Highway (see above /overleaf).

Anakim Sphinx – An ancient monument located beneath the surface of a deep lake inside Sanctuary Proper. Date of construction: unknown.

Anakim Arch – A massive crystalline structure located in Sanctuary Proper.

Arc de Triomphe – An iconic French monument located in Paris, France. It is the largest triumphal arch in the world (excluding Anakim structures as above).

The Parthenon – A spectacular building located in Athens, Greece. Constructed in the fifth century B.C., the Parthenon was used as a temple in an ancient citadel called the Acropolis of Athens.

Elgin Marbles – A wonderful collection of marble relief sculptures that once adorned the Parthenon in Greece (see above). Also called the Parthenon Marbles, and displayed in the British Museum in London since 1817, there is still dispute as to which country should have ownership of these precious works.

APPENDIX M - TECHNOLOGY, ARTEFACTS & OBJECTS

Thermal Density Reduction (T.D.R.) – Excavation technology utilised in the creation of large scale subterranean chambers.

Netcube – A storage device for computers using a state-of-the-art fluid drive instead of the cumbersome hard disc drives which preceded them. Used to store massive amounts of data, a Netcube is capable of storing the majority of mainstream data held on the World Wide Web. (Also known as a 'webinabox'.)

RV – Acronym used by the military for a rendezvous point. Also used as an acronym for a 'remote vehicle'.

Thermal sword – Darklight personal weapon.

SABRE – Synergetic Air-Breathing Rocket Engine, an engine that operates in both air-breathing and rocket modes. Developed by Reaction Engines / www.reactionengines.co.uk.

DPD – Digital Parchment Paper.

Stelae – Carved stone monuments, singular *stela*.

T.I.I. – Thermal Image Intensifier.

Air-shuttle – A specially designed vehicle which travels on rails and through a large transparent tunnel / tube. An air-shuttle is the fastest way out of the USSB and into Sanctuary Proper (and vice versa). Propulsion is in the form of gravitational pull, staged rocket burns and strategically placed air-jets (assisted by a low-resistance cushion of air).

Computer phone – Advanced mobile phone with the processing power to run advanced software packages. Acts as a personal computer as well as a smart phone. Computer phones are able to connect to wallscreens and monitors via induction ports.

United States Credits (USC) – Currency used in United States subterranean bases. One USC is equivalent to one U.S. dollar.

The Centipede – Remote operated all-terrain supply vehicle. Multiple wheels, low ground clearance and an articulated chassis enable the machine to scale near vertical climbs and all manner of obstacles.

Quantum processor – Super powerful computer processor based on a qubits (quantum bits) rather than bits. These processors can carry out a far greater number of computations than computer architecture utilised in the first two decades of the twenty-first century.

UAV – Unmanned aerial vehicle, also known as a drone.

Wallscreen – Large, interactive monitor attached to a wall, usually taking up the entire surface.

HUD – Head-up display, or heads-up display. Data projection onto a transparent screen / visor / window allowing a user to continue looking in the desired direction while being kept apprised of real-time information.

Deep Space Detection Array (D.S.D.A.) – NASA and U.S. military satellite in high Earth orbit. Categorised as an unacknowledged Special Access Programme / black project. Capabilities: satellite disruption technology and deep space surveillance imager.

OLED – Organic light-emitting diode. Utilised in monitors, televisions and other visual displays.

Monotube – Public metro transportation system in USSB Sanctuary. Utilising a high-speed mono-rail configuration, the train navigates the subterranean base via a network of transport channels and tunnels.

MX4 assault rifle – Advanced projectile weapon used by the U.S. military and Darklight security firm.

Beam rifle – Sophisticated non-projectile weapon capable of unleashing high-powered energy in the form of a beam.

Vacuum Lift – Super fast mechanism used to transport people up or down within a structure / facility.

Deep Reach helmet – High-tech headwear worn by S.E.D. Deep Reach personnel.

Multifunction card (M.F. card) – Given to permanent USSB residents, the MF card acts as a door key, sector pass, credit / debit card, data storage device and identity badge.

Mayan map – Dated at over a thousand years old, the dense metallic tablet was unearthed by Sarah Morgan in 2040 at the Ruins of Copán in Honduras. Consisting of Mayan hieroglyphs around a single line, the simple inscriptions portray a map linking together the ancient Mayan cities.

Anakim parchments – Collected by Sarah, Trish and Jason from a number of sources, these ancient scrolls are made from an unknown material which fails to degrade over time. They also have the capability to store large amounts of data and act like a digital display when activated using Sarah's pentagonal pendant.

Anakim orbs – Ancient relics unearthed in Sanctuary Proper by an S.E.D. archaeology team.

Anakim pendants – two metallic pentagonal pendants found by Sarah Morgan during previous archaeological digs. The larger of the two, measuring two and a half inches in diameter, enables the wearer to activate Anakim technology, although its use is limited by the operator's physical size.

Pentagon – Five-sided polygon.

Pentagram – A five-pointed star contained within a circle.

Anakim monolith / prism – Massive fifty foot high artefact removed from a 900,000 year old building. Unearthed and recovered by SFSD soldiers under the command of General Stevens. The monolith contains a single chamber full of a viscous liquid which is protected by a transparent material.

Anakim shield – Another ancient relic unearthed in Sanctuary Proper by S.E.D. personnel. Found in the same hoard as the orb (see above) and stored in the military vaults beneath the Museum of Sanctuary.

APPENDIX O - MAPS, DIAGRAMS & REFERENCE

GMRC SUBTERRANEAN PROGRAMME
Country / State of Origin
Suffix
Number of Subterranean Bases
UNITED STATES
SUBTERRANEAN BASE
USSB

GMRC SUBTERRANEAN PROGRAMME

Country / State of Origin	Suffix	Number of Subterranean Bases
UNITED STATES SUBTERRANEAN BASE	USSB	10
EUROPEAN UNION SUBTERRANEAN BASE	EUSB	10
PEOPLE'S REPUBLIC OF CHINA SUBTERRANEAN BASE	PRCSB	9
RUSSIAN FEDERATION SUBTERRANEAN BASE	RFSB	5
SUBTERRANEAN BASE BRAZIL	SBB	4
SUBTERRANEAN BASE *(Independents)*	SB	3
JAPAN SUBTERRANEAN BASE	JSB	2
SUBTERRANEAN BASE INDIA	SBI	2

TERMINOLOGY / MA

USSB – United States Subterranean Base
GMRC – Global Meteor Response Council
Darklight – World's largest private security contractor
SFSD – Special Forces Subterranean Detachment (*Terra Force*)
SED – Sanctuary Exploration Division
Deep Reach – Special survey team working within the SED
S.I.L.V.E.R. – An elite military unit available to the highest bidder
Sanctuary Proper – Ancient underground structure built by an extinct species of Hominid, Homo giganthropsis (the Anakim)

USSB
STEADFAST
NEVADA
UTAH
COLORADO
CALIFORNIA
Las Vegas
USA
Los Angeles
ARIZONA
NEW
MEXICO
TEXAS
MEXICO
USSB
SANCTUARY

POEM - I SEE YOU

I write
I sigh
I can
And do
Hope and pray
That someone
At some point
May brighten my day

At once
At night
The dark
No light
My mind a blur
Confusion astir
Words not worth writing
Some might say

It's clear as I create this verse
That poetry can be

As deep or light as I want to see
Whether or not it has meaning to me
To you, to them, to everyone
I sigh
I write, I ...
Pray

POEM - ENTER THE LIGHT

Darkest shores
Temptations past
I'm still to live
To breath, to love

I used to think
Motivation elusive
And yet ... now
Negative is conducive

My jealously, my failings
Another's complainings
A comment, belittling
I feel it, so crippling

And yet despite my yearning
I believe in my learning
That one or two failings
Can propel me up high

Determination afire
Heart aching desire
To reach dream's destination
My compassion now real

And so, as such, with clarity enhanced
Answer this question
Have I had my day?
Have you, what say?

Ancient Origins: Let There Be Light is dedicated with love to the human race, of which we are all a part.
May we find our way home.

ACKNOWLEDGMENTS

A massive thank you as ever to my parents for helping me stay the course and for their invaluable editing and insight into what works and what doesn't. Also, another big thank you to my copy editor, Julie Lewthwaite, who continues to keep me on the straight and narrow.

Furthermore, thank you to everyone who has given me their support and encouragement, which includes anyone who's been kind enough to contact me or leave a review for my books online or otherwise. It's your kind words and feedback that has kept me motivated through difficult times, both professionally and personally.

Robert Storey

2014

ADDENDUM

Fuse Books partnered with Terry and Maureen Storey, following the tragic death of their son Robert. It is our privilege to bring his Ancient Origins series to new readers.

In these books, Robert lives on.

As Rob himself noted above, and we can confirm from our time working together, these books would not have made it to publication without the support of Terry and Maureen.

Wonderful, devoted parents who could not have done more for their son.

James Blatch & Mark Dawson
February 2020

First published in Great Britain in 2015

2nd Edition 2020

Fuse Books

Made in the USA
Monee, IL
04 June 2021